CHASING OLIVIA

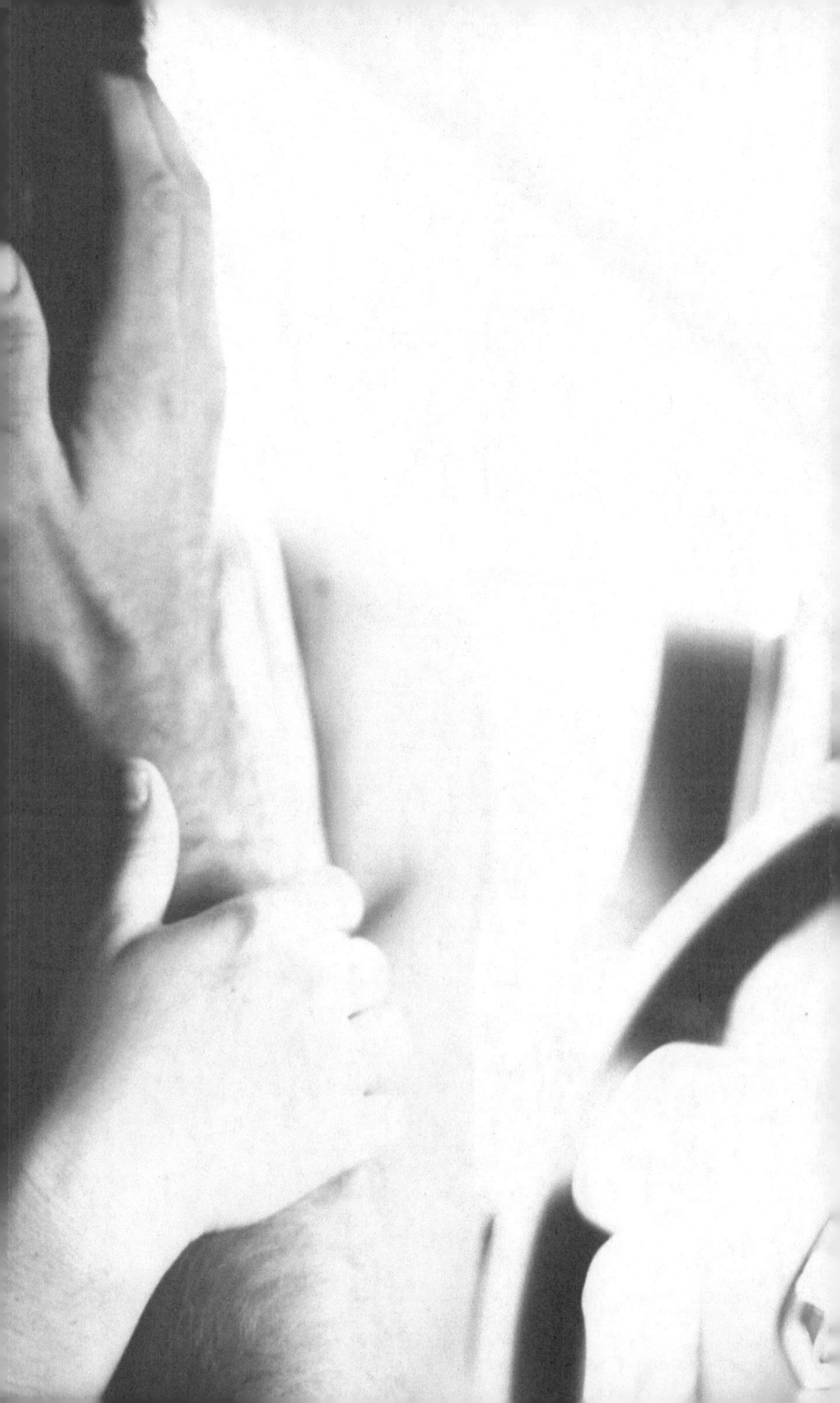

CHASING OLIVIA

THE TRACE AND OLIVIA SERIES

FINDING OLIVIA
CHASING OLIVIA
TEMPTING ROWAN
SAVING TATUM

Copyright © 2013, 2016, 2017 Micalea Smeltzer

All rights reserved.

This book or any portion thereof may not be reproduced or used in any manner whatsoever without the express written permission of the publisher.

This is a work of fiction. Names, characters, businesses, places, events and incidents are either the products of the author's imagination or used in a fictitious manner. Any resemblance to actual persons, living or dead, or actual events is purely coincidental.

Cover Design: Emily Wittig

Photography by Regina Wamba

Edited by Wendi Temporado of Ready, Set, Edit

Formatting by: Micalea Smeltzer

*This book is for everyone who fell in love with a shy girl and cocky plaid-shirt wearing mechanic.
I hope you enjoy the rest of their journey.*

CHAPTER ONE

I wiggled in my itchy dress as the sun beat down on my back. Whose idea was it to have a wedding at the end of May? The humidity was about to suffocate me.

"We are gathered here today, to celebrate the wedding of Nickolas and Nora," the minister stated.

Yep, my mom was marrying my best friend's brother, a guy that was only two years older than me.

It was weird, but I'd had two years to get used to it.

What I wasn't used to was the fact that in five months, I'd be a big sister.

I'd been an only child for all of my twenty-two years of life, so it seemed weird to be getting a sibling now. One day I'd have kids, and it would be awkward explaining why my brother or sister was so much younger than me.

I shuddered at the thought, but quickly sobered.

Today was my mom's wedding day and I needed to act happy. Well, not *act*, because I *was* happy for her, I just couldn't seem to get over the weirdness of the situation.

It wasn't right of me to judge my mom or Nick for loving each other. Love shouldn't be determined by your skin color, gender, or age. When you love someone, others shouldn't question your decision, they should respect it.

I gripped the bouquet tighter in my hands, wishing the minister would speed up the ceremony. This dress was some kind of itchy and if I didn't get to scratch myself soon, I'd go crazy.

They exchanged their vows, gazing lovingly into each other's eyes, as they stood under the flowered arch. Bright green grass surrounded us since the wedding was being held in the park.

I turned my head slightly when they kissed, eyeing the ground.

It might be awkward having a step-dad that was only two years older than me and the same age as my boyfriend, but I knew Nick loved my mom, and that's what mattered most.

Applause echoed around us and I smiled.

Nick took my mom's hand and they walked back down the aisle as the minister declared them, "Mr. and Mrs. Nickolas Callahan."

I took a huge sigh of relief as the wedding party began to disperse, heading to the tent set up for the reception.

When I was sure no one was looking my way, I scratched the itchy spot on my back, sighing in relief.

"Hey, beautiful." Trace, my boyfriend, grinned, grabbing me by the waist and spinning me around. My strapless lavender dress fanned around me. "You looked good up there." He kissed my cheek.

I rolled my eyes, hoping he hadn't seen me moaning in pleasure from *finally* scratching my back. Damn itchy dress. "You're such a liar. I know I looked terrified, I was scared to death I'd do something wrong."

"How could you possibly do something wrong?" he questioned, rubbing his stubbled jaw. "You stand there and look pretty."

"Knowing me, there's a number of things I could do wrong," I grumbled as we walked toward the large white tent. My heels kept getting stuck in the soft ground and Trace had to lift me up.

"You *are* clumsy." He chuckled, just as he had to grab me around the waist to keep me from toppling face first into the ground.

"Thanks," I mumbled.

"It's not a problem."

We made it to the tent where a dance floor, a stage, and tables were set up.

Paper flowers hung from the roof of the tent and soft music played. Everything was very simple and understated, just the way my mom and Nick wanted it.

This was the first wedding I had ever been to, and I was at a loss as to what I was supposed to do.

Trace gave my waist a slight squeeze. "Stop chewing on your lip, Olivia. You're going to make it bleed."

"Sorry." I let my lip go with a pop. I was a nervous ball of energy.

More people began to trickle into the tent and I felt more at ease. Some started dancing while others took a seat at one of the tables scattered under the tent.

I saw my mom and Nick come into the tent, and he pulled her onto the dance floor, one hand was at her waist, while his other hovered protectively over her small round stomach.

"Are you okay?" Trace whispered, his lips skimming my ear, and sending a shiver down my spine.

Even after two years, I was still affected by him. I think I always would be. After the man I'd grown up believing was my father nearly killed me, our bond grew even closer.

Trace had been there for me through the good, the bad, and the in-between. He was my rock. We had some hard times over the last two years but we stuck it out. Trace saw me at my worst after my near-death experience ... I said some not very nice things to him—to everyone, for that matter. But it never fazed him.

Eventually, I grew strong enough to let go of my past with his help.

Those first few months we were together, he taught me how to be wild and spontaneous, how to make mistakes, and most importantly, he taught me how to *live*. And that's what I'd been doing ever since.

"What are you thinking about?" he asked, rubbing my neck.

"You," I answered.

He smirked. "Are you thinking about the three orgasms I gave you this morning?"

I smacked his side. "*Trace*," I groaned, my cheeks coloring.

"What? You looked like you were really enjoying them." He wet his lips. "At one point, I thought you passed out."

"Shut up," I pleaded with him.

He chuckled. "Fine, no more orgasms for you."

"Are you trying to make me die of embarrassment?" I squirmed in his arms. "Someone could hear you."

"Eh" —he waved a hand— "I don't care."

"But *I* do," I hissed. I'd been with Trace long enough to know and respect the fact that he had no filter. But when he started saying certain things in very public places it became a bit difficult for me to handle.

"Ah, there it is." He grinned.

"What?" I asked.

"Your ears are turning red," he chortled, gazing down at me. Someone bumped into me, pushing me further into his body.

"Are not," I groaned, self-consciously reaching up to touch my ears. Sure enough I could feel the heat infusing them.

Trace chuckled in reply. Shaking his head, he stepped in front of me, holding out a hand as he bowed dramatically. "May I have this dance?"

I let my hands drop from my ears and placed one in his. "You should know by now that you don't need to ask."

He wet his lips. "I'm a gentleman, and a gentleman always asks for permission." He winked, leading me out onto the dance floor.

I wrapped one arm around his lean shoulders while he held my other hand. We swayed back and forth to the romantic music, while my mom and Nick danced nearby along with other couples.

"In case I haven't told you today, you look beautiful, Olivia," he whispered huskily in my ear and my stomach rolled. *God, how is it still possible for him to turn me on with a few words?*

"You've mentioned it a few times already." I smiled up at him.

He bent down so his lips were beside my ear. "Olivia," he whispered, "you deserve to be told you're beautiful every second, of every day, because it's true."

I blushed, leaning my face against his chest where his heart beat proudly. "You're such a flatterer."

"I'm no such thing," he murmured. "I'm honest."

My eyes flutter closed. "I love you." Three words had never been truer. I loved Trace Wentworth with every fiber of my being.

"I love you too," his chest rumbled beneath my ear with his words, "so much."

I knew he did. He told me and showed me every single day how much he loved me. I often wondered how I got so lucky finding Trace … or maybe he found me. Regardless, Trace was it for me. I hadn't had to suffer through tear-filled breakups. It had only ever been Trace and that's all it ever would be.

He gently grabbed my right arm and pulled it away from his shoulder, placing a light kiss on the tattoo that emblazoned my wrist. It was a fairly new tattoo and spelled out his name.

"You really like my tattoo, don't you?" I laughed.

He grinned, his eyes twinkling. "I *love* it. It lets all the other guys know you're taken."

I rolled my eyes. "You sound like a dog marking his territory."

He chuckled. "I have your name close to my junk, so you've taken my man-hood," he reasoned.

"*You're* the one that wanted it there." I glared.

"But your name looks so good there, peeking out of the top of my pants." His eyes were playful, holding back laughter.

"You ... You ... Ugh!" I stuttered.

He continued, "This way, guys know you're taken, girls know I'm off the market and that my—"

"Trace! We're at a wedding!" I cut him off.

"—cock belongs to you." He smirked.

"You just *love* embarrassing me." I buried my face against his chest, willing the blush staining my cheeks to leave.

"You'd think by now you'd be used to the things I say." I felt him shrug.

I shook my head and looked up into his green eyes. "I am," I grumbled. "But when you start saying certain things in public—" I trailed off, lifting my shoulders in a small shrug.

He chuckled, his lips lifting up into a smile. "I like to keep you on your toes ..." He paused. "Actually, I prefer to keep you underneath me but that's a different story."

"You are on a roll today." I shook my head rapidly back and forth, praying that the people around us couldn't hear our conversation.

He grabbed my chin between his thumb and index finger, tilting my face up. "I promise, from now on ... or at least until we get home, I'll be on my best behavior." He grinned cheekily.

I rolled my eyes at him. "I'll believe that when I see it."

"I can be good!" he exclaimed. I eyed him. "Okay," he paused, "I can be good if I try *really, really, really*, hard."

"Stop talking and dance." I shook my head, unable to hide my smile, and glanced down at my feet to make sure they didn't get tangled in his.

"So bossy." He chuckled. "I like it."

I bit down on my lip to hold back my retort.

"Hey." Nick appeared behind Trace and tapped his shoulder.

Trace and I stopped dancing, and he wrapped an arm protectively around my waist.

"Sorry to interrupt." Nick smiled sheepishly, sweeping his blonde hair from his eyes. "I was hoping to dance with Olivia."

Trace glanced down at me and I nodded that I was okay with that.

"Sure." Trace released me and placed my hand in Nick's.

"Nora, would you like to dance?" Trace asked my mom.

She smiled and accepted his offer.

I watched them sway onto the dance floor before I tilted my head back to look at Nick. God, he was a giant. I felt like a midget standing next to him.

"I wanted to talk to you," Nick whispered, glancing around to make sure my mom and Trace were out of earshot.

"I figured," I muttered, trying to keep the bite out of my voice. Nick *was* a nice guy, so I needed to stop acting like he wasn't. He and my mom deserved to be happy.

His hand flexed where it rested above my waist. We swayed awkwardly to the music, almost a foot of space between us.

"I know … that this has been … "

"Difficult?" I supplied with a raised brow.

He took a breath. "I know this has been *difficult* for you, Olivia. But I really do love your mom with all my heart and I'm ecstatic to be her husband. I can't wait to bring our son or daughter into this world and become a father. Nora's told me everything about Aaron and Derek." I flinched at the mention of Aaron's name. "I'm sorry that you've had to go through so much, Olivia. I really am. But I want you to know that I'm *nothing* like—"

"I know that," I interrupted him before he could say that name again.

He swallowed. "Good."

In the beginning, when I first learned of Nick and my mom's relationship, I'd wondered why she was so quick to jump into dating after *finally* getting away from her abusive husband. But now, I understood. There's a part of all of us that no matter what, never stops believing in the power of love. Love, makes us human. It's what drives us.

The song changed but we continued with our awkward dance. I felt like he was waiting for me to say something, so I opened my mouth and let the words tumble out. "I truly am happy for the both of you. I can see how much you love my mom and how much she loves you, I'd be an idiot not to. I think it's great that she's found someone to love and she's moving on with her life ... I'm sorry that I haven't been the most supportive person of your relationship, it's just awkward. I mean you're—" I floundered for a better way to explain but came up empty.

"I get it." Nick smiled and his dimple appeared in his cheek. "I could be your brother."

"Exactly!" I agreed.

Nick *was* my best friend's brother, which made this whole thing even weirder.

Nick chuckled. "I don't want you to ever think that you're not welcome, or anything like that, Olivia. Just because your mom and I are married now and the baby will be here in a few months, it doesn't mean you're not still her daughter."

"I know," I mumbled.

"Do you?" he questioned.

I sighed. "It's weird," I admitted reluctantly. I felt like my mom was replacing me, like I wasn't good enough. I knew in my heart that wasn't true, but it didn't stop me from thinking it.

"I don't want you to feel weird about this, Olivia." Nick's eyes narrowed.

"How could I *not* feel weird?" I countered. "What if the situation was reversed? How would you feel if your mom was marrying your best friend's brother and having his baby?"

He shrugged. "When you put it that way. I get it. I do."

"I'm a big girl, Nick," I told him jokingly. "Seriously, don't worry about me."

"I want you to be okay with me and your mom being together," he whispered.

It was kinda too late for that. But I didn't tell him that. "Nick, you love my mom and that's what matters the most. I'm *okay*."

He stared down at me for a moment, not believing me.

"Really," I added.

"All right," he sighed, his eyes zeroing in on something across the room. "I better get you back to your boyfriend before he bites my arm off or something."

I glanced over my shoulder to see Trace standing with his hands shoved into his pockets, glaring at Nick. My mom was speaking to Resa, Nick's mom.

I shook my head and smiled at Nick. "Did he miss the wedding or something? I'm pretty sure you just said 'I do' and it wasn't to me."

Nick chuckled. "Yeah, he must have missed that part."

The song ended and Nick released me. "Thanks for talking with me, Olivia." With a smile, he disappeared off the dance floor in search of my mom.

"Somebody was a Chatty Kathy." Trace appeared at my side.

I grabbed his hand and pulled him to an empty table. "He wanted to talk," I told Trace, sitting down beside him. "So, we talked. There was no need for you to glare at him like that. He *is* my step-dad." *Ew.* That word seemed too strange to comprehend.

"Sorry," Trace mumbled, bowing his head. "I know that. I'm just very overprotective of you."

I swallowed thickly, feeling like he'd punched me in the gut. Trace had always been protective of me, but after I was nearly murdered he gave that word a whole new meaning.

"I highly doubt Nick's going to kill me," my voice was barely above a whisper.

"I'm sorry," Trace repeated. "I can't help but freak out a bit when it comes to you."

"It's been two years, Trace. I've moved on—" *somewhat* "—and you should too."

His fingers tapped restlessly against his knee.

"I wish that bastard hadn't killed himself. He deserved to rot in prison for what he did to you," Trace seethed, his teeth gritted.

"At least he can never hurt anyone else now," I whispered, feeling very small. For some reason, whenever the conversation turned to Aaron, I always felt like a small child and wanted to curl into a ball.

Trace sighed, rubbing his hand over his stubbled jaw. "Yeah, I guess that is a good thing. I still think it's completely fucked up that he took the easy way out."

Shortly after I was released from the hospital, things were moving along with Aaron's trial. When he found out that he might be stuck behind bars for most of his life, he found a way to end it. The police officers found him hanging in his holding cell by the sheet from his bed.

When I first found out ... it didn't seem real. I felt like it was some kind of joke. I didn't feel like it should have been possible for him to commit suicide. That made me angry for quite a while. While I suffered with recovering from what he did to me, Aaron was dead and free from suffering for his actions.

"Can we stop talking about this?" I pleaded, looking up at Trace through my lashes. "Today is my mom's wedding day and the last thing I want to be thinking about is that—that—monster."

Trace swallowed, his eyes sad. He reached for my hand, placing a tender kiss on it. "I'm sorry, Olivia. I shouldn't have brought it up."

"It's okay." I forced a smile, but my words were weak.

While Trace's way of coping was to talk about what happened to me, I preferred to pretend it never happened.

"What are you two doing sitting over here looking so sad?" Avery asked, plopping into the seat beside me and kicking off her high heels. "Trouble in paradise?"

"No!" Trace and I both exclaimed.

"Ugh," Avery grumbled. "I *wish* you two weren't so perfect together. You make relationships look so easy."

For the past two years, Avery and Luca, who happened to be Trace's best friend, had been in an off-and-on relationship. I really wished they'd get their crap figured out and get together permanently. They were perfect for each other. Things had gone well for them for a while and then things went sour. Avery would never tell me what happened which led me to believe *she* was the one with the problem. I asked Trace if he knew what happened, but he told me that guys don't talk about that kind of stuff. Whatever.

"That's because relationships are easy when you love the other person and you communicate," Trace eyed Avery.

"Whatever." She rolled her eyes, crossing her legs and massaging the sole of her foot. "That's so not true."

I shook my head at her.

I sat up straight and reached for Trace's hand. I wasn't going to let Aaron or Avery make me sad today.

"Want to dance again?" I asked him.

"Sure." He grinned crookedly. "Any excuse to have you in my arms is a good one."

Avery made a choking sound. "I think I threw up in my mouth. That was way too sweet for me."

"And that's why you're single right now," I whispered in her ear as I passed by her on our way back onto the dance floor.

Putting our previous conversation behind us, I smiled up at him as I crossed my arms behind his neck. "You look really good in this suit." He wore a light grey suit with a button-down pale blue shirt, a thin black belt, and a navy tie.

"Babe, I look good in anything and nothing at all." He chuckled.

"Even after two years, you're still as cocky as ever." I smiled.

"*Confident*, not cocky. There's a difference." He laughed, his eyes light and playful.

I rolled my eyes. "I'm pretty sure you've told me that before."

"That's because it's true." He smiled down at me.

After dancing to a few more songs, everyone was cleared off the dance floor for dinner and cake.

I sat at the lone rectangular table beside my mom. Thank God Trace was on my other side. Nick was to my mom's left with his best man, his brother Ben, beside him. Ben and I were both expected to give speeches ... I was pretty sure I'd throw up before I could give mine. Public speaking was *not* my forte.

"Babe. Babe. *Babe*." Trace wrenched his hand from mine under the table.

"What?" I glanced over at him.

"You cut off my circulation, I think my hand is asleep," he groaned, waving his hand in the air.

"Sorry." I bowed my head, eyeing the white tablecloth. "I'm nervous."

Hearing my words, my mom turned toward me. "Honey, I told you that I don't expect you to give a speech. Don't worry about it, sweetie."

"Mom, it's my job as your maid of honor to give a speech, so that's what I'm going to do." I steeled my shoulders.

"You always were a stubborn child." She chuckled, fingering a loose curl beside her cheek.

Trace leaned around me so he could see my mom and squeezed my knee. "She's a spitfire."

"You've got that right," she huffed.

"Um, I'm sitting *right here*." I pointed to myself. "You realize that I *can* hear you?"

"You mean," Trace paused, "you have ears? That's shocking."

I narrowed my eyes. "Wanna sleep on the couch tonight?"

"Come on." He squeezed my knee. "I'm no good to you on the couch."

I blushed. Sometimes, I couldn't believe the things he said, especially when my mom was right beside me. Ugh.

"You're blushing." He poked my cheek.

"And you're about two seconds away from losing your hand," I snapped.

He leaned over and whispered in my ear, "Is it that time of the month or something? 'Cause you're super grumpy today."

"I'm stressed," I replied, wiggling in my seat. I had been worried about doing something stupid during the ceremony and now I was worried about my speech that I hadn't even written.

The stress of writing it had been too much, so I hoped I could come up with something decent off the top of my head.

If not, I was screwed.

"Allow me to," he whispered huskily, "relive some of that stress." His finger trailed up my thigh, higher and higher.

My eyes fluttered closed, but before I lost all sense, I smacked his hand away. "Not here," I hissed.

He sat back and smirked. "Later then. I'm sure I can locate a closet or something."

"We're outside," I stated. "No closets."

"A tree will work." He waggled his eyebrows.

"You're impossible." I shook my head, turning to my mom, praying that she didn't hear us. Luckily, she was engrossed in conversation with Nick and Ben.

Our food was brought out, and while it looked delicious, I was too nervous to eat. I merely pushed it around the plate with my fork. It was like there was a clock in my head and I could hear it ticking down the seconds until I made a fool of myself.

When the food was cleared away Ben stood to give his speech, sending my stomach plummeting out of my body.

Everyone listened intently to his speech but I didn't hear a single word. It was like my ears decided to stop working.

When he sat down, I knew my time was finally up.

I stood shakily, and Trace reached up, putting a supportive hand on my lower back. He was probably afraid I was about to fall.

I swallowed, turning away from the crowd and facing my mom and Nick. After all, what I was about to say was for them and no one else.

Clearing my throat, my fingers wiggled restlessly against my side.

"First, I think it's necessary for me to say that I am so extremely happy for the both of you. Mom, you deserve to love and be loved, and I'm glad you've found someone that loves you completely. Nick," I said his name shakily, and his eyes met mine. "I truly mean it, when I say, there's no one else I'd rather have seen my mom marry. The love you feel for her is palpable. I'm honored to have you become a part of our family and I'm excited," I paused, "to see you create your own family together." I smiled significantly at my mother's small bulge. Nick laid his hand protectively over her stomach.

I did a small curtsy and took my seat.

Wait ... I curtsied?

Trace snickered beside me.

Oh, God.

Before I could dwell on my embarrassing curtsy, Nick reached for my hand. "Our family."

"Huh?" I looked at him questioningly.

"You said, and I quote, 'create your own family together,'

but you're a part of this family, Olivia. Don't ever think you're not." He eyed me.

I smiled at him and my mom. "My bad, *our* family," I enunciated the word.

"That's better." Nick grinned, his dimple popping out on his cheek. "Now that that's cleared up" —he turned to my mom— "let's dance the night away."

CHAPTER TWO

"Ugh, my feet are killing me," I groaned, kicking off my heels and reaching for the zipper on my bridesmaid's dress. It pooled on the floor beside the door and I breathed a sigh of relief to finally be out of that dress.

The apartment was dark and our black lab, Ace, scurried forward. His nails clacked against the floors.

"Hey, buddy." I petted his head as I passed by him on the way to the bedroom.

Trace came into the bedroom behind me carrying the fluffy lavender dress. "I didn't want Ace to mess it up," he explained.

I looked over at Ace, who'd jumped up on the bed, and then back at Trace. "You know Ace would never do that. He's a good boy."

Trace chuckled, hanging the dress over the top of the open closet door. "You never know."

I removed my bra and pulled on a sleep shirt and sleep

shorts. I was so exhausted that I was sure I'd be asleep the second my head hit the pillow.

I pulled the covers back and climbed into bed. Ace lay down beside me with his head on my stomach. I loved that dog so much.

Trace stripped down to his boxers and got in bed. We were quiet, listening to the symphony of our breaths.

I rolled to my side toward him and he put his arm around me, pulling me close. My ear rested over his heart and the beat calmed me. I felt his lips press tenderly against the back of my head, right over the scar that my hair kept hidden.

My eyes shut.

Even two years later, the memories of that day still haunted me. Sometimes, I closed my eyes and it was like Aaron was hovering over me once more with his fist raised. On those nights, Trace comforted me, sometimes staying up until the wee hours of the morning. I don't know how he didn't get tired of it. I think, maybe because of what he went through with his dad, that he understood it was going to take me a long time to get over it. It was easy for others who'd never been through something traumatic to judge me. They thought I should magically be over what happened. But that's not how it works. Healing takes time ... a long time. It takes patience. It takes love. Thankfully, Trace had all the love and patience anyone could ever need.

"I love you," he whispered, believing I was asleep.

I smiled. I knew he did. He didn't have to tell me, but it was nice to hear.

KNOCK.

Knock.

Knock.

Bang.

Knock.

With a groan, I sat up. What the heck was going on? It had to be the middle of the night.

I climbed from the bed to investigate the strange sound. I couldn't decide if it was someone knocking on the apartment door or something else. The noise was strange ...

Once I was out of the bedroom, it was easy to deduce that the noise was, indeed, someone at the door. But they definitely weren't knocking on it with their fist. It sounded more like they were using their whole body ... or head.

Scared to go to the door—because let's face it, I wasn't exactly the strongest person on the planet—I went to wake up Trace.

"Trace." I pushed his shoulder, trying to rouse him from sleep. "Trace." I shook him a bit harder.

"Huh?" His eyes cracked open a bit, just a thin slit of green showing through.

"There's someone at the door," I hissed.

"What time is it?" He rubbed his eyes, yawning.

"Two," I muttered, looking at the clock beside the bed. "I don't know who it is and I'm scared to open the door," I admitted reluctantly, playing with the ends of my hair.

He sat up and rolled out of bed, pulling on a pair of jeans, which he left unbuttoned. "I'll check it out," he assured me, kissing the end of my nose.

I tiptoed behind him and out of the bedroom. He undid the deadbolt and slowly opened the door.

Whoever was standing there fell into his arms.

"Avery?" I gasped, taking in the vibrant red hair.

"Mhmmmmitsme," she slurred drunkenly.

Since she seemed to have lost the ability to move her legs, Trace picked her up and gently laid her down on the couch.

I grabbed a bottle of water before kneeling beside her. She was completely wasted and the dress she'd worn to Nick and Nora's wedding was ruined. It was covered in grass and mud stains, as was her body.

My eyes widened, zeroing in on something wrapped around her neck. I gasped when I realized what it was.

"Avery! Why is your underwear around your neck?" I bit my lip to hold back laughter. I mean, it wasn't every day your best friend showed up at your place drunk with underwear around her neck.

"Huh?" She looked at me with bleary eyes and fingered the silky string of fabric around her neck. "Must have taken 'em off."

"Obviously," I snorted. "What were you doing?"

"I'm pretty sure it involved beer and sex in a field. By the way, don't ever try that," she warned Trace and me, pointing at us with a shaky finger, "it really itches."

I covered my mouth to stifle my laughter, but quickly sobered. "Wait, who'd you have sex with?"

Last I'd heard, she and Luca weren't together ... unless they'd gotten together tonight.

"The guy I bought the beer from was getting off work and we both wanted to have some fun. I think his name was Austin. Or maybe it was John? Brad? Anyway, he wasn't very good," she pouted. "Hey, is that water for me?" She reached for the bottle in my hand.

"Oh yeah, sorry." I handed it to her.

She slurped at it greedily and when the bottle was empty she let out a very undignified burp.

"I miss Luca," she began to cry. "I keep trying to forget him, but I can't, Libby," she slurred my name. "I lub him." She wrapped her arms awkwardly around my shoulders and sobbed. I'm pretty sure she drooled on my neck too.

I bit my lip and looked up at Trace helplessly. I had no idea what to do with her.

"Uhm." I patted her back. "I'm sorry?" It came out as a question.

"All I d-d-do is p-push p-p-people away," she cried.

"That's not true," I tried to comfort her. "Um, Avery?"

"Yeah?" She pulled away and looked at me with shimmery green eyes. I wrinkled my nose.

"I hate to tell you this, but you smell *really* bad."

We looked at each other and neither of us could contain our laughter.

I pulled a strand of grass from her hair and glanced up at Trace, who was still standing by the couch with his arms crossed over his chest.

"Can you help me get her in the bathtub?"

"Yeah." Avery looked up at Trace with wide eyes. "Help me, Tracey-poo."

He chuckled and shook his head. "I'll carry her, but I'm not stripping her. You're on your own with that part."

"Good, I didn't want your help for that." I smiled at him. I stood and pointed a finger at Avery. "Don't grope my boyfriend."

"Not making any promises." Her giggle ended in a hiccup. "He has a nice ass."

I rolled my eyes. Only Avery.

I pushed open the bathroom door and flicked on the light, yawning. I yanked the shower curtain open and started a bubble bath.

Trace came into the bathroom with a half-asleep Avery in his arms. "For someone that looks so little, she's kinda heavy."

"It's the boobs," Avery mumbled into his shoulder, "they must weigh fifty pounds."

Trace chuckled and sat her on the edge of the tub.

"Thank you," I told him, kissing his stubbled cheek.

"I'll sleep on the couch." He pointed a thumb over his shoulder. "She'll be more comfortable in our bed and from the looks of it, she's going to have a killer headache in the morning. So, let's not add a sore back to her list of ailments."

"You're too sweet."

"I try." He smiled crookedly.

"Danks Tracey," Avery slurred, leaning her head against the tiled wall, her eyes closed.

He shook his head and closed the bathroom door behind him.

The bathtub was about halfway full of hot water and smelled of vanilla bubble bath.

"Come on," I coaxed Avery into a sitting position instead of her slumped one. "Lift your arms."

I helped her out of her dress and removed the underwear from around her neck. She wasn't wearing a bra and I figured she'd probably lost it in whatever field she'd been rolling around.

"I can't believe I'm doing this," I grumbled, helping my drunk and very naked friend into the water.

"That feels nice," she murmured, a content smile lighting her face.

"You so owe me for this." I laughed, grabbing a handful of bubbles and blowing them at her face.

She swatted them away and smirked. "I reward you with my fabulosity on a regular basis. You owe *me*."

"Whatever," I laughed.

"Any special plans for graduation?" she asked, her eyes twinkling, hinting that she knew something that I didn't. Our graduation was in two days and classes had ended last week.

"No." I shook my head. "Nothing special."

"I know something you don't know," she sing-songed in a very off-key pitch. "Trace—"

"Shut up, Avery!" Trace yelled from the living room. "So help me God, I will come into that bathroom and see your goods if you don't stop talking!"

Avery giggled. "Trace wants to see my goods."

I looked between my best friend and the closed door. *What the hell is going on?*

"What do you know that I don't?" I asked her.

She opened her mouth but Trace came busting into the bathroom. "She knows nothing! Nothing! Right, Avery?"

She looked up at Trace with bleary eyes. "Oh, right. It's a surprise."

He smacked his face with the palm of his hands. "Never again," he grumbled under his breath. "Don't say anything." He pointed a finger at her and then turned to me. "And don't you *dare* try to get it out of her."

I couldn't help laughing. I raised my hands in surrender. "Fine."

He looked between the two of us. "Don't make me find a roll—or six—of duct tape."

Avery mimed zipping her lips and giggled.

Trace sighed and ran his fingers through his hair so that it stuck up in random directions. Shaking his head, he left the bathroom, closing the door quietly behind him.

I was tempted to try and pry the information out of Avery, but since I figured Trace was listening closely, I decided not to. It wasn't worth it.

I opened the cabinet under the sink and grabbed a washcloth. I wet it and added some mango scented body wash.

"Here." I handed it to her. "I'm not scrubbing you down but you really need to get the dirt off of you."

"Some best friend you are." She took the cloth from me. Her eyes were looking a little less glazed and I breathed a sigh of relief.

The door opened a crack again and Trace's tan arm poked through. In his hand was a loose gray t-shirt.

"I thought this would be more comfortable than her dress," he mumbled.

I stood and took it from him.

"Thanks," I said as he closed the door once more.

"I'm so sleepy," Avery muttered. "And lonely. I'm really lonely, Livie."

I sat on the bathroom floor and eyed her. "Why are you lonely?"

I drew my legs up and rested my arms on my knees as I waited for her answer.

"I miss Luca." She leaned back in the tub, staring at the ceiling.

"Then why don't you tell him that?"

"Because, I don't deserve him. I don't deserve anyone."

"Avery, that's the dumbest thing I've ever heard. Of course you deserve him." In my opinion, Avery and Luca were perfect for each other. He was the first guy that ever seemed to be able to handle her. Our freshman year of college, she'd had a different guy in her bed every night—the library had been my best friend at that time.

"No, I don't." She bit down on her lip and—*oh, my gosh, are those tears in her eyes?* Avery never cried. "I'm ruined."

I had never heard her say anything like that before. Maybe all the alcohol in her system was giving her loose lips.

"You're not ruined, Avery." I shook my head. "You're definitely not normal." I laughed. "But I wouldn't consider you 'ruined'."

"You're too nice to be my friend." She frowned.

I stood and grabbed a fluffy towel. "You look like you're clean, and I'm exhausted. Let's get you dry and in bed."

She reached under the water and pulled the drain plug. I had to help her out of the bathtub since her legs were on the shaky side.

I dried her with the towel and helped her into Trace's t-shirt, before brushing out her red hair.

"Thank you," she whispered. "You're the bestest friend of all the bestest friends in the world."

"That's a pretty big compliment." I laughed, opening the door.

Trace sat up and I laughed at his makeshift bed on the couch. Ace was asleep on the floor beside him. "Need help?"

"I think I've got her." I shuffled along with Avery clinging to my shoulders.

I got Avery into the bed, and by the time I pulled the sheet up over her, she was already snoring.

"Figures," I snorted.

I got into bed and in no time exhaustion consumed me.

WHEN I WOKE, Avery was still sound asleep.

I eased from the bed, not wanting to disturb her. I quietly closed the bedroom door behind me.

I smiled when I turned and saw Trace in the kitchen making breakfast. Between sips of coffee from his beloved Yoda mug, he was singing and feeding Ace pieces of bacon.

"Morning, beautiful." He ceased his one-man musical when he noticed me. "Coffee." He handed me a steaming mug, full of sugar and cream, just the way I liked it. I was a sugar addict, but what sane female wasn't?

I took a seat at one of the barstools that overlooked the small kitchen.

"Whatcha' making?" I peered over the edge of the bar top to try and catch a peek.

"Pancakes from scratch, because I'm awesome like that." He smirked, leaning a hip against the counter.

"Of course." I laughed. "How could I forget your awesomeness?"

"Why do I feel like you're mocking me?" He put a hand to his chest.

"Because I am." I peered at him over the rim of my coffee mug.

"You wound me." He chuckled, grabbing an old bottle of ketchup that contained the pancake mix.

"Really, Trace?" I raised a brow and pointed at the bottle.

"I was being resourceful." He smirked, squirting several dollops of pancake mix onto the hot griddle. "See? It's so much easier."

"Do you want a round of applause?"

"Normally" —he leaned across the counter so that our faces were only inches apart— "people don't ask. They automatically applaud my awesomeness."

"You're one of a kind." I couldn't hide my smile.

"There's no point in being like everyone else. That's boring." He shrugged and stepped back. He grabbed a spatula from the drawer and flipped the pancakes.

I slid from the stool and gathered the butter and syrup. I also swiped a piece of bacon while I was at it.

"I saw that." He laughed, pinching my side.

I danced away, but he reached out and grabbed me. He pulled me against him and proceeded to nuzzle my neck.

"Ugh," Avery groaned, stepping out of the bedroom, "you guys are too fucking sweet."

"Morning to you too," I said to her, trying to pry myself out of Trace's arms, but he was too strong. "Trace! Let me go!" I giggled.

"Fine." He turned me around so we were face to face, and kissed me loudly before letting me go.

I stumbled and he grabbed my arm to steady me.

"My kisses always make her dizzy," he joked to Avery.

I rolled my eyes. "He wishes."

Avery took a seat on one of the barstools and I sat beside her. Trace placed a plate in front of each of us and since there were only two barstools, he hopped up on the counter to eat.

"You made this?" Avery asked him, pointing at her pancakes with her fork.

He nodded.

"Like, it's not from the freezer section at Wal-Mart?"

He laughed. "I made it myself. Having a dick doesn't mean I can't cook."

"I'm impressed." Avery stared at her plate, nibbling on a piece of bacon.

"I am quite impressive." He chuckled.

Ignoring Trace, I turned to Avery. "Are you feeling better?"

"Yeah. Thanks for taking me in last night. I couldn't go home and just ... thanks." She wouldn't meet either of our eyes.

"You know you're always welcome here," I told her.

"Yeah," Trace agreed.

"I'm sorry for showing up drunk, though," she mumbled.

"It's okay." I shrugged.

She frowned, poking her pancakes with her fork. "No, it's not."

She looked so sad that I couldn't help reaching over and giving her a hug.

"You're much too good of a friend for me," she mumbled.

"Avery, stop being such a Debbie Downer." I smiled as I pulled away, hoping to lighten the mood.

"Sorry." She frowned, staring at her still uneaten pancake.

I looked up at Trace, silently pleading with him to leave so I could talk to her.

"Huh?" He raised a brow, a piece of pancake sticking halfway out of his mouth. Most people would've looked stupid like that, but not Trace. He looked like a model at all times.

I looked at Avery and back at him, then nodded my head toward the door.

"Oh!" he exclaimed, hopping off the counter. "Gotcha!" He saluted me. "Come on, Ace. Potty time." He headed toward the door.

Once he was gone, I asked, "Avery, what's going on? Please, talk to me."

She bit down on her lower lip, refusing to look at me. "I *can't*." Her voice cracked. "I'm sorry, Livie, but I can't talk to you about this. Not to anyone."

I tilted my head, studying her. Whatever was going on with her ran a lot deeper than I had originally believed.

"I'm your best friend. You can tell me anything."

"Not about this." She shook her head back and forth rapidly. Swiftly, she stood, the barstool almost falling over from her quick movements. "Tell Trace I said thanks for breakfast." Not meeting my eyes, she asked, "Do you have some clothes I can borrow? My dress is ruined and I don't exactly want to wear your boyfriend's shirt home."

"Sure," I said softly, slipping from the chair, and padding across to the bedroom. She followed closely behind me.

Avery was a lot curvier than I was but I managed to find a pair of jeans and an old t-shirt that should fit her. "Here." I handed it to her. "You—um—weren't wearing a bra and we aren't exactly the same size." I had a decent sized chest, but Avery's was a lot bigger. There was no way those were fitting in one of my bras.

"I'll make do." She smiled but it didn't reach her eyes. She let out a defeated breath as I closed the door behind me. I leaned my head against the door and closed my eyes. I was used to the crude, slutty, Avery I'd always known—this new sad and moody Avery was someone I didn't even begin to understand. I didn't know how to handle her.

The apartment door opened again and Trace poked his head inside.

"Where's Avery?" he asked me.

"Changing." I rubbed my hands over my face. I hadn't even finished breakfast and I was ready to go back to bed and start this day all over again.

"Is everything okay?" he asked, coming all the way into the apartment.

Ace scampered over to me and proceeded to slather my arm in dog kisses.

"I don't know," I whispered. "I just don't know."

CHAPTER THREE

"Do I look okay?" I asked Trace, coming out of the bedroom in my black cap and gown.

He laid his guitar to the side, sticking the pick between his lips, and sat up. After I started getting better, he'd taken guitar lessons. He said music helped him to cope with everything. My way of coping had been to pretend it didn't happen.

He was dressed nicely in a pair of slacks and a button-down shirt. I may have grown to love his plaid shirts, but he cleaned up good. He crossed his arms behind his head and looked me up and down.

"What do you *want* me to say?" he asked, taking the pick from between his teeth and placing it on the table. "I feel like this is a test, and I'd really like to pass so I can be rewarded later."

I rolled my eyes. "It's not a test, Trace."

"It's a cap and gown, Olivia. It is what is. But" —he stood

and strode toward me— "I know no one else will look as beautiful in it as you do."

"You're so full of crap you stink." I narrowed my eyes at him.

He threw his head back and his laugh filled the small apartment. "Oh, Olivia, you never cease to amuse me." He guided me toward the door.

"Is your family coming?" I asked, being extra cautious on the steps that led to the parking lot. While Avery had made sure I'd gotten used to wearing heels, heels plus the long gown equaled dangerous territory for me. Hopefully, Trace was paying attention and could catch me before I face-planted because that was a definite possibility. *Oh, gosh! What if I fell in front of the entire class?*

I took a few deep breaths. I'd done fine at the wedding, but my dress had been short so it wasn't like it could get tangled in my shoes.

"You have really got to stop worrying," Trace's voice broke into my thoughts. "You're going to get a wrinkle right there." He swiped his thumb between my brows. "And yes, they're all going to be there. You know Gramps wouldn't miss this."

I smiled. Trace's grandpa had welcomed me into their family with open arms and I honestly loved that man like he was a blood relative of mine. Trace's grandma, mom, and brother were amazing as well, but not quite like Gramps. Warren Wentworth was an all-around special person.

I stumbled into Trace's car. I made sure no part of the gown was sticking out of the car before shutting the door.

I smiled over at my "new to me" Ford Fiesta. It was purple and a nice upgrade from my old Ford Focus. Trace had been more than willing to buy me a fancy new car, he'd thrown around names like Mercedes and Land Rover, but I wanted to buy my car by myself. I didn't want to be dependent on Trace. I knew he meant well, but I was stubborn, and I didn't really like being showered in lavish gifts. I wasn't that kind of girl. Simple was my way.

I took the cap off my head and twisted it around in my hands.

"Ready?" Trace asked.

I nodded. "Mhmm."

He chuckled and pulled out of the parking lot, waving to a humped over Pete, the owner of the garage, who was scolding one of the mechanics for something.

Trace's apartment was fairly close to the University, but it took longer than usual to get there because of all the people trying to get into the school for graduation.

My phone rang and I pulled it out of the cup holder where I'd put it earlier.

"Hey, Mom," I answered.

"Where are you? Are you at the school? Nick and I are in the parking lot."

"We're almost there. Stuck in traffic." I frowned, craning my neck to see how much further we had to crawl before we could turn into the parking lot. "It'll probably take us another five minutes. I have a parking pass though. Wanna meet us at the student parking lot and we can all walk over together?"

"Sounds good," she replied and the line went dead.

We eventually made it into the parking lot and found a spot to park the car. Thank God I wasn't one of those girls that took forever to get ready, otherwise I probably would've missed my own graduation. It was set to start in thirty minutes. Knowing Avery, she'd rush in at the last possible second.

Trace held my hand as we walked toward my mom and Nick, who were standing beneath the shade of one the large trees dotting the campus. I had unzipped my gown and it flowed behind me. A slight breeze picked up and the air felt amazing against my heated skin. It had to be close to one hundred degrees outside and I was already nervous, therefore I was turning into an unattractive sweaty mess and graduation hadn't even started yet.

A flash went off and I glared at my mom as we joined them.

"Mom!" I whined. "At least give me a little warning."

She laughed. "Liv, I learned a long time ago that if I warned you I was taking your picture, you ducked and ran."

"That's because I hate having my picture taken," I defended, fighting a smile.

"You better get over that phobia real quick," Trace warned.

"Why?" The word had barely left my lips before he was pulling me against him and holding his phone out, snapping a picture.

He let me go and looked down at the phone. "Oh, that's definitely a keeper."

I stood on my tiptoes and peered around him to see the picture. "I look like a serial killer!" Trace looked amazing in the picture, of course, while I was cross-eyed and the look on my face screamed crazy person.

"You look cute." He chuckled.

"Oh, please." I shook my head.

"Well, well, well," Avery sing-songed, sauntering up to us, "if it isn't the old married couple" —she poked my side— "and the new married couple." She smirked at her brother and waved to my mom.

"Glad to see that you're back to your usual self." Trace laughed.

Avery frowned, remembering the other night.

"How are you feeling?" I asked her.

"Never better," she replied too quickly. Before I could comment, she grabbed my hand and began tugging me away. "We need to go get lined up. Like, now."

I waved over my shoulder to my mom, Nick, and Trace. "I'll see you guys in a bit," I called.

Once we were away from them I wrenched myself from Avery's grasp.

"What the heck is going on with you?"

"Nothing." She toed the ground with the pointed end of her heel.

"I'm your best friend, you know you can tell me anything, right?" I questioned, looking at her sadly.

"I know," she paused. "There are just some things that it's hard for me to talk about with anyone. It's nothing against you, Livie." She looked up at the sky and let out a shuddering breath. "There are things about me that *no one* knows."

"You can tell me, Avery." I reached for her hand. "I would never tell anyone."

"I know you wouldn't." Her green eyes were full of tears she wouldn't dare let fall. "But I *can't* talk about it. Okay?"

Reluctantly, I nodded in agreement.

"Thank you." She reached out and pulled me into a hug. "Now, we really do have to get lined up."

I HELD my diploma proudly in my hands and smiled widely as my mom took picture after picture. If she didn't quit soon, my face was going to be stuck this way permanently. My cheeks were already tired from all this smiling.

Trace held me close to his side and let her snap as many pictures as she wanted. *Traitor.* Wasn't he supposed to be on my side?

"Warren, Ellie, Lily, Trent," she called over the rest of Trace's family. "I want to get one of you all together."

After much directing from my mom, she finally got us lined up the way she wanted.

"Okay, are you ready? One, two, three—"

On three, Trent leaned over and kissed my cheek.

"Trent!" Trace scolded his younger brother.

My mom laughed, glancing down at the display on her camera. "Oh, I'm framing this one."

I groaned. Parents just loved to embarrass their kids.

"Let me see it." I stepped forward and reached out for the camera. "Oh gosh." I laughed. Warren, Ellie, and Lily were smiling happily, but my eyes were wide and my mouth was open in shock as Trent's lips pressed against my cheek. Trace was glaring daggers at his younger brother. "That is frame worthy," I agreed.

She took the camera from me and instructed us to line up again. This time, she put Trace on one side of me and Warren on the other. Smart lady. Trent was trouble.

"Hey, sweet pea," Warren whispered.

"I've missed you, Gramps," I said before smiling per my mother's command. At first, I had thought it would be awkward calling Warren Gramps. After all, he was Trace's grandpa, not mine. But now, I couldn't call him anything else.

"I've missed you too," he said in his gruff voice. Coughing, he added, "Tell that grandson of mine he needs to let you out of the house more often."

"I heard that, Gramps." Trace chuckled.

"What? It's true," Gramps stifled yet another cough with his hand.

"Are you okay?" I asked him.

"I'm fine, sweetie. When you're as old as me your lungs don't work as well as they used to."

I glanced at him skeptically.

After she'd taken over a hundred pictures of Trace's family and me, she waved Avery over.

Avery and I posed for a few pictures and then she relinquished the camera to Trace.

"I want some of Liv and me, and then a few with Nick as well," my mom told him.

"You got it." Trace nodded, holding up the camera. "Smile, Olivia."

I plastered yet another smile on my face, draping my arm over my mom's shoulder.

After about ten more pictures, she finally said she had enough. I figured her memory card was full.

"Are we all going to get dinner?" I asked. "What's the plan?" My stomach began to rumble at the thought of food.

"Actually." Trace stepped forward. "I have something planned … for just the two of us."

"Oh." I shook my head. "I assumed—"

"We'll see you two later." My mom smiled, hugging me. With that, her and Nick disappeared. Avery had already left and Trace's family was slowly backing away.

I narrowed my eyes. "What's going on?"

"Nothing." He smirked, his green eyes sparkling, and giving away the fact that there was *something*.

"Uh huh."

"Come on, we need to go home and change first. Slacks and a button-down are so not my thing." He plucked at the tight shirt.

"Maybe if they came in plaid you'd like them better," I joked.

"I'd definitely like them better then." He chuckled, reaching for my hand.

We made the trek back to his car, trying to avoid the other families still dotted around campus chatting and taking pictures.

"So," I started, "are you going to let me in on this *plan* of yours?"

"Not a chance." He winked.

"Ugh," I groaned. "Not even a hint?"

"Nope." He shook his head, a small smile playing on his lips.

"Will I like it?"

"I hope so." He chuckled. "Otherwise, well … "

"Well what?"

"I can't say." He opened the passenger car door for me.

I placed my diploma and cap in my lap as I buckled the seatbelt.

As soon as Trace was in the car I asked, "Is this plan of yours going to embarrass the crap out of me?"

"I hope not." He laughed. "But you are easily embarrassed."

Once at the apartment I changed into jean shorts, a tank top, and a purple plaid shirt I'd recently bought for myself because I knew Trace would like it. I rolled the sleeves up to my elbows and tried to make my hair look halfway decent.

"I approve," Trace said from behind me.

Turning, I laughed. "I thought you would." I plucked at the bottom of my shirt.

"I still think you look better in my shirts, though." He winked, pulling on a white wife-beater. He'd switched from slacks to a pair of ratty jeans. "Ready?"

I nodded, slipping on a pair of Converse.

He grabbed a cooler, adding drinks and sandwiches he'd made earlier. I'd noticed him making them this morning but I'd been too busy worrying about graduation to ask him about them. He slung the cooler strap over his shoulder, grabbed a soft blanket from the closet, and then picked up his guitar case.

I raised a brow in question.

He smirked. "Still not telling."

"Of course not." I sighed, holding my hand out to take the blanket from him and open the door.

He jogged down the steps while I locked the apartment door.

"Let's go in the Camaro," he called.

"Sure." I shrugged. I loved Trace's classic '69 Camaro. It may have been old, but it was extremely well taken care of.

I put the blanket on the back seat, along with his guitar case and the cooler.

I paid careful attention to the direction he was heading, hoping it would give me some kind of clue as to our destination.

"Are we heading back to the University?" I asked after a minute.

"No," he chuckled, "but close."

"Tell me," I pleaded.

"Not happening, woman. Patience." He rubbed his hand over his stubbled jaw.

"Wait, are we going to the park?"

"Ding, ding, ding! We have a winner!" He grinned.

He pulled into the gravel parking lot a few minutes later. We gathered our stuff, and he took my hand, leading me in the direction he wanted to go.

A huge smile spread across my face when I spotted the picnic table we'd sat on more than two years ago when I told him about my Live List. It had been hard for me to tell him about it, but even then I'd known I could trust Trace.

He didn't stop at the table like I thought he was going to.

Instead, he found a shady spot under a nearby tree. He dropped the cooler on the ground and gently laid his guitar down as well. He took the blanket from my hands and spread it on the ground.

"Sit," he commanded, pointing.

"Okay, bossy pants." I laughed, but did as he said.

He dropped down beside me and opened the cooler. He handed me a bottle of sweet tea and a packet of sugar. "Just in case."

He pulled out a bottle of water for himself and got out the sandwiches.

"So, this is your special plan?" I asked, unwrapping the sandwich and taking a huge bite. Not very ladylike, but I was starving, so screw manners.

"Oh, how you doubt me. The specialness hasn't even begun yet." He grinned mischievously. *Uh oh.*

"If you're not trying to woo me with your mad sandwich making skills, what are you up to?" I questioned, finishing my sandwich. I hoped he had another hiding in there. I was still hungry.

Sure enough, he tossed me a second sandwich.

"I love you." I leaned over and kissed his cheek before starting my second sandwich.

He chuckled. "Do you love me or my sandwiches? Because right about now I'm feeling a little jealous of the turkey sandwich." I blushed, suddenly not wanting to finish it. Only Trace could make eating a sandwich sound sexual. "I do make a pretty good sandwich, which shouldn't surprise you, because I'm awesome at everything I do."

I sighed. "Sometimes, I think you talk just because you love the sound of your own voice."

He bumped my shoulder with his. "My voice is amazing. I can't help it if I think everyone should be gifted with listening to the sound of it."

I shook my head but couldn't help laughing.

I finished eating and put my trash in the cooler.

We lay back on the blanket, looking up at the blue sky through the tree branches. I curled against his side, resting my head on his shoulder.

"This is nice," I murmured.

"It gets better," he whispered, turning his head toward me. His lips were so close that I couldn't resist closing the distance and kissing him. When I moved back, his eyes were closed, and there was a small smile on his lips.

"What was that for?" he asked, slowly opening his eyes.

"Because I can," I answered.

He rolled over so he was on top of me, holding his weight above me in a push-up position. "And why can you?"

"Because you're mine," I murmured.

"And you're mine." He flexed his arms and lowered himself, pressing his lips against mine. My eyes fluttered closed and an embarrassing breathy gasp escaped from me. He nipped my lower lip lightly with his teeth and my fingers tangled in his hair. He pulled away, running his nose along my collarbone and leaving a trail of small kisses.

He gazed down at me with lust-filled green eyes and my whole body responded to that look. My heart beat faster, my breath faltered, and my body arched up, desperate to meet and connect with his.

But we were in public and that was a *huge* mood killer ... at least for me.

"Does it get better than that?" My words were barely audible. Trace had that effect on me, stealing my thoughts, my breath, and now my voice.

"Better." He grinned, climbing off of me. He unzipped his guitar case and grabbed a pick. I sat up, crossing my legs under me.

He closed his eyes, and his whole body shuddered, like he was scared of what he was about to do.

Then he began to play, and when he sang, tears sprung to my eyes.

He stared into my eyes as he sang his slowed down version of Jason Derulo's song "Marry Me".

The look in his eyes of complete and total love had me sobbing. People in the park were beginning to stare at us, but I didn't care. I dabbed at my eyes, biting my lip to quiet my cries. I didn't want to miss a moment of this.

The last lyric ended in a whisper as he put his guitar to the side and pulled a small black box out of his pocket. He bent down on one knee in front of me and opened the box. My eyes widened.

"Olivia, that day is today. Will you marry me?" After the words left his mouth, he bit his lip, and there was fear in his eyes. I didn't know how that crazy man could ever think I'd say no.

Words failed me. I brushed my tears away and did what any logical person would do in my situation. I tackle-hugged him.

"Whoa," he cried, catching me as we fell in the grass.

I brushed my lips lightly over his before kissing him deeply. "Yes," I breathed in-between kisses. He kissed me fiercely, grabbing me by the neck with one hand and by the waist with the other, pressing me into him. His tongue brushed against my lips and my mouth opened in response.

Clapping echoed around us.

Heat infused my cheeks and I pushed myself off his chest. He sat up, cradling me in his lap.

"I believe this belongs to you." He grabbed the fallen jewelry box. He pulled the ring out of the box and slipped it on my finger. It was a beautiful ring, with three emerald cut diamonds. I stared down at it in awe.

"Congratulations!" someone called from the crowd that had formed around us.

"I'm putting this on YouTube," another said.

"Thanks." Trace waved, chuckling.

I buried my face in his neck, inhaling his manly scent.

The crowd gradually disappeared and we were left relatively alone in the park.

"That was—" I floundered for words. "Beautiful."

He kissed my forehead and tucked a stray curl behind my ear. "I'm glad you think so."

"You're amazing," I whispered, kissing his jaw.

"I thought we'd already established that."

"Did we really just get engaged?" I asked him. I honestly was still in disbelief that the last five minutes of my life had actually happened.

"Mhmm," he murmured, "we did."

"It feels like a dream," I breathed.

"I have been told that I look like I could only exist in a dream."

I smacked his shoulder. "Don't ruin my moment with your cocky remarks."

He chuckled, his chest rumbling beneath my ear. "Sorry, I'll keep quiet."

I reached up, cupping his jaw. "I love you, cocky remarks and all."

"Glad to hear it." He smiled. "And I love you too, Olivia. So much."

I snuggled closer to his body. Between the warm temperature of his skin and sun shining down on us, I was getting hot, but I refused to move.

"Was everyone in on this?" I asked, running my finger along the skin just above his shirt.

"Yeah." He grabbed my hands, entwining our fingers together.

"I don't know how you managed to keep them quiet. They're not exactly the most secretive bunch."

"It was difficult. Avery almost spilled the beans."

"Was this what she was talking about that night?"

"Mhmm." He nodded. "I thought I was going to have to

tape her mouth closed. The little blabbermouth. I wanted you to be surprised, and you were, weren't you?"

"Very. I honestly didn't have a clue," I whispered.

I was still in shock that I was actually *engaged*. Not that I didn't love Trace with all my heart, but marriage had been the furthest thing from my mind. I'd been so focused on getting better for so long then graduating and finding a teaching position that I'd sort of put any thoughts of our future on the backburner. But this felt *right*. Everything with Trace felt right, he completed me in every possible way.

We stayed in the park, watching the sunset, before we finally gathered our stuff and left.

As Trace held my hand, he kept twisting the diamond ring around on my finger.

"You like that there, don't you?" I smiled.

He opened the car door for me and as I slid inside he peered down at me, crossing his arms across the top of the door.

"Very much. Even more than your tattoo." He winked.

I shook my head, laughing. "That surprises me."

"It shouldn't."

We were quiet on the drive back to the apartment, reveling in this new step in our lives together.

When the door closed behind us, he pushed me against it and kissed me deeply, before taking me to bed and showing me exactly how much he loved me.

CHAPTER FOUR

The next morning my muscles were sore, but I was so deliriously happy that I didn't care.

I stretched my arms above my head. Light filtered in from the open curtains, making the diamond on my ring finger sparkle. A smile spread across my face as I gazed at it.

That smile turned to a frown though when I looked at the clock.

"Crap!" I exclaimed, throwing the covers off of me. I was supposed to be at work in twenty minutes. There was no way I'd have time to shower. Marcy, the owner of the jewelry store I worked at, probably wouldn't care if I came in late. I'd never been late once since I started working for her, but I didn't plan on starting now.

I grabbed a pair of jeans and shimmied into them, then grabbed a loose tank top with a flowered print on it. I was lucky to have a boss that wanted her employees to dress casually. Marcy truly was one of a kind.

I slipped my feet into a pair of shoes and darted out of the bedroom, straight into the bathroom. I heard Trace chuckle from the kitchen.

I brushed my hair and teeth, then pulled my hair to the side and quickly braided it. I added some gloss to my lips and mascara to my lashes, but there wasn't time for anything else.

"I can't believe you didn't wake me up," I groaned, dashing into the kitchen and dropping a piece of toast in the toaster.

"You looked too cute to wake."

I groaned in exasperation. "But now I'm going to be late." I opened the refrigerator and grabbed the tub of butter.

The toast popped up and I pulled it out, scalding my fingers in the process. I grabbed a knife from the drawer and slathered the toast with butter, before sticking it between my teeth.

"Bye," I said around the food in my mouth.

Trace chuckled in response.

I grabbed my keys off the table by the door and was about to leave when Trace said my name.

"Yeah?" I asked.

"I won't be home for dinner. Gramps needs to see me." He crossed his arms over his chest.

"Oh," I mumbled, pulling the toast from my mouth. "Is everything okay?"

He shrugged, pushing his hair out of his eyes. "I don't know."

"Well, I'll see you tonight then." I jogged across the room and stood on my tiptoes to kiss him. "Maybe I'll call Avery and we can order Chinese and just veg out."

He chuckled. "I think you're both overdue for some girl time."

"I *really* have to go now." I looked at him apologetically.

"Get gone then, woman." He smacked my butt and shooed me away.

"*Trace!*"

He was still laughing as I closed the door.

By the time I got in my car I had five minutes to make it to the store. That so wasn't happening.

When I made it to the store, I ran in the back door, apologies slipping from my mouth.

"Slow down." Marcy grabbed my arm, halting my steps. "You're going to hurt yourself."

"Sorry," I apologized yet again. "I'm late."

"Oh, honey, it's not a big deal. You look like you're about to have a heart attack. Sit down." She pulled a chair out and all but pushed me into it. "I'm actually surprised to see you up and walking today." She smirked, removing her purple reading glasses, and shoving them into her blond hair. She still had the ends dyed in a rainbow hue of colors.

"What do you mean?"

She laughed and looked down at my finger significantly. "Who do you think made that? He told me how he planned to propose, so I figured after that romantic gesture getting out of bed would be the last thing on your mind." She winked. "I mean, if I was engaged to that sexy man of yours I'd never let him leave the bed ... or put clothes on. A body like that should *not* be covered up."

I blushed profusely. Marcy may have been in her fifties and happily married, but she had no problem going on and on about how good-looking Trace was and what she'd like to do with him. If she was my age I'd probably be jealous.

"Mom!" Alba, Marcy's daughter, called. "Stop embarrassing, Olivia!"

"What? I'm only speaking the truth! Even his armpit hair is hot!"

I snorted. She did *not* just say that.

"Ew! Mom, that's gross." Alba wrinkled her nose as she pushed the beaded curtain that separated the front and back of the store aside.

"Eh, you'll get over it." Marcy dismissed her daughter with a wave of her hand. "Now" —she turned back to me "—what did you think yesterday when he proposed?"

"I was kind of in shock," I admitted with a small shrug. "I couldn't believe it was actually happening."

"Oh, I wish I could've seen your face." Marcy looked away, a wistful look in her eyes. "Especially since my so-called daughter is apparently never going to get married and gift me with grandchildren."

Over Marcy's shoulder, my eyes met with Alba's. She shook her head, and mouthed "crazy".

"Well," Marcy said as she patted my shoulder, "I need to go work on some designs."

"Of course." I stood, heading toward the front of the store.

Alba stopped me, pulling me into a hug. "Congratulations," she said. "Trace is a great guy. You're really lucky."

"Thanks." I smiled.

"I'll see you later." She waved, heading for the back door.

I HAD A RELATIVELY BUSY DAY. Marcy's store did a good amount of business, so I never had much down time, which I liked. People came from all over the tri-state area to buy her unique pieces. She made every piece of jewelry herself, often doing custom orders. I had never been much of a jewelry person; Aaron had forbidden my mom and I from wearing any, so even if I had wanted to I couldn't. But I loved my gold star necklace that Trace had gotten me for our first Christmas, and I'd later found out that Marcy made it. It pleased me to know that she'd made my engagement ring as well. In the past two years, Marcy had become an extension of my family. I loved that crazy lady.

I locked the door to the store and flipped the old-fashioned sign from Open to Closed. I closed the blinds on the door and windows and then turned the lights out.

I pushed the beaded curtain aside and stepped into the back room. Marcy was working feverishly on her latest project.

"Marcy," I approached hesitantly, not wanting to disturb her. She looked up at me, raising a brow in question. "You should really go home," I continued. "You look tired."

"I'm old, I always look tired."

"You're not old, Marcy." I shook my head. "But you do deserve a break every now and then. You're going to drive yourself into the ground if you keep staying here so late. Go home, have a good dinner, and take a hot bath. Please?"

"Fine." She flicked her desk light off. "But only because my eyes are tired and I'd hate to mess up this piece and have to start over."

"Thank you." I hugged her. "I worry about you."

"Don't waste your time worrying about me, child." She patted my cheek.

"I don't consider worrying about you as wasting my time." I moved toward the cubbies where we kept our personal stuff and grabbed my purse, slinging it onto my shoulder.

"You're too sweet, Olivia." She smiled, grabbing her own bag. I swear her purse was as big as a house. I didn't know how she lugged that thing around. I'd seen her pull an umbrella out of it before, and not one of those small ones that folded up.

We walked outside and I waited as she locked the door before we both headed toward our cars. It was seven o' clock and the sun was still bright in the sky.

"Bye, Olivia." She waved, climbing into her yellow Fiat. The bright colored car suited her bubbly personality.

I waved back, slipping into my own car. I immediately locked the doors. After what happened with Aaron I'd become a nervous wreck, anticipating danger everywhere. I wasn't afraid to admit that I was now the proud owner of a can of pepper spray—three cans, actually. I *might've* gone a bit overboard.

I pulled my phone out and sent Avery a text, asking if she was available for a girls' night.

Her text was immediate, saying she'd meet me at the apartment.

I was actually a bit surprised. I was expecting a half-assed excuse from her. I guess she was as much in need of some girl time as I was.

I called my favorite Chinese restaurant and ordered our takeout, swinging by to pick it up.

When I pulled into the parking lot of Pete's Garage, Avery's red Volkswagen Beetle was already there.

"Do I smell chicken fried rice?" she asked me when I got out of the car with the large takeout bag.

I nodded.

"Gimme!" She grabbed the bag from me, not giving me a chance to relinquish it.

"Geez, manners, Avery," I scolded lightly, grabbing my keys and trudging up the steps to our apartment over the garage.

"Bitch, I'm hungry." She glared. "Oooh," she exclaimed, peering into the bag, "they gave us extra egg rolls!"

"I figured if I only got two, you'd end up eating mine." I laughed, opening the door and waving her inside first. She set the bag down in the kitchen. "Come on, Ace!" I called.

The large black lab came running out of the bedroom and to the door.

"Hey, buddy, Mommy missed you." I scratched the top of his head, grabbing his leash off the coatrack, and attaching it to his collar. "Don't eat my sweet and sour chicken," I warned Avery.

She ceased pulling the boxes out of the bag. "Just one?" She pouted.

"The last time I told you that you could have one piece, I ended up starving because you ate it all, the answer's no."

"Fine," she grumbled.

I walked Ace around the block, letting him stretch his long legs. I would've walked him longer, but I was starving and afraid that despite my warning Avery would eat my food.

Ace bound into the apartment and over to his cushion, grabbing his favorite toy—a yellow duck—and proceeded to sling it around in his mouth.

Avery was sitting on the couch, the food spread out on the coffee table, flipping through channels on the TV.

"Don't even think about snagging one of Trace's skittles," I warned her, pointing to the bowl of skittles on top of the two crates that were flipped upside down and served as our coffee table. "I think he must have cameras in here somewhere. I ate like three one time while he was working, and when he came in he *knew* I'd eaten some."

"Maybe he counts them before he puts them in there." She giggled before taking a huge bite out of her egg roll.

"I have no clue, but since then I haven't touched them." I shook my head, grabbing a water bottle, and sat down beside her on the couch. "Anything good on?" I pointed at the TV.

"*Say Yes to the Dress* is on." She shrugged.

"That's not too bad." I grabbed my container of sweet and sour chicken.

"So, where's Trace?" she asked, looking around like he was about to magically appear.

"He's having dinner with his grandpa tonight." I shrugged.

"Aw, that's sweet. It's really cute how close he is with his family."

"Yeah, it really is. It's one of my favorite things about him," I admitted.

"Ugh," she groaned, "you guys are so in love it's not fair. Wait! You didn't tell me about the proposal!" She managed to stop shoving food in her mouth for five seconds in order to grab my hand and inspect my ring. "Oh, Tracey-poo did goooood. He wouldn't show it to me when he told me his plan. I told him that as your best friend it needed my stamp of approval, but the little fucker just laughed at me. Doesn't he understand the laws of the universe?"

I laughed. "You probably would've told him it needed to be bigger." The diamond ring was already plenty big, but I knew Avery.

"Guilty." She winked. "The bigger the better when it comes to *everything*."

"How did I end up friends with you?" I groaned.

"You couldn't resist my fabulousness. No one can." She grabbed another egg roll. I decided to snag one before she ate them all. Avery *loved* Chinese food.

A lot of people didn't like Avery. She was crazy smart and never afraid to speak her mind. But she had her wild side and had no problem jumping from one guy's bed to the next. We were polar opposites, but we clicked, and she was honestly the best friend anyone could hope to have. She had my back and I had hers ... even if she did drive me crazy a lot of the time, I wouldn't have her any other way.

"So," I ventured, hesitant of her reaction, "what's up with you and Luca?"

She sighed, running her fingers through her red hair. "I don't know, Livie."

"I don't believe that," I pushed.

"It's complicated." She shrugged, frowning.

"Avery" —I reached for her hand— "I'm your best friend, you can tell me." I'd said basically the same thing yesterday at graduation and it hadn't done any good. But today was a new day.

She shook her head. "Livie, it's not a big deal. Really. Sometimes people drift apart. I know you've only had Trace and you two are perfect for each other so you don't understand, but this is normal, I promise."

I knew she was evading telling me the truth by trying to make me feel like I was stupid when it came to relationships. Trace may have been my only boyfriend, but I wasn't dumb.

"All right," I sighed, grabbing a packet of sauce. I was done pestering her. If she didn't want to tell me, then I didn't want to know. I wasn't going to get into a fight with my best friend over nosiness. It wasn't worth it. "Want to watch a movie On-Demand?"

She grinned. "As long as I get to see Channing Tatum's butt."

I cringed. "Fine," I reluctantly agreed, because I knew she needed some cheering up.

Magic Mike began to play and it wasn't long until I'd completely lost my appetite and was hiding my face behind a pillow with Chewbacca on it. Trace had a Star Wars obsession, it was one of his cute quirks like his love of ketchup that was too adorable to complain about. Although, he'd probably be pissed if I told him I thought it was adorable. I'd just have to keep that tidbit of information to myself.

The movie ended and I hugged Avery goodbye, watching to make sure she got in her car and left the parking lot in one piece. My paranoia extended to everyone, not just myself.

I locked the door and grabbed some pajamas, heading into the bathroom to take a shower.

I pulled my wet hair back into a bun and called Ace into the bedroom. He jumped up in the middle of the bed, stretching out.

I rubbed his belly as I climbed under the covers. "Night, buddy, Daddy will be home soon." I yawned.

He wagged his tail at the mention of Trace. While getting a dog—any pet really—had been something I wanted to do, Ace had become Trace's dog. Their bond was special.

I turned the light off and snuggled under the blankets. The bed seemed too large and too cold without Trace in it.

As if sensing my distress, Ace curled against my side, his long pink tongue flicking out to lick my cheek.

I giggled.

I was beginning to drift off to sleep when I heard the door open. Seconds later, Trace strode into the bedroom, tearing off his clothes. His shoulders were taught and his jaw clenched.

I sat up, tilting my head.

"What's wrong?"

He sat down on the edge of his side of the bed with his back to me. I reached out, placing my hand on the smooth skin of his shoulder. The muscles in his back jumped at my touch. I had never seen him wound so tight before.

"Trace? Talk to me, please. What's wrong?" I begged.

There was a thickness in the air, like what he was about to say was going to change everything.

After a minute, he turned to me. The light from the moon filtered into the room, shining on his face, and making the tears in his glimmer. My heart broke and my chest clenched. *What is going on?*

He reached out and cupped my cheek, gazing at me. "You know how Gramps has been grooming me to take over the company?"

I nodded.

Warren had taken him under his wing about a year ago. Trace still worked at Pete's when he had the chance. He loved working on cars and didn't want to miss out on that. But with his dad dead and Gramps fast approaching his seventy-fifth birthday, it left Trace to run the business. I knew Trace struggled daily with what was right. Did he tell Gramps he didn't want the business? Or did he trudge on out of a sense of family duty and obligation? I hated that he had to choose. It wasn't fair. I knew Trace was much happier living simply, not as some big CEO. But this *was* his family business, and he didn't know if he was willing to hand it over to a stranger.

"I thought ..." He swallowed. "I thought it was just because he's getting older and wanted to retire, you know?" He pulled at his hair.

"But it's not?"

He shook his head, sniffling. "Gramps has cancer."

"*What*?" I shrieked, sitting straight up in bed. I hadn't expected those words to come out of his mouth.

"He didn't want me to tell you." He reached for my hand holding onto it tightly. "He hasn't told anyone, except me. But I had to tell you, Olivia. I couldn't keep this to myself. It hurts too much," he admitted, pulling his bottom lip between his teeth and looking away from me, ashamed of showing weakness.

"Cancer?" I squeaked. Tears clogged my throat and one cascaded down my cheek. Trace turned back to me, wiping it away with his thumb, his eyes full of sadness.

"It's lung cancer," he whispered, bowing his head. "The doctor's given him anywhere from a few weeks to a few months to live."

"No." I shook my head, a sob crawling my throat. I grasped his forearm, needing something to hold me up. "No. That can't be true." I didn't want to believe what he was telling me. I loved Trace's grandpa like he was my own. The thought that he might not be with us much longer tore me up inside. A few weeks or even months was *nothing*. How could you make yourself say goodbye to someone you loved so dearly? Goodbyes were never easy, especially when they marked the end.

Trace wrapped an arm around my shoulders, pulling me against him.

Ace grunted and jumped off the bed, unhappy at having his sleep disturbed.

I was angry with myself. I should've been the one comforting *him*, not the other way around. He rubbed his hand soothingly up and down my arm. A tear fell from his chin onto my cheek.

"No," I said again, as if just by saying that word it would make what he'd told me not true.

But nothing could undo this.

He lowered himself until we were lying on the bed and I pressed my face against his bare chest, smearing my wet tears along his skin.

He wasn't okay.

I wasn't okay.

And I wondered if we'd ever be okay again.

CHAPTER FIVE

I woke up still in Trace's arms. He was sound asleep, so I slipped from the bed carefully so I didn't wake him. He needed his rest after the news Gramps dropped on him last night.

My chest clenched.

I couldn't imagine a world without Warren Wentworth. There were some people that made the world brighter, and Gramps was one of them. Despite the amount of wealth he'd garnered he was still one of the most down to earth people I'd ever had the pleasure of meeting. He was *special* for so many reasons.

Tears sprung to my eyes.

Not again.

Nope.

No more crying.

With a shake of my head I padded out of the bedroom and

into the kitchen, determined to make Trace a delicious breakfast. While I could cook well, Trace usually made all our meals because he loved it. The man was perfect ... except for his dancing.

I pulled out the carton of eggs and set about making scrambled eggs.

By the time Trace came out of the bedroom, the eggs were ready and I'd fried bacon.

"I've been thinking," he started, leaning against the doorway to the bedroom, his hair sticking up adorably in every direction.

"About what?" I asked, placing our plates on the bar-top that overlooked the kitchen.

"I—*we* need to get away."

"We do?" I raised a brow.

"Yeah." He rubbed a hand over his stubbled jaw before stifling a yawn. Rumpled and straight out of bed, he was still the sexiest man I'd ever seen. It probably helped that he was shirtless and my mouth was watering at the sight of his bare chest. Seriously, how did guys get that V? It was a woman's undoing. It made smart girls do stupid things—I would know. "It's been a long time since we've been anywhere. You've graduated and I know Marcy wouldn't care if you took off for a bit." He shrugged. "Pete understands and Gramps ... well, he'll have to get over it."

"Where would we even go?" I questioned.

He smiled. "Nowhere. Everywhere. It doesn't matter." He strode across the room until he was in front of me. He grabbed me by both arms and bent his tall frame so he could look me in the eye. "We've both been going through the motions for so long, Olivia. We need to get our spark back."

"Our spark back?" I looked at him like he was crazy.

"Our spark for life. I miss all those crazy adventures we had when we were crossing things off your list. The spontaneity, the craziness, I *miss* that."

"I miss it too," I admitted.

While the past two years had been great, I understood what he meant. We'd become like an old married couple, content to stay in and do nothing. But when we'd been crossing things off my Live List, we'd had so much *fun*, and had so many crazy adventures.

Yeah, I wanted more adventures.

"But what would we do?" I asked him.

He surprised me by grabbing my cheeks and smacking his lips against mine. I'm pretty sure he slobbered on me too. Ugh, that was Trace for you.

His green eyes were full of excitement. "Let's go on a road trip."

"A road trip?" I repeated, mulling over the idea.

He nodded giddily, dancing on the balls of his feet. "Yeah, we could head north. Maybe visit the lake house in Maine."

"This is crazy." I shook my head. "We both have jobs, Trace, and what about Ace?" I pointed to the dog currently sprawled on the floor licking his paw.

"I already told you, they won't mind if we take off. As for Ace, Trent will take care of him. The freak has a ferret, I'm pretty sure he can handle a dog. Please, Olivia," he begged, even jutting out his lower lip. He wasn't fighting fair.

I decided not to think about it. Sometimes, thinking got you in trouble, and you needed to jump in feet first and think about the consequences later.

"Let's do it."

"Really?" He lit up, but there was hesitancy in his eyes, like I might pull the rug out from under him.

"Really." I smiled.

He grabbed me again, dipping me down and kissing me until I thought I'd pass out from lack of oxygen. "I love you."

"I love you too," I murmured, clinging to his arms so I didn't fall.

"We're really doing this?" he asked.

I nodded. "You, me, and a road trip. What could possibly go wrong?"

"We'll conquer those bumps along the way together, because that's what we do." He grinned.

"Now" —I pulled away, looking at him sternly— "if we're doing this, we do it right."

"What do you mean?" He grabbed a piece of bacon, taking a bite.

"No fancy hotels and five-star meals. I want this to be a *real* road trip. I want to rough it." I placed my hands on my hips, daring him to argue with me.

A huge smile spread across his face. "I knew I fell in love with you for a reason."

"What?" I shrugged. "In my mind, staying in fancy hotels does not constitute a road trip. I want to stay up late looking at the stars and sleep in the car. I want to go into dingy little diners and meet normal people. I want ..." *What was the word he used?* "Spontaneity, that's what I want."

"I'm so glad I stopped to help you with your flat tire," he whispered, his eyes growing dark with an emotion I couldn't decipher. "Best decision I ever made."

"I'm glad you stopped too." I wrapped my arms around his

shoulders, hugging him. "Even if I did sound like a bumbling idiot when I talked to you."

He chuckled, his chest rumbling against me. "It was adorable. Especially when you called me Prince Charming."

I blushed, burying my face against his shoulder. "You *are* my Prince Charming, even though you drive me nuts sometimes."

"Gotta keep things interesting, babe." He grinned crookedly.

"So," I asked as I gazed up at him, "when should we leave for this road trip?"

"I'd say tomorrow, but you'd probably kill me." He winked. "How about next week? That should be enough notice for Pete and Marcy. Gramps will be pissed at first, but he'll understand." He took a shaky breath. "I need to get away. I can't be here when he tells them, Olivia. I know I have to be strong for them and I *can't* do it right now."

"I understand." I cupped his stubbled cheek. I could see how it pained him to admit that to me and it broke my heart. "Next week sounds perfect. How long are we going to be gone?"

"Two maybe three weeks, tops."

I had several interviews lined up in July for teaching positions, so we'd be back in plenty of time. I'd been afraid, knowing Trace, that he'd say two months.

"Well, Ace" —I bent down to pet the dog— "I'm going to miss you, bud." He looked at me with sad gray eyes.

"He'll be fine." Trace bent down beside me, scratching the dog behind his ears. Ace's tail thumped loudly against the floor.

"What are you, the dog whisperer now? We've never left him for this long. I hope he'll be okay." I frowned.

"Trent will do fine with him, he's an animal lover. I'm surprised the kid isn't off somewhere preaching about saving the whales or some other shit. He used to drive my mom nuts when he was little because he was always bringing stray animals into the house. She wasn't happy when she found the snake in her bathroom."

"I wouldn't be, either."

"It was a garter snake, it wasn't like it was going to hurt anyone." He chuckled. "She ended up on top of the bathroom counter wielding a hairdryer as her weapon of choice. She wouldn't get down until the snake was out of the house."

I snorted. "That's funny."

"There's a picture somewhere." He stood, walking around the counter and sitting in front of his plate of food. It was bound to be cold by now. "Unless she's burned them all, which is possible."

I grabbed his plate before he could snag another bite and popped it into the microwave, then did the same with mine and sat down beside him.

"Good?" I asked him, pointing to his plate.

"Delicious." He leaned over and kissed my cheek. "Thank you."

I smiled, nibbling at my own breakfast. I wasn't very hungry. While I was excited at the prospect of a road trip with Trace, I couldn't help but wonder if now was a bad time. I understood what he'd said about needing to get away. When it was time for me to go to college, I'd picked a school in Virginia, about as far away as I could get from my home in New Hampshire. So, I knew running when I saw it, and that's what he was doing—running from his problems.

But I'd already agreed, and I *was* excited.

There was nothing I could do now but go along for the ride.

LILY, Trace's mom, pulled me into a hug. "It's good to see you. I'm sorry we didn't get to talk more at your graduation, but Trace—"

I held up a hand to silence her. "I know. Trace is Trace, and he had a plan, which left little time for chitchat. Although, my mom didn't help with her endless picture taking."

"You're her only child, of course she wanted lots of pictures."

"I won't be an only child for much longer." I laughed.

"No, I guess not." She guided me into the dining room.

"Look! It's my favorite granddaughter!" Warren exclaimed as I entered the room.

My heart clenched and tears threatened to fall, but I dammed them back, because Trace wasn't supposed to tell me and I'd hate to ruin dinner. Trace was already bound to ruin it with his announcement that we were leaving for a few weeks.

"Hey, Gramps." I left Lily's side and made my way to the head of the massive dining table, where Warren sat. I bent and kissed his wrinkled cheek. He grabbed my left hand, inspecting the ring. "'Bout time my lousy grandson put a ring on your finger."

I laughed, squeezing his hand.

"When's the wedding?" he asked.

"We haven't talked about—"

"Gramps!" Trace groaned, coming into the room. "Don't scare her, I just proposed."

"When you're as old as me, these questions are important." He coughed.

I looked up at Trace and saw several emotions war across his face. He met my gaze and tried to hide his frown.

I knew what he was thinking, because I was thinking it too, Gramps might not be alive to see us get married. I couldn't imagine not having Gramps there. Since I didn't have my own dad, and had never met my grandparents, I'd assumed Warren would walk me down the aisle. If that didn't happen it would break my heart.

Trace stopped beside Gramps chair, on my other side, and patted his shoulder. "I'm sure we'll talk about it soon."

"Make it snappy."

"Will do, Gramps." Trace chuckled, taking a seat.

I took the seat beside him as Cecilia brought out the food. My eyes widened at the sight of the food. It was always a feast at the Wentworth's.

"Where's Trenton?" Lily looked around the room, realizing that her youngest son had yet to arrive.

"Probably sleeping." Trace shrugged.

"It's one in the afternoon!" she shrieked. "I'm calling him and he better get his butt here."

Before she could get her phone, Trent breezed into the dining room. "Sorry I'm late," he grumbled, pulling his baseball cap low over his eyes. "I was up late studying last night."

Lily narrowed her eyes. "Your classes ended a few days ago, Trenton. What could you possibly be studying?"

He smirked. "The female anatomy."

"Trenton Carson Wentworth! Don't speak that way!"

Throwing her hands in the air, she mumbled, "I miss the days when I could put you in time-out."

"I don't." Trent chuckled, sliding into a seat. "You used to forget about me and I'd spend hours sitting in a corner. Some people would consider that child neglect, Mom."

"Oh, please." She rolled her eyes, fighting a smile.

"It's true." He grabbed a roll, slathering it in butter, and sticking half of it in his mouth. "And I'd hate for you to go to jail. Orange is definitely not your color."

"You're so kind to me." Lily laughed, joining the rest of us at the table.

Ellie, Trace's grandma, watched Trent with an amused smile. The Wentworth boys were one of a kind.

Sometimes it still blew my mind that Trace and Trent had grown up in this mansion and were so normal. You'd think the kind of wealth they had would have gone to their heads, but the whole family was completely down to earth.

I nibbled on a piece of roasted chicken, trying not to moan in pleasure. Cecilia made the most delicious meals. Even Trace couldn't top them.

Trace and I tried to have dinner with his family every week. It was something I always looked forward to. I'd heard horror stories from other girls about their boyfriend's family not accepting them, but the Wentworth's had taken me in with open arms from the moment they met me.

As the meal wound down and Cecilia brought out a homemade cheesecake, Trace cleared his throat.

"So, uhm, there's something Olivia and I need to tell you guys," Trace said, draping his arm across the back of my chair.

Everyone looked up in interest. I stared down at the table to avoid their curious stares.

"We're going on a road trip. We leave Monday."

Well dang, he didn't waste any time sugar coating it. I waited with bated breath for the uproar that was bound to ensue.

I wasn't prepared for what Lily had to say though. "Oh, thank God," Lily breathed, "for a second there I thought you were pregnant."

I blushed, taking a huge bite of cheesecake so I wouldn't have to say anything.

"Calm down, Mom. No babies for like ... another year." He winked at me.

My eyes widened. *A year? Is he crazy?*

I began to choke on my cheesecake and he beat my back.

"A year?" I squeaked when I could talk.

"You never know." He grinned.

To avoid a panic attack I ate more cheesecake. Yeah, that was better. I was sure cheesecake could solve all the world's problems.

Trace slid his desert plate my way. *Smart man.*

"Where are you going on this road trip?" Lily asked with interest.

"North." He shrugged. "I don't know where we'll stop along the way, but I thought maybe we'd head to the lake house and stay for a bit."

"You should, it's lovely there. I'm sure Olivia would love it. How long will you be gone?" she asked, taking a sip of wine.

"Two or three weeks, which means Trent needs to watch Ace."

"Whoa!" Trent exclaimed, tipping his chair back on two legs and waving his hands. "No way! I didn't sign up for that, get someone else to do it!"

"Dude, you have a ferret, I think you can handle a dog."

"My townhouse has a one pet limit, sorry," Trent argued.

"That's bullshit and you know it. Did you forget who's paying for your townhouse?" Trace eyed his brother.

"Shit."

"Come on, Ace isn't a bad dog. You can handle it," Trace pleaded.

"But Bartholomew likes to run around on the floor. If Ace steps on him, that giant will kill him."

"I think Bartholomew will survive two weeks in his cage and you could always put Ace in your bedroom and let the little carpet shark run around," Trace shrugged. "Problem solved."

"You have an answer for everything," Trent snorted. "Fine, I'll do it. But only because Ace is cute and I've always wanted a dog."

"I knew you'd come around, little brother," Trace smirked.

"Yeah, yeah, yeah, whatever." Trent took his hat off and twisted it around in his hands. "You owe me for this." He pointed a finger warningly at Trace. "I don't know what it is yet, but it'll be big."

"You're ridiculous." Trace shook his head.

"Boys," Lily interrupted in a warning tone. "Stop it. I mean it."

"Sorry, Mom," Trace bowed his head.

"Sorry," Trent grumbled reluctantly. Despite the way they might sometimes act, I knew they both hated disappointing their mom. "I better get going." He stood and kissed his mom's cheek. "Thanks for lunch." With that, he brushed out of the room without a backward glance.

"What's got his panties in a bunch?" Trace asked his mom.

"How am I supposed to know? He's nineteen, Trace. He hasn't told me anything in a long time." She sighed, finishing her wine.

"I'm gonna go talk to him," Trace mumbled, looking toward the doorway. "I'll be right back," he told me.

"Mhmm." I nodded.

Trace had been gone a minute, when Warren said, "Olivia, can I speak with you?"

Automatically, I felt like a small child who was about to get scolded, which was silly.

"Of course." I wiped my mouth free of crumbs and took a sip of water.

He stood up and waited for me to do the same before guiding me out of the grand dining room and into his office located toward the middle of the mansion.

He closed the door behind us and motioned for me to sit on the large leather couch.

I'd only been in Warren's office a few times, but I loved it. Every wall was covered in floor to ceiling built in bookshelves stained in a rich dark color. It was sophisticated but warm and welcoming. It was the kind of room that I would love to curl up in and read a good book.

Clearing his throat, Warren sat down beside me.

"There's something I need to tell you, Olivia," he started. "I'm sure Trace has already told you, even though I asked him not to, but in case he hasn't I'm just going to say it." He took a deep breath. "I have cancer."

Even though I'd been prepared to hear those words, having Warren say them brought back everything I'd felt when Trace had told me—only this was a hundred times worse.

Not being able to help myself, I opened my arms and dove at him. He wrapped me in a hug, rubbing my back soothingly.

"Please, don't cry." He kissed the top of my head. "I don't want you to cry for me, sweetie. I've lived an amazing life and it's time for me to go. There's no need to mourn that."

I put a fist against my mouth to stifle my sobs. Gramps was the one *dying* and he was comforting me.

"I need you to listen to me, sweet pea." He took me by the shoulders and pulled me away so I was forced to look in his eyes. "Can you do that?"

I nodded, taking deep breaths in the hopes to quiet my sobs.

"I've known about the cancer for a long time now, more than a year, and I chose to forgo treatment. I didn't want to wither away. I wanted to enjoy every last moment with all of you. I hope you can understand that."

My lower lip shook with the threat of tears.

"You and Trace are the only people that know. I'm not telling anyone else. I don't want any of you to look at me differently. I plan to enjoy these last few weeks of my life as if nothing's wrong."

"Weeks?" I squeaked. "Trace said you had anywhere from a few weeks to a few *months*," my voice cracked.

"I told him that to give him *hope*." Warren took my hand, holding it tightly in his. His skin was warm and a healthy color. Nothing about him screamed that he was *sick*. Nothing but that cough. How could someone appear outwardly healthy but be fighting such a vicious disease on the inside? "I know my death is going to be hard on my family, you included, but it's going to be hardest on Trace. He already lost his dad." Warren took a shaky breath. "I need you to be strong for him. I need you to comfort him and keep him grounded. Can you do that?" His eyes held a shimmer of hesitance. I knew it was hard for him to ask me this, because he knew I was hurting too.

"Of course. I'd do anything for Trace and I'd do anything for you, Gramps." I hugged him. He smelled slightly like peppermint—like comfort and home.

"You're a strong girl, Olivia. Stronger than Trace gives you credit for."

"I don't know about that." I tried to laugh around the tears.

"You are," he whispered. "Sometimes it's the quiet strength that we have to watch out for."

CHAPTER SIX

"I THINK THAT'S EVERYTHING." TRACE GRINNED, closing the trunk of his Camaro, and pushing up his thick-framed black glasses. He grabbed me around the waist, plastering my body against his. My hands landed against his chest. The thin cotton tank he wore did little to mask the amazing muscles he was hiding underneath it. "Are you ready to be stuck in a car with me for weeks?" He smirked, bending his head and grazing his lips against my chin, before biting gently with his teeth. Every time he did that it left my brain a pile of mush.

"Mhmm," I murmured, closing my eyes. "It'll be fantastic if you keep doing that."

"This?" he asked a moment before he placed a kiss on my collarbone and then bit it.

"Yeah, that."

"I think I can arrange to do that often ... all over your

body." His lips glided over my shoulder, up my neck, and settled over my own.

I felt slightly lightheaded when he stepped back. "You're way too good at that," I groaned.

"There's more where that came from."

I smiled, shaking my head. "Is Trent picking Ace up here or are we dropping him off at his apartment?"

"Dropping him off. We'd wait forever for that loser." Trace chuckled. "I'll be right back." He held up a finger and dashed up the steps into the apartment. He appeared a moment later with Ace on a leash and the bag of dog things I'd packed.

"Did you put *everything* the dog owns in here? This is heavy!" he grumbled, awkwardly making his way down the steps.

I laughed, taking the leash from him.

"No, but dog food is heavy," I informed him, ushering Ace into the backseat.

"*Did you put a blanket down so he doesn't scratch the leather?*" Trace exclaimed from behind me, trying to peer over my shoulder.

"Calm yourself." I laughed. "Of course I did."

Not only was Trace a mechanic, but he was a car enthusiast. Heaven forbid he think there was a knick on one of his "babies".

"Before we leave, are you *sure* you have everything?" he asked.

I rolled my eyes. "Just as sure as I was the last ten times you asked me."

"Just checking." He chuckled, getting in on the driver's side. He patted the dashboard and said, "Let's roll."

TRENT'S TOWNHOUSE was surprisingly nice. I shouldn't have been surprised, though. Even before I came along, Trace's apartment had been pristine and didn't resemble the typical bachelor pad.

While the furniture and wall colors were of a masculine variety, nothing screamed that he was a college freshman living on his own.

A furry creature ran between my feet and I let out a yelp.

At my cry, Ace began to bark and tried to pull the leash from Trace's hand so he could run after it.

"Bartholomew! Come back!" Trent chased after the ferret. "I swear I put him away," Trent called to us. "He's a little escape artist. Aha! Got him," Trent exclaimed, grabbing up the furry little creature. "Bad," he scolded the ferret, before putting it back in its cage. He ran his hand through his hair and smiled crookedly. "Sorry about that."

"Yeah, well," Trace said dryly, "are you sure you can handle this?"

"Having doubts about me so soon?" Trent batted his eyelashes. "I'm offended. Especially after you forced me to agree to this."

"I didn't force you," Trace groaned.

Trent raised a brow.

"Okay, so maybe I *was* a little pushy." Trace shrugged.

"A little?" Trent shook his head and then smiled at me. "I don't know how you put up with this idiot."

"Sometimes I wonder myself." I laughed.

"We need to get on the road." Trace held the leash out for Trent to take.

I bent and said goodbye to Ace then hugged Trent.

"Thank you for doing this," I whispered in his ear so Trace couldn't hear, "I'm sorry he was so bossy."

"It's fine," he whispered back, "I like to give him a hard time."

Trace was watching us with narrowed eyes. "I know you two are talking about me. I'm not stupid."

"Never thought you were." Trent smacked his brother on the shoulder. "Now get out of my house. I don't want to see your sorry ass for at least two weeks."

"How I got stuck with you for a brother is beyond me." Trace shook his head as he left.

"Have fun." Trent chuckled, waving goodbye to me.

I waved back, closing the door behind me.

Trace was already waiting in the Camaro with his sunglasses on and the windows rolled down.

"Where are we heading first?" I asked, buckling my seatbelt.

"Pittsburgh," he answered, speeding out of the neighborhood and making a sharp turn. If he slung me against the door so help me—

"Trace!" I groaned, when my shoulder slammed against the door. "Don't do that! It hurts!"

"Sorry." He grinned, so I knew he really wasn't sorry.

"Why are we going to Pittsburgh?" I rubbed my shoulder.

"It's a surprise." He sat back, a small smile playing on his lips.

"You and surprises. I'm not sure I'm fond of this idea."

"It's nothing *bad*. I promise."

"Now I'm scared." I pulled my hair to the side and began to braid it. Leaving it down to whip around my face was not an option in my book. I didn't want to spend an hour having to untangle the wavy ends because Trace had the windows down.

"It's okay to be scared." He took my hand. "That makes the end result all the more fun."

"You have a twisted sense of logic." I laughed, tucking my legs underneath me.

"There's a method to my madness." He squeezed my hand. "Wait and see."

———

AND THAT'S how I found myself parked outside of the old Heinz factory that now served as a museum on the company and the city of Pittsburgh. There was a large lit up ketchup bottle that was filling up the Heinz sign with ketchup.

"Really, Trace? Really?" I placed my hands on my hips and stared him down. "Ketchup? That's the first thing you want to do on this road trip?"

"It's a *museum* dedicated to the founder of the *best ketchup*, of course this was the first thing I thought of. Don't ever doubt my love of ketchup." He grinned, sliding out of the car and opening the trunk.

I followed, eyeing him with suspicion.

"What are you doing?" I asked as he rummaged through his suitcase.

He held a hand, halting me.

I sighed, taking a step back and crossed my arms over my chest.

"Found it!" he cried, pulling out a red piece of fabric and zipping his suitcase closed. Much to my dismay he began to remove his trusty plaid shirt and wife-beater in the middle of the parking lot. He dropped the garments in the trunk and closed it before putting the red shirt on.

I snorted when I saw that it was his *I Love Ketchup* shirt I'd bought him a few years ago.

"What?" He grinned, his eyes a light playful green. "I can't come to the former Heinz ketchup factory without my ketchup shirt. It would be blasphemy."

"Of course it would." I laughed, letting him lead me into the building.

He paid the ten-dollar entrance fee and then dragged me around like an excited little kid. He oohed and ahhed, pointing out things here and there that he thought was fascinating.

"I like your shirt," one guy said in passing.

"Thanks!" Trace called after him. "See?" He smirked at me, fighting a laugh. "People love my shirt."

"Are you forgetting I bought it for you?"

"No" —he draped his arm over my shoulders— "I'm just pointing out its obvious awesomeness since you can't seem to see it."

We completed the tour and then he dragged me into the store area.

He raced straight toward the apparel section and grabbed a shirt. He turned and held it out to me. "Look, Olivia! We can be twinsies!"

"Oh, God," I groaned, burying my face in my hands. "There's no way I'm wearing that." I glared at the red shirt with the Heinz ketchup label on it.

"Please, for me?" He pouted.

Ten minutes later I found myself wearing the stupid shirt. Damn him and his persuasive ways. Those pouty lips and green eyes were always my undoing.

I tugged on the shirt as I followed him outside and toward the car.

"I can't believe I let you talk me into this," I grumbled, staring down at the shirt.

He chuckled. "You look cute in it."

"You're a liar. I look ridiculous." I shielded my eyes from the sun with my hand.

He stopped in his tracks in front of me. He stared down at me, cupping both of my cheeks in his large hands. "I would never lie to you, Olivia. You are cute, and beautiful, and smart, and amazing, and a thousand other things."

"Now someone's just trying to get laid."

"Don't get me wrong," he said with a smirk, "the sex is great, but it's not why I love you."

"Good to know." I smiled up at him.

"Hungry?" he asked, opening the passenger car door for me.

"Starving," I admitted just as my stomach let out a very unladylike growl.

He laughed at the sound.

He entered something into his phone and a minute later it was directing us to a restaurant.

We pulled up in front of a place with a large lit up sign in blue letters that declared it as Primanti Brothers.

"Have you been here before?" I asked him as I got out of the car. I knew Trace and his family used to travel a lot, especially when his dad was still alive.

"Yeah." He nodded. "You're about to feast upon a heart attack on bread."

"I'm a bit afraid now." I eyed him apprehensively.

"Don't worry, it's delicious and you'll love it."

"*That's* what I'm afraid of." I laughed. I glanced down at my new shirt and then at his. "People are going to think we're so weird."

"Weird is beautiful." He kissed my cheek.

"You have such a way with words." I poked his side as he held the door open for me.

"I once won a poetry contest." He smirked, adjusting his glasses as we stepped into the dim restaurant.

"Sure you did." I laughed in disbelief as we picked a table. I grabbed one of the menus off the table and began to flick through it. "Wait, they put fries and coleslaw *on* the sandwich, not on the side?"

Trace nodded, tapping his fingers against the wood tabletop as he perused the menu.

I studied a picture of one of the sandwiches, my mouth dropping open in disbelief. How the hell were you supposed to take a bite of that monster? It was huge!

Trace slammed his hand down on the menu, blocking my view of the picture.

"Don't look at it. You'll get overwhelmed and it's not like you have to eat it all."

"I'm not sure I'll be able to eat one bite."

"Trust me" —his tongue flicked out to wet his lips— "it's delicious. Want me to order for you?"

"Sure." I shrugged as he slid my menu away. Trace had known me long enough to know what I liked and didn't like.

A waitress came and he placed our order.

Once she had walked away, I asked, "What are we doing next? Are we staying here a bit longer or heading somewhere else?"

"So many questions." He chuckled, spinning the pepper-shaker along the tabletop. "I thought maybe we'd head toward Philadelphia. I'm a big history dork. It probably comes from living where there's so many Civil War battlefields and museums. Anyway" —he crossed his hands behind his head and leaned back in the chair— "I've never been to Philadelphia and I've always wanted to see the Liberty Bell and go to the museums in the area."

"Sounds good to me." I shrugged. "I'm down for anything."

He grinned widely and I knew I was in trouble.

"I'm glad you said that."

"As long as it's not something that might possibly get me killed," I warned him. "Or arrested."

"Done." He crossed his arms over his chest. "You know," he added as he leaned toward me, "I should probably be offended that you think I might possibly subject you to something dangerous. You're the one that made me get in a hot air balloon that one time."

"*You* surprised me," I argued. "You didn't have to do it."

"But I did." He grinned, pushing his hair from his eyes.

"Don't complain about it then."

"You're mean."

"You know" —I leaned toward him conspiratorially— "it surprises me that you were scared, what with the tattoos and bad boy demeanor you're always sporting."

"Hey," he defended with a grin, "I'm not afraid of heights. I just couldn't handle the teetering basket thing. What if it tipped all the way over and we fell to our death without any protection?"

"If that was the case, then I don't think anyone would ever get in one. They're safe," I explained as the waitress set our drinks on the table. Mmm, sweet tea. I'd never tried the stuff until I moved to Virginia, but I was now an addict.

"Obviously." He smiled in amusement. "We're still alive, aren't we?" He raised his glass of water, taking a sip.

"Yeah, we are," I mumbled, overcome by sadness. We were alive, we were healthy, and we had our whole lives ahead of us. But Gramps ...

"Olivia?" Trace said my name hesitantly, placing his hand over top of mine where it rested on the table. "What's wrong? What did I say?"

"It's nothing." I took a shaky breath.

"Oh." He frowned as realization hit him. "You're thinking of Gramps."

I nodded.

"You know," he started, biting down his lips, "I understand that every life has a limit. I watched my dad die and I almost did the same with you." His eyes grew sad. "But that doesn't make it any easier. When you look at someone, you don't see an expiration date. You see *life* and that makes death so much harder to accept."

His words were true. I turned my hand underneath his so that it was palm up and gave it a squeeze.

"You're so wise." I smiled.

"Hardly," he snorted. "I've just had way too much experience with this. Seeing my dad killed tore me apart, Olivia. You *never* get over something like that. Then having to watch you dying in front of me, and being unable to do anything to save you, was another blow. Watching you in that hospital, waiting for you to wake up" —the lines of his face darkened and his lips turned down— "I vowed then to never watch another person I loved have to suffer that way. I *can't* do it. I know that's weak of me." He laughed humorlessly. "But it's true. Going on this road trip might be taking the cowardly way out. But I *have* to. I can't stay home and watch Gramps wither away. Especially with the others not knowing." He took his hand from mine and rubbed his stubbled jaw. His eyes had a faraway look in them.

I looked down at the table, overridden with guilt as I remembered what Warren had told me. He hadn't told Trace the whole truth, but he had told me for some reason. By the time we got back from our road trip—I couldn't even think about it.

After what Warren had confessed to me, I'd told him that I would talk Trace out of the road trip. But he hadn't wanted that.

He'd taken me in his arms, given me a great big bear hug and said, *"Don't do that, Olivia. Trace needs this. I see it in his eyes. Go and have fun. Live for me."*

It had been hard to say goodbye to him after that, but I'd done it, because that was what he wanted.

I gazed across the table at Trace. We were both lost in thought. Slowly, his eyes met mine. The sadness that swirled in the green depths was reflected in my own.

I knew he was thinking, not only of Gramps, but of his dad and what had happened to me.

I knew it was selfish of me, but I'd never really stopped to think about how he had been affected by what happened to me. I could see in his eyes how much he had suffered watching me lie in that hospital bed and then with the slow recovery process. At the time, I'd only been able to think about how *I* was hurting. But Trace had hurt too.

The waitress set our food on the table and we both snapped

back to reality. He forced a smile and pushed his glasses further up his nose since they kept slipping down.

I hated seeing him so sad. I only ever wanted him to be happy. When you love someone unconditionally, when they hurt you hurt, and right now I was in so much pain that I couldn't stand it. From now on, I was going to make sure this road trip was only about the two of us and all the fun we could have.

I eyed the massive sandwich in front of me and smiled at him, hoping to lighten the mood. "I still don't know how you expect me to eat this."

"You'll manage." He chuckled, picking up his own sandwich and taking a massive bite. "Delicious," he said around his mouthful of food. A dollop of coleslaw sat in the corner of his mouth. I reached across the table and wiped it away with a swipe of my thumb. His eyes dilated as I took my thumb between my lips and sucked it away.

"Woman, we're in a restaurant and you're purposely trying to turn me on. That is so not fair."

"I didn't do it on purpose. Honestly."

He narrowed his eyes. "Mhmm, *suuure.*"

I shook my head, fighting a smile. I picked up the sandwich and attempted to take a bite without the whole thing falling apart.

"Mmm," I moaned, "this is actually really good."

"See?" He brightened. "Don't doubt me."

"When have I ever doubted you?"

"You doubt my awesomeness on a regular basis. It wounds my delicate heart." He placed a hand over his chest.

"There's nothing about you that's delicate," I snorted.

"I am delicate ... like a little flower," he joked.

I was glad that we were both able to put our earlier conversation behind. But that was one of my favorite things about Trace. He was always genuinely happy and able to make jokes. He didn't like to dwell on bad things.

Something I had learned was the bad things don't matter; it's our reaction to them that does.

CHAPTER SEVEN

Darkness had fallen by the time we made it to Philadelphia. Trace found a small motel and pulled into the parking lot.

"You said you didn't want five-star. Does this suffice?" he asked.

The place definitely wasn't the best, but it didn't appear to be the worst, either; it was perfect.

"It's great." I smiled.

The truth was, I didn't need fancy hotels or cars or lots of money. I had Trace and that's all I'd ever need. Everything else was just the icing on the cake, as some people liked to say.

"I'll be right back," he said, slipping out of the car. "Lock the doors just in case," he warned. "This area seems a bit sketchy."

"Sure thing." I saluted him, causing him to chuckle.

He returned a few minutes later with the room key and I

unlocked the doors, stepped outside, and stretched my sore muscles. Riding in a car practically the whole day was not the most comfortable thing.

Trace grabbed both of our duffel bags, carrying them easily. I put a hand over my mouth to stifle my giggle at the sight of him carrying my flowery bag. It was a stark contrast compared to his plain black one.

I followed him down the pathway a short ways. He stopped in front of a room that had once been labeled 3, but now half of the number was missing, its imprint still visible in the slight discoloration of paint on the door.

"Here goes nothing." He pushed the door open.

I immediately pinched my nose closed. "Oh, my gosh! Did something die in there? It smells awful!"

His lips turned down in a frown and his brows furrowed together. "The dude seriously wants to charge me a hundred dollars a night for this dump?" he asked incredulously.

"I'd rather sleep in the car." I took a step away, gagging at the pungent smell, too scared to glance in the room and see what it actually looked like. If it was as frightful as the smell—I shuddered at the thought.

"I think we might have to." He closed the door. "I know you said no fancy hotels, but I refuse to sleep anywhere that smells like five people died in it."

He put our bags back in the car and then went inside to argue with the man working there in the hopes of a refund.

I buckled my seatbelt and then double-checked to make sure I'd locked the doors. After smelling that room, Trace was right to be concerned about possible creepers.

Ten minutes later, he came outside shaking his head. I

unlocked the doors and he settled himself inside. "That fucker only wanted to refund me fifty percent of what I paid."

"Is he crazy?" I gasped. "We didn't even go inside the room!"

"But apparently, since we opened the door housekeeping has to clean the room." He shook his head in exasperation.

"What housekeeping?" I grumbled. "If they actually had someone to clean the rooms they wouldn't smell like that."

"Exactly!" he exclaimed with a small chuckle.

"Please tell me you got all your money back?"

"After threatening to call the cops and report this place he finally gave me the money back." He put the car in reverse and drove around, looking for somewhere else to stay.

"I can't believe they wanted to charge you a hundred dollars in the first place." I shook my head in disbelief. "That's ridiculous."

"It really is." He sighed, scanning the streets for another motel to stop.

Everything was either full or looked too gross to even contemplate.

Finally, when were both about to give up, we spotted a place.

Trace pulled into the parking lot and instead of sitting in the car, I followed him inside.

The place wasn't grand, which I knew it wouldn't be, but it was clean and didn't smell like decaying flesh. I almost gagged at the thought of the putrid smell that the other motel had possessed.

I found a vending machine and got a packet of Skittles for Trace and M&M's for myself.

"Hey." He grabbed me by the waist when he spotted me. "Don't take off like that. I thought someone took you."

"Sure you did." I rolled my eyes.

"If they had, I could take them." He flexed his arm muscles. While Trace was tall and lean, he was also muscular. It was a lethal combination, especially when he whipped out his panty-dropping smile. I hadn't stood a chance against his charms when I met him.

"I know you could." I smiled up at him. He had already proved that he was more than capable of protecting me when Aaron attacked me and he managed to get the psycho off of me. He'd punched Aaron so hard he'd given him a concussion. The jerk deserved more than that, but he was dead now, so there was no point in dwelling on it.

Trace was my hero in more ways than one. Not only did he save my life that day, but from the moment I met him he taught me how to live ... and, eventually, how to love.

His lips brushed against my forehead and my eyes fluttered closed at the feather-light touch. Even something as simple as that managed to make me feel so many different emotions.

"Come on," he murmured, his lips brushing against my skin with his words, "let's get our stuff."

He grabbed the duffel bags and we headed toward our room.

I crossed my fingers, praying that this one was nothing like the other one.

The door squeaked open and like a chicken I closed my eyes.

"Olivia?" Trace's voice sounded from inside the room. "Why are you standing outside?"

I hesitantly cracked one eye open.

The room was bathed in a pale orange glow from the ugly bedside lamp. The bed covers looked like they were from the nineties, with some kind of palm leaf design on them, which made no sense seeing as we were in Pennsylvania, not Florida.

"It's not bad." I stepped inside, looking over the carpet and walls for mysterious unexplainable stains. Thankfully, there weren't many, but I'd be keeping my shoes on anyway.

The place was about as nice as any motel could be, and it didn't smell bad, which was a plus. Not even the scent of cigarettes lingered in the air.

Trace stepped behind me and closed the door, latching the deadbolt. I made sure the blinds were completely shut before stripping out of my clothes.

Trace had his back to me, completely oblivious to what I was doing.

I unclasped my bra and threw it at his back.

He turned sharply, his eyes widening in surprise. A grin spread across his face as he said, "My little vixen."

At one time I would've blushed at his words. But I was a different, more confident, woman now.

I grabbed him by the shirt, pulling him into the bathroom and closing the door.

"I like where this is heading." He smirked before lowering his head and pressing his lips to mine.

He picked me up and I wrapped my legs around his waist, clasping the hair at the nape of his neck between my fingers. He shuffled toward the shower, reaching inside to turn it on. I pulled his shirt off and tossed it into the corner of the bathroom, then gently removed his glasses and set them on the counter.

He nipped at my lips and chin gently with his teeth, driving me crazy like he knew it would.

I slid down his body, unbuttoning his jeans. He grabbed a condom packet from the pocket and kicked them off.

Both still in our underwear, he pulled me into the shower.

I shrieked at the cold temperature but he silenced me with a kiss. The water began to warm, or maybe it was my internal temperature, but it didn't matter.

Our lips moved in sync, our bodies melded together. We truly were made for each other in more ways than one.

He kissed me slowly, teasing me. His tongue slipped between my lips and I gasped in pleasure.

A part of me had thought that after all this time we might get bored with each other or something, but honestly, we were more in love than ever.

I cupped his stubbled cheeks in my hands, deepening the kiss. "Trace," I pleaded between breaths of air. "I need—"

"What do you need, baby?" he cut me off. "Tell me."

"I need you," I pleaded.

"You have me." He kissed the sensitive skin of my neck, causing me to shiver. I had forgotten about the water beating down on us and was completely absorbed in the moment.

He tore my panties off and they landed on the bottom of the shower with a wet thud. His boxers soon followed. Then he was lifting me, pressing my back against the tile, and slipping inside me. An embarrassing moan of pleasure escaped me and he hummed in response.

My eyes met his lust-filled green ones and my muscles tightened. That look in his eyes, the one that said he loved me completely, always managed to get to me. I never thought I'd have a man look at me the way Trace does. With so much love and devotion. I thought that kind of love only existed in fairytales. But it was real. I had it and everyone should get to experience it.

A breathy moan escaped my lips and I gripped his shoulders.

"You're so beautiful," he breathed against the skin of my neck before peppering it with kisses.

I wanted to tell him that he was wrong. *He* was the beautiful one. Not just on the outside, but on the inside as well. I didn't believe there was anyone else as kind, amazing, and pure of soul as Trace. From tidbits he'd confided in me over the years, I knew after his dad died he'd gone off the deep end, and even before that he'd been more concerned with being the rich party boy, but somehow he found himself and the person he truly was, was quite remarkable. More people should aspire to be like him.

"Trace," I moaned, my hold on him tightening.

"Let go, baby," he murmured. "It's okay."

He kissed me deeply and I couldn't hold back any longer. I let go, clinging to the high, knowing he'd catch me when I came crashing back down.

TRACE PULLED a loose blue and gray plaid shirt on over his wife-beater, leaving it unbuttoned. Grinning, he shook his head like a dog, spraying water droplets from his hair all around the room.

"That's a cute look." I giggled, assessing the mess he'd made of his hair. It was currently stuck up in random directions.

"Thought I'd try something new." He smiled proudly. "You don't like it?"

"It's ... interesting." I tilted my head, studying him, as I leaned against the doorway to the bathroom.

He reached up, brushing the strands down. "Better?"

"Better." I crossed the room, flopping on the bed. "I'm so tired and I didn't even drive any," I groaned, stretching my aching and sore muscles. Although, they were tired for a completely different reason now.

"Get up." He reached for my hand, pulling me into a sitting position. "We're not going to sleep yet."

"We're not?" I frowned, looking at the bed longingly. All I wanted to do was curl up in the bed and go to sleep.

"Nope." He shook his head. "Today's fun hasn't ended yet."

"Ugh." I covered my face with my hands. "How are you always so ... chipper?"

"I have a lot to be happy about." He kissed my cheek. "There's no point in wasting time on being sad or miserable when there are so many amazing things you can be doing instead."

"At least let me put on some mascara and eyeliner," I pleaded. Thankfully, I was dressed in shorts and a tank top. If I had already put on pajamas, no amount of pleading on his part would have gotten me to agree to leave.

"Fine," he said as I stood. "But make it snappy, woman." He smacked my butt.

"Trace!" I groaned. "Honestly." I shook my head back and forth as I squatted on the floor to search through my duffel bag for my makeup case.

"What? You have a nice ass. My hands can't control themselves." He held his hands in the air, smiling like an innocent little boy. But we both knew he was far from innocent.

"Sure they can't." I rolled my eyes, heading for the dingy little bathroom. I put some mascara and eyeliner on, like I said I would, and then fluffed my damp hair. It still looked like crap so I ended up pulling it into a side bun and securing it with a ponytail holder. It still wasn't great, but it was better than nothing.

"I'm ready—are you wearing a fedora?" I stopped in my tracks, staring at Trace like he'd grown three heads.

"I am." He took it off doing some kind of fancy trick with it on his hand before replacing it. "I think I look mighty sexy in it."

"You say that about everything." I laughed because it was true. "I have to admit you look pretty hot though. Did you steal that from Luca?"

Trace stretched his legs out on the bed and crossed his arms behind his head. "Yes, yes I did, and you better not tell him or he'll kill me for stealing one of his beloved hats. He has about—"

"He has as many fedoras and vests as you have plaid shirts and ripped jeans," I interrupted.

"Exactly, so he shouldn't notice."

"He's probably already called the police." I laughed, tying the laces of my Converse sneakers.

"What can I say? I like to live dangerously." He swung his legs over the side of the bed and stood. "Ready?"

I nodded, curious as to what he had up his sleeve, but I knew better than to ask. Besides, surprises could be fun. Sometimes.

He got in the car and we drove a few miles away from the motel, parking outside a bar.

"A bar? Really, Trace? No. Just no." I shook my head. A bar was definitely not my scene. True, I was twenty-two and legal to drink, but I didn't enjoy contending with annoying drunk people. I had better things I could be doing, like sleeping.

"Calm yourself," he snorted, "it's not what you think."

I pointed to the lit up sign in the window of the establishment. "See that? It says bar. B-A-R."

"Now's not the time for your adorable sarcasm. See *that* sign?" He pointed to one above it, nearly smacking me in the face by accident. "It says, *music lounge*. Now untangle your panties from the wad they're currently bunched in and get that cute ass in there."

"So demanding," I sighed, fighting a smile as I opened the car door and stepped outside.

He grabbed his guitar case and we headed inside.

The place was packed with people. I didn't know how they all managed to fit inside. Trace took my hand, pulling us through the crowd. The walls and bar were covered in a dark wood, and the concrete floor was painted black. Instead of the typical white or yellow light bulbs, they were all blue, giving the space an almost ethereal glow.

Trace found an empty high-top table and snagged it before someone else could.

A waitress came along, looking frazzled and exhausted, to take our order.

"Can I get a drink for you guys?" she asked, fumbling for her pen.

"Sweet tea, please." I smiled at her.

"Uh ... " Trace paused. "A beer."

"What kind?" she asked.

"Surprise me." He grinned, showing his ID. "I'm adventurous. Oh, and we want an order of cheese fries."

"All right." Her hand fluttered over her notepad and she seemed even more flustered than before. I wasn't sure if it was because she was nervous over his request or his appearance. I'd probably looked much the same when I met him the first time. "I'll be right back with that." She smiled, tucking wispy pieces of blonde hair behind her ear.

"So ..." I nodded toward his guitar case. "I take it you're going to play."

"Of course." He smiled, his eyes crinkling at the corners as he played with the fedora. "And I'm hoping this really hot girl I know will sing with me." He batted his eyelashes.

"Flattery will get you nowhere." I snorted. "Nice try, bud."

"Aw, come on." He bumped my shoulder with his and then ran his hand up my thigh. "I can be very persuasive," he whispered huskily, his lips brushing against my cheek.

My eyes fluttered closed and my breath faltered. Damn him.

"Quit it." I pushed his hand away before he had me agreeing to things I shouldn't be.

"You have such a beautiful voice, Olivia." He ran his finger lightly up my bare arm and I shivered in response.

"But-but," I stuttered, "there are a lot of people here."

"They don't matter," he coaxed. "*Please*, one song?" His eyes pleaded with me to give in.

"I-I-I don't know." I closed my eyes to avoid his gaze.

"You know you want to," his voice grew husky as his lips tickled the curve of my ear. "I'll reward you later, and trust me, it's a prize you don't want to miss out on."

"O-o-okay," I agreed. I was a weak person, but I didn't know anyone on the planet—especially one with ovaries—that could resist his charms.

"I knew you'd agree." He removed his hand from my body and sat on his barstool looking mighty proud of himself.

"You don't play fair." I glared at him.

"No one said I had to." He smirked, taking a bite of one of the cheese fries.

I stared at the food and drinks in shock. I hadn't known the waitress even brought them. Trace had managed to make everything else disappear. It was an annoying talent he had. Although, it might prove useful since I'd agreed to sing and I would need to be sufficiently distracted so I didn't throw up on anyone. Talk about embarrassing.

"Not bad," he muttered after taking a sip of beer. "Want some?" He held the bottle out to me.

"No thanks." I slid my glass of sweet tea closer to me. "This is fine."

"Suit yourself." He shrugged, taking another sip. "It might ... loosen you up a bit." He winked.

"Gosh," I groaned, "how do you make *everything* sound like a sexual innuendo."

"I'm *very* talented," he waggled his eyebrows.

"You're a pain in my ass, that's for sure. I'm not sure about talented, though." I reached for a fry covered in cheese and drenched it in ranch.

"That hurts." He chuckled, his lips turning up in a small smile.

"I didn't know your ego could be bruised," I joked, adding a sugar packet to my supposedly sweet tea.

"My cockiness is a ruse to hide the hurt little boy I am

behind the handsome face." He stared at me seriously for a moment before busting into laughter.

"How do you come up with this stuff?" I asked rhetorically, but he answered me anyway.

"My mind works in mysterious ways." He smirked, grabbing a handful of cheese fries and stuffing them into his mouth.

I wrinkled my nose in disgust. "That's gross, Trace."

"What?" he mumbled around a mouthful of food. "I'm hungry. *Somebody* had me working off all my energy earlier."

"Oh, please." I rolled my eyes. "You're insatiable and you know it."

"Only when it comes to you." He smiled widely, his green eyes light and playful.

"Good to know." I laughed.

Between the two of us we managed to eat almost all of the cheese fries. I think we'd both been starving. "Well," he said, grabbing his guitar case and standing, "I better get ready."

"You already signed up to sing, didn't you?" I questioned. "Before we even got here?"

He nodded. "I always have an agenda, babe." He kissed my cheek before heading for the stage area. He bent to speak with someone, who I assumed was a manager at the bar, and then he was escorted behind the stage.

I *really* hoped he didn't do something to humiliate me. But knowing Trace, the lengths to which he'd go to embarrass me were endless.

I turned in my barstool so I could see the stage better.

Somebody's arm brushed mine and I jerked in response.

"Sorry," they said, and their voice was way too close for comfort. I turned my head sharply and found a guy about my age sitting in Trace's vacant chair. He had curly blonde hair and pale blue eyes clouded over from alcohol.

"Can I help you?" I questioned, giving the guy the benefit of the doubt.

"I just saw you sittin' here and thought you looked lonely," he slurred with a grin, leaning much too close to me. Somebody needed to teach this guy the rules of personal space because he was all up in my bubble, and if it popped, I could not be held accountable for my actions.

"I'm not lonely," I said sternly, glaring at him, "so run along now." I waved my hand in dismissal, hoping he got the message.

He grabbed my arm, squeezing much too tight. I bit down on my lip, breathing in and out sharply, hoping to avoid a panic attack. I hadn't done well with strangers touching me after what Aaron did to me.

"There's no need to play hard to get." He flipped a stray blonde curl out of his eyes.

"I'm not playing anything." I tried to yank my arm from his grasp but he was too strong. "Let me go!" I screamed as panic crawled up my throat. Tears burned my eyes. I pulled my arm again and this time I managed to get him to let go, but I went falling from my seat in the process and landed on the ground, smacking the side of my face sharply against the concrete floor.

"Olivia!" I heard Trace yell, his voice echoing around the whole bar as he yelled into the microphone. I'd been so preoccupied with Mr. Touchy Feely that I hadn't seen him come out on stage.

Before I had a chance to move, Trace's familiar scent surrounded me, and his large hands were on my body picking me up.

"Olivia," he whispered, looking me over. "You're bleeding."

I reached up and felt around my eye. My fingers came away with a small smearing of blood. "It's not that bad." I shrugged.

His jaw was clenched tight and his eyes screamed murder. "You're *hurt*." He shoved me behind him and glared at Mr. Touchy Feely who was still sitting in his former seat.

"I didn't do anything." He held his hands up in surrender. "She just fell."

"She didn't just *fall*," Trace seethed. "You grabbed her arm and you wouldn't let go. When a girl says no, it means *no!*" Suddenly, he was reaching out and grabbing the guy by the shirt collar and lifting him out of the chair.

Holy shit, I knew Trace was strong, but this guy was double his size and built like a linebacker.

"Dude, let me go." Mr. Touchy Feely tried to pry Trace's hands off of him, but it was pointless. Trace was in a rage and there was no stopping him. "I wasn't gonna hurt her."

"I don't care what your intentions were," Trace growled, right up in the guy's face as he shoved him into a wall. "When a girl tells you to let her go, guess what? *You let her go!*" He shook the guy forcefully.

I hadn't seen Trace get this angry in a long time—not since Aaron attacked me. Trace was an easygoing guy and it took a lot to get him riled.

"Trace," I whispered, placing my hand on his taut arm. "I'm okay."

Slowly, he turned his head toward me, and some of the anger drained out of him. He released the guy, but not before giving him a hard enough shove that he went sprawling to the ground. The guy looked up in disbelief. For a second I thought he might attack Trace but instead he chose to pick himself up and walk away. I guess he wasn't as dumb as he looked.

"Stay here," Trace growled, bowing his head as he walked away. The brim of the fedora hid his gaze from me and I chewed my lip nervously.

Within seconds he was back, his guitar case slung over his shoulder. "We're leaving." He took my hand and practically dragged me out of the building.

People stared as we passed, the blue lights in the bar making them look strange—almost alien.

We drove back to the motel in silence, his grip so tight on the steering wheel that his knuckles turned white, and his jaw was clenched. I wanted to say something, but I figured silence was better.

He opened the motel door, letting me in first. I sat on the edge of the bed, nervously fiddling with the edge of my tank top. "Trace—"

"I'll be back," he said in a steely tone, slamming the door closed behind him as he left. I jumped at the noise.

My bottom lip trembled with the threat of tears, but I wouldn't cry. I *couldn't*.

Frustrated, I tore off my clothes and changed into pajamas.

I climbed under the itchy covers; eyes wide open.

Let him leave.

I didn't care.

Honestly, I didn't.

Okay, I did.

And that's why it hurt.

CHAPTER EIGHT

"Baby, wake up. Wake up." Someone shook my shoulders, but I didn't want to wake up. I'd been dreaming and it had been so good. "Olivia, wake up. I need to see your face. Come on. That's my girl."

My eyes opened to see Trace smiling down at me.

Why the heck was the jerk smiling at me when he'd left me in a rage?

I scooted away from him, my brows furrowing in anger. "Leave me alone," I snapped, glaring at him.

"Olivia," he whispered my name, reaching over to turn on the light. "I went to the drugstore and got some things." He held up a plastic bag, shaking the contents.

"You just ... *left*," I seethed.

He bowed his head, his forehead wrinkling. "I'm sorry. I was angry, but not at you, never at you." His green eyes pleaded with me for forgiveness. "That guy *hurt* you, Olivia. It made me mad and I'm sorry you had to see me like that. But I'm not sorry for protecting you." He reached a tentative hand out to me. After a moment, I placed my hand in his. "Come here," he coaxed.

I closed my eyes and took a deep breath before scooting close to him.

He brushed a piece of hair behind my ear, his fingers skimming over my cheek and hovering there.

Anger flashed in his eyes again.

"You're going to get a black eye," he growled.

I placed my fingers just below my eye and winced. The skin was surprisingly tender. I didn't think I smacked the floor *that* hard. I guess I was wrong.

"I fell," I said with a frown, "it's not like he hit me or anything."

"If he hadn't grabbed you, you wouldn't have fallen," he growled, the tension returning to his body.

I grabbed his forearm. "I'm fine, Trace. I promise. It doesn't hurt."

"Whatever," he grumbled, standing. He strode into the bathroom and I heard the faucet running. He returned a moment later, kneeling in front of me. He reached up, gently rubbing a wet washcloth against my face. I closed my eyes, letting him work. When I opened them, he was staring down at the pale pink smear on the white cloth with an angry look on his face.

Shaking his head, he grabbed the shopping bag and pulled out a bottle of Advil and water. He shook two into his hand and gave it to me. "Take this so you don't get a headache."

I felt fine, but I took it anyway to make him feel better.

Then he pulled out one of those instant cold packs and

gently laid it against my eye. I hated to admit it, but it actually felt pretty good.

I put my hand overtop of his. "Thank you."

"Don't thank me," he growled. "If I hadn't left, you wouldn't have gotten hurt."

I rolled my eyes. "Trace, you can't blame yourself for every bump or bruise I get. This wasn't your fault."

"Yes, it was."

I pushed his hand off my face, the cold pack falling to the bed, and cupped his cheeks in my hands as I stared into his eyes. "Why do you insist on taking the blame for everything?"

"When things are my fault, I like to accept responsibility."

"What happened back there wasn't your fault, it wasn't mine, and it wasn't even really that guy's fault." Trace growled at my words. "Okay, maybe it was a little bit his fault."

He forced a smile. "That's better."

"But you're not my bodyguard, Trace. You can't be there for me all the time. I'm going to stumble and fall and have to pick myself back up sometimes. You can't save me."

"That doesn't mean I'm ever going to stop trying." He leaned in, resting his lips against mine. He didn't really kiss me; he just held his lips there, brushing them against mine. It was the sweetest *almost* kiss I'd ever experienced ... even if I was still mad at him.

He pressed his lips more firmly against mine before pulling away. His gaze dropped and he picked up the ice pack. "Ice your eye" —he handed it to me— "it'll help with the swelling."

I did as he said, crawling back under the covers. The cold from the ice pack made me shiver. He climbed into bed and wrapped his arms around me. I probably should have pushed him away since he was being so weird but I was cold and his arms felt like heaven around me. The truth of the matter was I wasn't really mad at him. I understood where he was coming from. If Trace was hurt, I wanted to be there to pick up the pieces.

I felt his lips brush against the back of my neck, his stubble scratching my sensitive skin.

Time passed and I thought he'd drifted off to sleep, but then he spoke.

"I'll always keep you safe. No matter what."

———

I WOKE up covered in a thin sheen of sweat since Trace was plastered to my body. He had me hugged against his chest like a human-sized teddy bear. It would be cute if *I* wasn't the teddy bear.

I pushed his heavy arm off me, sliding out of the bed and falling on my butt. So much for trying to be stealthy. I could never be a ninja.

Luckily, Trace didn't stir at the sound of my fall. He was sound asleep, his mouth slightly open. It was completely unfair that he was cute even when he slept. I woke up every morning looking like Medusa. Boys had it so much easier.

I picked myself up off the floor and tiptoed across the room and into the bathroom. I eased the door closed behind me and locked it.

My eyes widened when I saw my face. "Holy crap." I frowned at my bruised eye. It looked like someone had punched me, not like I'd tried to hug the floor. I knew I'd have to hide it before Trace woke up but none of the makeup I'd packed would cover up this purple sucker.

I decided to shower first and then head across the street to where I remembered seeing a drugstore—probably the same one Trace had gone to last night.

I secured my hair into a messy bun on top of my head and dressed as quietly as possible before snatching the room keycard off the dresser and slipping outside. Now I had to hope he didn't wake up while I was gone. Knowing Trace, he'd wake up thinking I'd been kidnapped.

I avoided looking at anyone directly as I grabbed a bottle of liquid foundation and checked out. I knew people would think my boyfriend had hit me, and since that definitely wasn't the case, I'd rather avoid awkward question-and-answer sessions.

Trace was still asleep when I came back into the room and I let out a sigh of relief. Usually, Trace didn't sleep long after I'd gotten out of the bed. He must have been really tired.

I had just finished hiding the bruise on my face when he woke and strode into the bathroom.

"Hey," he muttered groggily, hugging me from behind and pressing his hips against me.

"Trace," I groaned, prying myself from his arms.

"It's morning. I can't help it." He yawned. "You already showered," he stated, taking in my wet hair and fresh clothes.

I nodded. "I wanted to get the bar smell off of me."

He reached up and smoothed his thumb beneath my left eye. I hoped he didn't wipe the makeup away. "I thought for sure that would bruise," he whispered to himself.

"It didn't," I said a bit too quickly, backing out of the bathroom and away from him. "I'm ... uh, going to get us some breakfast while you shower."

He eyed me suspiciously. "Ooookay," he drew out the word. "My wallet's on the dresser, grab some cash."

"I notice you didn't say to grab your car keys," I taunted with a grin.

"No one but me drives the Camaro. Ever." His eyes were serious but he was fighting a smile. "It won't take me long to shower. Why don't you wait and we'll go together?"

"I can do that." I crossed my arms over my chest. "But there's a McDonald's right next door. I won't be far, so you don't need to worry."

"I don't worry—"

"Your pants just caught on fire with that lie." I grabbed his wallet and snagged a twenty-dollar bill. "I'll be back in five minutes. Stop treating me like I'm two and you have to babysit me."

His eyes narrowed and his tongue flicked out to wet his lips. "Oh, I know I don't have to babysit you, trust me."

I chose to ignore his comment. "Go shower. You smell."

"Thanks, sweetie. Love you too," he called after me sarcastically.

It was early so there wasn't much of a line at McDonald's. Besides, this didn't strike me as the hot spot in town anyway. I grabbed the bag of food and drinks and walked back to the motel. They were literally right beside each other. The smell of the greasy food was making me hungry, though. The cheese fries we'd had last night hadn't been enough to eat. If I kept eating all this cheesy grease-filled food on this trip I'd end up gaining fifty pounds.

I had the keycard with me but my hands were full and I couldn't get it out of the pocket of my jeans. I knocked on the door with my shoulder.

Trace opened it a moment later, standing there in nothing

but a towel and wet water droplets sticking to his sculpted chest. I wanted to lick him.

"Whoa." He grabbed the drink carrier that I almost dropped because I was staring at his chest. It would have been a worthy cause, though. He had such a nice chest that you couldn't keep yourself from staring at it.

"Sorry." I stepped around him as he closed the door.

He placed the drinks on the dresser and tossed the cardboard carrier into the trashcan.

By the time I had our breakfast sandwiches laid out he'd put on a pair of boxers and loose jeans. My eyes roamed over his body, memorizing each dip and curve of his muscles and tracing the lines of his tattoos.

"You know" —I smiled as he sat down beside me and grabbed his sausage egg and cheese biscuit— "you've never told me why you got a four-leaf clover when I got my first tattoo."

He swallowed, wiping his mouth with a napkin. "I thought it was pretty obvious." He shrugged. "You're my lucky charm."

I wasn't sure if I should hug him or punch him for his cheesiness.

I eyed him. "Don't mess with me."

"I'm serious." He crumbled up his wrapper and dropped it in the paper bag. "From the moment I met you my life had meaning again." He looked at me seriously. "I'm not one to confess all my feelings and be gushy, but it's true. When I met you ... " he paused, his brows furrowing together. "I was finally getting over what happened to my dad and seeing the damage I'd caused to my family. But meeting you is what truly changed me. You made me *laugh* again, Olivia. That may seem like something simple, but when you go years without laughing at anything ... when all your thoughts and feelings are only *bad*. Laughing takes on a whole new meaning. So, yes, you're my lucky charm."

"I-I-I don't know what to say," I stuttered, shaking my head. I hadn't been expecting a deep meaningful answer from him. But I should've known. All of his tattoos meant something important to him.

"Don't say anything." He reached for my hand and entwined our fingers together. "Words aren't always necessary."

I swallowed thickly. "Do you ever think," I whispered, "that we met for a reason?"

He brought our joined hands up to his heart and I could feel its steady beat. "Every single day of my life."

I laid my head on his bare shoulder. "Before you came along, I never thought about falling in love or marrying someone." I glanced down at my engagement ring. "But now I can't imagine not having that."

"I know what you mean." He kissed the corner of my mouth. "Some things come along when you need them most, and at the time, you don't even realize that you need them."

"Exactly," I whispered.

Fate worked in mysterious ways. The night I'd met Trace, I'd wanted nothing more than to get back to my dorm without being raped or murdered. When Trace had come along, I hadn't known how much that single moment would change the rest of my life. But, boy, am I glad that it did.

"Are you gonna finish that?" He pointed to my half-eaten egg McMuffin.

"No." I handed it to him. "You can have it."

"So, besides seeing the Liberty Bell, what else do you have

planned?" I asked, gathering up our stuff and putting it in our duffel bags.

"Independence Hall, maybe some museums." He shrugged, finishing the last bite of my sandwich.

"Are we only visiting museums on this road trip?" I raised a brow. "I thought we were going to have fun, not be bored to death."

"Museums are fun!" he defended. "But, no, we're not just visiting museums. After this, I don't know which way the wind might blow us."

"Except north," I stated. "You keep saying we're heading north."

He looked like deer caught in headlights for a moment, but he shook his head and the look was gone. "Yeah, uh, I want us to go to the lake house. Remember?" He stood, pulling on his shirts.

"Mhmm," I muttered, eyeing him suspiciously. "What are you up to?"

"Nothing," he replied a bit too quickly, "nothing at all."

"Trace," I said his name warningly. "Is there something you need to tell me?"

"Absolutely not." He shook his head, grabbing our bags.

He grabbed the room key as well as his car keys, picked up our bags, and breezed out of the room. I knew avoidance when I saw it, and that's exactly what he was doing. *What the hell is he up to?*

I wasn't sure I wanted to know.

I scanned the room several times and even looked under the bed to make sure we weren't leaving anything behind. When I was sure we had all our belongings I headed out to the car. Trace already had the car started and his sunglasses on. He was fiddling with his phone as I slid inside.

"What are you doing?" I asked.

"I made a playlist for our road trip," he mumbled, pushing a button on his phone. The sounds of Lifehouse's "Gotta Be Tonight" blared from the speakers. For an old car it had one heck of a sound system. For all I knew Trace had upgraded it. I knew absolutely nothing about cars.

Trace seemed to know where he was going and since I didn't want to be the annoying, nagging girlfriend—fiancée, I kept my mouth shut.

Maybe in a few days I would finally realize that we were engaged. It was still so new that I kept forgetting.

"All right." Trace parked the car. "We should be able to walk to the Liberty Bell from here as well as the museums."

"Walking's fine with me. Especially since I'm going to be cooped up in the car with you for a couple of weeks." I laughed.

He frowned, removing his sunglasses and hooking them into the collar of his shirt. "I don't know why you say that like it's a bad thing. I'm awesome to be around. You should be happy that you're being rewarded with my presence twenty-four seven. Not many get that pleasure."

I shook my head. "You're too much to handle sometimes."

"And yet" —he smirked, tapping my nose with his finger like I was a small child— "you're still here."

"There's no place I'd rather be," I taunted, getting out of the car before he could say anything else.

A light breeze swirled around me, ruffling my hair. It was only ten in the morning but I knew it was going to be a scorcher. I'd need to find some sunscreen so I didn't end up looking like a lobster.

"Which way should we head first?" Trace asked from behind me.

I looked over my shoulder at him, squinting from the sun. "Does it matter?" I asked, shading my eyes.

"I guess not," he said, shrugging out of his plaid shirt and tossing it in the car, leaving him in only a wife-beater. "Geez it's hot out," he grumbled. "You'd think it was Florida or something."

"It's not *that* hot." I laughed.

"Maybe not," he said as he locked the car, "but it's still pretty hot."

"It is," I admitted. Sweat was already dampening my skin and we'd only been outside for a few minutes. Hopefully, it would get cooler as we headed north. Scorching hot temperatures weren't my thing.

"I think Independence Hall is this way," he pointed as he spoke. "I already got tickets before we left." He pulled two pieces of paper from his back pocket.

I narrowed my eyes, glaring at him. "I'm beginning to think you've had this whole trip planned before you even asked me."

I was only joking, but his posture stiffened and he wouldn't meet my gaze. "That's just silly," he chuckled, trying to play it off.

"Huh," I muttered to myself. *What is going on with him?*

"Come on, this way." He grabbed my hand, pulling me after him.

There was a line to get into the tour but Trace bypassed it, flashing something I couldn't see. I gave him a peculiar look and he explained, "Sometimes having money comes in handy."

I hated to admit it, but the tour was actually pretty interesting. It made you feel so small to be surrounded by so much history. It blew my mind to think about all the important decisions that had been made in that building, in this city. It was crazy. Those people were long gone but I was sure if they knew the state we were in now, they'd think we were all a bunch of screw-ups.

As we left the old brick building, Trace grabbed my arm, halting my progress.

"What?"

"I want a picture," he explained, holding out his phone and taking a few pictures of us. He'd done the same yesterday at the Heinz museum. I think he was determined to document every moment of this trip.

We headed to the Liberty Bell next.

Tickets weren't necessary so we strolled straight on through the gates.

I gazed at the bell for a few minutes in awe and read the plaque located in front of it that explained its history.

"*Proclaim liberty throughout all the Land unto all the inhabitants thereof,*" I read from the plaque in a whisper. I looked up at Trace and said, "Those words must have meant so much to them at that time."

He didn't hear a word I said, though; he was still staring at the bell. He tilted his head from side to side. "You know, I thought it would be bigger."

I laughed. "It looks plenty big to me."

"That's because you're small, like a little doll."

I snorted. "Thanks," I said sarcastically. "You sure know how to make a girl feel good about herself."

"What? It's true." His lips brushed against the top of my head. "You're short and tiny. You do have a nice chest and ass, though. I especially love your ass." He reached down and grabbed it.

"Trace!" I squealed, darting away from him. "There are *people* here." I looked around at the different families. One husband and wife was staring at us with a look of contempt. I half expected them to pull out a Bible and throw it at us.

"What? It's true!" He raised his hands in surrender, grinning like an idiot.

"You are impossible," I growled over my shoulder, striding toward the exit. "You need a muzzle and a leash."

"I didn't know you were so kinky," he chuckled behind me. When I turned around to glare at him, his laugh turned into a fake cough. "You know," he commented, shoving his hands into his pockets, "I wasn't quite done back there."

"Then go back." I shooed him away with my hand. "I'll be here."

He narrowed his eyes and, before I knew what was happening, he scooped me up and tossed me over his shoulder. "Trace!" I shrieked as my stomach dropped out from under me. "Put me down!" I beat at his back but he was completely unfazed. People were staring and heat infused my cheeks ... or maybe my face only felt so hot since all the blood was currently rushing to my head.

He didn't put me down until he was standing in front of the Liberty Bell again, and even then he held on tightly to me. Before I could run away, he pulled out his phone and snapped a picture of us.

He chuckled at the screen. "I'm sending this one to my mom." He was already typing madly on his phone.

"Let me see." I stood on my tiptoes to peer at his phone.

When I saw the picture I gasped. "Don't you dare send that to your mom!"

"Too late." He grinned boyishly, shoving the phone in his pocket.

"I'm glaring at you in the picture like I want to kick you ... or worse."

"Exactly, she'll think it's hilarious. Give her about five minutes and I'm sure she'll call me and ask what I did to you."

"Yeah, right—" I was cut off by the sound of his phone ringing.

He pulled it out and smirked at the caller ID. "Told you." He showed me the name lighting up the screen. "Hey, Mom," he answered. "Why do you assume I did something? Oh, really? I only picked her up and carried her back to the bell so I could get a picture." He was quiet for a moment and then said, "I am being a very good boy, Mom." He grinned at me. "Love you, too. Bye." He hung up his phone and smiled. "That went better than I thought it would."

"And how did you think it would go?" I asked, walking out of the gate once more. I found a bench and sat down.

He took the spot on the bench beside me. "I figured she'd chew me out for at least thirty minutes. But I guess by now she knows I am who I am and there's no changing me."

"If I've figured that out in the three years since I've met you, then I think your mom is bound to have figured it out in twenty-five." I snickered, tapping my shoes against the ground in a random beat.

"*Almost* twenty-five," he amended. "Don't go making me older than I am, woman."

"Whatever." I laughed. "And it's not like twenty-five is old."

"Easy for you to say." His nose wrinkled as he tried to pretend to be mad.

I rolled my eyes. "Trace, you'll be forty and still act like you're fifteen."

"True," he said on a laugh. "I don't see the point in acting my age. I want to have fun, so I do."

No longer irritated with him, I took his hand in mine. I frowned down at his reddened knuckles. "Trace," I breathed, "you hurt your hand." I looked up at him with worry in my eyes as he snatched his hand from my grasp.

"It's nothing," he mumbled, looking at a spot over my head.

"It looks like it hurts." I grabbed his hand again, inspecting it. "Why didn't you tell me you hurt yourself?"

He forced a smile. "It's not a big deal. I didn't realize I punched the guy *that* hard," he mumbled under his breath.

"You don't need to act so macho all the time," I scolded him, running my finger lightly over his injured knuckles. "I'm not going to love you any less."

"Honestly, I didn't even notice it until you pointed it out. I was too concerned about you."

I closed my eyes and swallowed thickly as he played with a piece of my hair. That was the kind of person Trace was, though. He was always concerned about everyone else, not about himself.

I opened my eyes and found him staring curiously at me. "What?" I asked.

"Nothing," he whispered, shaking his head. Standing, he reached for my hands and hauled me up. "Let's get out of here."

CHAPTER NINE

I WOKE WITH A START AS THE CAR JERKED TO A STOP. I turned groggy eyes Trace's way. "What's going on? Why are we stopping?"

"Just something I want us to do." He grinned mischievously, unbuckling his seatbelt.

I yawned, rubbing my eyes, then I glanced at the clock as I massaged the back of my neck. I'd been asleep about an hour. It was one in the afternoon and the sun shone through the windows.

I looked around at the bridge we were parked on and at the group of people up ahead in—*is that a harness?*

"What. The. Hell?" I gasped, scrambling out of the car just as one of the guys from the group jumped off the freakin' bridge. His cries of joy echoed around us. I wanted to scream in terror. I peered over the bridge railing as the guy was released from the cord and dropped into the water.

"I-I-I ... No way." I shook my head, putting the puzzle pieces together. Trace would've only stopped if he wanted us to do this. I wasn't afraid of heights, but if Trace thought I was going to jump off a bridge, he had another thing coming.

"Adventures, remember?" Trace grinned crookedly, pinching my hip.

"Adventures, yes. Falling to my death? No."

"It'll be fun," he coaxed, looking at me with wide green eyes. "We'll do it together. You fall, I fall. Always."

"Don't try to sweet talk me." I pushed his shoulder. "It's not going to work."

"Oh, it'll work." He skated a finger over my collarbone. "Just give it a second. My powers of persuasion are too much for you to resist."

I looked over my shoulder at the group of people on the bridge. Most of them were men but there were a few women too.

I'd never thought about bungee jumping before ... but it could be fun ... maybe ... if I didn't throw up from fear.

"Fine," I met his gaze once more as I spoke, "but we're doing it together. There's no way I'm jumping by myself."

He grabbed my cheeks and lowered his head, kissing me passionately. He pulled away, breathing heavily, and rested his forehead against mine. "I love my little spitfire."

"Yeah, yeah, yeah," I groaned. "Let's get this over with before I change my mind."

"You got it." He grinned, kissing me quickly, and walked toward the group. "Hi, I'm Trace." He held his hand out to shake the man's hand that seemed to be in charge. "This is my fiancée, Olivia." My heart did a little happy dance at that. "Are you Marcus?"

"That's me." He was probably in his thirties, tall and lanky, with black hair and kind brown eyes. "You ready to jump?" He addressed me, not Trace.

I nodded, hoping I didn't look like a big-eyed frightened rabbit.

The guy clapped me on the shoulder. "It's okay to be scared; that makes the fall even better."

He meant for his words to be comforting, but they weren't.

"Mhmm," I mumbled, letting him guide me over the equipment scattered around. A few cars passed us, completely oblivious to the jumpers. I figured this was a regular occurrence around here. Wherever *here* was. Marcus helped me into the gear, explaining what each piece was for to calm my nerves, while another guy helped Trace. "How did you know about this?" I asked him.

His green eyes met mine and a slow smile spread across his face. "There was a sign a few miles back, and I thought, why the hell not."

"Lovely," I groaned.

"You'll be fine," Marcus assured me. "It's not scary. People spend too much time worrying about what it's going to be like, instead of enjoying the moment. When you fall ..." His eyes got a faraway look in them. "For a moment, it's like you're free ... Nothing can stop you."

I looked across at Trace with a frown. *Is this dude high or something?*

"I know I probably sound crazy, but wait and see."

After we were both in our harnesses, we hopped over the bridge railing and they hooked us together. Marcus double-checked everything, and his thoroughness managed to make me feel a bit better.

"Whenever you're ready just ... fall." He stepped away from us with a smile.

I looked up into Trace's eyes as my body shook from fear.

"Don't be afraid," he whispered, "I'm right here." He wrapped his arms around me, holding me close.

I pressed my face against his chest and closed my eyes.

"Let's do this," I said with more confidence than I possessed.

"One, two," he counted and before he said three, we were falling.

A scream tore through my chest and the shrill sound of it probably busted Trace's eardrum, but he simply laughed in elation.

My stomach was in my throat but Marcus was right. I felt like I was flying. Like nothing could touch me or stop me. In that moment, we were invincible.

My eyes had opened and I looked down at the water shining below us—if I reached my hand out my fingers would graze the top of it, but I was too scared to let go of Trace.

The cord rebounded and we went flying up in the air again. I held on tight to him, burying my face in his shirt to muffle my screams.

Eventually, the cord settled and we swung back and forth slowly.

"Ready?" Marcus yelled down at us.

Trace must have given him a thumbs up—or maybe he said something and I was still in shock and couldn't hear him. Regardless, we fell into the icy water.

I hadn't expected the water to be *that* cold and came up sputtering. My teeth clattered together as I looked around for

Trace. He surfaced in front of me, shaking his hair out of his face.

"It's freezing," I said unnecessarily as we swam to shore. Somehow, when they'd released us from the bungee cord we'd come undone from each other. "And now we're in wet clothes."

I stretched out on the shore, taking a moment to let the hot sun shine against me.

"Yeah …" He shook his head like a dog, sending droplets of water everywhere. "I didn't think about that part."

"Obviously." I wrapped my arms around my chest as a shiver rocked my body.

"Come on, they have towels up there."

He located a path that led back up to the bridge and took my hand to keep me from slipping.

We rounded the corner and the group faced us with wide smiles.

"How was it?" Marcus asked, appearing with two towels. *Bless him.*

"Awesome." Trace grinned, drying his hair with the towel. Guys had it so much easier. It wasn't fair.

"Spectacular," I admitted reluctantly, accepting the towel from his outstretched hand. "I'm sorry if I hurt your ears." I laughed, looking up at Trace.

"I'll live." He winked, removing his shirt and drying his chest. I'm pretty sure I heard one of the girls gasp.

I dried my arms with the towel and wrapped it around my shoulders for a bit of warmth. I had an elastic on my wrist and used it to secure my wet hair in a messy bun.

I found a spot to sit down in the sun and Trace joined me, stretching out his legs, kicking off his boots.

"Still want to kill me?" he asked.

I giggled, unable to answer him. A stubborn piece of hair was sticking straight up on top of his head. I reached up, smoothing it down before answering him.

"No." I smiled at him. "I'm glad you made me do that."

His grin widened. "Can I get that in writing?"

"Quit it." I punched his arm lightly. "You know, it's fun to do stuff that most people are afraid to do. I like that you push me to try new things and to not be so ... scared."

"That's my job." He grinned crookedly. "What's life without a little excitement?"

"Boring," I answered unnecessarily.

"Exactly, and who wants boring?"

I giggled. "Not me. That's why I'm stuck with you."

"Stuck?" He raised a brow. "I should be offended."

"But you're not?"

"No." He shook his head. "I know exactly what you mean. I'm stuck with you too, because there's no one else that could handle all of this." He shimmied awkwardly, since he was sitting, as he pointed to himself.

"Yeah," I agreed with a laugh, "I don't think there's anyone else that could handle you ... or put up with your horrible dancing skills."

He gasped, draping his towel on top of me since I was still shivering, and then wrapped his arm around me. "My dancing is *awesome*. Just because you aren't familiar with the style doesn't mean it isn't good."

"You look like you're having a seizure when you dance. That isn't normal."

"I don't need rhythm on the dance floor when I have it in the bed." He grinned, thrusting his hips for good measure.

"Can you—I don't know—*not* do that in public?" I groaned, fighting a blush.

His smile widened. "What difference does it make when you're the one reaping the benefits?"

"Do you think before you speak?" I buried my face in my hands, shaking my head back and forth in disbelief.

"No," he snorted. "Where's the fun in that?"

"Sometimes, you're as bad as Avery, and that's saying something," I groaned, kicking at a pebble.

"There's no point in sugar coating things."

Marcus came over and smiled down at us. "I noticed your license plate and saw that you guys are from Virginia. Are you passing through or might you stay here a bit?"

Trace shrugged. "Maybe. We're on a road trip and we don't exactly have much of a plan."

"Excellent." Marcus smiled. "I'm having a bonfire down by the lake tonight if you want to stay and hangout. There's also room at my house if you want to stay the night. My wife won't mind. I think she's sick of me anyway and would like some company," he chortled.

Trace looked at me skeptically. I shrugged in response to his look.

"Sounds good." Trace smiled at Marcus. "A bonfire would be nice and we just might take you up on your offer for a place to stay."

"Great." Marcus clapped his hands together. "I better get back over there. We have a group of college kids coming. They can be a bit rowdy; they tend to show up drunk."

Trace chuckled. "Have fun with that."

"Oh, I will," Marcus cackled as he walked away.

"You hungry?" Trace asked me, raking his fingers through his slightly damp hair.

"Yeah, but I'm still wet."

"We'll go through a drive-thru then." He stood, shaking off the pebbles that clung to his jeans.

"You really want to get your beloved Camaro's seats wet?" I eyed him questioningly.

"Damn," he muttered, "I forgot about that." He put his hands on his hips, lips pursed in thought. "Why don't we just change? A bra and panties is equivalent to a bikini."

"Are you kidding me?" I protested. "I'm not stripping down in front of strangers. You're insane."

"Fine" —there was a challenge in his eyes as he marched toward the Camaro— "I will."

"I hate you so much right now," I growled as I stood, stomping after him.

"Hate is a passionate word," he sing-songed, "and I will be rewarded with all that passion *later*." He glanced at me over his shoulder, holding back laughter.

"I'm sure you'll think I'm real passionate when I pull your hair." I glared, stopping by the trunk.

"Oooh, you wanna get rough? I'm down for that." He smirked, unlocking the trunk.

I punched him as hard as I could and was pleased when he let out a grunt.

"I'll show you rough," I mumbled, looking through my duffel bag for dry clothes. I wasn't at all pleased about the idea of almost getting naked in front of all these strangers, but Trace was kind of right, it *was* like a bikini. Or so I kept telling myself. "Give me one of your shirts," I pleaded.

He handed me one of his long-sleeved plaid shirts and I

pulled it on, quickly doing the buttons and rolling up the sleeves. While I would've loved to change out of my wet tank top, people were watching us, and I just couldn't stomach it.

Since his shirt almost came down to my knees, it made it easy to get the wet shorts off and replace them with dry ones without anyone seeing.

Trace, apparently, didn't have an ounce of modesty. He was smiling crookedly at me as he stood in just his boxers.

I rolled my eyes. "Put some clothes on."

"Yes, ma'am." He saluted me, grabbing a pair of jeans and a dry shirt.

I shook my head and got in the car. I knew if I stood there, it would only enable him to do something stupid and embarrassing.

Instead of getting in the car, he jogged over to Marcus and they exchanged phone numbers.

"What was that about?" I asked when he got in the car.

"Thought it would make it easier when we meet up later." He shrugged, pulling away from the group.

"Oh, of course." I looked around at the bright green leaves on the trees and the grazing cattle. "Where exactly are we?"

"New York," he answered.

It was crazy to me that we had just left home and were already several states away. But we had a lot farther to go before we reached Maine.

Trace found a small diner and pulled into the parking lot. Several eighteen-wheelers were parked in back and there were few cars in the front.

"You did mention no fancy restaurants," he reminded me.

"Yeah, yeah." I eyed the place with suspicion. "I know."

We stepped inside the small diner and a bell chimed pleasantly above the door.

"Take a seat anywhere you'd like," a voice called out from the back.

We found an empty booth in the corner by a window. The table was sticky and looked like it hadn't been cleaned in years. I tried to hide my frown, but it was impossible.

Trace laughed at my expression.

"Don't tell me you're not grossed out," I challenged.

"It's not the best but spontaneity is what we agreed on."

"I didn't agree to get a strange flesh-eating disease," I countered, wishing I had a bucket of Germ-X and a spray can of Lysol.

He snorted. "You'll live."

"I didn't even know places like this existed in New York."

Trace chuckled. "You do realize that New York is more than just Manhattan?"

I narrowed my eyes. "Yes, I know."

"Just checking," he said with a smirk.

The waitress came striding up to us with a pleasant smile on her wrinkled face. "Can I get you guys something to drink?" she asked.

I frowned. "Bottled water." That seemed safe enough.

Trace snorted.

"What?" I glared at him.

"Nothing." He waved his hand in dismissal. "I'll have the same."

"Sure thing." The waitress smiled. "And menus are right there" —she pointed to the other end of the table— "look things over and I'll be back with your drinks."

I picked up two menus and handed one to Trace.

When the waitress came back with our water, I ordered a B.L.T. That seemed safe enough. Trace ordered a cheeseburger. If he got mad cow, well ...

I took a sip of water and said, "If I die from this, I hope you miss me."

He chuckled. "You're not going to die from the food or the water." He eyed the bottle in my hand. "I'm sure you'll be pleasantly surprised by how good it is. Truckers wouldn't stop here if the food sucked," he reasoned.

I hoped he was right, because I was hungry.

It didn't take us long to get our food and it actually looked pretty yummy ... but I still had to taste it.

Trace took a bite of his burger, which he'd covered in ketchup, and was very dramatic about how good it tasted. "Mmm, mmm," he hummed, "delicious."

I took a deep breath and picked up half of my sandwich. I took a small hesitant bite.

"This is actually really good," I admitted.

"See?" He smirked. "You got all worked up for no reason."

"Well ..." I looked pointedly at the dirty floors and then the table. "I think had reason to."

"You worry too much."

"Someone has to," I replied.

"Are you implying that I don't?" He took a bite of a French fry, his face suddenly serious. There was no playfulness in his eyes or tone of voice. "Because I can assure you, I do worry. A lot. About you. About Gramps. About my idiot brother. I worry if I'm good enough for you." He leaned toward me, staring into my eyes. "I worry that I'm not a good son or grandson. I worry that I'm not the right person to take over my family's business.

I worry about disappointing them if I tell them I don't want to take it over."

"Whoa," I whispered. I hadn't expected him to ... open up so much. Trace was a closed-off guy. He didn't talk about his feelings with me. I was usually able to pick up on what he was thinking or feeling because I'd known him so long. But I hadn't known he carried all of that around with him.

I placed my hand on top of his. "Trace," I whispered, "you don't need to worry about *any* of that. I love you, unconditionally, and so does your family. We could never be disappointed by the decisions you make."

He entwined our fingers together and stared at our joined hands for a moment. "That doesn't stop me from wondering."

"Do you really not want to take over your family business?" I asked hesitantly.

"No," he answered immediately, "I don't. I hate it. Bossing other people around is not how I want to make a living."

"Then *tell* them."

"I can't," he murmured. "I won't disappoint them like that."

"So, what? You'll be miserable for the rest of your life?" I questioned him, trying to meet his gaze but he refused to look at me.

"Sounds about right," he muttered.

"*Trace*," I said his name sternly, "that's the dumbest thing I've ever heard."

"Yeah, well, it's what I have to do."

"No, it's not," I countered. "We're in control of our own destinies, Trace. If you don't want to run the company, don't do it. Simple as that."

"And do what? Sell it? Put a stranger in charge? Gramps is *dying*; this is my responsibility now."

"Gosh, you're so stubborn," I groaned. "Do you even hear yourself? You're being ridiculous!"

"I'm not—"

"If the situation was reversed, you'd tell me I was being dumb," I interrupted.

He clenched his jaw, having no comeback for that since he knew it was true.

After a few minutes, he let out a breath. "I have a lot to think about," he mumbled, unable to meet my gaze.

"You do," I replied, squeezing his hand, which I'd never released, "and I hope you make the right decision for *you*."

CHAPTER TEN

THE FIRE CRACKLED AND SPARKS FLEW THROUGH THE air. I sat in-between Trace's legs with my head lying against his chest.

"This is nice," I murmured. "I'm glad we decided to stay for this."

"Me too," he whispered, his lips brushing over the scar my hair kept hidden. "There're no lakes in Winchester to do something like this ... but it's not like that stops people from having bonfires. This is just ... nicer."

"Mhmm," I agreed as his lips passed over my scar again. "Why do you do that?" The words tumbled from my mouth before I could stop them.

"Do what?" he asked, his chest rumbling against me.

"Touch my scar ..." I paused. "Does it ... bother you?" I tilted my face up to see his reaction.

"Is that what you think?" His brows furrowed together and he seemed shocked that I would come to that conclusion.

I frowned. "It bothers me." I reached up, running my fingers along the bumpy scar on the back of my head. "So it's understandable that it would bother you."

"Absolutely not." He shook his head forcefully. "You wanna know why I touch it? Why I kiss it?" he asked, his eyes dark with an emotion I couldn't decipher.

I nodded.

"Because," he said forcefully, "it reminds me of what I almost lost and how precious life is."

That hadn't been the answer I'd been expecting. I don't even know what I thought he'd say, but it hadn't been that.

Continuing, he ran a finger lightly over the scar, making me shiver. "I watched you bleed out from here ... and I knew then exactly what it means to be helpless."

"Trace," I breathed, reaching up to cup his cheek, but he caught my hand and kissed the palm.

"When I watched my dad get hit by that truck, there was nothing I could do. With you, I could do something, but I wasn't sure if I was doing the right thing and that scared me more than anything."

"I'm here," I whispered into the night. "You did everything right."

"It's been two years." He rested his chin on top of my head. "Two whole fucking years, and I still have nightmares about walking in on him beating the crap out of you."

I let out a shaky breath. "I still have nightmares," I admitted. "But I didn't know you had them."

"I know you have them," he stated, which surprised me. He ran his fingers down my neck, causing me to shiver.

"You do?" I had thought I'd done a pretty good job of hiding my continual nightmares from him. Early on, after it happened, it had been impossible to keep them from him. But as time passed, I thought I had been sneaky enough that he didn't know. I should have known, though—Trace being Trace, he knew everything.

"Yeah," he sighed. "Sometimes, while you're sleeping, you whimper and break out in a sweat and I *know* you're dreaming about what he did to you. When you have those nightmares, no matter what I do, I can't get you to wake up."

I frowned, staring at the bonfire. "Why do you think that is?"

It had been a few weeks since I'd had the last nightmare, but they were always the same. Aaron was above me, his foot kicking into my side and his fists battering my face. Trace never came to save me in my nightmares and I couldn't wake up until Aaron had delivered the fatal blow.

"I don't know." I felt him shrug. "I guess you're in such a deep sleep that you can't wake up."

"We're one messed up pair," I mumbled.

He chuckled, playing with a piece of my hair. "We're not messed up. We're perfect for each other, Olivia. Absolutely perfect."

"And why is that?" I asked, tilting my head back to smile up at him.

He kissed the end of my nose. "Because there's perfection in everything."

"I thought you told me perfection doesn't exist." I flattened the collar of his shirt as I remembered a conversation we'd had several years ago when we were crossing things off of my list.

"It doesn't, not in the way people believe."

"What do you mean?" I gazed at him quizzically.

He took a deep breath, gazing at the fire for a moment, before looking down at me. "There's beauty in everything, Olivia. So, why can't there be perfection too?" His tongue flicked out, moistening his lips. "People spend too much time dwelling on the bad in a situation when if they dug a little deeper they could find something good in it."

"Does that mean you found something good in what happened to your dad? To me?" I asked. I wasn't asking the question to be mean, I was curious.

His jaw tightened and his eyes narrowed but eventually he answered. "It took me a while, but yes."

"And what was it you found?"

He tightened his arms around me. "If my dad hadn't—died," he choked, "I would've probably been at some party or doing something stupid, and I wouldn't have been there to help you with your tire. Hell, I wouldn't have even been a mechanic." He brushed his nose against my hair. "I miss my dad *every single day*, but I know that if he hadn't died I wouldn't have *you*." I was surprised that he was being so open with me. Trace wasn't one to talk about his feelings; I knew that and I respected it, but it was nice to hear how much he cared. But I hated that he felt he had to lose his dad in order to gain me.

"And what good did you find in what Aaron did to me?"

"This is going to sound so cheesy." A smile played on his lips as he looked to our right where there was a forest and Marcus' kids were playing hide and seek.

"I promise not to mock you for your cheesiness." I rested my head against his chest, looking up at the stars.

"Mhmm, sure," he hummed.

"Tell me."

"I knew I was in love with you before that day, I was just a pussy and wouldn't tell you," he chuckled. "But what Aaron did to you made me fall even more in love with you, because after that I knew we could get through anything ... together."

"That *is* cheesy." I giggled.

"Woman, you said you wouldn't mock me." He nibbled on my earlobe.

"Sorry, I couldn't help myself." My eyes fluttered closed as he trailed light kisses down my neck.

"Hey, lovebirds!" Marcus called over to us, waving his hands. "Come get something to eat!"

I scooted out from between Trace's legs and stood, dusting the grass and dirt off my legs. I shivered as a breeze gusted around us. Being on the water, the nights were cool. It was nicer than the heart-attack-inducing humidity I had grown used to in Virginia, but I hadn't packed for cooler weather. Which was dumb, since we were heading all the way up to Maine.

"Here." Trace shrugged out of the plaid shirt he was wearing and draped it across my shoulders. I'd ditched the shirt I'd borrowed from him earlier and left it in the car.

"Thanks." I smiled as I pushed my arms through the large sleeves.

"Can't have you getting sick." He kissed my forehead, placing a hand on my waist and guiding me toward Marcus.

Apparently, Marcus had a bonfire once a week, where he grilled and hung out with his friends and family. He was a nice guy and his wife, Rebecca, seemed sweet but I'd only been introduced to her briefly. She was pretty with short, light-blonde hair and kind blue eyes. She almost seemed too calm to handle Marcus' boisterous personality. Their two kids, Sarah and Jamie, were adorable and reminded me of their dad. Both were currently trying to climb the trees to see who could make it the highest.

"Sarah! Jamie! Get down from there!" Rebecca scolded, looking like she might pass out if they climbed any higher.

"Becks, they're kids. Let them play." Marcus waved his hand in dismissal, flipping a burger on his portable grill.

"Tell me that when we end up spending the night in the emergency room." She glared at her husband. "Tell them to get down. They'll listen to you."

"Kids!" Marcus yelled. He didn't have to say anything else. They immediately started climbing down. "Sorry about that. The burgers will be ready in a minute. Buns are over there and Rebecca made some side dishes." He nodded to the open trunk of the SUV parked behind him.

I grabbed a plate and a hamburger bun, squirting a dollop of mayonnaise on it and adding lettuce and tomato. Rebecca had made macaroni salad and coleslaw; I scooped a spoonful of each onto my plate. Trace took enough to feed at least two other people. I looked his athletic body up and down. Seriously, where did he put all that food?

"What?" He glanced over at me. A slow smile—the panty-dropping one—lit his face. "Are you checking me out?"

I snorted. "Don't flatter yourself."

"You are." He smirked, licking some mayonnaise off his finger.

"Not for the reason you think." I shook my head.

"You mean, you're *not* undressing me with your eyes? Damn."

"I heard that," Marcus interrupted before I had a chance to

retort. "Keep it clean." He eyed Trace sternly. "My kids are here and they still think the opposite sex has cooties. I'd like to keep it that way until I'm dead."

"Sorry." Trace hung his head to hide his laughter. "Won't happen again."

"You bet it won't." Marcus laughed. "I *am* offering you a place to stay tonight that doesn't look like it belongs in a horror movie."

When we first arrived at the bonfire and accepted Marcus' invitation for a place to stay, we'd told him about the first place we'd stopped at in Philadelphia. He'd gotten quite a laugh from that. I'm happy we didn't end up staying there. I shuddered at the thought. The place probably had roaches crawling out of the drains.

Trace chuckled. "Yeah, thanks for that."

Marcus turned back to the grill, removing the burgers and stacking them on a plate. He put it in the trunk with the rest of the food.

I grabbed a plastic fork and used it to lift one of the burgers onto my plate.

"I can't believe you had a cheeseburger for lunch and now you're having one for dinner." I shook my head.

"I need protein." Sobering, he added, "I didn't really eat my lunch anyway."

That was true. After the conversation about taking over his family's business, neither of us had much of an appetite. I hated that Trace felt ... obligated to take over the business. His family—they were good people—and I knew they'd respect his decision if he chose to carry on as he was.

We found a spot close to the edge of the lake and sat side by side.

With the darkness, the lake appeared to go on forever. The only disruption on the surface was the reflection of the crescent moon. It was beautiful. Peaceful, even.

Marcus had set up small outdoor lanterns and spread them around so that we weren't completely in the dark.

I wasn't used to eating dinner this late—at home Trace and I usually ate dinner around four or five, not nine-thirty—but it was nice to do something different.

Someone sat down beside me and I turned to see one of the guys from the bungee jumping group. I couldn't remember his name, though.

"Hey." He smiled at me and then Trace. "What did you think of your jump?"

"It was pretty awesome." Trace grinned. "That adrenaline rush I got when we fell—there's nothing else like it."

"It's addicting," the guy agreed. "What about you?" He nodded at me.

"I'm glad I did it. It was pretty spectacular."

"Marcus said you guys were just passing through?" he questioned.

"Road trip," Trace replied.

"I've always wanted to go on a road trip," the guy said, stretching his legs out in front of him. "Never had the time, though." He stared out at the water for a moment and then jumped up. "Well, I'll leave you two alone." And with that, he sauntered off.

"That was ... weird," I mumbled.

Trace chuckled. "He thought you were hot and wanted to talk to you. You're lucky I'm not the jealous type."

"Oh, please." I rolled my eyes. "He did not think I was hot."

"Trust me, he did. I'm a guy, I know these things." He set

his empty plate to the side. "He was trying not to look at your breasts. At least he didn't look at your ass, 'cause that's *all* mine."

"You are ... " I shook my head, looking out at the lake. There were no words to describe Trace. He was one of a kind, and I wouldn't have him any other way.

"I'm what?" he prodded. "Sexy? Amazing? A great singer? Because I already know all of that." He turned on his side, looking up at me.

"You're just ... you." I shrugged, wrapping my arms around my legs.

"And there's no one else I'd rather be."

Sarah, Marcus' six-year-old daughter, walked up behind Trace and tapped him on the shoulder. "Hi." She waved at him.

"Hello, Princess Sarah." Trace grinned crookedly as he rolled over to face her. "What can I do for you?"

"Will you dance with me?" she asked sweetly, holding out a small hand for Trace to take.

Marcus had turned on his iPod and hooked it up to a docking station. Music pumped around us and I found my head bobbing along as I smiled at the scene playing out before me.

"Sure, sweetie." He smiled at her and I swear she blushed. Apparently, even small children weren't immune to Trace's charms.

He turned to me and whispered, "Don't be jealous," before hopping up and taking Sarah's small hand. She led him away and I heard Trace tell her she was a bit too short for him. He swept her up into his arms, holding her close. Her giggle filled the air. She wrapped her arms around his neck as they swayed to the music. My heart swelled. In my mind, Trace wasn't holding Sarah. Instead, he was holding our daughter. I had always known Trace would make an amazing father, but I'd never seen him around kids before. He was a natural.

I watched them closely, choked up on an emotion I couldn't begin to describe. If it was possible, I fell a little bit more in love with him in that moment.

Jamie appeared in front of me, blocking my view of Trace and Sarah. He smiled, displaying a gap in his mouth from missing teeth.

"Come on." He grabbed my hand, trying to pull me up. "They're dancing. We should too."

I laughed, taking his hand. Jamie was eight but he was almost my height. That's what I got for being short.

"You're pretty," he said to me.

I laughed. "Thank you, Jamie. You're quite handsome yourself."

He beamed at that. "Dad says you're staying the night at our house. You can sleep in my bed. I promise I don't snore like my dad."

I laughed. "Thanks for the offer, but I don't think that will be possible."

"Why not?" He frowned, his nose crinkling.

"I think my fiancé might not like that very much," I whispered, like I was letting him in on a secret.

Jamie glanced to his right, where Trace and Sarah were currently spinning in circles, and looked Trace up and down as if sizing him up.

After a moment, he looked back at me. "I can take him." He shrugged nonchalantly.

I threw my head back in laughter. "I'm sure you could," I

assured him, before I hurt the little boy's feelings with my outburst.

"I'm very strong," he boasted. "My dad says I'm going to be a fighter one day. He doesn't like it when I fight with my sister, though."

"Fighting with sisters isn't very nice," I told him.

"I know, but she's always taking my stuff. Doesn't she know my toys are for boys and hers are for girls?" He looked at me seriously, waiting for an answer.

I smiled down at the eight-year-old boy. "Sometimes, siblings take each other's stuff just to make the other one mad."

Jamie glared at his little sister in Trace's arms. "Well, that's not very nice. I don't touch her Barbie's. Those things are gross."

"I'm sure you're not always nice to your sister."

"Well, there was that one time I colored on her dolls. But she stole my Pokémon cards. So it was only fair," he reasoned.

Ah, sibling logic. I hadn't had to deal with that growing up, but I'd learned a few things being around Trace and Trent, as well as Avery and her brothers. Even as adults they were still picking on each other. I mean, Trace was twenty-four and Trent was nineteen, and those two were always arguing over something goofy and irrelevant.

"Do you have a brother or sister?" Jamie asked me.

"Not yet." I shook my head. "But I will soon."

"How?" He tilted his head. "You're old."

I frowned. I would've been better off to have told him no. Now, I was stuck explaining my complicated life to an eight-year-old. "It's a long story," I finally said, hoping that sufficed.

"I like stories." He shrugged his small shoulders. "You can tell me. I'm a good listener, promise."

"I'm sure you are." I smiled at him. "But it's not something I like to talk about."

"Oh …" He frowned. "That's okay."

The music cut off and we stopped dancing.

"*Dad*," Jamie groaned. "We were dancing."

"Sorry, bud" —Marcus smiled at his son— "but it's way past your bedtime. We need to get home."

"Fun sucker," Jamie grumbled, heading toward his dad with a lowered head.

"What did you say?" Marcus' voice was stern but he was fighting a smile.

"Nothing, Dad," Jamie mumbled as he climbed into the SUV.

I turned to find Trace still holding Sarah, carefully rocking her in his arms. She was holding on tightly to his neck and her eyes were closed as she breathed deeply. I think my heart stopped beating for a moment before kicking into overdrive.

He carried her to the car and strapped her in her booster seat.

"We'll follow you," Trace said to Marcus.

Marcus didn't live that far from the lake—we had only driven about five minutes when we pulled into the driveway of a modest sized home.

Sarah had woken up on the ride home and when she got out of the car, she came running to Trace. He immediately bent down so that he was on her eye level.

"What is it princess?" he asked.

"Will you read me a story? Mommy normally reads to me, but I want you to." She twisted her shirt between her small fingers, looking bashfully at the ground as she waited for his reply.

"Sure, as long as that's okay with your mommy and daddy."

"Thank you!" She hugged him tightly.

Marcus held the front door open and Sarah went running inside.

Trace grabbed our bags, refusing to let me carry mine.

"The guestroom's this way." Rebecca smiled pleasantly, leading us past a homey family room and nice kitchen. Kids toys were scattered about. "I'm sorry for the mess," she apologized. "I can never get them to put their toys away, and the minute I clean them up they drag another fifty out." She stopped in front of a door at the back of the house and opened it. "It's not much, but it's clean and there's an attached bathroom."

I hugged her. "Thank you so much for opening your home to us. Most people wouldn't do that."

"It's not a problem, honestly." Looking at Trace, she added, "You don't need to read Sarah a story. I know she can be pushy."

"I want to," Trace said quickly.

"Are you sure?" Rebecca asked hesitantly.

"Positive."

"Well, okay then." She smiled, heading back toward the kitchen. "I'll get her ready for bed. There's shampoo, conditioner, and body wash in the shower. Feel free to use it."

I stepped into the bedroom and Trace closed the door. The carpet was plush under my feet and the room smelled of fresh linen, courtesy of one of those plug-in outlet things.

I couldn't believe we'd lucked out in meeting Marcus, even if I did end up jumping off a bridge in the process.

"You can shower first," I told him, sitting on the edge of the bed. The mattress was nice and soft, nothing like the rock we'd slept on last night.

"Or" —he bent down and pressed his forehead against mine— "we could shower together."

"Nice try, but we're in someone else's house."

"I'll be a good boy, I promise," he coaxed.

"Mhmm, I'll believe that when … well, never."

"Thanks for believing in me." He released my cheeks and backed toward the bathroom. "I'm glad you have so much faith in me."

I tossed one of the pillows from the bed at him.

"Oooh, you want a pillow fight?" He waggled his brows.

"No, I'd like for you to shower so that I can. I smell gross." I frowned.

He wrinkled his nose playfully. "Is it *you* that I've been smelling?"

"Stop it." I rolled my eyes, falling back on the bed.

He chuckled as he gathered something to change into. "It's a legitimate question."

"Don't act like you don't smell either," I grumbled.

"That's my natural manly musk. Don't diss it," he chortled, closing the door. A moment later, the shower started up.

I didn't have anything to do so I figured I should be a nice daughter and call my mom so I could give her an update on our progress. Before we left, she'd told me to call her every day. So far, I was sucking at that.

"Liv?" she answered on the second ring.

"Hey, Mom," I replied, lying back on the bed and staring at the ceiling.

"You didn't call me yesterday. I was worried, but I thought maybe I shouldn't call you."

"Yeah, I'm sorry about that, Mom. I suck. I was so tired that I forgot." I stifled a yawn.

"You sound like you're tired now," she laughed.

"I am."

"What have you been up to?" she asked.

"Trace made me jump off a bridge," I said nonchalantly.

"He *what*?" she screamed so I had to hold the phone away from ear.

"We went bungee jumping. It was actually pretty fun."

"Geez, way to give your mom a heart attack, Liv."

"Sorry. I didn't think about the way that would sound," I apologized. I didn't need to scare my poor mother into going into labor early.

"So, besides bungee jumping, what else did you do?" Her tone was clipped and I knew she was still fretting over the bungee jumping. I shouldn't have told her. Lesson learned.

"We went to the Heinz museum yesterday, and this morning we saw the Liberty Bell and toured Independence Hall."

"Where are you now?"

"New York." I adjusted one of the pillows behind my back.

"At least you're making progress," she commented. "I better get to bed."

"Of course." I looked at the time, feeling bad that I'd called her after ten. "Love you, Mom."

"I love you too, Liv."

I had just put my phone away when the bathroom door opened and steam billowed out. Trace stood in a pair of low-hanging pajama bottoms and a t-shirt.

"Gotta keep it decent for the kiddos." He winked, heading for the door. He turned back to me and swiped his thumb across my lip. "You had a little drool there. I didn't know my plaid pajama pants would turn you on so much or I would've whipped these bad boys out a long time ago."

I blushed at his words. *Curse you, traitorous cheeks!*

"Now that you're sufficiently flustered, I have a story to read." He opened the door.

"I hate you," I spat playfully before the door closed.

"Sure you do," he called.

I grabbed a clean pair of pajamas and stepped into the bathroom. It was nothing like the bathroom we'd had to use at the motel yesterday. It was fairly large to be attached to a guestroom and kept tidy and clean. I turned the water on and stripped out of my clothes, more than happy to *finally* wash the lake scum off of me. I pulled the ponytail holder out of my hair and let it fall down my back. I stuck my hand under the spray to test the temperature and when I found that it was perfect, I stepped inside.

An embarrassing gasp of pleasure escaped my lips. I had taken for granted just how great a nice shower was.

I lathered my hair with the shampoo and scrubbed my body with the blueberry scented body wash. *Goodbye, lake scum!*

I rinsed the shampoo from my hair and then slathered it with conditioner. If I didn't use the stuff, my hair knotted into a curly ball that was impossible to tame.

When I got out of the shower and into clean pajamas I felt like a whole new person.

I wiped the condensation from the mirror and gasped at the nasty bruise around my eye. It hadn't been pretty this morning, but it was even worse now. I hadn't brought my makeup into the bathroom because I'd forgotten about the bruise. But I knew I had to hide it. Not just for Trace's sake, but because if Rebecca and Marcus saw it I knew they'd assume that Trace had hit me. Which was *so* not the case.

I locked the bathroom door, just in case Trace came back, and went to work hiding the bruise. The skin around my eye was extremely tender and I found myself wincing when I applied too much pressure. Only I could fall on the floor and get a black eye from it. That took major skill.

I eyed my reflection carefully, inspecting my face to make sure none of the bruise showed. When I saw that it was completely covered up, I put the foundation bottle back in my make-up bag and zipped it up. I knew it was only a matter of time until Trace learned about the bruise, but I figured the longer I could keep it hidden, the better.

I ventured out of the bedroom, hoping to get a glass of water before I went to bed. I stopped in the hallway outside a door when I heard Trace singing and pushed the door open slightly with the tips of my fingers.

I bit my lip to stifle my soft sigh.

Sarah was curled on top of Trace's chest as he ran his fingers through her soft dark hair. I didn't know what song he was singing, it wasn't a lullaby, but it was a slow sweet song. A book lay forgotten to the side.

He cracked his eyes open and spotted me in the doorway. He brought a finger up to his lips in a shushing motion. I stood there for a moment longer, watching him sing to the sleeping girl.

I didn't want to rifle through Marcus and Rebecca's things

so I was lucky enough to find them in the family room watching TV.

"Hey," I said quietly and Marcus turned at the sound of my voice. "Do you mind if I grab a bottle of water or something."

"Help yourself." Rebecca smiled pleasantly. "You're our guest."

"Thank you." I smiled, backing into the kitchen. I couldn't believe that Marcus and Rebecca were being so kind to us. I mean, they didn't *know* us. I guess they thought we seemed trustworthy. I know Trace had that effect on me. It was the only reason I ended up blabbing to him about my *Live List*. He was one of those people that upon meeting them, you knew you could trust them with anything and they'd never judge you.

I grabbed two water bottles and padded back to the guestroom. After today's adventures, I was exhausted and the bed was calling my name.

Trace had stopped singing and I stuck my head inside Sarah's room to find him asleep. Her small body was curled against his. I hurried to bedroom and came back with my phone, snapping a picture. Seeing Trace interact with Sarah … It was too adorable for words.

I climbed into the bed and fell asleep with a smile on my face. For the first time in a few weeks, I was genuinely happy.

CHAPTER ELEVEN

"You made all of this?" I gasped as I stepped into the kitchen and saw the breakfast Rebecca had prepared.

"I don't normally do all this—" She pointed to all the food prepared. "But I figured you could both benefit from a good home-cooked meal since you've been traveling," she explained.

"Rebecca, you didn't need to do all of this." I shook my head. I'm pretty sure she'd made a bit of every breakfast food known to man. "Trace and I were just going to hit the road and get something to eat while we drove. We didn't want you to go to all this trouble."

"It wasn't any trouble at all. I love to cook, but my kids only ever want to eat Pop-Tarts so I don't get the chance very often," she said as she flitted around the kitchen, putting food on plates. "Grab one, help yourself."

"Thank you for doing this." I smiled kindly as I took a plate and glass of orange juice she'd already poured.

"No need to thank me."

I pulled out a seat at the kitchen table and sat down.

Trace came into the room with Sarah clinging to his back like a monkey, her giggle filling the air.

He'd never come to bed last night and when I woke up, I found him in the same spot he'd been when I went to bed. Sarah didn't appear to have moved, either. It was one of the cutest things I'd ever seen.

"What do you want to eat?" Trace asked her.

She tightened her arms around his neck. "I want that plate." She pointed to one that had scrambled eggs with cheese on it.

"You got it, princess." He grabbed that plate and one for himself, carrying them over to the table. He went back for orange juice and finally sat down. Sarah had released his neck, but instead of sitting in her own seat, she sat on his lap.

I grabbed my phone from my pocket and snapped a picture of the two of them.

A sleepy-eyed Jamie strolled into the kitchen. He frowned at the food. "Mom, I don't want—"

"Here's a Pop-Tart." She handed him a pack before he could finish speaking.

He took it from her and scurried over to sit beside me.

"Manners, James," Rebecca scolded. "What do you say when someone gives you something?"

"Thanks, Mom," he mumbled, ripping open the packet.

"Mmm, something smells good." Marcus rubbed his stomach as he stepped into the kitchen. He kissed Rebecca on top of the head and her eyes closed as a small smile graced her face. "Thanks, Becks."

They joined us at the table and Rebecca shook her head when she spotted Sarah in Trace's lap.

"You'd never believe that she's normally wary of strangers," Rebecca told me. To Trace, she said, "You're a natural."

Trace smiled at Sarah. "I like kids and they like me."

I snorted. "That's because you act like a kid yourself."

"Exactly. There's nothing wrong with never growing up."

"Don't go getting any ideas," Rebecca warned her son when he brightened at Trace's words.

Jamie frowned, his small shoulders slumping. Being a kid though, he quickly got over it. Looking at me, he asked, "Are you going to live with us now?"

I tried to hide my smile. "No, Jamie. We're leaving today," I explained.

"Oh." His frown deepened. "I don't want you to leave."

"Me neither," Sarah chimed in, hugging her arms around Trace's neck. "Stay! Stay!"

"Sorry, princess, but we can't." Trace tucked her small head under his chin.

"No." She began to cry. "Don't leave."

Trace rubbed her back soothingly, looking at me with panic-stricken eyes.

I was more clueless than he was. I'd rarely been around small children growing up and had no idea what to do with the tear-fest.

"Please, stay," Sarah pleaded. "You can live in my room. My dolls won't care."

Trace chuckled and pried her arms from his neck so he could look into her wide brown eyes. "I'm sorry, princess. But I have to go home to my family."

"But" —her lower lip trembled as she fought more tears— "we can be your family."

"I know you could," he comforted her, "but my mom and brother would miss me. You don't want that, right?"

"No." She shook her head, dark-brown ringlets brushing against her shoulders. She looked at her own parents, as if thinking about how they'd miss her.

"Don't forget about me." She placed her head against his chest.

"Never, princess." He kissed the top of her head. "That would be impossible."

I NEVER KNEW it could be so hard to say goodbye to people you'd just met. But it was. I was sad to leave Marcus and his family.

"Thank you so much for everything." I hugged Marcus and Rebecca. "If you're ever in Northern Virginia, call us."

"We will," Marcus assured me.

"Bye, Jamie." I bent slightly to hug the boy.

"Are you going to visit us again?" Jamie asked.

I shrugged. "You never know."

"I hope you do."

"I hope so too." I smiled, meaning it.

"Bye, Sarah," I said to the girl, but she was too busy sobbing into Trace's shoulder to hear me. I swear I saw tears in Trace's eyes too.

Finally, Marcus pried Sarah from Trace's arms so we could get into the car. Sarah clung to her dad as she sobbed. Trace bowed his head and ducked into the car.

"Bye, guys," I said one last time.

Trace didn't waste any time in pulling away.

I looked over at him. "Are you crying?" I gasped.

"No." He turned his face away from me.

"Liar."

"There's something in my eye," he defended.

I rolled my eyes, fighting a smile. "That's the oldest excuse in the book. It's okay to cry, you know."

"I—" He shrugged, floundering for words. "I feel bad. I didn't think she'd be that upset by us leaving."

"She likes you, of course she's upset. She's only six," I reasoned.

"Yeah," he said, gripping the steering wheel harder, "but I don't want to be responsible for breaking a six-year-old girl's heart."

I laughed. "It's your own fault. You're too charming for your own good. I'm pretty sure everyone falls in love with you on sight."

"It's the scruff." He rubbed his jaw. "No one can resist the power of my facial hair."

"It is pretty amazing." I reached across and rubbed his cheek.

"So …" His brows furrowed as he became serious. "Where do you want to go next? I've picked the last three places, so I think you deserve a turn."

"Hmm," I pondered. "I really want to see the Statue of Liberty."

He grinned. "Done."

A FEW HOURS later we parked in New Jersey and rode the subway into New York City. I didn't like the subway. At all. There were some strange people on there, but Trace had insisted that we ride it for, in his words, "experience's sake". Whatever. That was one experience I could've done without. There was one man that wasn't wearing any pants. When we finally got off the subway, I dug Germ-X out of my purse and drenched my hands in its gooeyness. Trace watched me with a raised brow, fighting a smile.

"Here, take some." I shoved the bottle in his hands.

"Nah, I'm good," he leaned casually against the wall, crossing his feet at the ankles.

"If you ever want me to touch your hands again, you'll use it," I warned him.

"Fine." He took the bottle from me, squirting a small amount in the palm of his hand.

"More than that!"

"Woman," he groaned, adding some more. "Does this suffice?"

I eyed the amount in his hand. "That's better."

After I was sure that every germ on our hands had been killed, I followed him up the stairs, careful not to touch the railing, and outside.

I dug sunglasses out of my bag and put them on.

"Which way do we go?" I asked.

"Give me a second," he muttered, looking for a map. When he found one, he studied it for a moment before saying, "This way."

I had to jog to keep up with his long-legged stride. "Slow down," I pleaded. "I'm short."

"Sorry," he chuckled.

"Thanks," I croaked when he slowed. "My throat hurts from all the singing," I groaned. The whole drive here, we'd been singing along, non-stop, to Trace's road trip playlist.

"That's because you don't sing enough. You should change that. Your voice is beautiful," he mused.

"You're only saying that to be nice." I rolled my eyes.

He stopped, grabbing my arm to halt me. "Olivia, I would never lie to you. It's not a part of my personality. If I thought you sounded like a dying cow, I'd tell you. I'm honest like that."

"That's so comforting," I snorted.

"It should be." His lips spread into a smile. "Now come on, we have to hurry so we don't miss the ferry."

"Ferry?" I squeaked. "You mean we have to get on a boat thing?"

"Um, yeah." He looked at me peculiarly. "Is that a problem?"

I gulped. "I, um, get really sea sick."

He chuckled. "You mean to tell me that you're not afraid of heights, but a boat is what gets your stomach in knots? Interesting."

"It's a legitimate illness!" I complained. "One time, we went on a fishing trip when I was younger, and I spent the whole time throwing up over the side of the boat."

"Olivia," he said my name calmly, "it's the Statue of Liberty. It needs to be appreciated up close. Not from far away."

I shook my head rapidly back and forth. "No, no. I can't do it."

He eyed me for a moment. "Don't make me throw you over my shoulder caveman style."

"Don't even think about it," I warned him, walking away. "You're not getting me on that boat ferry thing."

"How did you think we got to the statue if you didn't know we had to take the ferry?" he asked, fighting a smile.

"I don't know," I answered honestly. "I never thought about it. But I'm not getting on the ferry."

I was already nauseous at the thought. I spotted a bench and snagged a seat, breathing deeply in and out, hoping to settle my rolling stomach.

"Olivia?" Trace questioned, squatting in front of me, his hands on my knees. "Are you okay?"

"Give me a minute," I warned him, taking another deep breath.

Anyone that had never experienced motion sickness of any sort would think I was crazy, but just the *thought* of stepping on a ferry had me feeling sick. I *couldn't* do it.

I slowly brought my head up to meet his worried gaze.

"Are you okay?" he asked, smoothing his thumbs over my cheeks.

"As long as I don't get on the ferry."

"No ferry." He grinned. "I would never make you do anything you absolutely didn't want to do."

"You made me jump off a bridge!" I exclaimed.

"Yeah, but that's because I knew, in the end, that you'd love it. It's my job to push you out of your comfort zone."

"I'm not getting on that ferry. It has nothing to do with a comfort zone."

"Woman, did you hear what I said? I would *never* force you to do anything. Not that I'd have to."

"You're so full of yourself." I playfully pushed his shoulder.

"I have a lot to be proud of." He waggled his eyebrows as he took my hands and hauled me up. "Come on, we have a statue to see."

I let him lead me to a better viewing point. The statue was quite spectacular, and I would've loved to see it even closer, but I wasn't going near the ferry.

"I'm sorry," I said after we'd been standing there for a few minutes.

"What for?" He looked at me questioningly.

"I know you would've liked to have gone." I pointed to the ferry pulling away. "You could've gone by yourself."

"But I didn't want to." He smoothed his hands up and down my arms. "I'm perfectly fine standing right here with you. *This*" —he motioned around us— "makes me happy."

I swallowed thickly. "Sometimes, I feel like I'm holding you back from things. Without—"

He silenced me with his lips.

"Why do you do that?" I gasped breathlessly when he pulled away.

"Do what? Kiss you senseless?" He smirked, pleased with himself.

"Yes, that," I snapped.

"Sometimes, you need to shut up and kissing you is the most pleasing way to do it."

"You have one strange thought process," I commented, fighting a smile.

"You say strange, I say spectacular. Any excuse to kiss you is a good one." He chuckled. "But what I was going to say to you is, in no way do you ever hold me back. How could you ever think that? Look at all the crazy shit we've done."

I laughed, feeling lighter. "I guess you're right."

"I'm *always* right. I'm a Wentworth, after all."

We gazed out at the water and statue for a little while longer before he said, "Ready to go?"

I nodded. "Yeah."

Since I wasn't getting on the ferry, there was no point in hanging around here any longer. At least I'd gotten to see it.

"Wanna head into Manhattan?" he questioned.

I gazed up at the New York City skyline. "Would you think I was weird if I said no?"

He laughed, shaking his head. "I won't think you're weird."

"Then no, I'm not interested. Big cities aren't my thing."

"God, you're perfect." He grabbed me, kissing the top of my head.

"I'm far from it, but I'm glad you think so." I smiled as we started back to the subway station. I was already dreading what we might encounter on there.

By the time we got back in the car, my stomach had completely settled, and I was ready to do something else. Seeing monuments and museums was interesting, but it was time for something a little more ... exciting. Like bungee jumping.

Trace plugged his phone in and—wait ... *Is that? No way.*

Trace looked at me with wide eyes as I began to laugh hysterically. I clutched my stomach, struggling to breathe, as tears coursed down my face from laughing so hard. "Oh, my gosh, I can't believe you have the Spice Girls on there."

"I didn't put it on there, I swear—"

"This is too funny." I wiped my face free of tears and began to sing.

Trace shook his head and then joined in.

When the song ended, he turned the volume down.

"The Spice Girls." I giggled, shaking my head back and forth. "What else do you have on there?" I eyed his iPhone.

"Once upon a time I had a big crush on Ginger Spice. Don't judge me, woman," he joked, changing the playlist. "And there might be one Britney Spears song on there." I eyed him. "Okay, maybe two. But don't tell me you never had a crush on one of those 90s boy bands."

"I did."

"Which one?"

"Backstreet Boys," I admitted.

"And who was your favorite?" he asked, fighting a smile.

I squirmed in my seat. "Brian," I muttered.

He began to sing one of their more popular songs and I shook my head.

"I can't believe you know that song," I bit my lip to stifle my laughter.

"I think every kid growing up in the 90s knew that song, not to mention countless other pop song." He shrugged. "You couldn't escape them. Don't worry, my parents still exposed me to the classics."

"What's your favorite song then?" I asked.

He bit his lip, his eyes narrowed in thought. "Don't make me choose. I love all kinds of music so it's impossible for me to pick one."

"That's a sucky answer." I frowned. "But I don't think I have a favorite song, either."

"See?" He grinned, finally backing out of the parking space after our impromptu Spice Girls sing-along. "There are too many good ones to pick only one. I don't even have a favorite artist or band. Picking one over another would be like … " he paused, thinking. "Like picking a favorite child. Impossible and unfair."

"Do you think your taste in music has changed since you were younger? I know mine has." I kicked my sneakers off, getting comfortable since I had no idea how long it would be until we stopped.

"Hell yeah." He chuckled, changing lanes. "I used to sing "Farmer in the Dell" *all* the time. It drove my parents nuts. Then I moved on to the Spice Girls," he joked. "After that, I listened to a lot of heavy rock music; I call that my angst years. Now I like pretty much every genre of music. If it has a good beat and lyrics I can appreciate then I'm cool with it." He glanced over at me for a moment and then said, "I like how different types of music can set a certain mood, or make something even more memorable. You know what I mean?"

"Yeah, I do."

"For example, when I took you to karaoke night, to cross singing off your list, I picked "Just a Kiss" for a reason. I was too scared to tell you what I was feeling, so I chose that song."

I snorted. "Then you did kiss me and ran away." I looked out the window, avoiding the look I knew he was bound to be giving me.

"I'm still sorry about that," he whispered. "It was a pussy move for me to make. I was scared of what I felt for you, Olivia. I had *never* felt that before."

"Felt what?" I asked, curiously.

"Like I'd be lost without you," he murmured. "I know that sounds like such a chick thing to say, but it's true. I knew you were different from the moment I met you. You're not like other girls, Olivia. You're just ... you, and that's why I love you. There isn't one thing in particular that I love about you. It's everything. You're beautiful and smart, and you don't mind the random shit I say, or my crappy dancing. "

"Whoa," I breathed. "That was deep."

"Hey, I can be a deep guy. Give me some credit, woman."

"Oh, please." I rolled my eyes. "Your 'deep' moments are few and far between. I need to soak this in while I can."

He frowned. "I can be serious."

"You were watching *Dora the Explorer* while eating Trix cereal last week." I rolled my eyes.

"I like the "Backpack" song."

"Of course you do," I laughed.

"Seriously, though, I meant what I said."

"I know you did." I smiled. "And in case you were wondering, I feel the same way about you." I leaned over and kissed his stubbled cheek.

His eyes were a dark forest green when he looked down at me briefly. "I love you, and I can't imagine my life without you in it." Slowly, he brought my left hand up to his lips, kissing the top of it before grazing his lips over my engagement ring. "I can't wait until you're Mrs. Wentworth."

"Me either." I laid my head on his shoulder, a smile on my face, a smile that rarely ever left thanks to him.

CHAPTER TWELVE

Rain beat down on the car and a crack of thunder roared, causing me to jump. I hadn't seen a storm this bad in a long time. The rain was so heavy that I could barely see out the window.

Trace came running back to the car, completely soaked.

"They're full too," he groaned, leaning his head back as he stared at the car ceiling. "Apparently, the storm has caused all the motels to fill up. There's not another one for at least fifty miles and I'm exhausted. I can't keep driving."

"I can—"

"No." He pressed a finger over my lips, shushing me. "Only I drive the Camaro."

I glanced at the backseat and then at him. "We can sleep in the car. The backseat is bigger than most."

"I don't think we have much choice." He rubbed his eyes then buckled his seatbelt. "I'll try to find a safe place to park."

I jumped again as lightning lit the sky.

"I don't like this," I admitted reluctantly.

"I'll keep you safe."

"How?"

"Cover your body with mine. Problem solved."

"I should've known." I forced a smile, because not even Trace's sense of humor could make me feel better right now. Thunder growled ominously, and I prayed we made it through this storm alive.

Trace drove at a snail's pace as the windshield wipers worked overtime to clear the glass. The rain was coming down so fast that we could only see a few feet in front of us. I hoped the wind—that was currently trying to push the car into the wrong lane—would blow the storm passed ... and quickly.

Trace pulled the car as far off the side of the road as he could manage without crashing into one of those wire fences they used to keep cattle back and turned the flashers on.

"This is g-g-good enough." He shivered, his teeth clacking together. His hair was plastered to his head and water dripped off his chin. His clothes were soaked and if he didn't change into something dry, he was going to get sick. Unfortunately, our clothes were in the trunk, and there was no way to get to them without getting out of the car ... which would lead to the dry clothes getting wet. "There's enough gas to let the car run," he muttered, turning up the heat.

I guess that counted for something.

I unbuckled the seatbelt and climbed into the back.

"Are you coming?" I asked him.

"Y-yeah." His body trembled with another shiver. He cupped his hands over his mouth, blowing hot air against them. "I'm cold," he said unnecessarily.

"I know you are, come here." I patted the backseat.

His wet clothes made a squishing sound against the leather seats as he climbed in the back.

"You need to get out of your clothes," I told him, already reaching for his plaid shirt and pushing it off his shoulders.

He grinned crookedly. "You l-l-love any excuse t-t-to get m-m-me out of m-m-my clothes."

"Right now, I'm more concerned with getting you warm before you get sick."

"Oooh, are you going t-t-to wear a n-n-nurse's outfit and feed me by hand?" Despite the fact that he was shivering uncontrollably the man was still making jokes and there was a mischievous glimmer in his green eyes.

"Sorry" —I spread my arms wide— "no nurse's outfit here."

"D-d-darn," he shivered, letting the plaid shirt drop to the floor.

I pulled his white t-shirt over his head and it fell to the floor as well. His jeans were the next to go.

When I curled my body around his, he stuck his thumb in the elastic of his boxers letting it snap against his skin. "A-a-are these s-s-staying o-o-on?"

I laughed weakly. "Yeah, they are."

"A-a-and h-h-here I thought y-y-you had an u-u-ulterior m-m-motive for g-g-getting me n-n-naked."

"You are something else," I muttered, laying atop his chest and wrapping my arms around his neck. Only Trace would make sexual advances while freezing to death.

"S-s-so I-I-I've b-b-been t-t-told."

I pressed my face against his chest, hoping my body heat

would help him get warm. It wasn't working, though. His body was so cold that *I* was becoming chilled.

Another loud clap of thunder had me letting out a squeal.

"I-I-It's o-o-okay." His large hand spread across my back, rubbing up and down in comfort.

I ruffled my fingers through his hair, trying to dry it.

"I-I-I'm f-f-fine."

"No, you're not. Stop trying to be Mr. Tough Guy and let me take care of you."

"O-o-okay, b-b-bossy p-p-pants."

"Stop talking," I mumbled, moving my hands across his chest, trying to transfer my warmth to him.

"M-m-maybe y-y-you s-s-should k-k-kiss me and w-w-warm my l-l-lips."

"Nice try, Trace. Now seriously, shush."

I took my tank top off and his eyes widened. "Don't even think about it," I warned as I balled the shirt up and used it as a makeshift towel to dry his body.

I dried his chest and arms first then scooted down his body to dry his legs. I gasped in surprise when I felt the prominent bulge. "Trace," I gasped his name in shock.

A crooked smile graced his lips for a moment. "I c-c-can't help it. It has a m-m-mind of it's own."

I rolled my eyes but I was pleased that his teeth weren't chattering as much. The car was quickly building in heat, and I wasn't sure if it was from the heaters blowing full blast or us.

After I dried his legs, I somehow ended up straddling his chest. He grabbed my legs, just below my butt, his fingers grazing against the edge of my shorts. "I think I'm warm now." Lust-filled green eyes gazed into my own.

A shaky breath rolled through my body as he sat up and I slid down until my center was pressed right up against him.

"You know …" He tucked a piece of hair behind my ear that had escaped the confines of the braid I'd put it in earlier. "I've never had sex in a car before."

"Really?" My voice shook. Funny, how only minutes ago *he'd* been the one shaking. Now, with a few words he had me shaking like a leaf.

"Really." His lips brushed lightly against mine, causing a soft moan to escape me.

"Are you sure we should do this?" I questioned, my eyes fluttering closed as he nipped at my neck.

"Do what?"

"Have sex in your car," I gasped as he pressed kisses to the tops of my breasts.

"I don't think I've ever had a better idea." He pulled down the cups of my bra. "I think this is the perfect way to warm me up." His mouth closed over one of my nipples and I was lost. My fingers tangled in his damp hair. He unclasped my bra and tossed it to the floor of the car. With deft fingers, he unsnapped the button of my shorts and eased the zipper down. They too joined the rapidly growing pile of clothes on the floor.

He reached down for his jeans, grabbing his wallet, and pulling out a condom.

"Always prepared," I joked.

"You never know." He grinned wickedly, then reach for my panties, ripping them from my body.

"Trace!"

"They were in my way." He smirked, sliding his boxers down.

I took the condom packet from him and tore it open. I

slowly rolled it on him, smiling in satisfaction when he twitched against my hand.

"I need to be inside you." He pushed my hands out of the way and finished putting it on himself.

I squealed when he grabbed me by the waist and slowly lowered me down his length.

"Oh, God," we both moaned simultaneously.

His mouth descended on mine, and his tongue pressed against my lips, seeking entrance.

He rocked me slowly against him, setting the rhythm.

Everything except us ceased to exist in that moment.

I was consumed by the feelings he was creating inside me.

His hand skated up my back, making me shiver. He pulled the ponytail holder from my hair and let it fall forward to conceal us. He cupped my face in his hands, kissing me deeply and making my stomach flutter in the process. Before Trace, I never thought anyone would ever make me feel the way he does, make me want to expose myself in such an intimate way. I might not have been a virgin when I met him, but my first time didn't really count. A drunken encounter at a party wasn't comparable to the bond I shared with Trace. What we had was special. I knew enough to see that.

I clasped the ends of his hair in my hands. Laying my head on his shoulder, I rocked my hips slowly against him.

Our gasping breaths filled the car. All thoughts of someone seeing us had long disappeared.

"I love you," I murmured, pressing my lips against his throat.

Until I met Trace, I hadn't understood how powerful those three words were. Some people tossed them around like they were nothing, when they meant everything. When you love someone as completely as I love Trace, you can make it through everything as long as you're together.

"Not as much as I love you," he gasped, cupping my cheek and forcing my eyes to meet his.

I closed the distance between us, kissing him deeply.

There was no talking after that.

Nothing else needed to be said—we only needed to feel our love for each other.

SOMETHING WAS BRUSHING against my skin and it was super annoying. I swatted at it and laughter met my ears. With a groan, I opened my eyes slowly.

I was sprawled on top of a grinning Trace and he was tickling the bare skin of my shoulder with a piece of my hair.

"I was sleeping."

"And my body is numb. Did you know you're kind of heavy when you're sleeping?" He tapped my nose with the chunk of my hair he was still playing with.

"Did you know that you're annoyingly peppy in the mornings?" I rolled my eyes, reaching for my shorts and scooting off of his body. I'd put my bra, tank top, and ripped panties on before we fell asleep. After I got my shorts on I crawled over the seats and into the front of the car.

"Face it, you love my cheerful personality."

I looked back to see Trace sit up and stretch. The ways his muscles flexed and rippled when he did that left my mouth watering. I never thought I'd be one of those girls constantly checking out guys—or in my case, *guy*—but I had a hard time taking my eyes off of Trace.

He pulled his jeans and shirt on and climbed over the seats like I had. He sat in the driver's seat, staring out the windshield. I looked too, wondering what had captured his attention. A dancing cow, maybe? But there was nothing there.

"Tr—"

"Marry me?" he cut me off.

"Uh ..." I raised a brow. "Did I dream that, or didn't you already propose? I'm kind of confused right now." I frowned, looking at him like he'd grown three heads.

He chuckled, shaking his head. "That's not what I meant. What I mean is, marry me ... today." There was no playfulness in his gaze or smile. He was dead serious and I was shocked.

"Today?" I whispered, my voice fleeing me.

He nodded. "Today."

"Why?" I gasped. When he frowned, I hastened to add, "Not that I don't want to marry you today, but our families aren't even here. Why now?"

"Why not now?" he questioned, taking my hands in his. "It's not that I don't want them here, but this is about the two of us and our commitment to each other. We can have a wedding with a dress and cake and all that other crap, when we get back. I'm sure they'll insist. But I don't want to go another day without you as my wife." His hand glided up my arm, causing me to shiver, and then rested against my cheek.

My eyes closed and a shaky breath gusted between my lips.

I had always thought I'd get married with my family surrounding me while wearing a white dress, but what Trace said was making me think differently. Marriage was between the two of us—everything else was just pomp and circumstance.

"Your mom is going to kill us."

He kissed me quickly and pulled away grinning. "I don't care."

"You know," I said as I glanced down at my shorts and plain white tank, "I never really imagined getting married dressed like this."

"Here" —he shrugged out of his red plaid shirt— "put this on."

I laughed as I put it on. "I didn't picture getting married in your plaid shirt, either."

"Who wouldn't want to get married in plaid?" he scoffed, throwing a wink my way.

I shook my head, fighting a smile. "Are we really doing this?"

"We are." He entwined our fingers together and brought our joined hands up to his lips, kissing my knuckles.

"I really hope your mom doesn't kill us," I mumbled.

He chuckled. "I think we should be more worried about your mom. Pregnant ladies can get pretty crazy."

I snorted, gazing out the window as he pulled away. "You're probably right."

"Now, we need to find the nearest courthouse."

CHAPTER THIRTEEN

Unfortunately, our rumbling stomachs ceased our search for a courthouse, at least for the time being.

"How are you feeling?" I asked, taking a bite of my egg sandwich. "You were really cold last night and I was scared you might get sick.

A boyish grin lifted his lips as he leaned back casually in the booth. "I'm fine. Lucky for me, I had someone to warm me up."

"Stop it," I groaned, throwing my wadded up napkin at him.

"What?" He batted his eyes innocently. "You did a really good job."

"You just—ugh." I buried my face in my hands. I was going to have to start leaving Trace at home, or in this case, the car if he kept talking like that in public.

"Don't be embarrassed. You were hot last night—no pun

intended." He smiled crookedly. "It was nice having you on top for a change."

"Trace!" I shrieked, causing an elderly couple to glance our way. I knew my cheeks were bright red but I didn't care.

"I mean, don't get me wrong," he continued, "I prefer being on top, but it's nice to mix it up every now and then."

My heart was about to race out of my chest as I looked around to see if anyone had heard him.

Based on the smirk the guy in the booth next to us was wearing, it was safe to assume he had.

"I can't believe you," I frowned.

"Hey, you knew what you were getting into when you met me."

"That I did," I groaned. "I must have been insane."

"Or wowed by how amazing I am."

"How about amazingly immature?" I retorted.

He leaned forward so there was little space between us. "Look at us, we're already bickering like an old married couple and we haven't even signed any official documents. The next seventy or so years of our lives seem so promising."

"Where do you come up with this stuff?"

"My mind. It's a spectacular place to reside. Mere mortals like you can't fathom it." He bit his lip, eyeing me.

I tried not to, but I couldn't help laughing. I was weak and it was impossible for me to stay mad at Trace, even if he was speaking publicly about our sex life. That was the power of his charm.

"Your mind is bound to be a strange place."

"Strangely fascinating. Unicorns and dragons frolic here while drinking tea and discussing the winner of the latest quidditch match." Grinning, he tapped his forehead.

I shook my head, at a loss for words. What *did* you say to that?

"What? No response?" He grinned, crossing his arms over his chest. "Have I rendered you speechless?"

"Pretty much." I laughed, finishing the last bite of my egg sandwich.

"Wow, normally you always have a witty comeback for me. This day is one for the record books."

Before I could reply, my phone began ringing. I saw my mom's name on the caller ID and cringed. I was being a horrible daughter and not keeping her updated on our road trip. With her hormones she was liable to hunt me down and drag me back home.

"Hey, Mom," I answered.

"Liv, is everything okay? You didn't call yesterday."

"Everything's fine. We got caught in a bad storm last night so it slipped my mind to call you. I'm—"

"Don't you dare say you're sorry," she said, her voice stern. "I've been worried sick and now you're telling me that you were driving through a bad storm. Do you want to send me into preterm labor? One day, you're going to have your own daughter, and then you'll see just how worrisome children are. I thought you were in an accident or something."

"Mom," I said calmly, "don't be dramatic."

I heard her take a deep breath. "Sorry. Forgive me, Liv. This whole being pregnant thing is messing with me." She sighed and I pictured her hanging her head in her hands. "Last night I was crying over an Oreo commercial because I wanted an Oreo and we didn't have any." I couldn't contain my laughter at that. "Anyway," she huffed, "what's your plan for today?"

"Uh—" I stalled. There was no way I could tell my mom

that we planned on getting married today. She'd lose it. Before we left for our road trip she'd already showed up at the apartment three different times with stacks of those wedding catalogs and asking me about colors and cake flavors. I mean, it wasn't like we were eloping in Vegas but it *was* kind of a shotgun wedding. If I told her, she'd try to talk me out of it, and I didn't want that. Like Trace, I was ready to be married.

"No plans," I finally said after a lengthy pause.

"What are you two up to?" she questioned curiously. Moms always knew when something was up. It was like they had radar or something.

"Nothing," I blurted and ended the call, dropping my phone straight into my glass of water by accident. "Crap."

Trace snorted. "Well, that was effective." He pointed to my swimming phone.

"Shut up," I groaned, fishing my phone out of the ice water. The screen was a rainbow of colors before going completely black. I sighed. "At least she can't call me back now."

"That's for sure."

"Oh, no," our elderly waitress said as she stopped by the table. "Did you get your phone wet?" She nodded her head at me, where I was currently drying it with a napkin.

"Yeah. It fell out of my hand."

"I'm so sorry about that."

"It's not your fault." I shrugged, glaring at the black screen. "I'm the idiot that dropped it."

Choosing not to comment on that, she laid our receipt on the table and said, "If you need anything else, just holler. Pay whenever you're ready."

"Thanks." Trace smiled, already pulling out his wallet. Nodding to me, he added, "We'll stop by the Verizon store and get you a new phone ... maybe one with a waterproof case."

I narrowed my eyes. "Not funny."

"Why did you drop it?" he asked, laying his credit card on the table.

"Because," I groaned, "she wanted to know what we were doing today and I couldn't tell her we're getting married."

"Then you should've lied."

"I *can't* lie. Besides, she's my mom. She would've known," I reasoned. Leaning my head back against the booth, I said, "Our moms are *so* going to kill us."

"That's what you keep telling me."

"Gramps will be pissed too."

Trace frowned at that but didn't comment.

The waitress came by again and took his credit card. He grabbed his phone and looked at the screen intently.

"What are you doing?"

"I'm looking for the nearest place to get a marriage license. No one's going to perform the ceremony without the license," he mumbled, scrolling through his phone.

"Oh." I nodded. I hadn't thought about that part.

"Looks like there's a clerk's office just around the corner." He smiled triumphantly. Sobering, his emerald eyes met mine. "You are sure about this, aren't you?"

"I've been sure about you since I trusted you with my list," I confessed. "I wasn't sure where it would lead us, but I knew you were special."

Chuckling, a smile spread across his face. "Oh please, you wanted me from the moment you saw me. I saw you licking your lips when I got out of my car."

I rolled my eyes. "It was the tattoos."

"*Sure.*" He smirked cockily, taking the pen and receipt from the waitress. He wrote down the tip amount and scrawled his signature. "Come on." He stood, holding out his hand for me. I placed mine in his larger one and let him pull me from the booth, giggling. "We have a marriage license to get." He pecked me on the lips in front of the whole restaurant, but I didn't care who saw. I was getting married to the man of my dreams today. Nothing could dampen my mood now.

"You want a marriage license?" The balding clerk eyed us. "Aren't you a little young?"

I rolled my eyes. "We're both consenting adults that want to get married. I don't understand what the hold up is," I said sassily.

"Neither of you are from New Hampshire." He glanced down at our Virginia driver's licenses.

"Obviously," I snorted. "Although, I did grow up here."

"Well, there's nothing stopping you from getting a license as long as you're getting married in this county." He adjusted his reading glasses.

"We can arrange that," Trace assured the man.

"Well, then, let me get everything organized. I'll need both of your social security cards."

I pulled mine out of my wallet and handed it to him. Trace did the same.

The man, I think his name was Jim, forced a smile and went in search of the documents he needed.

Trace grabbed me around the waist and hugged me to his chest. "Ready to be married to me for the rest of your life?"

I giggled. "You make it sound so ominous."

"There's nothing ominous about waking up next me." He waggled his brows.

"You are so full of yourself." I shook my head.

"When you've got it like I do, there's no point in sugar coating it."

I buried my face in my hands, stifling a laugh. "What have I gotten my myself into?" I asked rhetorically.

He removed my hands from my face and grabbed my chin between his thumb and index finger, forcing my gaze to his. In a serious tone, he said, "I promise to make every day of our lives together better than the one before it. I know we're going to have our ups and down, life's a roller coaster and that's expected, but I'm always going to look for the bright side even in the darkest situations."

"Wow," I breathed. "That was beautiful."

"I can be deep when I want to." He winked, kissing the end of my nose.

Jim came back into the room, clearing his throat.

I pulled away from Trace, blushing, which was silly. It wasn't like we were doing anything inappropriate. But the look on Jim's face suggested that he thought otherwise.

"I have some papers for you to sign," he muttered gruffly, settling behind his desk once more. The wheels on his chair squeaked shrilly. "Sit." He pointed to the chairs in front of his desk.

My eyes widened and Trace coughed to stifle his chuckle.

"Here." Jim slid a stack of papers to Trace. "You fill this part out and she fills this out." He handed him a pen. "Sign down there—" he pointed to the bottom of the page.

Trace filled the information out quickly and pushed the

documents my way. I signed my name beside his and stared in awe at my name for a moment. This was the last time I would be signing my name as Olivia Owens. From this moment on I was going to be Olivia Wentworth. That knowledge filled me with a giddy warmth.

Jim stood and puttered around his office. Minutes later, he returned and said, "This is your copy. Show this to whoever is administering your wedding and you're good to go."

"Thanks." Trace took the papers from him and shook his hand.

"Good luck to you," Jim muttered.

Trace stood, smiling down at me. "Ready?"

"You know it," I answered immediately.

He chuckled. "Glad to know you're ready."

"I'm more than ready." I smiled, following him out of the building.

"Oh, really?" He raised a brow.

I nodded. "Marriage is just another adventure."

"That it is." He grabbed me by the waist, kissing me. "Last one before we're married." He winked. "I hope that will hold you over."

"I think I'll live." I giggled.

"Good, 'cause I'm not into necrophilia."

"Ew, Trace." I wrinkled my nose.

"What?" He grinned, unlocking the car. "Shouldn't you be *glad* I'm not into that?"

I gagged. "Stop talking."

He chuckled as he slid in the driver's seat. "We haven't even said 'I do' and you're already telling me to shut up." He shook his head. "Should I run now?"

"Stop it." I fought a smile, pushing his shoulder. "Oh no!" I exclaimed suddenly.

"What?" Trace responded, looking wildly around him to locate whatever had caused my outburst.

"We don't have wedding rings!"

He chuckled. "Dang, woman. I thought something bad happened."

"Sorry," I muttered with a frown.

"I actually have your ring," he admitted.

I grabbed his arm. "What? Let me see it."

"No way." He shook his head, fighting a smile. "You're not seeing it until it goes on your finger." He frowned. "I don't have it with me, anyway. It's at home in my sock drawer."

"Your sock drawer?" I snorted.

"I knew you wouldn't look there!"

"True," I laughed. "But I don't have a ring for you."

"It's okay." He waved his hand in dismissal. "I *just* proposed and now I'm dragging you off to marry me. I understand why you don't have one."

"No, it's not okay," I insisted. "I want you to have a ring. Surely there's a jewelry store around here somewhere." I looked out the car windows like I thought one would magically appear in front of me.

"I think Marcy would kill us if she didn't make my ring." He grabbed my shoulder so I was forced to look at him and cease my scanning.

"You're right," I agreed. "She would hunt us down. What if we get a temporary ring?"

"Why waste the money?" he reasoned. "Besides, like I said, your ring isn't with me."

"Says the billionaire," I snorted.

"Hey ..." His smile faltered and I instantly felt bad. His family's money had always been a touchy subject. While the Wentworths had more money than I'd like to even think existed, none of them were *different* because of it. Money certainly hadn't gone to their heads like some people. "It's not my money, it's my family's."

"I know." I placed my hand against his stubbled jaw. "I'm sorry. I shouldn't have said that."

"It's okay." He turned his head into my hand, kissing my palm.

"So, no ring?"

"Not yet. When you put a ring on my finger, I intend to never take it off. I don't want a placeholder ring. I want the real thing."

I bit my lip to stifle my laughter but it was of no use.

"Why are you laughing at me?" he questioned.

"Because," I tried to breathe around my giggles, "that's quite possibly the cutest, but cheesiest, thing you've ever said to me."

He put a hand to his chest, feigning anger. "Woman, I can be romantic."

"Surprising me with a room filled with lightsaber nightlights is not romantic, Trace," I snorted.

"It was *one* time!" he chortled. "And I thought it was cool."

"It was definitely cool," I agreed, "but not exactly as romantic as you'd thought. Next time, try candles."

"That's a fire hazard, Olivia."

I stuck my tongue out at him.

Ignoring my protruding tongue, he continued, "So, are we really doing this thing?"

"Having second thoughts, Mr. Wentworth? I'm shocked."

"Never, I just …" He swallowed thickly, his lashes fanning against his cheeks, "I want to know that this is what you want. That *I'm* what you want."

"Of course," I gasped. "How could you ever doubt that?"

His tongue flicked out, moistening his lips. "Even the most confident people have doubts."

I wrapped my arms around his neck and scooted as close to him as I could get in the car. "You're exactly what I want, Trace. Bad dancing and all. I accept you as what you are, which in my eyes, is everything."

A huge grin lit his face. "Now look who's getting corny."

"What can I say?" I grasped the dark hairs that curled against his neck. "We bring out the cheesiness in each other."

"And I wouldn't have it any other way."

CHAPTER FOURTEEN

I let Trace lead me into the courthouse and through security. My heart was racing and my hands shook. I was nervous, but not because I was unsure of Trace. I was excited too. And scared. Yeah, definitely scared. Marriage was a big commitment, and while I was ready to be married to him, it still frightened me. So many marriages these days ended in divorce, and I didn't want to be another statistic. But I knew in my heart and soul that what Trace and I had was special. We were the exception to the rule and I was incredibly lucky to have found him. All it took was one flat tire to completely change the course of my life. It's quite amazing how life works like that.

Trace was speaking with the security guard, asking for directions, but I was completely zoned out.

In a matter of minutes, Olivia Owens would cease to exist and Olivia Wentworth would take her place.

"Thank you," Trace said to the guard as he headed for a set of stairs.

I hurried behind him—actually, he kind of dragged me since he held my hand and both of us were smiling goofily. This was it.

He turned right, heading a short ways down a hallway. He stopped in front of a set of double wooden doors, blowing out a breath between his lips. He put his hand on the knob but didn't turn it.

"Ready?" He looked down at me with happy green eyes.

"Do you even need to ask?" I responded.

With a grin, he pushed the door open and we stepped inside.

There were wooden benches set up and I was surprised to see several couples scattered around. Some had friends and family with them, but most were like us and had no one.

Trace sat on one of the benches and pulled me down beside him. The Justice of Peace finished performing the ceremony for one couple and they quickly left the room with huge smiles in their faces.

He called another couple up and my heart raced even faster. I counted three more couples ahead of us.

"Your hand is sweating," Trace whispered in my ear.

"Sorry." I blushed, trying to pull my hand from his but he wouldn't release it.

"It's cute. Are you nervous?" he asked.

I nodded. "Aren't you?"

"Baby, I never get nervous."

"Of course not." I rolled my eyes, my lips twitching as they threatened to turn up in a smile.

"I don't want you to be nervous, either." He grazed his thumb over my cheek.

"It's a good kind of nervous," I assured him. "I promise."

He smiled at that and then jumped as if frightened. I looked around thinking something in the room had caused his reaction. It would be my luck that his ex, Aubrey, would show up. Or something as equally ridiculous. But that wasn't the case. He pulled his vibrating phone out and frowned at the screen. I could see that it was his mom calling. He pressed a button, directing her call straight to voicemail, and turned the phone completely off.

"I'll call her later," he whispered.

"Are you going to tell her?"

He nodded, releasing my hand and rubbing his on his jeans, a nervous habit of his. "Yeah. No point in waiting. She's going to get pissed either way."

"We can wait." I placed my hand on his forearm. The muscle was tight from tension.

"No. I want to marry you today. I'm sick of putting everyone else's happiness before mine. This is for *us* and no one else."

"Trace—"

"I'm fine," he assured me.

"Are you?" I questioned worriedly. "I don't want you to do this" —I motioned to the courtroom— "just because you feel it's the only way to establish control. I love you, Trace. I don't care when or where we get married. If you want to walk out those doors right now, that's—"

He silenced me with a kiss. Damn him.

"You've really got to stop doing that," I groaned when he released me.

"Well, you talk too much." He smirked. Sobering, he added, "It hurts me that you'd think that. All I want is to be married to you, I swear. No hidden agenda here. When we get back home, I'm going to make sure you get a traditional wedding with a white dress, cake, and flowers. Whatever the hell you want, it's yours."

I fought a smile. "That's quite a promise."

"It's one I can keep," he responded, biting his lip. He didn't bite his lip often, but when he did it sent my tummy fluttering. He wasn't even trying to be seductive, but it was working.

We were quiet as the rest of the ceremonies were performed. When we were called up, I thought my heart was going to race right out of my chest.

The Justice of Peace smiled pleasantly at us. "Do you have any witnesses with you?"

I shook my head.

"No," Trace answered, "do these lovely people count?" He pointed a thumb over his shoulder to more couples that had come in after us.

"They sure do." The kind gray-haired man smiled.

He began speaking and I wasn't sure if I was supposed to repeat after him, or Trace, or was I just supposed to say I do? Oh, crap, I was panicking, and therefore sweating in places no one should ever sweat.

When the Justice of Peace paused, waiting for me to respond, I shouted, "I do!"

Trace threw his head back in laughter and the other couples in the room joined in. I was sure my face was red as a tomato. Lovely.

Stifling his laughter, Trace said to the Justice of Peace, "At least she's excited to marry me."

The man chuckled, one of those hardy belly laughs that always made me think of Santa. "That's for sure."

And I officially wanted to crawl in a hole and die. *Could* you die from embarrassment? If you could, I was sure I was a few seconds away from being cosmically struck by lightning.

"It was my turn to say, 'I do.'" Trace winked.

My face reddened even more. "Oops." I shifted my eyes guiltily to the floor.

"Would you like me to start over?" the man asked.

"No need." Trace smiled pleasantly. My eyes were still downcast and he grabbed my chin, forcing my face up. "Don't be embarrassed."

That was easier said than done.

I nodded, though, to make him feel better.

"I do," Trace said, squaring his shoulders, and holding my hands in his.

I forced myself to listen to what the man was saying this time, so I didn't say anything I wasn't supposed to.

"Olivia Camille Owens, do you take Trace Alexander Wentworth to be your husband? Do you promise to love, honor, cherish and protect him, forsaking all others and holding only to him forevermore?"

"I do," I answered softly but without hesitation.

"I now pronounce you husband and wife. You may kiss your bride." He clapped Trace on the shoulder.

"About time." Trace grinned, taking my cheeks between his hands and kissing me deeply. He dipped me down and my hair skimmed the floor.

He pulled away, breathing heavily. "Hello, wife."

"Husband," I replied with a quiet giggle.

He took my hand and we ran out of the room and all the way out to the parking lot. When we reached the car, he pushed me against it and caged me in with his arms. His head lowered and his lips pressed softly against mine at first, then grew more urgent. My fingers knotted in the fabric of his wife-beater as I tried to get as close to him as possible.

"We're not staying in some crappy motel tonight." His lips fluttered over the curve of my jaw.

I nodded in agreement.

"Tonight is our wedding tonight," he murmured, "and you deserve the best."

Before I could reply, he was kissing me again and all coherent thoughts disappeared.

I wrapped my legs around his waist and my back pressed roughly into the car. It wasn't the most comfortable position, but I didn't mind.

His hands roamed down my body, settling beneath my butt as his hips pressed firmly into me. I gasped and his tongue flicked against my lips. He kissed the corner of my mouth and pulled away. I lowered my legs but he kept a firm grip on my waist.

"I think we better find a hotel. I'd really hate to get arrested for indecent exposure on my wedding day."

"That would ruin the mood," I agreed, my words coming out breathless.

He kissed me lightly once more and opened the car door for me.

He drove for ten minutes and pulled into the parking lot of a Holiday Inn. "It's not the fanciest, but it's better than a smelly motel."

I laughed in response. I loved that we were still joking about that first motel.

"Be right back," he assured me. I watched him jog into the hotel, shaking my head. Someone was in a hurry and the reason was pretty obvious. *Men*.

He returned a few minutes later, spinning a room keycard between his fingers. He opened the passenger door and held his hand out for me to take. "Come on, wifey."

"I take it someone's ready to consummate this marriage," I joked.

"You make me sound like a horndog," he said as he frowned. "Okay, maybe I am," he admitted. "But only for you."

"Mhmm," I murmured, heading for the trunk, but his hold on my hand kept me from getting there.

"I'll get our stuff later."

Before I knew what was happening, he swept my legs out from under me.

"Trace!" I exclaimed, causing people in the parking lot to turn our way. "What are you doing?"

"Carrying you over the threshold," he responded, heading toward the sliding glass doors that led into the hotel.

"I don't think it counts as a threshold unless we're home."

"Well, we'll just have to repeat the *whole* process over when we get back." He chuckled, his lips brushing dangerously close to mine as he spoke. My eyes fluttered closed at the feel of the feather-light touch.

He carried me through the lobby and the few people mingling stared at us curiously. He pushed the button for the elevator and I tried to get down but he wouldn't let me go.

"Trace," I groaned, "let me down. I'll get too heavy."

He rolled his eyes as he snorted. "Woman, you're light. I'm fine. Stop worrying so much."

"I don't want to break you," I mumbled.

He laughed at that. "It'll take a lot more than that to break me. I assure you."

The elevator doors opened and a family stepped out, looking at us like we'd grown three heads.

Once in the elevator he still wouldn't put me down. Stubborn man.

I wrapped my arms around his neck and laid my head on his shoulder. I might as well get comfortable. I knew he wouldn't put me down until he was good and ready.

He pushed the button for the fourth floor and the doors slid closed.

My heart rate spiked with the knowledge of what was coming. I pulled back and gazed up in wonder at him. Suddenly, he wasn't just Trace—the scruffy, fun-loving, sucky dancer I fell in love with. He was my husband—the man I'd be spending the rest of my life with. The man I knew I couldn't live without.

"What?" he asked when he noticed my staring.

"Nothing," I whispered, laying my head against his shoulder once more.

My eyes closed and a smile of satisfaction graced my lips.

The doors dinged open and he started down the hallway, murmuring room numbers under his breath. "A-ha." He smiled in triumph as he stopped in front of one. He slid the keycard into the slot and it blinked with a green light. He opened the door and stepped inside, letting it slam closed behind him. He carried me to the bed and dropped me on top.

I giggled, scolding him, "Trace!"

He dropped on top of me, but caught his weight on his hands. I bounced from the momentum, biting my lip to stifle my laughter.

"Hey," he murmured in a husky voice, his green eyes darkening to a forest green color.

"Hi." I smiled, reaching up to trace my finger over his lips. He opened his mouth and playfully nipped at my finger. "Did we really get married?" I cupped his stubbled cheeks between my hands.

He nodded. "Already regretting it?"

"Never."

"I know we're young," he whispered, lowering his head to skim his nose along my collarbone and up my neck, "but I feel like I've been waiting for this day since the moment I knew you were the one."

"And when did you know I was the one?" I dared to ask.

He pulled back slightly, gazing at me thoughtfully. "It wasn't just a single moment that I can name. It was an accumulation of moments that added up over time and I knew that I'd never be happy with anyone else. You were made for me, Olivia."

"And you were made for me." I wrapped my arms around his neck.

"Glad you think so."

"I *know* so."

He placed a kiss on the end of my nose and whispered huskily, "I think we should stop talking now."

I nodded in agreement as my back arched off the bed so that I could kiss him.

He cupped the back of my head, his fingers tangling in the wavy strands of my hair. I lightly bit his bottom lip and he growled low in his throat, causing my stomach to flood with warmth. His free hand skimmed over my cheek, down my neck, and over my shoulder. He pushed the plaid shirt he'd lent me off of my shoulders. It pooled at my elbows and I released my hold on him long enough to remove it.

"Your turn," I gasped breathlessly.

With a raspy chuckle he pulled away and stood in front of me. He hooked his fingers into the back of the shirt and pulled it off.

I stared at his beautifully sculpted body and the tattoos that adorned his skin. I couldn't believe that he was mine.

"Come here." I crooked a finger, beckoning him forward.

He wet his lips, fighting a smile, but lowered his body over mine once more. I felt so small and protected cocooned beneath him like this.

I ran my fingers greedily over the hard lines of his abdominal muscles. I smiled in satisfaction when a tremor rocked his body and his eyes fluttered closed as his breath gusted between his lips. I loved that I could affect him this way. It pleased me to know that our relationship wasn't just one way. He was as affected by me, as I was by him, and that was a beautiful thing.

"Make love to me," I breathed and his eyes opened at my words.

"I thought you'd never ask," he murmured.

He eased his fingers under the edge of my tank top and I shivered at his touch, goosebumps breaking out across my skin. He tapped a finger against my belly button ring and then his hands began to venture higher. Before reaching my breasts, his hand descended once more, and he grasped the bottom of my tank. He tugged it over my head and tossed it behind him.

He unsnapped my bra and threw it behind him as well.

"That's better." He smiled, taking my breasts in his hands, testing the fullness.

"Trace," I whined, lifting my hips slightly.

"Patience," he whispered in my ear, his voice raspy. "Good things come to those who wait, Olivia."

I mewled in protest.

Waiting is torture.

"Please," I begged.

"No," he growled, pulling my earlobe between his teeth and nipping it.

I whimpered, not because it hurt, but because he wasn't giving me what I wanted.

I grasped his dark hair between my fingers and gasped when one his fingers delved into my shorts.

Now we were getting somewhere.

But when I was close to an orgasm he pulled his hand away. I cried out in displeasure.

"Trace, please," I cried.

"Not yet. Not until I'm inside you."

"Then hurry up," I demanded.

"Not yet," he repeated, kissing his way up my stomach, over my breasts before finally reaching my lips.

My mouth opened beneath his and his tongue flicked against my own.

My hands found his belt and undid it with ease. I popped the button and slid the zipper down, brazenly running my hand over the curve of his erection. Two could play this game.

"Olivia," he gasped my name, the sound of it filling my body with warmth.

He kicked his jeans off and grasped me by the waist, moving me so that my head was on one of the pillows.

"You'll be the end of me," he whispered, "but I wouldn't have it any other way."

I could say the same about him, but all coherent thoughts had gone out the window.

His lips glided over mine before nipping at my chin and down my neck.

I was getting impatient, but I knew from past experiences that if I complained too much about his slow pace, he'd only go that much slower. I think he liked torturing me.

He moved down my body, hooking his thumbs into the sides of my panties and pulling them down. When they reached my ankles I kicked them off.

"I think you're a bit over dressed." I pointed to his boxers.

"Not yet."

Ugh. If he said that to me one more time I might lose my mind.

He kissed the sides of my thighs, spreading me open.

"Trace," I gasped.

"Olivia," he chuckled my name as his tongue flicked out.

My back arched off the bed and I reached up, gripping one of the pillows tightly in my hand.

Just like before, when I was close he pulled away.

I groaned in protest, squeezing my eyes shut in frustration.

When I finally opened my eyes, he was braced above me, staring.

The tip of him nudged my entrance and I whimpered.

I wanted to beg, but I bit down harshly on my lip to keep any words from leaving.

He adjusted his weight and lifted a hand to pull my bottom lip from between my teeth. "You'll make yourself bleed," he whispered and then tenderly kissed the lip I'd almost injured.

He stared at me for a long moment, his gaze causing a tremor to shake my body, and slowly slipped inside me.

"About time," I gasped, causing him to chuckle lightly.

He sat up, bringing me with him. He cradled me against his chest, looking into my eyes. It was extremely intimate but I didn't shy away. I trusted Trace. He knew the real me.

He kissed me deeply, sucking on my bottom lip as I rocked my hips against his. I ran my hands over his muscular chest before settling them around his neck.

"I love you," he said fiercely as he stared into my eyes and straight down to my soul.

"I love you too."

I knew what we had was a special kind of love. You have to love someone at their worst to truly love them at their best. Trace had seen me at my worst, my best, and everything in between, and he still loved me. That's true love. The kind that lasts for eternity.

———

AFTER ROUND THREE we were both exhausted and unable to move. My body was curled around his, our legs entwined together, and my head rested on his shoulder with my long hair fanning around us.

"Is it just me, or is it even better now that we're married?" he panted.

I lightly traced my finger over his chest in a random design, mulling over what he said. "I think you're right."

He chuckled at that. "Maybe living in sin was weighing on me."

"Hardly," I snorted, moving my index finger over the tattoo on his heart that he'd gotten in memory of his dad.

"Eh, you're right. I didn't care." He placed his hand over mine to cease its movements. "It's still better, though, because now I know you're really mine and you're not going anywhere."

"I wasn't going anywhere before. Besides, if I had run away ... again," I added, thinking of the times I'd become insecure because of his ex, "you wouldn't have let me get very far."

"Damn straight. If you're not by my side, I will chase you down, woman." He grinned, tucking a piece of hair behind my ear and gliding his fingers lightly over the curve of my cheek. "I would go to the ends of the Earth for you, because *I love you* and when someone owns your heart, like you do mine, you don't let them get away."

"Whoa."

"What?" He rolled over so that he was above me. "It's the truth. My life was 'okay' before you came along. But from the moment I met you, I finally understood what it meant when people said someone 'owned you'. It's not necessarily about ownership. It's about caring more for that person than you do for yourself. When I saw you standing by your car, with those big sad brown eyes, I *knew* the sadness had nothing to do with your tire and that something else was eating at you. I wanted to get to know you and unravel your secrets so that I could slay your dragons and be your Prince Charming."

I giggled, covering my face with my hands. "I'm *never* going to live that one down."

"Your stuttering about Prince Charming was adorable," he assured me, pulling my hands from my face, "especially since you were referring to me. Although, most princes aren't as ruggedly handsome as I am." He ran a hand over his stubbled jaw. "You got lucky."

"I know."

"I'm glad you agree." He smirked, rolling off of me.

"You're something else." I laughed, rolling onto my side and propping my head in my hand.

He waggled his brows. "Something spectacular."

"Stop talking," I mumbled, laying my head on his shoulder once more.

"I can do that."

"Yeah, right," I snorted.

He mimed zipping his lips.

My eyes grew heavy and, surrounded by his body heat, I found myself being lulled into a peaceful sleep.

CHAPTER FIFTEEN

My hand reached out, patting against the sheets as I searched for Trace. When my hand kept connecting with cool sheets I finally forced my eyes open. Early morning light filtered in through the flimsy hotel curtains. I peeked at the clock, groaning at the time. Six o' clock was too early for me.

I sat up, holding the sheet over my chest, and looked around the room. Trace wasn't anywhere to be found and there were no sounds coming from the small bathroom.

I slipped from the sheets and showered, changing into my clothes from yesterday since our bags were still in the car. I chose to forgo the tank top, opting to wear his plaid shirt open over my bra.

I had just sat down on the bed and was turning on the TV when the door opened. He came inside with our bags slung over his shoulders and two cups of coffee from Starbucks.

"My hero!" I exclaimed, reaching out with grabby hands for one of the cups of coffee.

"Cinnamon Dolce Latte." He smirked, handing it to me.

I took a tentative sip of the liquid, fearing it might be a scalding temperature, but it was perfect.

"If I'm going to be up early" —I pointed at the clock— "I need my coffee."

He shook his head, laughing under his breath at me. "Why do you hate mornings so much?"

"Because," I said, drawing my knees up to my chest, cradling the precious coffee close to me, "I like my sleep. You, on the other hand, seem to be fine with no sleep."

He shrugged, taking a sip of his coffee. "I've never needed much sleep. Much to my mother's dismay. I'm sure if you asked she'd tell you stories of how I used to keep her up all night as a baby."

"I'm sure you were a very interesting child."

"Is that your nice way of saying weird?" he questioned, his lips twitching into a smile.

"You *are* weird. But I wouldn't have you any other way."

He frowned at his cup of coffee. "I hate these stupid cups they give you. Who wants to drink coffee with a lid? I want my Yoda mug."

"Of course you do." I laughed, scooting back in the bed so that I could rest against the headboard.

It may have been a Holiday Inn but the room was clean and didn't smell. The walls were painted a buttery yellow with maroon carpet. The covers on the king-size bed were in a similar color palette and the pictures on the walls were the typical floral ones all hotels seemed to have.

"Yoda makes everything better," he joked, sitting down beside me and stretching his long legs out. "Your mom tried to call me."

"She did?"

"Yeah. I, uh, had turned my phone off yesterday after my mom called, so I didn't see it until now."

"She probably wonders what happened." I laughed. "I still can't believe I dropped my phone in the glass of water."

"That was hilarious," he chortled, setting his coffee cup on the bedside table.

"It was funny," I agreed. "Except, now I don't have a phone."

"We'll get you one today," he assured me, "before your hormonal mom tries to track us down. Our road trip isn't quite over yet."

"Where are we going next?"

He shrugged, looking away from me. It was evasive behavior from him and it piqued my curiosity immediately.

"Trace," I probed.

"I thought we'd stay here for another day," he mumbled, plucking at the white sheet. "Then head out."

"M'kay." I eyed him. "What are you hiding?"

"Nothing," he insisted. "I just want to hang here with my wife." He batted his eyes innocently.

"Yeah, right. Come on, spit it out. I'm not dumb, Trace. What do you have up your sleeve? You're not going to make me jump out of a plane are you? 'Cause I'm definitely not doing that."

He laughed at that, shaking his head. "No planes," he promised when he had regained the ability to speak.

"So, what is it then? And don't you dare say, 'nothing,'" I mimicked his tone.

"It's a surprise," he admitted, glancing toward the window so he didn't have to look at me. "Be patient."

"Fine," I reluctantly agreed. I knew there was no point in pushing him. If Trace said he had a surprise for me, then his lips were sealed.

"I'm gonna head down and get some breakfast," he said after we'd been quiet for a few minutes. "Do you want to come with me? Or would you rather I brought food up here?"

I stretched out, letting the plaid shirt I was wearing fall open. "I think here sounds like a pretty good idea to me."

His eyes widened, scanning over my stomach and up to my breasts concealed behind a lacy black bra.

"Oh, fuck the food."

Two hours later we were sitting in bed, finally eating breakfast. I was starving. By the time I was full, there wasn't a single crumb left on my plate.

"Ugh." I placed the plate on the end table and laid my head down on the pillow. "I'm so full."

"You were hungry." He chuckled. "That happens when you burn a lot of calories."

I smacked his arm lightly.

"I'm sleepy now." I crooked an arm over my eyes, shielding them from the sunlight streaming in through the window.

"No." He pried my arm away. "We don't have time for sleepiness. We should go explore the town. This place seems … cute."

"Ugh," I groaned. "I don't think I can move for at least five hours."

"You can do it. I believe in you." He winked, beaming at me. Damn him and his cheerfulness. I wish I felt that peppy. But I was exhausted and my muscles were sore.

He kept smiling at me, willing me to cave and, eventually, I did. I never could resist his charms. "Fine." I sat up, smoothing my hair back.

"I knew you'd eventually agree." He hopped off the bed, rifling through his duffel bag.

"You're hard to resist," I grumbled, forcing my tired body from the bed.

He smirked over his shoulder at me. "Impossible, actually."

"Your cockiness will be your downfall," I muttered, unzipping my duffel bag and looking for something clean to wear. I couldn't wait to get to the lake house in Maine so we could wash our clothes. I knew the hotel probably had a laundry area guests could use, but I was weird and kept imagining some strange bacteria ending up on my clothes from them.

"Not cocky, just confident," he reminded me.

"You keep on telling yourself that," I retorted.

"Is this our first martial spat?" He looked over at me, pulling clothes from his duffel bag.

"Oh, please." I shook my head. "This is hardly a fight."

"Good to know." He chuckled, changing into clean jeans and yet another wife-beater and plaid shirt. I swear he had an endless supply.

I grabbed a clean pair of shorts and shimmied into them. Then put on a plain white V-neck t-shirt. Simple was my way.

I had already brushed my teeth earlier, but I did it again

since I'd eaten breakfast. My hair was a wavy mess, and since I didn't want to take the time to make it look presentable, I pulled it to the side in a fishtail braid. I had put on foundation when I got out of the shower. I was still continuing in my efforts to hide the slow fading bruise from Trace. I added some mascara to my lashes and deemed myself ready enough.

I put on my favorite pair of old Converses and said, "I'm ready."

Trace was reclined on the bed with his hands crossed behind his head. He looked me up and down, his eyes lingering over my mostly bare legs. He wet his lips. "Yes, you are."

"Trace," I scolded. "Don't look at me like that or we're never going to leave this room."

"Why *did* I want to leave? That was a dumb idea. I should've kept you chained to this bed all day." He shook his head and heaved himself off the bed.

"I think I might break apart if you keep at it," I warned him. "I'm sore."

"Sorry." He strode over to me, grasping my elbows. "I'll try to keep myself under control."

"Good luck with that." I patted his chest condescendingly as I backed away.

"Oh, is that a challenge?" He wrapped an arm around my waist, hugging me against him, and swiped the room key off the dresser with his free hand.

"Nope, no challenge. I'll end up being the one that gets burned then." I tried to wiggle free from his hold but he was too strong.

He opened the door and we stepped into the hallway.

Before I had walked two steps, he was hauling me over his shoulder.

"Trace!" I shrieked, beating his back. "Put me down."

"If my wife is so sore—" he smacked my butt "—I'll have to carry her."

"You're embarrassing me."

"A little embarrassment never hurt anyone." He laughed and I heard the elevator door ding.

"Are you going to put me down now?" I asked as the doors slid closed.

"Not a chance."

"They're so going to kick us out," I pouted.

He adjusted his grip on me. "Don't be such a Debbie Downer."

"How am I being a downer? I'm simply stating the obvious. Now, *please* put me down. I'm getting light-headed."

"Fine." He lowered me to the ground, but didn't release his hold on me. He kissed my forehead, a small smile on his face.

"I swear," I grumbled, pulling my shorts down, "I think you get some kind of sick enjoyment out of embarrassing me."

"You're so adorable when you get pissed." He chuckled, crossing his arms over his chest.

"The fact that you think I'm cute when I'm angry says a lot about our relationship." I couldn't help laughing.

The elevator doors slid open and I followed him out to the car.

"Where are we going first?"

"To get you a new phone," he answered, unlocking the car, as his own cellphone began to ring. He pulled it out of his pocket and glanced at the screen. "It's my mom. I better answer it. Your mom probably told her that she couldn't get ahold of you."

"Yeah, go ahead," I replied, buckling my seatbelt.

"Hey, Mom," he answered. "Yeah, we're good. Really? No, I haven't talked to him. I'll call him later and check up on Ace. Nothing much, just got married—" He held the phone away from his ear and I flinched at his mother's shrieks. I couldn't tell if they were good or bad. He clicked the button to put it on speaker and said, "Mom? Are you okay? Should I alert the paramedics of a possible heart attack?"

"Married?" she asked breathlessly.

"Yeah," Trace replied, looking at me guiltily.

"When?" She gasped for breath. He must have really shocked her.

"Yesterday afternoon. It was a lovely ceremony in a New Hampshire courthouse. You should've been there, Mom," he joked.

"Trace Alexander Wentworth, now is not the time for your smart mouth remarks. I can't believe you got married without your family there. Your grandpa is going to be so mad when I tell him."

"How is Gramps?" Trace questioned, swallowing thickly. "Is he okay?"

"He's fine. Why wouldn't he be?"

"No reason." Trace stared out the window.

"I'm really sorry, Lily," I spoke up.

"There's no need for you to apologize, Olivia. I know this wasn't your idea."

"Hey," I said, looking at Trace questioningly, "we didn't exchange rings, so maybe when we get back home we can have a ceremony at the mansion for everyone. We can even make Trace wear a tux. Think you can plan something nice on short notice?" I asked her. Trace *had* said I could have a traditional wedding ceremony. Hopefully, he hadn't promised that just to sweet talk me into getting married yesterday.

"I've been throwing parties since I was twenty. I can put together a nice wedding ceremony in no time. Are you thinking the end of the month? That would give you plenty of time to get home," Lily said.

"Sounds good to me."

"Do I really have to wear a tux?" Trace asked.

"Yes," Lily and I said simultaneously.

"*Great*." He pinched the bridge of his nose. "Look, Mom, we've gotta go. I love you."

"Love you too. And, Olivia, keep your phone on. I'll be calling you to ask for details. Okay?"

"Uh—"

Trace snorted. "Olivia drowned her phone. We're going to get her a new one now. She'll call you with her new number."

"Oh, okay! I love you guys! Bye!" she chimed and then the line went dead.

"I can't believe we just agreed to that," he mumbled.

I punched his shoulder. "You're the one that said we could have a real wedding when we got back. This way, we can exchange our rings and still have the typical ceremony with our friends and family there. I hope your mom doesn't go all out, though." I frowned, wiping my hands on my legs in a nervous gesture. "I'd prefer to keep it simple."

"Don't worry." He leaned over and placed a tender kiss on my cheek. "My mom knows our taste."

I giggled. "There better not be any plaid."

He scoffed. "Plaid is delightful. You looked beautiful in it yesterday when you said, 'I do'."

I shook my head, at a loss for words. Finally, I said, "Do you think Gramps is going to be upset with us?"

When Trace had come up with the brilliant idea of getting married yesterday, I hadn't thought at all about what Gramps would think or feel. But Gramps was *dying* and he deserved to be there. What we had done was selfish; there was no other word for it.

Trace's hands tightened around the steering wheel as he pulled out of the hotel parking lot.

A muscle in his jaw twitched and I wasn't sure if he was going to answer me, but after a minute he said, "Yeah. He'll be pissed. He, uh—" His gaze flicked toward me. "He told me, before we left, that he hoped we might consider getting married before—" he swallowed thickly, his Adam's apple bobbing "—before he dies." He bit his bottom lip and I knew he was fighting tears. I reached out and placed my hand on his thigh, hoping to offer any comfort that I could.

"Well then, I guess it's a good thing your mom's going to plan a ceremony for when we get back."

"Yeah." He nodded stiffly, turning into the parking lot of a strip mall. He parked and sat there for a moment, staring out the windshield as if he was searching for something.

After a few minutes he shook his head and got out of the car. I did the same, following him into a Verizon store. He gave his name to one of the techs working there and then sat on a bench to wait.

"Trace—"

He shook his head. "I don't want to talk about it."

"Not talking about it doesn't make it go away," I whispered, rubbing a hand soothingly up and down his back.

"I know that," he mumbled, resting his elbows on his knees and burying his face in his hands. "But I'd prefer not to think about it."

I could understand and respect that. After what Aaron did to me, I'd preferred to push it to the back of my mind. Thinking that if I convinced myself that it hadn't really happened then somehow that would eventually be true. It was an unhealthy way of thinking, but a coping mechanism that many clung to.

"Trace, we have to face reality. Gramps is dying. Not thinking about it doesn't stop it from happening. We have to brace ourselves for the inevitable. I know what you're feeling is ten times worse than what I'm feeling," I whispered, trying not to cry. "But I love him too, Trace. He welcomed me into your family like I was of his blood. He never treated me differently or looked down at me. Not many people are as exceptional as Gramps is."

"Stop making me feel bad," he mumbled, looking away from me.

I grabbed his chin, forcing him to look at me. "I'm not trying to make you feel bad. I'm just trying to get you to understand."

"I *do* understand. But it's easier not to feel," his voice shook. "Maybe that's weak of me, but it's what I have to do. I need to be numb."

I shook my head. He was being a stubborn idiot. But I didn't want to piss him off so I shut my mouth hoping the opportunity would present itself and I could bring it up later.

A FEW HOURS LATER, we left the store and I was the proud new owner of the latest iPhone. My previous phone had been a cheap touchscreen that didn't at all compare to this.

"I think I'm in love," I gasped, playing with the settings.

Trace chuckled, starting the car. "Should I be jealous?"

"Maybe." I smiled, setting a picture of us as my wallpaper.

"So," he started, "I was thinking ..."

"Yeah?" I prompted when he trailed off.

"You agreed to sing with me at the bar the other night, but since ... well ... you know," he growled, "that fucker pushed—"

"He didn't push me," I interrupted.

"Well, he might as well have," Trace snapped. "Anyway," he cleared his throat, softening his tone, "I thought you might sing with me tonight. There's a coffee shop not too far from here that has live music and patrons can sign up to sing."

"How do you find these places?" I asked incredulously.

"I saw it this morning when I went to get you Starbucks. Soooo? What do you say?"

I frowned. I didn't really want to sing. But the jerk was pouting and giving me puppy dog eyes. Besides, I *had* agreed the other night.

"Fine." I tossed my hands in the air. "I'll sing."

"That didn't take much convincing." He smiled, pleased with himself.

"Yeah, well, don't make me regret it." I crossed my arms over my chest, taking in the small town as we drove through. It was cute and quaint, kind of reminding me of home. "Are we going back to the hotel?"

"Nah. Thought we'd drive around for a bit. Get some lunch. See the sights."

"What sights?" I replied sarcastically.

"There are unique things in any place." He poked my cheek to annoy me. "You just have to know where to look."

"And somehow you know how to find these places? Does Dora teach you how to find them?"

He threw his head back in laughter. "First off, Dora is highly educational and I like to brush up on my Spanish. Secondly, I can sing the "Backpack" song better than anyone. Thirdly" —he held up three fingers "—I happen to be a very awesome explorer."

"You ... Ugh," I groaned, at a loss for words. Trace truly was one of a kind. When we had kids one day, they were going to have the coolest dad ever.

"Have I rendered you speechless?" He scratched his stubbly jaw. "It's okay. It happens to a lot of people. They don't know how to handle all of this—" he motioned a hand to his body. "Don't worry. I'll give you a minute to compose yourself." He smiled boyishly.

I put my hand over my mouth to hide my smile.

A few minutes later, he found a parking spot along the street and parked the car. He hopped out, rifling through the pocket of his ratty jeans for some change to put in the meter.

When the meter was full, he took my hand and we started down the street, ambling in and out of the little shops.

"Let's go in there." I pointed to a unique looking little store that had quote plaques in the window and handmade paper stars.

When we stepped inside, I looked up in awe. More paper stars, in varying sizes and color, adorned the ceiling. It was one of the most beautiful things I'd ever seen. My neck began to hurt with the craning I was doing but I couldn't stop looking. They were mesmerizing.

"Beautiful, aren't they?" a voice said, snapping me back to reality.

I straightened my neck and found myself gazing at a kind older lady. Her gray hair hung to her shoulders and her blue eyes were kind with crinkles at the corners. Laugh lines wrinkled her mouth. She smiled sweetly at me, waiting for me to reply.

"Amazing," I gasped when I finally found my voice.

"My son and I made every single one of those. He's gone now, though," she said sadly. "I find origami very relaxing. Have you ever tried?" she asked, clasping her hands together.

"No." I shook my head. "I don't think I'd have the patience. And I'm sorry about your son," I added.

She waved her hand in dismissal. "Ah, but maybe it would teach you to have some," she laughed quietly. "I could teach you, if you'd like. Or I have some instruction books and starter kits." She pointed to a far corner of the room. "The starter kits have precut strips of paper to make it easier."

"I'm not sure."

"We'll take one," Trace said, appearing at my side, draping an arm over my shoulder. "I think Olivia would be good at origami."

The woman's smile widened. "What a pretty name. I always liked that name."

"Thank you."

"I'm Margaret." She held out her hand. "My husband and I own this store."

"Well, it's lovely. You already know I'm Olivia, and this is my husband, Trace." My heart stopped beating for a moment when I said *husband*. It was strange to think that I was actually married, but wonderful at the same time.

"Nice to meet you both." She shook each of our hands. "Look around, take your time. If you need anything, I'll be here." She smiled kindly, moving behind the register where she appeared to be organizing something.

I scanned down the aisles, picking up things here and there. I came to a small plaque, about as long as my hand and not very wide. It was wood and painted blue on all the sides except the front where a Volkswagen Beetle was painted. But that wasn't what had caught my eye. It was the quote.

"'Life is but a breath—live it well,'" I whispered, reading it off the plaque.

"What's that?" Trace asked, appearing over my shoulder. I held it up where he could see and he read the quote aloud as well. "Huh. That makes you think."

I nodded, thinking of how my own life had almost been snuffed out and Gramps' was coming to a close.

Nothing guaranteed that we'd get to live to be old and gray. Each of us was only allotted so much time here on earth and it was up to us to decide how to live it. I wanted to make every moment count. I didn't want to have regrets.

"I'm buying this," I informed him, holding onto the small plaque.

"No." He took it from my hand. "*I'm* buying it for you. I'm your husband now." He kissed the corner of my mouth. "You better get used to me spoiling you. I know you don't like it and I let you off the hook while we were dating. But now we're married. So, it's my job to take care of you."

"Fine," I agreed, "but only because it's cheap."

"It wouldn't matter if it wasn't. I'd still buy it." He sauntered off, investigating another part of the store.

I laughed under my breath at him.

I came to the book Margaret had been talking about. I picked it up, flipping through the pages. I didn't think I'd ever be able to turn pieces of paper into art, but a part of me wanted to try, so I tucked the book under my arm and grabbed one of the kits she'd also told me about. I didn't think a kit was actually necessary, but if it could help me not suck at origami, then I'd give it a shot. After all, I needed a hobby. With school over, and no permanent teaching position, I needed something to distract my mind.

I met Trace at the register and he paid for the items.

"I'm glad you decided to try the origami," Margaret commented as she bagged our stuff.

"Me too." I smiled kindly at her. "Hopefully I won't suck at it."

"Origami isn't that hard, but it does take patience. It'll take you a couple of tries until you get it right. Just don't give up."

"I'll make sure she doesn't," Trace assured her, taking the silver bag from her.

"If you live nearby and have any trouble, feel free to swing by and I'll help you. I'm here every day." She leaned her elbows on the counter.

"Sorry, but we're not from here."

"I didn't think you looked like locals." She laughed. "Enjoy your time here."

"Thanks." I waved lamely at her as I started toward the door. I looked up at the paper stars one more time before exiting onto the street. There was something about looking at them that made me feel at peace.

Trace's hand wound around my waist and his lips brushed against my forehead as we continued down the street.

"Did you bring a dress with you?" he asked.

"No." I shook my head. "Why? Do I need one?"

"Not necessarily. I thought if we were going to sing tonight you'd look beautiful in a dress."

I glanced down at my tank and shorts feeling underdressed. I didn't want creepy old guys staring at my legs and chest. At least a dress would cover more.

"A dress would be nice," I admitted.

"Good, I'm glad you see things my way. I was expecting an argument."

"Am I really that argumentative?" I questioned curiously.

"No." His nose wrinkled in thought. "But you're very stubborn."

"And you aren't?" I raised a brow.

"Baby, I'm a go with the flow kind of guy."

I laughed, heading inside a clothing store.

I scanned through the clothes, pondering what I'd like to wear.

"Hey, look at this!" Trace called from across the store, earning us a glare from the woman working there.

"Trace, keep your voice down," I scolded, heading his way.

"Sorry." He grinned so I knew he really wasn't all that sorry.

"What did you find?" I stopped in front of him, waiting for him to show me.

He pulled out a hanger, showing me a floral corset.

I paled. "No way. I'm not wearing a corset." I shook my head adamantly.

"Aw, come on, Olivia. You have the body for it. Please," he pouted, "for your husband?"

I closed my eyes, willing myself not to give into his demands.

"What would I wear with it?" I argued.

His smile was triumphant. "This." He pulled out a blush colored high-waisted skirt. It kind of reminded me of a tutu, but not as poofy.

"And tell me, how did you come to pick this out? You're not exactly the most fashionable guy." I pointed at his plaid shirt.

"It was on one of the mannequins in the window," he admitted with a small shrug of his lean shoulders, "and I thought it would look hot on you. Especially with those shoes." He pointed.

I turned to see the mannequin he was talking about. It was dressed in the corset and skirt with aqua-blue high heels.

"I'll die in those," I stated. "They have to be at least four inches."

"I would never let you fall." He sighed in exasperation. "Will you please wear it?"

It *was* pretty cute.

"Fine," I agreed after making him sweat it for a moment. "I'll wear it."

"Good." His eyes darkened and his voice grew husky, "Because as much as I want to see you in it, I'm going to enjoy taking it off of you even more *later*."

I shivered at his promising tone.

"Go grab the shoes and I'll meet you at the register," he said, already striding away. "If you see anything else you want, get it," he called.

I shook my head, chuckling at his bossiness.

I found the shoes in my size and tucked the box under my arm. The store had a lot of cute clothes that kept catching my eye, and while I knew Trace would buy me anything I desired, I didn't want that. I didn't like being spoiled. It made me feel … dependent. I knew Trace was only being sweet, but I liked working and having my own money to buy things. I understood he had the money to blow, but I'd rather he buy himself something, not me.

"Didn't see anything else?" he asked when I met him at the register.

"No."

The look he gave me told me that he didn't believe me.

"Honestly," I added, leaning against the counter.

"All right." He shrugged, smiling at the sales girl who was currently checking him out. I was used to girls swooning over Trace, so it didn't really bother me, but it was annoying when they stood there gawking instead of doing their job.

"We'd like this." Trace pointed to the items on the counter when she didn't move.

She shook her head harshly, snapping herself out of a daze. "Oh, right. Of course. I'm sorry."

Trace ignored her, pulling his wallet out of his back pocket. He smiled at me sheepishly.

"This is all?" she asked, ringing up the items. "We have some perfumes on sale." She pointed a finger at a round table set up near the door.

"Olivia?" Trace prompted.

"I don't want anything else," I assured him.

Trace laughed. "You heard the woman."

The sales girl's gaze flicked my way and jealousy sparked in her eyes. I wondered if Trace was wearing his *I Heart Ketchup* shirt if she'd still feel that way.

She totaled the items and rattled off the price. Trace handed over his shiny black credit card and let her swipe it. The receipt printed out and she put it in the bag along with the other items. "Have a nice day." She forced a smile as she handed me the pale pink shopping bag.

"You too," I said, trying to be polite.

When we stepped outside, Trace grabbed his phone from his pocket, looking at the time. "Let's head back to the hotel and get ready. That way, we can grab a nice dinner before we head to the coffee shop. I'm sick of fast food."

"Sounds good to me." I shrugged, turning in the direction to head back to the car.

Luckily, when we made it back to the hotel, he didn't try to carry me inside. I dropped my shopping bags on the bed, kicking off my sneakers.

"I'm gonna shower. Care to join me?" He grinned cheekily.

"I already showered," I replied, pulling off my socks and knotting them into a ball.

"All right, fine, your loss." He shrugged as he entered the bathroom and closed the door.

I knew it wouldn't take Trace long to get ready, he was a guy after all, so that meant I better get a move on.

There was a floor-length mirror hanging on the wall beside the dresser. I stood in front of it, pulling my hair out of the braid and trying to tame the wavy strands by running my fingers through it. I knew from experience that brushing it would only make it turn into a poofy mess. When it was smoothed out I parted it in the middle and took two sections, which I braided and pulled back, securing it with a ponytail holder. I let the rest of my hair hang down past my shoulders. I added some gloss to my lips and some more mascara before touching up the foundation around my eye.

When that was done, I stripped out of my clothes and cut the tags off of the outfit Trace had bought me. The corset was black with varying shades of pink roses. The leaves on the flowers were an aqua blue that matched the shoes. I knew I was going to have to forgo a bra so I really hoped my boobs didn't fall out. That would be mortifying.

I put the corset on, zipping it closed in the front, and slipped on the skirt. The corset ended above my belly button and since the skirt didn't come up that far I was left showing more skin than I was used to. I assessed my appearance in the mirror, my belly button ring shimmering in the light. I chewed nervously on my bottom lip.

"A bathing suit shows more skin, Olivia. Calm down," I told myself, fisting my hands at my sides.

"Are you talking to yourself?" Trace asked as he opened the bathroom door and stepped into the room. Steam billowed out behind him and his dark hair was damp.

"No," I said a bit too quickly, causing him to smile. "Okay, yes," I admitted. "But only because this is a bit ... revealing." I frowned at my reflection. "I don't want people gawking at me." I had thought I'd get a dress that covered a lot more. Leave it to Trace to pick out something that left me feeling naked.

He strode up behind me and wrapped his arms around my chest, resting his chin on my shoulder.

"You're beautiful, Olivia. Don't ever doubt that. Besides, if anyone starts staring at you, I'll take care of it. You're mine," he growled huskily, nibbling on my earlobe, "and I'll make sure they know it." He skimmed his nose along my neck and murmured, "Your boobs look really good in this."

"Trace!" I giggled his name.

"What? It's true." His hands skimmed over my stomach and up to cup my breasts. He gave them a light squeeze and stepped back. "Hungry?"

"Yeah." I nodded, sitting on the edge of the bed to slip the heels on. "We didn't eat any lunch."

"I think there's an Italian restaurant not too far from here. Sound good?" he asked.

"Mhmm." My stomach growled. "I love pasta."

"It's settled then." He smiled, grabbing his keys and spinning them around on his finger. "Let's go." He held the hotel room door open for me.

I wobbled unsteadily in my heels and he grasped my forearm. "Careful there," he chuckled, releasing me when he was sure I wasn't going to fall over.

"Sorry, but these are really high."

"I guess I have the perfect excuse to hold you all night." He winked, letting the door slam closed behind us and setting his large hand above my waist.

"Since when has that stopped you?"

"Good point." He pushed his hair out of his eyes. He was in need of a haircut but I kind of liked his hair shaggier so I hadn't said anything. Feeling my eyes on him, his gaze flicked down at me. "Why are you staring at me? Do I have toothpaste on my mouth or something?" He scrubbed the back of his hand over his mouth, stepping into the elevator.

"No," I laughed. "That's not what it is."

"Then what is it?" His hand fell away from his mouth.

"Nothing." I shook my head, fighting a blush.

"Tell me," he coaxed in a raspy voice, pushing me against the wall of the elevator and skimming his hands up the bare expanse of my arms.

My eyes fluttered closed and I swallowed thickly.

"Olivia," he murmured, his lips brushing against my cheek.

"I just ..."

"You just what?" he prompted when I lost my voice.

"I like your hair longer," I admitted.

I opened my eyes to see him smiling. "See? Now that wasn't so hard, was it?"

I shook my head.

He chuckled, sweeping his fingers over the curves of my breasts. I shivered in response. My mouth fell open slightly and a breathy gasp escaped.

"I love how even after all this time, you're still affected by everything I do to you."

I bit my lip to hold back a moan as the elevator doors opened.

I opened my eyes to find a family of four standing in the lobby looking at us with disgust. *Oops*.

Stifling a laugh, I let Trace lead me out of the elevator and to the car.

"I'm really glad I didn't have you pinned against the wall, screaming my name. I don't think they would've approved," he mused.

I punched his stomach and he grunted from the impact.

"What was that for?" he asked, trying to regain his breath.

"What do you think it was for?" I countered. "Can't you make things sound ... not so sexual?" I squirmed.

He grinned boyishly, unlocking the car and holding the

door open for me. "Come on, Olivia. Where's the fun in that? Besides, I totally and completely meant that in a sexual way."

"You are something else." I smoothed my skirt down and buckled the seatbelt.

"If by 'something else' you mean wickedly sexy and hilarious, then yeah, that sounds about right."

I didn't have a comment for that, so I chose to steer the conversation in a different direction. "What song have you picked out for us to sing?"

He squirmed in the driver's seat, taking an extra-long time to put his blinker on and turn.

"I know you've picked one. Tell me," I coaxed. "I agreed to sing. You don't need to worry about me running away. Besides—" I pointed to the heels I was wearing "—I don't think I could run in these if I tried."

He chuckled at that, scratching his jaw. "I, um, actually was hoping you'd sing by yourself." My jaw dropped open and he hastened to add, "I'll play guitar and I'll be right beside you. It's not like you'll be alone."

"No." I crossed my arms over my chest. "No way. That's not happening. I agreed to sing *with* you. Not by myself. I won't do it," I glared out the window, fighting an internal panic attack. He *knew* I hated singing in front of other people and it was completely unfair for him to try to trick me like that.

"Olivia," he coaxed, "your voice is amazing. There's nothing for you to be insecure about."

"I'm sorry." I shook my head. "But I won't do it. We can't all be as self-assured as you."

He sighed deeply. "It's not like I'm going to force you to do it, but I'd really appreciate it if you did."

His tone of voice tugged at my heartstrings and made me

feel bad. I could do it, couldn't I? He'd be there. It wasn't like I'd be alone.

"I'll think about it," I said quietly, almost hoping he wouldn't hear me.

"Thank you." He put his hand over mine and squeezed it.

"Yeah, well, I haven't agreed yet. So don't get too excited," I warned.

"Noted," he laughed, turning into a parking lot.

Since it was still a bit early, the restaurant wasn't packed and we could be seated right away.

"Want any wine?" Trace asked.

I rolled my eyes and set my menu aside. "Do you *think* I want any wine?"

His lips quirked. "No."

"Then why'd you ask?" I cupped my chin in my palm.

He shrugged, scrutinizing the menu. "I thought if I could get you drunk, you'd be more likely to sing."

"If you got me drunk, that would result in making me more likely to throw up on you," I warned, taking a sip of water.

"You're not going to throw up if you sing. Once you start singing, all your nerves disappear. I don't know why you make such a big deal out of it." He put his menu down so he could look me in the eyes.

I fidgeted under his gaze. "I don't like people staring at me."

"It's not like they're *staring* at you," he argued. "They're listening to the music."

"They're staring." I took another sip of water to have something to do with my hands.

He shook his head back and forth, chuckling under his breath. "Only 'cause you're hot."

I unrolled the cloth napkin, fanning it across my lap. "I told you I'd think about it. Can you drop the subject?"

He chuckled, tapping his fingers rhythmically against his water glass. "I know you 'thinking about it' entails you coming up with ways to get out of it. Just. Do. It." He leaned across the table, gazing at me from beneath long lashes.

"Are you a Nike sponsor now?" I retorted.

He laughed at that, leaning back in his chair. His tongue flicked out, moistening his pink lips. Gosh, why did he have to be so freakin' kissable, even when he was irritating the crap out of me?

"That was a good one." He drummed his knuckles on the tables.

"I can be witty," I responded.

"I must be rubbing off on you.".

The waitress chose that moment to stride up to the table. "Have you decided what you'd like?" She smiled pleasantly, looking between the two of us.

"I'll have the seafood Alfredo." I handed her the menu.

"Same." Trace handed her his menu as well.

"I'll put that in. It shouldn't take too long. I'll bring you some breadsticks while you're waiting." She smiled and headed over to another table.

"Do you like your new phone?" he asked me.

"I love it, but—" I bit my lip, not wanting to continue.

"But what?" he prompted with a wave of his hand. "Spit it out."

"It was expensive," I squeaked, knowing I was in for a lecture.

"Olivia," he growled my name, rubbing his hands on his jeans, "why does it bother you so much when I buy you things?"

I swallowed thickly, looking away from him. "Because I can't do the same for you."

"Do you think that matters to me? I *want* to buy you things. It brings me joy to see you happy." His green eyes seared into me.

"It's just that ..." I took a deep breath, bracing myself. "Aaron used to buy my mom stuff and then hold it over her head. I know you're not like that, Trace. I do. But that's what I grew up with and—"

"I love you, Olivia. You're my wife, for God's sake." He smacked his hand against the table, causing me to jump. "When I get you something, there are no strings attached."

"I know—"

"Obviously you don't know." He pinched the bridge of his nose. Breathing deeply to calm himself, he said, "You need to let go of that silly notion. Aaron was a *bastard* and he shouldn't have been allowed to *breathe*," he seethed. Not caring that other people were around, he added, "If that fucker hadn't hung himself I would've killed him. No one like him deserves to live." His hands were fisted on the table and his breathing was ragged. "I *hate* that he treated you and your mom the way he did. I *hate* that I couldn't do anything sooner. And most of all, I *hate* that because of him, there's a part of you that's always going to be broken."

My bottom lip trembled as I fought tears.

"Please, don't cry, Olivia," he begged.

A single tear slid down my cheek and I hastily swiped it away but more replaced it.

"Ah, fuck. I'm such an ass," he muttered under his breath as he pushed his chair back. He squatted in front of me, taking my face between his large hands and forcing me to look at him. "I'm so sorry, baby. I didn't mean to make you cry."

"But you're right," I sobbed. People were staring and I did my best to ignore their gazes.

"No, I'm not." He shook his head. "I shouldn't have said that."

"But you *did*," my voice cracked. "And you were right," I repeated.

"You're not broken, Olivia. I was wrong to say that. I—"

"But I am." I placed a hand over his, taking a deep breath. "You *should* be able to buy me things without it making me feel guilty or sending me into a panic. I need to let go of what he did, but I haven't gotten to that point yet. What if I never get there, Trace?"

"Then I'll continue to love you just the way you are." He swiped his thumb over my lips.

"I don't deserve you." It was the truth. I didn't deserve Trace. No one did. He was far too good, even though he didn't see himself that way.

His eyes closed. "Olivia, it's *me* that doesn't deserve *you*."

"How about we agree to disagree?" I forced a laugh, trying to lighten the mood.

"Sounds good to me." He laid his head in my lap.

"Um, Trace," I cleared my throat.

"Yeah?"

"People are staring at us," I mumbled, glancing around in discomfort. Couldn't people mind their own business?

"Let them. What they think of us doesn't matter, Olivia. This is only a blip in time, something they'll all forget about in a few hours. You need to stop worrying so much about what people think of you." He raised his head, looking into my eyes as he let his words soak in.

"You're right," I whispered, my fingers tangling in his hair.

"I'm always right." His lips twitched as he fought a smile.

"Now, can you please get up off the floor," I begged.

"I can do that," he chuckled, rising slowly. Before returning to his seat, he kissed my forehead. He glanced around at the people in the restaurant who were still watching us with curious eyes. "Go on," he waved his hand in dismissal, "continue on with your regular scheduled activities. Nothing more to see here."

I snickered, pretending to cough into my hand to hide it.

The waitress breezed by our table, setting down a tray of food. "Seafood Alfredo," she announced. "The plates are hot so be careful," she warned, setting them on the table. "And here's your breadsticks. I, um, brought them by earlier but I thought I'd be interrupting something."

"It's okay," Trace assured her.

With a small smile she picked up the tray and left quickly.

"I think we've frightened our waitress," I informed him, swirling my pasta around.

"Don't worry." He ripped a breadstick in half and took a huge bite of one end. "I'll give her a big tip."

"I think she deserves one." I laughed. "Mmm," I hummed. "This is really good." I pointed at my bowl of pasta. "You know," I started, mulling over what he'd said about this being a blip in time, something everyone would forget in a matter of hours. "I think I'm going to sing. By myself," I clarified unnecessarily.

A huge smile spread slowly across his face. "Are you serious?"

I nodded. "Just one, though." I held up a finger. "I might sing more than that, but don't push your luck."

"God, I want to kiss you so bad right now," he gritted his teeth, "but I think these people have had enough of a show for one night."

I nodded in agreement.

Since we were so hungry, it didn't take us long to finish our meal and get out of there.

My knee bobbed up and down nervously on the drive to the coffee shop. Trace didn't say anything, probably scared to push his luck. But I wasn't going to back out now. This road trip was about recapturing our spark, and I couldn't do that if I didn't branch out.

I hadn't realized we'd made it to the coffee shop, but suddenly Trace was saying, "Ready?"

I swallowed thickly as my heart picked up speed in my chest. I could do this. This wasn't a big deal. All I had to do was sing.

I took a shaky breath and nodded as I opened the car door. I forced my stiff body out of the car.

"You'll do great," Trace assured me, kissing my cheek. "You have absolutely *nothing* to be worried about, okay?"

I nodded again since my voice had temporarily fled me.

"I have to grab my guitar," he said, jogging around to the trunk. I stood rooted in my spot. I stared at my feet, willing them to move, but they were frozen.

"Move," I whispered as I glared at them.

"Olivia?" Trace questioned with a raised brow. "Are you okay?"

"Yeah, I'm fine." I took his extended hand and let him drag me inside.

The coffee shop was large but not quite packed with people. At least, not yet.

Trace found a table near the stage and plunked down. I took the seat beside him and wiped my sweaty palms on my skirt.

"Breathe, Olivia," he whispered in my ear.

Oh, right, I was holding my breath. It probably wouldn't be good if I passed out *before* I got on stage. I exhaled loudly, giving him a shy smile.

"You'll do great," he assured me with a hand on my cheek.

I was glad one of us thought so.

"I don't even know what to sing." I chewed on the edge of my fingernail, looking around at the coffee shop. It was decorated like most, with warm colors and pictures of steaming hot cups of coffee.

Trace grabbed my hand, pulling it away from my mouth. "Don't do that," he scolded. "Why don't you sing "Starry Eyed" by Ellie Goulding?"

I looked at him in disbelief. "How do you know that song?"

"First off, I don't live under a rock. I know who she is. Secondly, I came into the apartment one day while I was working and you were in the shower singing it." He waved two fingers in front of my face to further drive home his point.

"Okay." I played with a piece of my hair. "I'll sing that."

"Good." He grinned and his eyes crinkled at the corners.

"What are *you* going to sing?"

"You'll see." He tipped the chair back on two legs and crossed his arms behind his head.

"Ugh," I groaned. "Why won't you tell me?"

"Where's the fun in that?" he countered. He smacked his hand on top of the table and stood. "I better go sign us up before all the slots fill up." He had walked a few feet when he turned back to me. Pointing to his empty chair, he warned, "Try not to let anyone steal my seat this time. I'd like to refrain from punching someone and enjoy my evening."

"If anyone comes along I'll keep them away with your light saber," I joked, pointing to the keychain on his key ring that laid on top of the table.

"Excellent," he chortled, disappearing into the crowd. We'd only been there a few minutes and at least twenty more people had arrived.

I kept my eye out for any potential creepers. I wanted to avoid having another situation like the one that occurred in Philadelphia.

Trace returned a few minutes later with two bottles of water. "I thought you might be thirsty," he handed me one.

"Thanks." I took it and twisted the top off. I didn't dare ask him how long it would be until I took the stage. It would only serve to make me more nervous. I was definitely better off not knowing.

There was a clock hanging on the wall beside us and my gaze flicked its way every few seconds. I needed to stop.

"Hey, there's nothing to freak out about."

"That's easy for you to say." I frowned. "You don't get nervous."

"I don't care what people think of me," he reasoned. "Good or bad. Their opinion doesn't matter to me. I *do* care what you think of me, and my family, of course. But these people" —he gestured to the crowd— "they're not important, Olivia."

I absorbed his words, letting them soak in as I repeated them silently. "Why do you always have to be right?"

"I'm not always right. But I'm glad you think so. That makes my life easier." He chuckled, fighting a smile. He took a sip of water and pointed to the stage. "My turn."

He grabbed his guitar from the case and hoped up on stage.

Gripping the microphone in his hand, he smiled out at the crowd. "How are y'all doin' tonight?"

The crowd, mostly high school and college kids, hollered in response.

"I'm going to sing a couple of songs for you before my lovely wife takes the stage."

I blushed profusely as all eyes turned toward me.

"Hi," I squeaked, waving.

"This first song is one you've all probably heard. It's a big hit right now, but I'm going to slow it down." He lowered the microphone and sat down on a plain wooden stool. "This is "Wake Me Up" by Avicii."

He strummed the guitar, a smile on his face, and began to sing.

The crowd was getting into it, swaying to the beat. Trace had some kind of magnetism that seemed to capture everyone.

I sat riveted for the rest of the song, my mouth agape. He was so good and I wondered why he'd never pursued a career in music.

When the song ended, I clapped along with everyone else, jumping enthusiastically to my feet.

"I'm going to do a faster song with this next one." He adjusted the guitar in his lap. "Feel free to dance and sing along. Look at the person next to you and make friends.

Tonight is about making memories that will last a lifetime. This is "Here Ya Say" by Tony Lucca."

I propped my chin on my hand as I watched him in fascination. He was so amazing up there, closing his eyes with a smile on his face, and just ... letting go. When he sang, he was free. I wanted to feel that freedom too, but I wasn't sure I could let myself.

The song ended and I clapped along with everyone else, still in a trance.

He cleared his throat and said, "I have one more song to sing before my wife gets up here. This is a song that every time I hear it, I think of her." A chorus of "awws" echoed around the coffee shop from the girls. He scooted the stool a bit closer to the microphone. "This is "Mirrors" by Justin Timberlake. Olivia, this one's for you." He looked into my eyes and began to sing. Everyone else disappeared and it was only us.

He stared into my eyes for the whole song. But it wasn't like he was just *looking* at me. He was *seeing* me and there was a big difference for those that understood it.

I don't know if he knew it would have that affect, but the love that shown in his eyes as he sang erased all my fears. When he finished the song, I didn't hesitate to stand and stride toward him. "That was beautiful. Thank you." I bent, placing a light kiss on his lips. I wasn't one for public displays of affection, but I couldn't stop myself.

"Glad you enjoyed it."

I grabbed another stool and sat down beside him. He lowered the microphone so it was at my height.

"Hi," my voice cracked as I addressed the crowd.

I took a deep breath. I could do this. I might not have had

the charisma on stage that Trace possessed, but I could do it. I could. In a minute. *Okay, no more stalling.*

"I'm going to sing "Starry Eyed" by Ellie Goulding," my voice shook and I prayed that it didn't shake when I sang. The last thing I needed was to sound like a dying cow.

I glanced at Trace and he smiled reassuringly, giving me a thumbs up.

I closed my eyes and placed my hand around the microphone. I needed *something* to hold me up.

My voice was soft and hesitant at first, but I grew more confident and by the time the song ended, I was grinning like a fool. I was always so scared to get up on stage and sing, but after I actually did it, I felt like I was unstoppable. It gave me a rush and nothing else could compare to it.

The crowd applauded us and I said, "Thank you."

A slight blush stained my cheeks at the attention.

"You were great," Trace assured me, taking my hand and kissing my cheek. He'd already put his guitar back in the case and it was slung over his shoulder.

"Thank you," I told him. Shaking my head, I hastened to add, "Not for the compliment, but for convincing me to do that. There's nothing else quite like it," I explained, letting him lead me out of the shop. "And you," I gasped, shivering as the cool night air touched my skin, "you're so amazing, Trace. Why have you never pursued music?"

He shrugged, popping the trunk open. "It's a hobby. It's something I enjoy doing, but not something I want to make a living at."

"But cars—"

"Cars are my passion," he finished for me. He rubbed the finish on the Camaro affectionately. "Fixing something that's broken and making it beautiful again ... It's amazing. When my dad and I fixed this together, it was one of the best times of my life. Watching this piece of junk get a new life, seeing it shine again, brought me joy."

I turned away from him, chewing on the edge of my fingernail to hold back a lecture. His eyes had lit up when he was talking about cars. That was where his passion lay. I knew he still felt like it was his responsibility to take over his family's company, but don't we owe it to ourselves to be happy? Isn't that more important than the feeling of *duty*? I didn't want to argue so I opened the car door and slipped inside. I would bring it up again, eventually, because I loved him and I wouldn't sit back and let him be miserable for the rest of his life.

CHAPTER SIXTEEN

It was well into the afternoon by the time we started on the road. We'd lounged around in bed for most of the morning and eaten a late breakfast before packing our bags.

I smiled fondly as we drove through the town one last time. This would always be the place where we got married, and therefore, it would always hold a special place in my heart.

"What are you smiling about?" Trace's gaze flicked my way as he pushed his aviator sunglasses further up his nose.

My smile widened further. "I was thinking about how this will always be the place where we got married."

"We'll have to come back ... if you'd like that," he suggested.

"I would." I nodded, pulling the bottom of my tank top down. We were fairly close to the town where I had grown up but I didn't feel bothered by that. My life had been far from perfect, and anyone looking from the outside in had been oblivious to what was happening behind closed doors, but it had still been my home. While I had no desire to see the house I'd lived in, it didn't bother me being here. It was ... nice, and I knew that this wasn't my home anymore. I'd been in Virginia for so long that sometimes it felt like I had always been from there.

Trace turned down a street and I looked from side to side.

"Uh, this doesn't look like the way to the highway." I hated to sound like a nagging wife, but I didn't want to spend an hour getting lost either.

"I know," he answered simply.

"Where are we going then?" I looked at the houses surrounding on us each side. "Are we buying a house or something?"

"No," he chuckled, scratching his stubbled jaw.

"Trace," I groaned, "what's going on?"

I hated being kept in the dark, but Trace was always trying to surprise me.

"I'm not telling." He mimed zipping his lips.

I crossed my arms over my chest and watched as we passed even more houses. I racked my brain, trying to figure out what he was up to, but I kept coming up empty.

He parked in front of a cute Cape-Cod style home. The siding was gray and the shutters were painted a dark green. The front door was wood with two lights beside it. Flowers and bushes lined the walkway. It was a comforting friendly-looking home.

"Why are we stopping here?" I asked, still staring at the home.

"You'll see." He climbed out of the car.

I pushed the door open and stood staring at the house.

"Are you coming?" he asked as he started up the walkway.

"Yeah." I shook my head. "So, who lives here?"

"You'll see." He reached behind him for my hand. I reluctantly let him lead me to the front door. He pushed the doorbell and we waited.

After a minute, I said, "No one's home," and tried to walk away.

He tightened his hold on me. "Nuh-uh, stay here."

I opened my mouth to protest but the door was opening. The man pushed the storm door open, glaring at Trace, and then his gaze flicked to me.

Those eyes.

That nose.

That *face*.

I was staring at Derek Wynn, the man who was my real father, and the one my mother had told me was dead.

"Dad?" I gasped and everything went black.

MY HEAD WAS POUNDING and I couldn't seem to get my eyelids to open. I heard murmuring in the background but couldn't make out what the voices were saying.

A warm hand pressed against my face. "Olivia? Wake up," the voice coaxed.

I wanted to tell the person that I was trying, but I couldn't open my mouth to speak.

A cool cloth was spread across my forehead. The feel of it soothed me.

"Olivia," the voice started again. "Wake up. There's someone that would like to meet you."

Oh, holy shit!

The moments before I blacked out came rushing back at me.

"Dad!" I exclaimed, sitting straight up. The wet cloth plopped in my lap and Trace's tan arm snaked out to grab it.

My dad squatted in front of me, laughing under his breath. "I'm not your dad, kid."

"You're lying." My brows furrowed together and I glared at the man. "You're Derek Wynn. You're my dad. My mom told me so. We *look* alike." I couldn't believe I was looking at my *dad*. My mom had told me he was dead, but here he was in front of me alive and well. I wondered if she'd lied to me or if—

"I'm not Derek." The man shook his head. "I'm his brother, Dexter. But call me Dex." He held out a hand for me to shake.

"So, Derek really is dead?" I squeaked, staring at his hand. After a moment, I took it.

"He's been six feet under for twenty-two years. He's dead. Very dead. As in not coming back, dead."

Trace laughed, pointing at Dex. "I like this guy."

"So, you're my uncle," I stated.

"Seeing as how I was your dad's older brother, yes, that makes me your uncle." Dex rubbed a hand over his light beard. His dark hair and beard was speckled with gray.

"I-I-I—" I stuttered, looking at him. Finally, I forced my eyes to Trace. "How?" I had meant to ask him how he'd found Dexter, but I'd only managed to get the one word out.

He pretended to pick dirt out from under his fingernails. "I hired a private investigator. It didn't take them long to track down the Wynns. The problem was in figuring out how to get you here without telling you."

My mouth fell agape. "This whole road trip was a ruse, wasn't it?" I demanded.

Trace had the forethought to appear sheepish. "Yeah, kind of. I was going to wait and do it later, but after what happened with Gramps ..." He cleared his throat. "I needed to get away."

"I, uh, need some air." I stood shakily with a hand against my throbbing head. I shuffled to the door and turned to find Trace behind me. "Alone," I added in a harsh voice.

Pain flashed in his green eyes, but he nodded, ducking his head.

I pushed open the storm door and sat on the steps, breathing deeply in from my mouth and out from my nose.

There was a harsh pain in my chest and I grasped at my heart. Panic was rising from my stomach, up through my chest, clawing to get out. I hadn't had a panic attack in a year, but one was hitting me now. I fought desperately to regain control of my body, but I couldn't breathe.

The screen door slammed closed and Trace rushed around me, squatting in front of me. He took my face between his hands. "Breathe, baby. Just breathe."

I tried to even out my breathing but it wasn't working. Tears escaped the corners of my eyes and he wiped them away.

"It's okay, Olivia," he said soothingly. "Everything is okay. All you have to do is breathe."

My gasps began to quiet and my chest didn't heave near as much, but the panic attack hadn't passed yet, and if I didn't get myself completely calmed down it would start up again.

"I'm so sorry, Olivia." He brushed my hair away from my eyes. "I should've told you. I thought you deserved to know about them. They're your family. I wanted you to find that part of yourself. I didn't want you to feel like you had no one. I know how often you look at your dad's pictures and I know how much you wish you knew him. But he's gone, and if you can't know him, then I was going to be damned before I kept you from your grandparents and uncle," he spoke fiercely. "I really thought I was doing the right thing," he pleaded with me to believe him. "I didn't tell you because I know how shy you are with meeting new people and that you'd get yourself too worked up to meet them. Clearly, I was wrong; you got upset anyway."

He quieted after that, breathing slowly with me in an effort to keep me calm. His hands soothed up and down my back. He watched me with worry in his eyes. Once, I'd woken up from one of my nightmares and had such a bad panic attack that he had to take me to the hospital. I didn't like scaring him like that.

"I'm okay," I said after a few minutes. My voice was hoarse, almost sounding like a smoker.

"Are you sure?" he asked hesitantly.

I nodded.

He took my hands and helped me to stand.

"Dexter probably thinks I'm so weird." I frowned, glancing at my reflection in the glass door. I looked horrible. My hair was sticking up wildly, my skin was deathly pale, and my brown eyes were wide like a frightened rabbit.

"No, he doesn't think that." Trace chuckled.

"Of course he does," I grumbled. "First, I called him Dad and fainted. Then I ran out of the house having a panic attack. Did he—" I paused. "Did he know were coming?"

"Not at all. After you passed out into my arms I explained

who you were and he let me inside. I was actually surprised to see him. This is your grandparents' house. He said your grandpa was gone to the hardware store and your grandma is working." He put a hand on my waist and I leaned heavily against him for support. Panic attacks always left me feeling drained and exhausted.

"What if they hate me?" I whispered. "What if they tell me to get out of their house?"

"Silly girl." He brushed my hair away from my forehead so he could see my eyes. "How do you not see how incredibly lovable you are?"

"Lovable has nothing to do with it. I'm their illegitimate grandchild. My mom never even told them about me. Why wouldn't she tell them? What if they're horrible people?" I frowned, staring inside the door at the homey living room. Surely horrible people wouldn't have such a sweet looking home?

"They were grieving," Trace reasoned, "and your mom *was* married to another man. I can understand why she didn't tell them. She was scared of Aaron and she'd lost your real dad. But don't you think they deserve to have you in their lives, as much as you deserve them? You're both missing out on something special." Tears pooled in his eyes and he swallowed thickly. I knew he was thinking of Gramps.

I laid my hand comfortingly against his jaw. "You are one of a kind, Trace Wentworth."

"Well, I've never seen the benefits in being normal."

I rubbed my hand against his stubbled cheek. "I love you," I whispered. "Even when you pull stupid crap like this, I still love you."

He didn't say anything, he didn't need to, and bent his head so he could press his lips against mine. Heat ignited in my belly at the feel of his lips. He lightly nipped at my bottom lip and a moan escaped me.

The harsh clearing of a throat had us pulling away.

"Feeling better?" Dex asked.

I nodded, untangling my fingers from Trace's shirt. How had they even got there? It was like they had a mind of their own. "Much better," I smoothed my hands on the jean fabric of my shorts.

Dex held open the storm door and nodded his head for us to go inside.

Trace and I sat side by side on the old floral couch. I looked around the living room, memorizing everything. The yellow walls, the scratched coffee table, the piano in the corner. Every single piece revealed a little bit about the family living there.

"So ... did you and my dad grow up here?" I asked Dex, finally venturing to speak.

He leaned back in the matching floral chair. "Yeah."

"Do you live here now?" I asked.

Dex laughed, his eyes crinkling. "No. I live about ten minutes from here. I'm here today helping my dad. He had this silly notion to build a bird house and he has no tools."

"Married?" I continued the inquisition.

"No." He ran his fingers through his wavy dark hair.

"Why not?" The words tumbled from my mouth before I could stop them. "I'm sorry," I stammered. "I'm not trying to be nosy. I just—"

"I understand." He smiled. "You want to get to know me. I *was* married, but turned out she was banging my boss as well. Real stand up lady. We have a daughter together. Here, I have a picture." He tugged his wallet out of his back pocket and opened it up.

I smiled at the girl's picture. She appeared to be about five or six, with straight dark brown hair that reached her shoulders and bangs straight across her forehead. A dimple indented each cheek. She was absolutely adorable and she was my family. My cousin. *Holy crap, I have a cousin.*

"She's beautiful." I handed his wallet back. "What's her name?"

"Ella," he answered.

"Do you see her often?" I ventured to ask, praying it wasn't a sore spot for him.

"Every weekend." He smiled sadly. "I wish it was more. She's such a joy. Can't say the same for her mother, though." He laughed humorlessly. "So," he started as he pointed a finger to Trace and me, "you two dating?"

"Married," Trace answered.

Dex narrowed his eyes at Trace's left hand. "I don't see a ring."

"That's because we got married two days ago," I supplied. "We'll exchange rings when we get back home."

"Mhmm," Dex hummed in disbelief, sizing Trace up. "Don't hurt her," he warned.

It secretly pleased me that Dex was putting on a father act. I had grown up believing Aaron was my father, but he'd never been very ... fatherly. I didn't know what it was like to have a normal father/daughter relationship. Heck, my relationship with my mother had been far from normal with the constant fear she lived with.

The sound of a garage door going up had me on edge.

"Showtime." Dex waggled his brows.

Trace's hand sought mine, entwining our fingers together. "It'll be okay," he said confidently.

I held my breath, waiting for one of my grandparents to enter the room.

"Dex? Where are you?" a man's voice called out. "That little punk at the hardware store was less than helpful. Honestly, America's youth. What are they teaching those kids in school these days? Obviously not manners," he grumbled. "And did you see that Camaro parked out front?" he continued to rattle as the sound of plastic bags being set down met my ears. "I haven't seen a ride that nice in forty years."

"Dad?" Dex called out. "Why don't you come into the living room, there's some people I'd like you to meet."

"What are they selling? Tell them I'm not interested. I might be old but I'm not stupid."

"Dad," Dex said a little more sternly. "They're not selling anything."

"Then why'd you let them in? Are they holding a gun to your head or something, son? Where's my shotgun?" he muttered and I heard his feet shuffling against a tile floor. I put my hand over my mouth to stifle a laugh.

"Dad, just get in here." Dex rolled his eyes and mouthed, "Old people."

"All right, all right, I'm coming. You don't need to be so demanding. What happened to treating your elders with respect? I did give you life, don't forget that."

An older man with a slightly stooped back and white hair appeared in the doorway. His face was heavily lined but there was a light in his eyes that made him seem much younger.

The breath left my lungs in a gust as his eyes met mine.

This man ... he was my *grandpa*.

He studied me with a look of puzzlement.

"Dexter, you have a kid I don't know about? Or am I getting senile and Ella's older than I remember?"

"Dad." Dex stood, putting an arm around the older man. "This is Olivia. She's Derek's daughter."

The man—my grandpa, I corrected myself—crumpled to the ground sobbing.

My mouth fell open and I looked up at Trace hoping he would tell me what to do, but he was as stunned as I was.

"Dad?" Dex knelt on the floor in front of him. "Dad, are you okay?"

He continued to sob and his tear filled eyes met mine. Reflected in his orbs was delight and wonder.

"I never—" He shook his head. "I can't believe this." Dex helped him to his feet and I stood, hesitantly making my way to him. He looked me up and down in disbelief. "You … you're beautiful … and you look so much like your dad. I can't believe you're real. I thought after he died—" he choked, pulling a handkerchief from his pocket and wiping his face free of tears. "Can I hug you?"

I didn't answer him. Instead, I wrapped my arms around him and buried my face against his robust chest.

"Olivia," he said my name softly, like he was testing the sound of it, and patted my head like one would a small child.

I pulled away and my eyes roamed over his face. He had thick brows and a strong jaw. He was handsome, and I'm sure back in the day he'd broken many hearts. I found that my cheeks were stained with tears I hadn't even realized I was crying. I wiped them away, laughing slightly in embarrassment. "I'm afraid you have me at a disadvantage. You know my name but I don't know yours."

"Douglas." He smiled. "But you can call me Dougie."

"Can I—" I stopped myself, scared to ask, but finally I forced the words out. "Can I call you grandpa?"

He started crying again. "I would love for you to call me grandpa." He wrapped his arms around me in another bear hug. "In fact, I'd be honored."

He took my hand and led me back to the couch. I ended up sandwiched between my grandpa and Trace as Dex plopped in the chair once more.

"I'm Trace." He held out his hand to my grandpa. "Olivia's husband."

My grandpa let his hand drop. "Husband? You're married?" he asked me. When I nodded, he said, "You don't look older than twenty."

"Twenty-two." I blushed.

"You're a tiny thing." He chuckled. "Stay around here long and your grandma will have you fattened up." He patted his round stomach. "She's an excellent cook."

I knew there were a thousand and one questions I should have been asking him, but at the moment all I could do was sit and stare at my grandpa in awe.

"Your grandma should be here any minute." He glanced at his watch. "She always comes home for a late lunch before going back to the shop."

My heart skipped a beat in excitement.

In a matter of minutes, I had gained an uncle, cousin, and grandparents. I had been content to carry on my life never knowing them, figuring they wanted nothing to do with me. In all honesty, it was unfair for me to have believed that. After all, my mom had confessed to me that she'd never told them about me.

"I'll call her and see where she is. And then you can ask us any questions you want to know and we can get to know you better." He heaved himself up from the couch and shuffled out of the room.

"Well—" Dex smacked his hands against the arms of the chair "—my day got a whole lot more exciting. This is like one of those bad soap operas that's always on TV."

I giggled at his words. How often in the last two years had I compared my life to a soap opera? A lot, that's for sure.

"You don't even know the half of it," I told him.

Douglas came back into the room a few minutes later. "Maggie should be here in a few minutes. She's going to be beside herself." He shook his head in disbelief. "I still can't believe you're Derek's daughter. He's been gone for twenty-two years. When someone's been dead for that long it gets kind of difficult to remember that they were ever even alive."

"That's just because you're old, Dad," Dex chimed.

Douglas eyed his son. "Even after all these years you're still a smart mouth."

"It keeps life interesting." Dex winked. "To be honest," he said as he laughed, scratching his beard, "when I opened the door, I thought you were my kid or something and that I'd knocked some girl up back in the day. Then you called me 'Dad' and I thought, 'Holy shit! She really is your kid, Dex!'"

"Sorry," I giggled. "I didn't mean to scare you."

"Nah." He waved his hand in dismissal. "I'm just happy to know that good ole' Derek didn't die a virgin. He was always a goody two shoes. He was their favorite," he whispered conspiratorially, pointing at his dad. "They think I didn't know, but it was obvious."

"That's not true." Douglas' face grew red. "We loved you

both equally. Derek never caused all the trouble you did, though. If I could get back all the hours I lost bailing your sorry as out of jail, I'd be a young man again."

"You're exaggerating." Dex chuckled with a roll of his eyes.

"Twelve times. Does that sound like an exaggeration?" Douglas countered.

I smiled at their familiar banter.

"Okay, so I was a bad kid." Dex shrugged. "At least I'll have some kick ass stories to tell my grandkids one day."

"I'm home!" a female voice called out. I hadn't heard the garage door open since I'd been so caught up in listening to my grandpa and Dex bicker.

I held my breath, bracing myself to meet my grandma for the first time.

Heels clacked against the floor and when they stopped I slowly brought my eyes up.

My mouth fell open and I'm pretty sure I choked on my saliva. Why? Because, I was looking at Margaret, the lady that owned the store with the origami stars. My eyes widened further as I recalled her mentioning a son that had died.

Margaret looked between Trace and me with a bewildered expression. "What are you doing here?"

"You know each other?" Douglas looked from Trace and I to his wife.

"I don't *know* them, but they came into the shop yesterday."

Trace began to whistle the tune to "It's A Small World" under his breath. I smacked my fist against his thigh to get him to stop.

"What's going on?" Margaret asked.

I couldn't seem to get my voice to work. I sat frozen, staring at her like a weirdo. I hadn't noticed yesterday, simply because I hadn't known to look, but we had the same slender nose that was upturned on the end. The same heart-shaped lips and slightly rounded cheeks.

"Mom, meet Olivia." Dex swept his hand from Margaret to me. "Your granddaughter. Oh, and she's Derek's daughter, not mine, FYI."

Margaret's mouth fell open and she looked at me with shock.

For a moment, she didn't move, then suddenly she was in front of me sobbing hysterically. Gosh, I was making everyone cry today.

"You? You're? Oh, my God!" She pulled me off the couch into a hug, swaying us back and forth. My arms wrapped around her, holding her close, and inhaling her scent of lavender and juniper. She patted my cheeks, tears streaming down her face. "Derek's daughter? I-I-I didn't know."

I didn't know what to say, so I chose to say nothing.

"You're so beautiful." She fingered one of my curls. "You look so much like him." She shook her head, gazing at me in disbelief. "I can't believe this."

"Me neither," I admitted.

"How did you find us?" she asked as we scooted around to make room for her on the couch.

Trace cleared his throat and her gaze flicked his way. Rubbing my back, he said, "I hired a private investigator. I wanted Olivia to know her family."

"Well, thank you." Margaret wiped her face with the backs of her hands. "This is very forward of me, but can I ask who your mother is?"

"Her name is Nora. If you knew her, you would've known

her as Nora Owens." My eyes flicked away from hers guiltily. If they knew who my mom was, then they would know that she was married to Aaron when she got pregnant.

"I remember her." Margaret smiled and my stomach plummeted. "She was very sweet but she always seemed so sad. She was married, wasn't she?"

I nodded reluctantly.

"Aaron, I believe his name was?"

I nodded again and Trace squeezed my hand in reassurance.

"Derek told me about him. He said he wasn't ..." she paused, unsure if she should continue.

"He was a bad man. I know." I sighed.

"Is your mom still married to him?"

"No," I answered.

"Good for her." Margaret smiled.

I swallowed thickly, debating on whether or not to tell them what had *really* happened to Aaron. In the end, though, I decided against it. They didn't need to know what I went through. I wanted them to look at me, and see *me*, not the girl who was traumatized by the abusive father figure who'd tried to kill her.

"Are you hungry?" Margaret asked us. Before we could answer, she went on to say, "I'm starving. Why don't I make us all a nice lunch and we can catch up some more?"

"Sounds good." I smiled.

"Would you like to help me?" she asked with a wide smile as she stood.

"Of course." I pushed myself up off the couch to help her. Before I left the living room, I turned to look over my shoulder at Trace, fearing he might be mad that I was leaving him alone.

But he was already carrying on a conversation with my grandpa, completely at ease.

The kitchen was bright and cheery with cabinets painted a pale green and a white tile countertop. It needed some updating, but it was cute and well maintained.

"I thought we'd make some sandwiches, nothing fancy." She opened the refrigerator, laying different items on the countertop. "Bread is over there." She pointed to a pantry.

I opened the doors and located the loaf of bread.

Margaret was already getting out plates so I undid the twist-tie and counted out the right amount of slices.

"Are you in college?" she asked, trying to make small talk.

"I recently graduated," I replied, taking the mayonnaise jar from her and untwisting the lid since she was struggling.

"Good for you." She clapped her hands together in excitement. "What's your degree in?"

"English," I supplied. "I'm going to be a teacher."

"That's really wonderful!"

"Really?" I questioned.

She frowned. "You don't think so?"

"No, it's not that. I'm excited to be a teacher. Some people tend to be really negative about it, though."

"People like ...?" she probed.

"Just people in general." I shrugged. "My mom's supportive and so is Trace but ..."

"But what?" she asked, spreading the mayonnaise on the bread.

"It's nothing." I opened the baggie full of deli meat and started pulling out slices of turkey.

"You can tell me, Olivia. I know you don't know me that well. But I'm a good listener and I am your grandma."

"Well, I once told Trace that I wanted to write a book. He's afraid that if I start teaching I'll never do it."

"Is he right?" She began laying slices of cheese on the bread.

"Probably," I admitted.

"If you want to write one, why don't you?"

"I don't know what I'd even write about," I groaned.

"Why do you have to have a story mapped out? Why can't you sit down and just ... do it?"

Trace had said basically the same thing the first time I'd ever mentioned writing a book. He'd brought it up several times over the years, especially in the months before I graduated. I think he was as concerned about me being stuck doing a job I hated, as I was about him.

She looked at me, waiting for me to respond.

"I don't think I could do that," I finally said.

"How do you know if you haven't tried?"

She had me there.

"Maybe one day." I shrugged as she put the food items away. I helped her set the plates on the table and she grabbed five water bottles.

"Lunch is ready!" she called and the three men joined us.

Trace took the seat across from me, letting my grandma and grandpa sit beside me.

"After we eat, Trace is going to drive me around in that Camaro," my grandpa announced proudly. "That's a nice car."

Trace chuckled. "I'm glad you approve, sir."

"Dougie. Not sir. Sir sounds like ... Well, I better not say what it reminds me of," my grandpa chortled.

My cheeks flamed and Trace snorted, turning it into a cough to cover himself.

"What do you do for a living, Trace?" my grandma asked.

"I'm currently working as a mechanic, but my grandpa is grooming me to take over the family business," he replied.

"And what exactly is your family's business?"

Oh, God. This was getting embarrassing. These people may have been my grandparents, but they didn't *know* me, and they were already giving my boyfriend the third degree. *Husband! Not boyfriend!* Hopefully, in a few days, I'd be used to the fact that Trace was now my husband. It still seemed surreal. We'd gotten engaged and then married so quickly that none of it had quite sunk in yet—maybe it never would.

"We make ammunition," he answered.

"Ammunition," my grandpa mused. "You hunt?"

"Some. Not as much as I used to." Trace shrugged.

"I like you," my grandpa announced, enthusiastically pointing a finger at Trace. Turning to me, he added, "You did good."

I smiled over at Trace, my body flooding with warmth. "I think so too."

"So," Margaret started, "I remember you saying yesterday that you weren't from here. But you grew up here, right?"

"Yeah." I tucked a piece of hair behind my ear. "I lived close to here. When it came time to go to college I … I needed to get away."

"Where are you living now?"

"Virginia," I answered.

"That far away?" Her eyes widened.

I frowned. "Yes."

Her lower lip trembled with the threat of tears. "You mean, I've only just met you and I'm going to have to say goodbye so soon?"

I nodded sadly.

"Please say you'll stay with us for a few days. We have a spare room ready for guests and I'd love to get to know you better before you leave," she pleaded with me.

I looked across at Trace and he nodded.

"We can do that," I answered. "You know," I ventured hesitantly, "when we get back home, we're going to have a wedding ceremony, since we didn't have a real one here. Our moms want to see us, you know, actually get married. You should come."

Margaret looked at Douglas and they seemed to communicate silently, a lot like how Trace and I did.

"We'll try to make it, sweetie," she assured me. "But we can't make any promises. It's a long way."

"I understand completely. No pressure."

"We want to," she added. "We definitely want to. But Doug isn't in the best shape for traveling by car and we can't afford plane tickets—"

"Say no more," Trace interrupted. "I'll get the tickets. One for you too, Dex, and your daughter, if that's okay."

"I'm sure I can get out of work for a few days." Dex shrugged. "Ella will be dying to meet you once I tell her," he told me. "She'll think you're her sister."

"I would love to meet her. I've always wanted a little sister," I confessed.

I smiled at Dex and then smiled at each of my grandparents. I had only met them today, but already the overwhelming sense of *family* was impossible to ignore. I felt *loved*. But most importantly, I felt like I belonged.

CHAPTER SEVENTEEN

"And this is the guestroom," Margaret concluded the tour. She flicked a light switch and the room was bathed in light. "You'll use the bathroom I just showed you, since this room doesn't have one connected. I hope you like it."

"It's great. Thank you." I smiled, stepping into the room and looking around. The walls were painted a periwinkle color and the furniture was all white. A quilt covered the bed and I glided my fingers over the surface. "Did you make this?" I asked her, pointing at the quilt.

"I did."

"It's beautiful." I studied the different patterns. Some were floral, other stripes, and even circles. It shouldn't have gone together, but somehow it worked.

"I have plenty of quilts I made lying around. If you see one you want, let me know, you can have it."

"Oh, I couldn't take one of your quilts," I said, glancing out the window at Trace and my grandpa. Douglas was looking over the Camaro and gesturing wildly with his hands. Trace threw his head back in laughter.

"I insist. I have too many anyway. Doug has threatened to burn some." She shrugged. "Take as many as you want."

"If you're sure." I turned away from the window to face her.

"I'm positive. You know ..." She shook her head, laughing lightly. "I can't believe you're real. This seems like a dream. I'm afraid to go to sleep because I don't want to wake up and find you gone."

I stepped toward her and wrapped my arms around her. Her gray hair hung down her back and it was surprisingly soft. "I'm not going anywhere."

"I'm sorry," she said when I pulled back as she wiped away more tears. "Today has been really emotional."

"It has been," I agreed. I'd probably be crying again too if I hadn't already cried so much.

"There's one last room to show you. If you're interested."

"Of course." I knew I couldn't stay here forever and that we'd be leaving in a few days. But while I was here, I wanted to get to know my family.

She crooked a finger and led me back into the upstairs hallway. She opened a door at the end that had a narrow staircase leading up to the attic. "This is where my craft room is. It used to be downstairs, but it started taking over the whole house, so Doug told me I needed to move it somewhere else. I like it up here. It's quiet. And since Doug is too lazy to climb the stairs I can get a lot done."

The stairs opened up into a spacious attic. The sides of the room were sloped but you could move freely around the middle of the room. There were lots of storage organizers and a desk with paper spread across the top.

"I guess I'll have time to show you how to make those stars." She laughed, bumping my shoulder lightly like we were friends.

"I guess so."

"You know, they call them lucky stars," she mused.

"I need all the luck I can get," I joked.

"Come here." She led me to the desk where there were pre-cut strips of paper. "Sit down," she insisted, pulling out a chair.

I did as she said and listened intently as she described the process of making the small paper stars. It didn't seem too difficult, but knowing me it would be impossible.

After giving me the instructions, she grabbed a strip of paper and I watched as she turned it into a star.

"Now you try." She handed me a piece of blue paper.

I made the knot and began to do the folds. When I finished, I glared at the monstrosity I had created.

"Mine looks nothing like a star," I grumbled.

"Try again," she coaxed. "It's not that difficult once you get the hang of it."

I tried again, watching her carefully as she folded her own small star. My second attempt was far better than my first, but still not perfect.

"See, you've almost got it."

Almost wasn't good enough.

Turns out, third time was the charm.

"Beautiful." Margaret clapped her hands together excitedly like I was a child that accomplished something mesmerizing.

She grabbed a piece of pink paper and began making another star. "You know" —she tapped her finger against the paper— "you can write a message on the paper before you turn it into a star."

"Like what?"

"Anything you want." She shrugged, pinching the points of the star. "Usually it's exchanged between couples." She winked and I blushed. "I have something I'd like to give you," she said softly, moving away from the desk and to a far corner of the room. She stood on her tiptoes, reaching for something on the top shelf of a large bookcase. She cradled a large mason jar in her hands. It was filled to the top with brightly-colored origami stars. "Here," she said, holding it out for me to take. "I want you to have this."

"Thank you." I smiled, gazing at all the stars as I turned the jar around in my hands.

"Your father made those." Her voice grew quiet and she looked away from me as tears pooled in her eyes.

"I can't take this." I tried to hand the jar back to her, but she refused.

"No." She shook her head hastily. "I want you to have it."

"I can't take this," I whispered. I *wanted* them, after all it was something my dad had made, and all I had to remember him by were the photos my mom gave me, but it didn't seem right to take them. They obviously meant a lot to her.

"I insist, honestly." She forced a smile. "I have plenty. I don't need these and you should have something of his."

I glided my finger over the metal top. "Tell me about him. Please."

Her gaze grew wistful. "He was the youngest child and he was always so ... *happy*, and he wanted other people to be happy too. He was kind and giving. He would go without, so someone else could have. I remember one time, where he came home from school, starving to death, or so he said, because he'd given his lunch to a boy in his class who didn't have one. He worried more about everyone else, than himself. He was just that kind of person."

"He sounds like a remarkable man," I whispered.

"He really was. He wasn't like most people, and he left the world much too soon." She laid a hand against my cheek and looked down at me, studying my face intently. "He would have loved you so much, Olivia. I want you to know that. I'm sorry you never got the chance to know him."

Both of us were crying freely now. She reached for a box of tissues, handing me one and taking one for herself.

"I'm so sorry. I don't have much time with you and here I am crying again."

"Tell me more," I pleaded. "Did he play any sports in high school?"

"Does the chess club count?" She chuckled. "Derek was always the studious one while Dexter was the rebel. Dexter used to try to get Derek to cover for him. But poor Derek, the boy couldn't lie to save himself."

"I think I got that trait from him then." I giggled around my tears. It hurt to hear about him since I would never have the chance to know him but I *needed* this.

"Have you seen any pictures of him?" she asked, already spinning around her office in search of one.

"Yeah. I have some that my mom gave me," I replied. "I-I look like him."

"You do." He stopped in the middle of the attic space. "You really do," she whispered the last part wistfully. "I can't believe I didn't notice the similarities when you came into the shop the other day. I guess, since I didn't know to look for them, you were just any other girl. I can't believe ..." She looked at the ground, fighting tears again. "I can't believe you could have left here, and I would've gone on, never knowing that I had you as a granddaughter."

I stood and went to hug her. "I guess we both have Trace to thank for that."

"We definitely do." She led me out of the room and down the narrow steps. "I have to get back to the store. I know you would probably love a home-cooked meal for dinner since you've been traveling but would you mind terribly if we ordered pizza tonight? That way we can spend more time catching up."

"That would be great." I smiled, dropping off the jar full of stars in the guestroom before going downstairs.

I hugged her again before she left. I had a feeling we would be doing a lot of hugging the next day or so.

I watched her drive away and the men slowly made their way back into the house.

"I couldn't talk him into letting me drive that sweet ride out there," my grandpa informed me when he shuffled back into the house, tossing a finger over his shoulder at Trace.

"Dad," Dex chuckled, "that's because you're not a very good driver."

Douglas cleared his throat as he took a seat on the couch. "He didn't know that until you told him!" he exclaimed. "You blabbermouth!"

Dexter laughed, shaking his head at his father. "You're a mess, old man."

"Old man?" Doug scoffed. "You have almost as many gray hairs as I do!"

"Don't remind me," Dex grumbled, grabbing a piece of his curly hair and tugging on it.

"How are you?" Trace whispered in my ear as he came to my side.

"I'm okay," I assured him.

He swiped beneath one of my eyes and I flinched at the tenderness still present from the bruise. "What the ...?" he muttered, staring at the makeup now coating his thumb. He looked down at me and his eyes widened. He started to say something but then shut his mouth, a low growl emanating from his chest. *Oh, crap.*

"We'll be right back," he said through gritted teeth, taking my hand and leading me upstairs. "Which room are we staying in?" he snapped.

I startled at his tone and pointed a shaky finger at the room.

He dragged me inside and closed the door.

"What the hell, Olivia?" he growled, hands on his hips as he paced the length of the room. "Why didn't you tell me about that?" He pointed at my black eye.

"I knew you'd get mad," I whispered, my eyes darting to the ground.

"Fuck yes, I'm mad." He stopped in front of me, breathing heavily. "I wondered why it didn't bruise. Turns out it did and you were hiding it from me."

"It's just a bruise," I mumbled.

He shoved his fingers through his hair, causing it to stick up wildly around his head. "It shouldn't have happened," he growled. "I should have—"

"You should have what, Trace?" I interrupted his tirade. "Stop and think for a second. There was nothing you could do to prevent this." I pointed at my eye. "It wasn't even really that guy's fault. I fell, so what? Lots of people fall and scratch themselves or worse. I don't know why you feel the need to make such a big deal out of it," my voice grew heated. "I'm going to get hurt, Trace. You can't bubble wrap me and send me out into the world."

His lips quirked as he fought a smile. "I can try."

"Let it go." I sighed, letting my hands fall to my sides. "I have a black eye. You can't wave a magic wand and make it disappear, so there's no point in getting so worked up about it."

"I'm sorry." He took me into his arms, holding me close. His lips grazed the top of my head. "I overreacted and I shouldn't have."

"You're right, you shouldn't have." My voice was muffled against his shirt.

Kissing the end of my nose, he told me, "Stay here. I'll go get our bags and you can do what ever it is you've been doing to hide that." He swirled his finger in front of my eye.

I laughed. "It's called makeup, Trace."

"Yeah, that." He chuckled, backing out of the room.

I sat on the bed as I waited for him to return.

I looked around, still not quite believing that I was in my grandparent's home. After my mom told me about my real dad, I'd never once thought about finding my grandparents. My mom had said they knew nothing of me, and since I was never one to put myself out there, it had never bothered me very much. Sure, I'd wondered about them, but I would've never had the guts to track them down. Leave it to Trace, though.

He came back into the room and sat our bags down.

"I'm sure Dex and my grandpa wondered why you dragged me out of the room and upstairs."

"They probably thought I couldn't control my animalistic male tendencies a minute longer and brought you up here so that I could ravish you." He shrugged nonchalantly.

"Trace!" I giggled.

"I'm sure they were surprised when I came back down," he continued. "With my pants on," he added.

I laughed, not having a comment for that, and grabbed my makeup bag.

I headed across the hall to the bathroom and Trace followed me, leaning against the doorway.

He didn't say anything as he watched me apply the makeup to hide the bruise. When I was done, he said, "Damn, that stuff is magical. I could use that to hide some of my scars." He held his arms out. Pointing to one, he explained, "I got this one when my dad was teaching me how to ride a bike. He didn't teach me how to brake, so when he let me go I had no clue how to stop."

I frowned. "Aw."

"It's okay," he chuckled. "I was a tough kid. Although, my dad wasn't happy when I cussed like a sailor when he dabbed my cuts with alcohol. That stuff burns."

I laughed heartily as I imagined a smaller version of Trace cussing at his dad. "Yeah, most parents wouldn't be happy about that."

I turned the light off in the bathroom and carried my makeup bag over to the bedroom.

When we made it back downstairs, Dexter and my grandpa were in the same spots we'd left them.

"Weren't you going to build a birdhouse?" I asked my grandpa when I sat down beside him.

"I was, but now I have a granddaughter to get to know."

He began asking me similar questions to the ones Margaret had asked when we made sandwiches. I answered every single one with a smile and asked him questions too. I found out that my grandparents were high school sweethearts and he'd fought in the Vietnam War. Once the war was brought up, he began telling different stories from his time in the war. Trace listened intently, his mouth hanging open in wonder.

I hadn't realized how much time had passed, but suddenly Margaret was home again, carrying in three large pizzas.

"I wasn't sure what you and Trace would like," she explained. "So, I got a bit of everything."

"Trace will eat anything." I laughed, grabbing a plate.

"Like most men." She squeezed my arm lightly as she passed by me to grab drinking glasses from the cabinet.

Dinner was much more relaxed than lunch had been. The newness of the situation had worn off and we were beginning to talk like we'd known one another forever.

By the time we cleaned up from dinner and said goodbye to Dex, I was exhausted and ready for bed.

I had taken a shower that morning before we left the hotel, so I didn't bother with one now. I changed into my pajamas and climbed into bed. Margaret had been kind enough to let us use their washer and dryer so Trace had taken our dirty clothes to the laundry room, muttering that he hoped they had, "mountain spring fabric softener". It was his favorite and he complained that his clothes didn't smell right if he used anything else. He was crazy, but if it meant he washed the clothes and I didn't have to bother with them, I'd let him have his quirks.

He returned a few minutes later, stripping down to his boxers, and climbing into the bed beside me. It was a full-size bed, so once he was in it I ended up sprawled on his chest.

He tucked my head under his neck and began to hum under his breath. I was beginning to drift off to sleep when he asked, "Are you mad at me?"

I sat up abruptly, banging my head against the underside of his chin. "Ow!" we both exclaimed.

Rubbing the sore spot on the back of my head, I replied, "Why would I be mad at you?"

"Well, I did track down your biological grandparents without telling you and planned a whole road trip around it."

Lying back down, I said, "I couldn't be mad at you if I wanted to. I understand why you did it and I understand why you kept it a secret. I was surprised, that's for sure. But thanks to you, I know my grandparents and my uncle now. I can't thank you enough for that. They're my …"

"Family?" he supplied.

"Yeah," I croaked. "I didn't know what I was missing out on until I met them."

Tears leaked from my eyes onto the bare skin of his chest. "Olivia," he murmured my name, "please, don't cry."

"They're happy tears, Trace. I promise." I reached up to wipe them away.

"I guess those are okay, then."

"I'm so happy I have you," I mumbled as I fought the sleepiness threatening to take over my body.

"I'm the lucky one," he whispered, and it was the last thing I heard before I fell asleep.

CHAPTER EIGHTEEN

"I closed the shop so we'd have all day together," Margaret announced when I stepped into the kitchen.

"Thank you, Grandma." I smiled widely, excited at the prospect of getting to know her and my grandpa even more today.

She burst into tears, sobbing, "You called me grandma! Doug! Doug! Did you hear that? Olivia called me grandma!"

My eyes widened and I backed into Trace's chest. His hands snaked out to grab me and keep me from falling. I hadn't expected me calling her grandma to cause such a reaction. If I'd known, I probably wouldn't have said it.

"Um " I paused, unsure of what to say. Did I apologize? Or hug her? Or run the other way? Running seemed like a good option at this point.

"I'm sorry." She fanned her face. "I didn't expect you to call me grandma."

"I don't have to," I mumbled, growing red in the face from embarrassment.

She scurried across the room and stopped in front of me, taking my hands in hers. "No, I want you to."

"O-O-kay," I stuttered.

"Maggie, stop scaring the poor girl." Doug chuckled, coming into the kitchen with a steaming mug of coffee.

"I haven't been this emotional in a long time," she explained, ripping off a paper towel and using it to dry her tears.

"It's understandable." Trace gently nudged me in the back so I'd stop standing in the doorway.

I willed my legs to move, since they were currently frozen, and took a seat at the oak kitchen table.

Margaret had made a simple breakfast of scrambled eggs and buttered toast. Maybe I was crazy, but I thought they were the best scrambled eggs I'd ever had because my grandma had made them.

My grandma.

I had a grandma.

And a grandpa.

An uncle.

Even a cousin.

I had a *family*.

Being close to my mom and Trace's family I hadn't known I was missing out on anything, but I had been.

So many people took their family for granted, not realizing how lucky they were.

I had finished eating my breakfast when my cellphone began ringing.

I smiled bashfully and pushed away from the table. "I better take this. I'm sure it's my mom."

"No problem," my grandma said as she gathered up the dirty dishes.

I unlocked door and stepped onto the front porch, sitting down on the steps before pulling out my phone.

I frowned at the caller ID. It wasn't my mom like I had expected. Instead, it was Avery.

"Hello?" I answered hesitantly.

"You bitch!" she shrieked venomously into the phone.

I startled at her tone. "What do you mean? What did I do?" I hesitantly brought the phone back to my ear, in case she had another outburst.

"You got married, that's what! How could you get married without me, Olivia?" Her voice softened and I could tell that she was genuinely hurt.

"It sorta just happened," I explained, squinting up at the blue sky and fluffy white clouds.

She snorted. "I can't believe you didn't tell me and I had to find out from Trace's mom this morning. She called me asking for my dress size. I, of course, said, 'Why the fuck are you asking me for my dress size?' She told me that y'all got married and are having a ceremony when you get back. She assumed I knew and that you'd asked me to be your maid of honor. All I can say is, after being so rudely left out the first time, I better be your fucking maid of honor."

I pushed my hair out of my eyes, fighting laughter. "Of course I want you to be my maid of honor. And I'm sorry I didn't call to tell you. I haven't even told my mom," I whispered the last part like it was still some kind of secret.

"She's going to be pissed," Avery stated in a matter of fact tone. "You better call her before Tracey-poo's mom beats you to it. "

"Ugh," I groaned, "I'll call her when I hang up from you." I chewed on my fingernail, already dreading that conversation.

"So," Avery's tone brightened, "I think, that as your maid of honor, you shouldn't subject me to one of those hideous fluffy gowns that look like they're the color of puke. I mean, I know it's your wedding day or whatever, but why should I have to look ugly?"

I laughed. "Avery, I would never make you wear an ugly dress. Besides, you'd probably slit my throat if I tried."

"You know it," she said. "As your maid of honor, it's also my duty to give you a kick ass bachelorette party. We need male strippers and—"

"Whoa, whoa, whoa," I stopped her. "No way. No party. And definitely no strippers. After all, I'm already married."

"God, do you have to be such a fun sucker!"

"Someone has to keep your crazy ideas reigned in," I commented.

"They're not crazy," she whined.

"Don't even think about it," I warned.

"We'll see," she sing-songed and hung up.

I looked down at the phone screen and shook my head. Avery was out of her mind if she thought I was going to let her drag me to a bachelorette party—a lonely one at that, seeing as how she was my only friend—then she was going to see a side of me she hadn't seen before.

I brought up my contacts and pressed the button to call my mom. I felt nauseous at the thought of telling her.

"Hello?" she answered.

"Hey, Mom." I stood, pacing the walkway. A light breeze ruffled my hair.

"What happened the other day? It was really weird. And why are you calling me from a different number?"

"Um, well, you see." I bent down and picked a dandelion out of the yard and twirled the stem between my finger, "I kinda dropped my phone in a glass of water."

"Honestly, Olivia," she laughed, "I don't know how this stuff happens to you."

"Me either," I mumbled. Deciding that stalling wouldn't help me, I said, "I have so much to tell you."

"Really? What have you guys been up to?"

Oh, crap. This was it. I had to tell her. I thought I might be sick.

"We got married," the words tumbled from my mouth and I slapped a hand over my lips.

Silence.

Then …? *Is she laughing?*

"Mom?"

"Oh, my God, that's the funniest thing I've ever heard! Married? I know you'd never get married without me there—"

"Well, we did."

"You're being serious?" she quickly sobered.

"As serious as the marriage certificate in Trace's duffel bag," I mumbled.

She started crying and I toed the ground uncomfortably. I didn't know what to say to make this better.

"Mom—"

"I can't believe you guys would do this to me! To his mom! His grandparents! It's selfish, Olivia!"

"It's what we wanted. We've already decided to have a ceremony when we get back. We haven't exchanged rings yet. It will still be a wedding, Mom," I hastened to explain, hoping to make her feel better.

"It's not the same," she sniffled.

"Yes, it is, Mom." I pinched the bridge of my nose. I could feel a headache coming on.

"I'm sorry," she cried. "I'm upset but I'm not *that* upset. I'll be okay. I'm sorry I yelled at you," she rambled.

"It's okay, Mom." I sighed. "I understand." She continued to sniffle and I added, "There's something else I need to tell you."

"I don't know if I can handle anymore." She forced a laugh.

"It's nothing bad, I promise." I sat back down on the porch steps.

"Okay," she said hesitantly, not believing me.

I traced my finger on the skin of my legs, creating random shapes. "Trace found my grandparents."

"What?" she gasped.

"Yeah. We stayed with them last night. I'm still in shock."

"Are they being nice to you? They're not angry, are they?" she rambled nervously.

"They're wonderful, Mom. I met my uncle too, Derek's older brother. He's funny, and I have a cousin too. Her name is Ella. I haven't met her yet, though."

"Wow," she breathed.

"I know." I propped my elbow on my leg and let my head drop forward into my hand.

"Are you enjoying yourself?" she asked.

"I am," I breathed. "They're wonderful people and if it wasn't for Trace I wouldn't have met them."

"I-I better go," she stuttered.

"Okay. I love you, Mom."

"Bye, Liv." The line disconnected.

I was a bit hurt by her abrupt departure from our conversation but I knew she was probably getting emotional over Derek. Even though she had moved on with her life, I knew a part of her would always love Derek and wonder what could have been.

I tucked my phone back into my pocket and opened the storm door. It creaked closed behind me.

"Is everything all right?" Trace asked as he sauntered into the living room from the kitchen. "You were out there for a while."

"Avery called," I explained, "fussing about how I didn't tell her we got married and she had to find out from your mom. I think she was more upset that she thought I might not want her to be my maid of honor."

He chuckled, shoving his hands into the pockets of jeans. "I bet that was an interesting conversation."

"It was." I nodded. "And then I called my mom, to tell her before someone else did."

"How did she take it?" he asked hesitantly, looking at me beneath his long lashes.

"She was mad at first, but I calmed her down. Then I told her that we were here." I sighed. "I think she's happy that I've gotten to meet them, but she doesn't really like to talk about Derek. I know she's moved on with Nick and she's happy, but I think there's a part of her that will always miss Derek and wonder what her life would have been like if he had lived."

"That's understandable." Trace shrugged. "I'm going to take your grandpa out in the Camaro."

I laughed. "Is he still bugging you?"

"He's not bothering me, and I can understand why he loves it so much. I mean, it *is* a '69 Camaro."

"You and your cars." I smiled as my grandpa stepped into the room.

"You ready?" Trace asked him.

"I've been ready since yesterday." He shuffled to the door and outside.

"I take it that's my cue to leave." Trace chuckled. He kissed me quickly before hurrying after my grandpa.

I found my grandma in the kitchen and helped her finish washing the dishes.

When that was done, she turned to me with a smile. "Would you like to help me make more stars? I need some more for the store."

"I'd love to," I replied giddily.

She squeezed my arm lightly as she passed me on her way out of the room.

There was a small loveseat with a coffee table in front of it in her attic workspace and that's where we ended up sitting. She had to show me how to make the stars again and after a few tries mine looked almost as good as hers.

"This is relaxing," I said after we'd been silent a few minutes.

"It is. Your grandpa doesn't quite understand why I love it so much." She shrugged, dropping a completed star into a jar.

She grabbed a pen, writing a message on the piece of paper before turning it into a star. I read what she wrote over her shoulder, "'Leap and the net will appear—Zen Saying.'"

"You can write something too." She smiled at me. "Whatever you want. It can be a quote from someone else or something you come up with. Anything, really."

I thought for a moment and took the pen.

Regret nothing, I scrawled on the piece of paper. I laid the pen aside and made my star.

"Why did Der—" I stopped and corrected myself, "Why did my dad want to be a doctor?"

"Oh." Margaret's eyes filled with warmth. "He loved helping people. He was the kind of person that wanted to save everyone."

"I, uh—" I bit my lip, afraid I might be stepping over a boundary. "I would like to get flowers and visit his gravesite."

Her eyes filled with tears and she patted my hand. "That would be wonderful. I know that Derek is in heaven smiling down on you. He'd be so proud to have a daughter like you."

"You think?"

"I know so." She looked away, finishing the star she was making. "I don't like going there, to the grave. But I'll give you directions and you can go there on your own or with Trace."

"Thank you," I whispered.

"Hang on." She stood, going to the same bookcase where she'd gotten the jar full of origami stars. She heaved a heavy looking book off the shelf and dropped it on the coffee table. "It's a photo album," she explained.

"Oh." My eyes widened. I reached out and stroked my fingers along the black leather cover.

Margaret sat back down and opened it up.

"That's Derek as a baby." She pointed to a picture of a cute baby with dark hair and chubby cheeks. "Wasn't he precious?"

"Adorable," I agreed.

"There we all are." She pointed to another picture. In it, she was holding a baby Derek with a hand on Dex's shoulder to keep him from running away, and Doug had his arm around her shoulder. They stood in front of this house, smiling proudly. "That was the day we moved into this house."

"You all look so happy," I commented, studying the picture.

"We were. I'm not saying we didn't have our moments and boys will be boys, but we were always so happy. We still are, but even this many years later we still feel Derek's absence like it was yesterday." She gazed at the photo sadly and turned the page. "Oh look, here's Derek in his first grade spelling bee. He won." She chuckled.

I grinned at the photo of my father as a small boy. He smiled triumphantly at the camera as a teacher put a medal around his neck.

Hours passed as we went through even more photo albums. When my grandpa and Trace arrived back home, they joined us in the attic. My grandpa chimed in with even more stories and details of my father as a young boy. It was only bits and pieces, but I felt like I was getting to know my father a little bit better. I would never have the chance to meet him in person, as much as I might hope and wish for that impossibility, but it was nice to hear more about him.

———

I DIDN'T KNOW it would be this difficult to say goodbye to people I'd just met. But they were my *family* and that bond was impossible to ignore.

"I'm going to miss you so much." Margaret held me close,

nearly suffocating me, but I didn't care. After all, I held her as tightly as she held me.

"I'm going to miss you too," I replied honestly. "But you guys are going to fly out for the ceremony, right?"

She smiled down at me, patting my cheek. "We wouldn't miss it for the world."

I hugged her again, feeling like a small child. I didn't want to let go, because a part of me was convinced that if I did I'd never see her again.

Finally, I had to release her and hug my grandpa and Dex.

"We'll see you soon, kid." Dex ruffled my hair.

I smoothed my fingers over the top of my head to fix my hair. "Bye." I frowned, backing away. My eyes flickered over their faces, trying to memorize every detail.

They waved. "Bye."

Fighting tears, I forced myself to turn around and get in the car.

"Are you okay?" Trace asked. "We can stay longer if you want."

"Two days was enough." I forced a smile. "I know we still have to get to Maine. Maybe we can stop by on our way back?" I asked hesitantly.

"We can do that," he assured me, taking my hand.

A few minutes later he stopped in front of a flower shop.

"Would you like to pick them out?" he asked.

At first, I wanted to say no. But if I was visiting my dad's grave, then I should be the one to pick out flowers, not Trace.

I nodded slowly and slipped from the car. He followed me inside, not saying anything, but his presence alone kept me calm.

I picked out an arrangement of all white roses and lilies. It was simple and beautiful. I didn't know what Derek would have liked, but I hoped wherever he was that he was happy with what I had chosen.

We paid for the flowers and, using the directions Margaret had given him, we drove to the cemetery.

He parked the car and looked over at me.

I bowed my head, staring at the flowers.

I knew I needed to get out of the car and face this, but I didn't want to. Seeing his grave would make it even more real.

I *knew* he was dead, but that didn't mean I wanted to believe it.

"Olivia," Trace said my name softly, like I was a small frightened rabbit that might run away at any moment.

"I need a minute," I whispered, taking deep breaths.

I could do this.

"Do you want to go alone? I don't have to go with you. I'll stay here."

I looked up then and shook my head. "No, I want you there with me. I ... I *can't* do this alone."

"Okay." He smiled and sat patiently waiting for me to get out of the car.

I watched the clock in the car, counting as five minutes passed.

I shook my head roughly and grabbed the door handle.

"I'm ready," I whispered unnecessarily.

He waited for me to get out of the car before he joined me, not wanting to push me.

I stood at the cemetery gates for a moment, gazing at the intricate design of vines.

Trace took my hand and waited for me to give the cue that I was ready to move forward.

Taking a shaky breath, I placed my hand on the gate and pushed it open. It squeaked loudly on its hinges and I flinched at the shrill sound.

We made our way down the path with slow steps.

The sun shined brightly in the sky, warming my skin. I felt like the sky should have been gray and dismal to reflect my mood.

I repeated Margaret's directions in my head and veered off the path. I counted the headstones and came to stop when I got to the fifth one.

DEREK ALLEN WYNN

I hadn't even known his middle name until I read it on the grave marker. How horrible was I that I hadn't even asked what his middle name was?

I sank to my knees and placed my hand against the cold stone. I was trying desperately to feel *something*. But I was empty.

The man that lay beneath the ground I sat on was my father. But I didn't *know* him. And I never would. That fact broke my heart. So many people took their family for granted, but up until a few days ago all I had was my mom. Trace's family was great; I loved them completely and I knew they loved me too. But it wasn't the same.

Trace's dad was dead now too, but at least he'd known him.

I didn't have that luxury. All I had was this headstone and a few pictures—the jar of origami stars too, but that wasn't enough to ever let me get a feel for the kind of person he was.

People could tell me stories about him, and I could listen, but they weren't *my* memories. I would never get to hold his hand. Or have him walk me down the aisle. I'd never hear him say my name or call him Dad. These were all simple things, but they were powerful moments in a person's life. Moments I would never experience.

I lowered my head, letting my hair fall forward to conceal my face, as a pain-filled sob escaped my throat.

Trace didn't say anything as I cried. I think he knew I didn't want to hear it.

I placed my hand on the stone, rubbing my fingers over his name.

The flowers lay forgotten at my side. I clutched my stomach in one hand as my sobs threatened to overwhelm me.

I didn't even know why I was crying.

Is it possible to mourn someone you'd never met? The answer was yes. Because somehow, in this messed up world, we're all connected.

Trace let me cry until all my tears were shed then helped me up and back to the car.

He turned the car on and sat there. After a moment, he looked over at me and there was pain in his eyes. "I don't like seeing you like this," he admitted.

"I'm okay," I tried to reassure him, but since my eyes were swollen and I barely had a voice, it didn't do much to make him feel better.

He ran his fingers through his hair and sighed loudly. "Maybe it was a bad idea coming here."

"No, I needed this."

He reached over and cupped my cheek, turning my face

toward his. "Are you sure?" He swiped his thumb over my lips. "Because this doesn't seem very beneficial."

I rubbed my swollen eyes. "I needed to see the grave. I guess a part of me didn't want to believe he was really gone. Silly, I know."

"No, not silly. It's understandable." His gaze was sad. "All the time, I want to think that what happened to my dad was a really bad nightmare. But it's real and I'll always have to live with his loss."

I scooted over and draped my leg over his so that I was straddling him. I laid my head against his chest and closed my eyes, listening to the steady beating of his heart. I counted the beats, letting the rhythmic sound calm me. His arms wrapped around me and he rested his chin on top of my head.

"Thank you," I murmured.

"For what?" His fingers tangled in my hair.

"For this. For everything that you do for me," I whispered

"It's not much."

"It is." I pressed my lips against his forehead and his eyes closed. I slid off his lap and buckled my seatbelt. "I'm ready to go."

"You sure?"

I nodded, braiding my hair and securing it with a ponytail holder. "It's time for our honeymoon."

He chuckled, pulling out of the cemetery parking lot. "I like the sound of that."

"You know, when you said *lake house* somehow I envisioned a cottage. This, is definitely not a cottage. It's huge." I craned my neck back, staring at the house.

"It's seven thousand square feet ... a lot smaller than the mansion," he reasoned.

"Yeah, but way bigger than the one house that most people own. It's a *second* home for Pete's sake. Why does it need to be so big? I might get lost." I frowned as he opened the garage door and pulled inside.

"You're not going to get lost."

"You don't know that," I argued. "I don't have a very good sense of direction."

"There's nothing wrong with your sense of direction. Stop making excuses. I know you're really going to love it here." With that, he slipped from the car and I was forced to follow.

Once we got on the road, it hadn't taken us long to reach the house in Maine. Like with the mansion, the house was located off the beaten path. There didn't appear to be any other homes anywhere near here. Just the woods. And a lake, I assumed. Why else would they call it the lake house?

He grabbed our bags from the trunk and I followed him up the steps into the house.

We entered a darkened mudroom and he flicked a switch, bathing the room in light.

The walls were covered in paneling, but not the cheap kind, this was definitely expensive. I kicked my sneakers off and he did the same with his boots.

"I'm going to take our bags to our room and then I'll give you the grand tour."

"Okay."

He left the room and I heard his feet smacking against wooden stairs as he headed to the second level.

Since I had no desire to stand in the mudroom and wait for him, I ventured further into the house. All of the rooms were dark, but it didn't have that unlived in smell that some homes got. I figured the Wentworths had someone stop by periodically.

I turned on a light and looked up.

A bloodcurdling scream escaped my throat and I slapped a hand over my mouth.

"Olivia?" Trace called from upstairs as his feet thumped against the floor in his haste to reach me.

"I'm okay!" I called out to calm him.

"Then why were you screaming?" His voice grew closer as he descended the steps. He stood in front of me with a raised brow, waiting for me to reply.

"Because, um, I looked up and saw that." I pointed to the giant moose head hanging above the fireplace. "I really hope that's fake." I wrinkled my nose.

"It is," he chuckled. "We may hunt, but do you really think Grammy and my mom would allow us to hang a real one?"

"No," I giggled, ashamed of my reaction, but that thing was really scary looking.

"I want to show you something," he said softly, placing a hand on my waist and guiding me to the back of the family room. The whole back wall was windows and French doors opened onto a deck.

He opened the doors and stepped back so I could go first.

"Wow," I gasped.

The deck led straight down to a dock and there were even jet skis.

But that wasn't what left me breathless. It was the view.

The forest surrounded the house, cocooning it like a blanket, but the back was open and for as far as I could see, there was water.

"That doesn't look like a lake," I breathed, placing my hands on the railing of the deck and leaning forward.

"It's not. It's the Atlantic Ocean. We just call it the lake house, because it doesn't really look like a beach house, so that seemed weird."

"Of course, because that makes so much sense."

The water lapped against the muddy shore. There was some sand, but not much, mostly mud, rocks, and grass.

Birds chirped incessantly and squirrels ran around the yard. It was peaceful, as if the chaos of the outside world hadn't touched this place.

"I'm glad you brought me here."

"You are?" He chuckled, leaning his hip against the railing. "It's not too country for a city girl like you?" He faked a deep Southern drawl.

"I'm hardly a city girl." I rolled my eyes. "Besides, I do know how to shoot a gun."

He chuckled at that. "And you learned from the best."

"Really?" I raised a brow. "Because I didn't think he was all that good."

"Oh, now you've done it."

I squealed as he tossed me over his shoulder and jogged down the deck steps.

"Trace!" I screamed. "You've got to stop doing this!"

"Never! It's too much fun!" He smacked my butt.

"You. Are. Ridiculous," I spat as he jogged straight for the water. When I saw what he was about to do I pleaded with him to stop but to no avail.

He tossed me straight into the chilly ocean water and I sank below.

I came up sputtering, holding my nose. "You jerkface!" I screeched. "Water went up my nose!"

He chucked from the shore, the bottoms of his jeans were wet from where he'd walked into the water to throw me.

He shrugged and held his hands out to his side. "You shouldn't have questioned my teaching techniques. I assure you, babe, you couldn't have learned from anyone better. And not only am I a beast with a gun, I'm also proficient with a cross bow, as well as a plain old bow an arrow. I'm a jack of all trades."

"What are you? Katniss?" I growled, rubbing my eyes as I trudged out of the water.

"Who's Katniss?" he questioned.

"You know, from *The Hunger Games*." I stopped in front of him. "Surely you've heard of it."

"Oh, yeah." He smiled. "But I'm a lot cooler than Katniss."

"And why is that?" Only Trace and I would argue over a fictional character. If there was an award for weirdest fight between a couple, we'd surely win.

"Just look at me." He plucked at his shirt. "I'm way hotter."

I glanced down at the muddy shore, fighting a smile. "Not as hot as Peeta."

"Peeta is a pussy, I am a man." He pointed to his chest. "If the Hunger Games were real, I could protect you ... even with my bare hands."

"Really now?" I tilted my head. "Please, explain exactly how you would do that."

"I'd snap their neck, of course. But I'd also use my hands for more important things."

"Like what?"

"Well, first" —he stepped in front of me and bent his head — "I would take your face in my hands like this ..." His hands came up to cup my cheeks. "Then I would lower my head like this ..." His head came closer to mine. "And then, when I knew you were sufficiently breathless, I would graze my lips lightly against yours ..." And he did. A small gasp escaped my lips and I shivered. "Then, when I knew you were good and ready, I'd kiss you, and it would be the best kiss of your entire life."

Before I could respond, he was kissing me. His tongue pressed against my lips and my mouth opened in response. My body curled against his and my hands pressed against his toned stomach. He didn't seem to mind that he was getting wet. His hands left my cheeks and he grasped my waist, lifting me up so that I could wrap my legs around his waist. I clutched his stubbled cheeks between my hands and deepened the kiss. Salt from the ocean water clung to my lips, mingling with our kiss. I lightly nipped his bottom lip with my teeth and he growled low in his throat. The sound sent warmth straight to my belly. He gently lowered me down his body and kissed the end of my nose as he tucked a wet strand of hair behind my ear. His chest heaved with labored breaths.

"Woman," he whispered, "you'll be my undoing."

"I think I could say the same for you," my voice was as breathless as his. "That was some kiss."

"I'm *very* skilled," he murmured huskily, lowering his head to press his lips against my neck. My pulse jumped in response. He chuckled and bit the skin there.

"Ow!" I jumped, grabbing my neck. "That hurt!" I smacked his solid muscular chest. "Way to ruin the moment."

"Oh, baby, the moment isn't over. It's only beginning."

With that, he tossed me over his shoulder once more and carried me into the house and into the bedroom.

I guessed I'd get the grand tour later ... and I was perfectly okay with that.

I PADDED into the state-of-the-art kitchen and opened the refrigerator doors. My mouth dropped open as I marveled at all the food. It was fully stocked with anything you could possibly want.

"Trace!" I called. "Are you hungry?"

"Um, yeah," he called back from the laundry room, "you helped me work up quite the appetite, woman."

"I don't know what to make," I responded.

A moment later he stepped into the kitchen with a puzzled expression. "Is the fridge not stocked? It's supposed to be."

"Oh, it is," I assured him. "There's a lot to choose from."

He peered into the refrigerator and pointed to a packet of hotdogs. "I'll grill those. Why don't you make some mac n' cheese?"

"Sure, I can do that. Do you mind telling me where everything is?" I motioned to the large kitchen. "If you leave me on my own it might take me a while."

He chuckled, striding across the room and opening a door. "Macaroni will be in here and—" he opened a cabinet and pulled out a small pot "—here's this. Think you can find the sink?"

"You're such an ass!" While my words weren't very nice, I couldn't keep the laugh from my voice.

Chuckling, he said, "You know you love me. I'll finish with the laundry and start the grill."

I stared at the industrial grade stovetop, wondering why anyone needed something so fancy in a vacation home. In fact, everything in this kitchen was a chef's dream.

Shaking my head, I grabbed the pot and filled it with hot water, placing it on the stovetop. I turned the knob and the blue flames sparked to life.

Trace came back a few minutes later and grabbed an apron, tying it around his body.

"Man Bib?" I read the slogan printed on the apron in red letters. "Really, Trace?" I arched a brow, trying not to snicker at the ridiculous piece of fabric.

"Yes, really. I thought I'd go for the less offensive one. There's another one that says, 'It's all fun and games until someone burns their wiener'. On second thought ..." He removed the apron he'd put on. "That one is much more appropriate."

Grinning, he grabbed the hotdogs, a plate and fork, and sauntered outside onto the deck.

The water started boiling and I dumped the macaroni noodles into it. I realized that I had a problem in the fact that I hadn't asked Trace where bowls were.

I looked around at all the cabinets, knowing it would take a while to find them.

By the time I found a large enough bowl to stir the macaroni in, it was ready.

Luckily, in my search for a bowl I'd also found a strainer.

I drained the water and dumped the noodles in the bowl,

adding butter, the powdered cheese, and a splash of milk. It took another minute, but I found a spoon to stir it with.

When it was ready, I carried the bowl outside, along with forks, and placed it on the table.

Trace was already taking the hotdogs off the grill. With a smile, he set them on the table and headed inside. He returned with two plates, hotdog buns, as well as ketchup and mustard.

The grill was part of an outdoor kitchen, complete with a refrigerator, which Trace grabbed two bottles of water from.

"Eat up." He smirked, pulling out a chair to sit down.

"You don't need to be so bossy." I smiled, fixing my hotdog, and sliding the ketchup bottle over to him.

"Oh, I think you like it when I get bossy."

"Puh-lease." I rolled my eyes, scooping some macaroni onto my plate.

He propped his elbows on the table, raising a dark brow as he watched me closely. "What?" I asked when he continued to stare. "Is there something on my face? My hair?" I looked down to see if I dropped something on myself, it really wouldn't surprise me, but there was nothing there.

"No," he murmured, "just looking at my wife." A slow smile spread across his face and he repeated, "My wife. You have no idea how much I love the sound of that."

"I hope you still like the sound of it ten years from now." I laughed, spearing some macaroni. For some reason, I'd always hated eating it with a spoon.

"Ten. Twenty. Fifty years from now, it doesn't matter." He spread his arms wide. "I will always be happy to call you my wife."

"Good."

"Will you be happy to call me your husband that many years from now?"

"Do you even need to ask?" I raised a brow.

He chuckled, scratching his chin. "No, I guess not. How could you ever get sick of me? I'm the coolest person ever."

By the time we finished eating and cleaned up, Trace had given me very detailed reasons why he was the coolest person ever, some of which made me blush.

After everything was cleaned up, and darkness was beginning to fall, I found myself mesmerized by all the fireflies in the yard.

I had never seen so many at one time before and I watched in awe as their lights blinked on and off, illuminating the sky like little fireworks.

"They're beautiful," I breathed.

"That's one of my favorite things about this place." Trace stood beside me, his hands in his jeans pockets. "When I'm here, it's like I'm a part of nature. The animals aren't scared of us and they're free to roam around undisturbed. Do you know, one time I was standing right here" —he pointed to the spot where he stood on the deck— "and a bear walked right by, stopped and looked at me, then went on its way."

"A bear?" I squeaked, looking around in fright. "There are bears in these woods?"

He chuckled, crossing his arms over his chest. "Of course there are bears. Those are woods, and that's typically where they live."

"Still," I shuddered, "I don't want to encounter a bear."

"Live a little." He reached for my hand, guiding me down the deck steps.

"Where are we going? You're not going to dunk me in the ocean again are you?" I tried to pry my hand from his.

"No," he chuckled. "Nothing like that."

He stopped in the middle of the yard, and surrounded by all the fireflies and the chirping of the crickets, he pulled me against him and began to sway us to the music of nature.

I closed my eyes and laid my head against his chest, breathing in the moment.

The salty ocean air swirled around us, and the fireflies blinked cheerily.

I smiled to myself as his warmth soaked into me and I knew that I'd be enjoying many more moments like this for the rest of my life.

CHAPTER NINETEEN

"Mmm," I hummed, stretching my legs and arms, but keeping my eyes closed. I didn't want to wake up.

"Wake up," Trace coaxed and his lips skimmed over my bare stomach where my t-shirt had ridden up. "I have somewhere I want us to go."

"I don't wanna." I tried to roll away from him, grasping onto the pillow.

"Trust me, you don't want to miss this."

"What time is it?" I mumbled.

"Early," he chuckled, his breath skimming against my bare skin and I shivered.

Slowly, I cracked open one eye and peered at the sexy man hovering above me. "How early?"

"That's not important."

"It is." I threw an arm over my eyes. "I want to sleep."

He swirled a finger around my belly button and my back arched off the bed as a small moan escaped my lips.

"Quit it," I warned.

"Nope." He jostled the bed as he climbed off.

I rolled over, thinking I had won, and curled my body against the other pillow.

But my victory was short lived.

Trace threw the covers off, grabbed one of my ankles, and pulled me from the bed.

I shrieked, thinking I was about to fall from the bed onto my face, but he caught me.

"You jerk!" I smacked his chest and pried myself from his arms.

He laughed heartily, clutching his stomach. "I know I've made you mad when you start calling me names."

"Yeah, well, I want to sleep."

"And I told you that I want to show you something. We have to hurry or we'll miss it."

"Maybe I don't want to see it," I grumbled, heading back to the bed.

"Nuh-uh." He grabbed my arm, halting my steps. "Get dressed and be downstairs in five minutes. I mean it." He pointed at me sternly like a father scolding a child. "Put a bathing suit on under your clothes and be sure to wear sneakers."

"I hate you so much right now." I stared longingly at the plush king-sized bed where I'd been dreaming so peacefully a few minutes before.

"You won't be saying that soon." He grinned, releasing me as he backed toward the door. "Remember, five minutes." He held up a hand, wiggling his fingers.

I glared at him as he left the room. A part of me was tempted to climb in the bed and go back to sleep, but I knew Trace would only wake me up again so it was pointless.

I scurried into the bathroom, brushing my hair and braiding it to the side. I brushed my teeth but didn't bother with any makeup since I was running short on time. I changed into my bikini. It was pale blue with a floral design and the bottoms had ruffles on the side. I'd been looking to buy a one piece but Avery had talked me into this one and I was actually happy I'd gotten it instead.

I pulled shorts on over the bottoms and grabbed a plain t-shirt, figuring the morning air would be cool.

Trace was starting back up the steps when I rounded the corner.

"Coming to get me?"

"I thought you fell asleep standing up." He smiled, waiting for me on the second to last step.

"No." I shook my head. "You might have spanked me if I did."

"Any excuse to touch your ass." He smirked, reaching for my butt. With a screech, I lurched away from his clawing hand.

"Nice try." I narrowed my eyes at him.

"There's always later."

"Now, what was so important that I had to get up while it's still dark?" I pointed to the window where the sky was black and stars still twinkled.

"Come on now, I can't tell you that. It would ruin the surprise." He opened the doors that led to the deck and waved me over.

"Outside?" I asked. "With the bears?"

"Yes." He rolled his eyes. "And the moose, squirrels, deer ... Shall I continue?"

I marched forward and out the door. He jogged down the steps and waved for me to follow him. Shaking my head, and grumbling unintelligibly under my breath, I reluctantly followed him.

He pulled a small flashlight from his pocket and turned it on.

"We need a flashlight because?" I prompted.

"We're going into the woods." He quickly grabbed my hand so that I couldn't make a run for it.

"The woods? In the *dark*? Are you crazy?"

"No." He stopped, looking at me seriously. "I'm a boy scout."

I stared at him a moment before laughter burst out of my throat. "You can't be serious?" I cried, wiping away tears.

He frowned, like I had offended him. "I was a boy scout until I was twelve. I was so awesome I didn't need to continue after that."

"Oh, please," I continued to laugh, trying to catch my breath.

"You don't believe me?"

"Hardly." I bit my lip to hold back more laughter.

He puffed out his chest and put his hands on his hips. "I was the best boy scout ever, I'll have you know."

"So, if a bear happens to wander by, what will you do?"

"I'll wrestle it to the ground, of course." He flexed his arm muscles. "No bear can withstand these."

Shaking my head, I said, "Your confidence never ceases to amaze me."

He chuckled, placing a hand to his chest. "Never doubt my

bear fighting abilities." He nodded his head toward the woods, coaxing me to follow him.

I was still a bit wary, but I knew Trace was bound to know these woods like the back of his hand and the chances of being eaten by a bear were minimal.

There didn't seem to be any discernable trail, and while I was an outdoorsy girl, hiking had never been my thing.

Trace helped me over fallen trees and always made sure he held my hand so I didn't fall. We'd been hiking for about fifteen minutes when I asked, "How much farther?"

"A lot farther."

"How much is a lot farther?" I skidded around a stick I was convinced was actually a snake.

"A lot farther," he repeated.

"You're not going to tell me?"

"Absolutely not," he replied.

Another fifteen minutes later, he said, "Almost there."

The sun was beginning to rise and bits of brightness peeked through the tree branches.

Trace stopped and turned to me. "Ready?"

"For what?" I questioned hesitantly. Lord only knew what Trace had up his sleeve.

"To have your mind blown." He grinned crookedly.

Nodding his head, he led me further into the trees. I was looking down at the ground, so I didn't see what was in front of me. He slammed his arm against my chest to halt my progress and I momentarily panicked, thinking there really was a bear or something.

With my heart racing, I looked up and my mouth fell open.

"Holy crap," I gasped.

The ground stopped suddenly, dropping straight into a

small river. I didn't know how I had missed the sound of rushing water, but it could probably be explained away by my thinking a snake, bear, moose, or other woodland creature was going to attack me.

The sunrise reflected on the crystal clear water, igniting it with oranges and reds.

I had honestly never seen anything more beautiful in my entire life. I wished I had a camera so I could take a picture and remember this moment exactly as it was. I didn't want to tell Trace, but this was definitely worth getting out of bed for.

He turned to me with a smirk. "Glad I woke you up?"

I reluctantly nodded. There was no point in lying. He could tell from the awe on my face that I was mesmerized.

"How did you know about this place?" I gasped, looking around me.

"Exploring." He shrugged, bracing a hand against a tree trunk. "Trent and I found it."

I toed the ground, kicking a rock and watching it fall into the water. I looked below and wondered aloud, "How far down do you think it is?"

He shrugged. "Twenty feet maybe, but I'm not really sure."

Before my brain could process what he was doing, he tossed his shirt off and started working on the belt of his pants. I noticed he was wearing swim trunks and it began to click as to why he had told me to wear a swimsuit.

"What are you doing?" I asked, hoping I was wrong.

He looked at me like I was the crazy one. "Jumping."

"Jumping? As in jumping down *there?*" I pointed to the water below.

"Yeah." He kicked his jeans off.

"Is that safe?"

He chuckled. "Olivia, I've done this every summer for practically as long as I can remember."

"That still doesn't make me feel better about you jumping."

"You're jumping too."

"What? No way." I looked down at the water churning below. "That water looks really rough."

"I'll hold your hand."

I swallowed, gazing at the water uneasily. "I don't think you holding my hand is going to save me from drowning." I gulped.

"Olivia ..." He took my face in his hands, forcing my stare away from the water. "It's the things that scare us that are the most worthwhile. Like falling in love." He rubbed his thumbs over the curves of my cheeks. "It scared the shit out of me, but it's been the best rush I've ever experienced. This is a memory I want us to make together. *Please.*"

I closed my eyes, repeating his words.

When I first met Trace, I had been desperate to *live, make mistakes, be wild* and *spontaneous*. Why did that have to suddenly stop after the list was complete?

I opened my eyes and smiled slowly.

"I'll do it."

"I knew you'd see things my way." He kissed me leisurely, purposely trying to make me forget what I was about to do. He more than succeeded.

I removed my shorts, lifted my shirt off, and kicked off my shoes. Before I could let myself think about it a second longer, I took his outstretched hand.

"One, two, three—" he counted.

With a scream, I jumped.

I hit the water feet first and its cool depths surrounded me, blanketing me. Somewhere along the way I'd lost my hold on his hand. I kicked for the surface and came up gasping for air. The water wasn't nearly as choppy as it looked from above.

Trace surfaced a few feet away from me and flicked his dark hair out of his eyes.

"You okay?" he asked, his shoulders rising and falling with labored breaths.

"Great." I smiled as he swam toward me.

He wrapped an arm around me and my legs automatically found his waist. My fingers tangled in his wet hair as I gazed at him with heated eyes.

"If you keep looking at me like that, I'm going to have to kiss you," he confessed as my eyes greedily watched a water droplet that clung to his kissable lips.

"Then do it," I challenged.

So he did.

The kiss was intense and passionate, but sweet at the same time, a lot like us.

He nipped at my lip and my mouth opened beneath his, welcoming him.

The water sloshed against our shoulders, moving us with the current, but we didn't care. I clung to his shoulders, tightening my legs around his waist.

His lips moved to my chin and he sprinkled small kisses down my neck.

"Was it worth the fall?" he asked huskily with warm green eyes.

"Yes," I answered, knowing he wasn't referring to the jump.

"Good." He kissed me again.

By the time we extracted ourselves from each other's arms and made it to shore, my fingers were wrinkled. Shivering, I said, "I'm not looking forward to walking back up there with no shoes."

"Stay here." He pinched my side as he passed me. "I'll throw your stuff down and then you can walk up."

The twigs on the ground didn't seem to bother his feet as he walked back up to the cliff. Maybe he really had been a boy scout.

He threw my shoes down and I ducked to avoid them.

"Sorry!" he called.

"Uh-huh, sure you are." I laughed, retrieving my shorts and t-shirt.

Once my shoes were tied I made my way back up to the top of the cliff; luckily, I managed to avoid falling and skinning my knees.

The trek back to the house went a little faster, but I was still on the lookout for critters that might be determined to take a bite out of me. I knew I was small and defenseless looking, the perfect target for a hungry bear.

When we stepped into the yard, I breathed a sigh of relief that I'd made it through alive.

Trace made us breakfast and we ate outside before settling on the big leather couch in the family room. He didn't turn the TV on, but he did turn the gas fireplace on low. It was completely unnecessary, but I loved it nonetheless. It would definitely be fun to visit this place in the winter and see all the snow. We didn't usually get much snow where we lived in Virginia and I actually missed it.

I curled myself against Trace's side but soon found myself sprawled on my back with him hovering above me.

"What are you doing?" I giggled.

"Nothing."

"You're up to something," I remarked.

His lips quirked at the corners. "That may be so."

Suddenly, he rolled off the couch, taking me with him. I landed against his chest and the air gusted out of my lungs.

"What was that for?" I gasped.

"I thought the rug looked mighty comfortable, of course." He spread out his arms and legs like one would if making snow angels.

"I'm sure it's very comfortable," I commented, going to move off his chest, but he rolled over again and pinned me beneath him.

"Seriously, what are you doing?"

"I don't know," he answered honestly. "Playing, I guess."

"What are we, five?" My body shook with laughter.

"Yeah, wanna wrestle?"

I snorted. "Yeah, because I'm really going to be able to take you on." I gripped his muscular arms.

"I'll go easy on you." He smiled boyishly.

"Fine." I smiled.

"One, two—"

Before he said three I brought one of my legs up and wrapped it around his waist. Leveraging my weight, I flipped him off of me. He landed on his back with me straddling him. His eyes widened in surprise. I grabbed his arms, forcing them above his head where I held them down. Bending my head, and letting my hair fall around us like a curtain, I closed the distance between us like I was about to kiss him. When my lips grazed his, I breathed, "I win."

He growled low in his throat. "You tricked me."

"I'm small, I have to use *something* to my advantage." I sat up, smiling down at him.

He narrowed his eyes. He reached up and placed his hand against my neck, caressing me. My eyes closed and before I could take another breath, gravity tilted and he had me beneath him. He lowered himself so that his whole body was pressed firmly against mine and I had no chance of escape.

I tilted my head up, pressing kisses against his collarbone and neck in the hopes of distracting him long enough to gain control of the situation. His lips found mine, and his fingers pulled at my hair, but not so hard that it hurt.

All thoughts of the game we'd been playing left my mind.

My hands skimmed under his shirt, over the smooth skin of his toned stomach. He sat up long enough to remove the shirt and then he was on top of me again. My hands greedily memorized every curve and dip of his muscular chest and stomach. God, he was like a work of art.

He raised my shirt over my head and kissed the dip between my breasts. His tongue flicked out, licking a wet trail down my stomach. My back arched off the rug. "Trace," I moaned his name as his tongue circled around my belly button ring.

He continued down my body, undoing the button on my shorts. I raised my hips so that he could tug them off. He kissed the skin of my stomach, just above the top of my bikini bottoms.

My heart rate accelerated in the anticipation of what was to come.

His fingers began to tug on the string holding my bikini top in place.

Before he could undo the knot, both our phones began to ring at the same time.

He pulled back slightly and from his expression I knew he

was tempted to ignore them, but when both calls ended the phones started ringing again.

"Fuck," he groaned, rolling off of me and into a standing position. He reached down to haul me up. "And just when it was getting to the good part."

He pulled his phone from his jeans pocket and answered it.

I found my phone on the kitchen counter and puzzled as to why Trent would be calling me. What if something happened to Ace?

"Hello?" I answered.

"Olivia," Trent sounded breathless, "you guys have to come home right now."

"Why?" I questioned, my gut telling me I didn't want to know the answer.

"It's Gramps," his voice was tense.

At his words I lost my hold on the phone and it crashed to the ground. I watched it shatter apart, exactly like my insides.

I looked up into Trace's pale face.

While we'd been happy and joking around, Gramps had ...

"Trace." I crashed into his arms, both of us crying.

My heart hurt as it broke. This wasn't fair. Why did Gramps have to die? He didn't deserve this. He was a good man, better than most people. Why did he have to get sick and suffer like this?

"I didn't get to say goodbye," my voice was muffled against his chest.

"There's still time," he murmured, his lips brushing against the top of my head.

"There is?" I tilted my head back, looking at him with wide eyes, scared to hope.

"That was my mom." He wiped away his tears with one

hand. "Gramps is in the hospital. Things are bad, Olivia. Real bad. He only has a few days left."

"We're not going to make it back in time, are we?" I began to cry harder.

"I'm going to make sure we're there." He took my face between his hands. "My mom's getting us plane tickets now. I'll pay someone to drive the car back to me."

His words relieved me. We'd get to see Gramps again. There was so much I wanted to tell him, but none of it mattered. All I wanted to do was hug him.

"We need to pack," Trace whispered, "and get to the airport."

I nodded. "You get our stuff from the laundry room and I'll head upstairs and get a head start there."

He wrapped his arms around me, hugging me close. "I need you," he said softly.

I realized then, that sometimes those words were even more powerful than *I love you.*

CHAPTER TWENTY

Trace's leg bounced up and down restlessly as we waited to board the plane. I kind of wished I had some drugs to knock him out with. He was *that* worked up.

"Why aren't they boarding yet?" he asked through gritted teeth.

"I don't know." I placed my hand on his knee to stop his shaking. "We still have a while until we're supposed to leave."

He buried his face in his hands and growled, causing more than one person to look our way. "God," he groaned. "I should be *there!* Not here!"

I went to place my hand on his back, but he stood abruptly, pacing in front of the seats.

"Trace, you need to calm down. This isn't solving anything," I said in as soothing of a voice as I could manage. I was stressed and it was giving me a tension headache. It wouldn't be long before I snapped at him and he didn't need me giving him a hard time right now. What we needed was each other.

He paced back and forth in front of me a few more times before sitting down. He leaned his head back and stared at the plain white ceiling of the airport.

"This isn't fucking fair," he snapped.

"I know it's not." I took a deep breath, fighting tears as images of Gramps filled my mind. "But it's *life* and life is never fair."

"I feel like I need to smoke or something," Trace announced. "And I don't even smoke. I just ..."

"You need something to take your mind off what's happening. I understand."

"What I need is to be there," he whispered. "I should have never talked you into that fucking road trip. But I needed it ... you know?" He waited for me to nod before he continued, "And I wanted you to meet your grandparents."

"Trace." I placed my hand over his where it rested on his leg. "We can't dwell on the things we wish we could change. Besides, would you really want to undo our whole trip? We had some really great times."

"No, I wouldn't," he admitted.

I cupped his cheek in my hand. "We're going to get there in time."

"How do you know?" he asked, tears swimming in his eyes.

"Because, he's a Wentworth." I forced a smile, repeating the words Trace told me often. "And he's stubborn. He's going to wait to say goodbye."

"You're right." He forced a small smile.

About that time they called for us to line up for boarding. Trace heaved both of our duffel bags onto his shoulders.

He handed the lady our tickets and she motioned us through.

"First class, really?" I eyed him upon entering the plane.

"My mom bought the tickets." He shrugged, taking the seat by the window.

I sat down beside him, buckling the seatbelt even though it would be awhile before the plane actually took flight.

Trace was still on edge, but he had calmed down a little bit since we got on the plane. I knew he wouldn't feel better until we saw Gramps, and even then it wouldn't ease the burden of knowing that Gramps was going to leave us very soon.

WHEN WE LANDED in Dulles it was almost ten at night. Trace's mom was waiting for us in her white BMW SUV. She got out, hugging each of us. Her blue eyes were bloodshot with bags underneath. She kissed Trace's cheek but didn't say anything. There wasn't much that *anyone* could say to make this situation better.

Once we were seated in the back of the car, Lily said, "We'll go straight to the hospital. He's in a private room so no one can complain about it being too late for visitors."

"How is he?" Trace asked shakily, reaching for my hand.

"He ... he's *dying*, Trace. So, not good." She pinched the bridge of her nose as she pulled away from the curb. "He's laughing and joking, but it's not good."

"He ... he told us, a few weeks before we left, that ... that he had cancer," Trace admitted.

Lily's hands tightened around the steering wheel. "He told

you, but not anyone else? Why would he do that? Your grandma is beside herself, clearly he hadn't told her."

"I guess he didn't want you and Grammy fussing over him." He rubbed his free hand nervously on the fabric of his jeans.

"Of course we would have fussed over him!" Lily exclaimed and I saw tears begin to stream out of her eyes. "He shouldn't have been working so hard! He should have been home relaxing and trying to get better!"

"Mom." Trace leaned forward from the backseat and placed a hand on her shoulder. "Gramps. Didn't. Want. That."

"I don't care." She wiped her eyes free of tears and looked over her shoulder before changing lanes. "I know he's not my dad, but I feel like he is. He and your grandmother have always been there for me. Especially after Trey died."

Trace looked at me and back at his mom. "I know none of us want to face reality, but the truth is, he's going to die. Everyone dies. It's not a matter of *if* it's *when*. That doesn't make it any easier to accept, but it's the truth. I don't want to lose Gramps but it's inevitable."

We all grew quiet after that. It took an hour and a half to make it to the hospital and when Lily parked the car my stomach plummeted. This was it.

I had never had to watch someone I loved wither away and die. I wasn't sure I was strong enough for this, and I knew I needed to keep my head together for Trace.

We followed Lily into the hospital with our hands clasped together like we were the only things keeping the other person from falling apart.

I inhaled the sickening scent of alcohol and disinfectant, and images of my time in the hospital came flooding back to me. I pushed them aside though. I *couldn't* think about that right now.

We ended up on the top floor of the hospital and Lily came to a stop in front of a closed wooden door.

"He's probably sleeping, but at least you can see him," she said. She hugged each of us and headed down the hall to where the waiting room was.

Trace looked down at me questioningly.

I nodded and he opened the door.

Gramps wasn't sleeping. Instead, he was sitting up in the bed smiling widely at us. His skin was pale and gray in color. He'd lost weight since the last time I saw him and more wrinkles lined his face. But his eyes were exactly the same and the happiness that shone there almost brought me to my knees.

"Well, if it isn't my favorite person in the whole world and my shitty grandson."

I laughed, despite feeling like I'd rather curl up in a ball and cry, and leaned my head on Trace's shoulder. "He's not that shitty. I kind of like him." I smiled at Gramps as we stopped at the end of his bed.

"Come here, the both of you. I'm not contagious. It's not like you can catch cancer if I breathe on you."

Only a Wentworth would crack jokes as he faced death.

Trace and I separated, standing with one of us on each side of the bed.

"I've missed you." Gramps looked at us both.

"I've missed you *too*." I started to cry, because I knew that in a matter of time I'd be missing him for the rest of my life. I would never forget Warren. I looked up at Trace, and my heart broke at the look of hopelessness in his eyes. One day, when we had kids, I was going to make sure they knew how remarkable their great-grandfather and grandpa had been. I had never met Trey, Trace's dad, but I knew if he was anything like the rest of the family he was a special person and the world wasn't nearly as beautiful of a place because he was gone.

"Don't cry." Gramps reached up shakily to wipe my tears away. "An old man like me doesn't deserve your tears."

"You deserve everything," I sobbed, reaching down to hug his small frame.

I never wanted to let him go. A part of me was convinced that I could keep him alive by sheer will power.

I pulled away, wiping at my wet face. I don't think I had ever cried this much or this hard in my whole life.

Gramps looked at me sadly and I blurted, "I'm sorry."

"Don't be sorry, sweetie." He looked up at Trace and took one of his hands as well as one of mine. "I hear you two went and got married without me."

"Sorry, Gramps," Trace mumbled, bowing his head in shame.

"Don't be sorry," Gramps repeated the same words he'd spoken to me. "I'm happy this one" —he squeezed my hand lightly— "is finally a true Wentworth, but I do have something to ask of you both."

"Anything," I gasped. "We'll do anything you want."

With a shaky breath, he explained, "I only have a few days left to live, and if it's not too much to ask—" He became overwhelmed by a coughing fit and couldn't continue for a moment. When he recovered, he said, "All I want is to see you walk down the aisle, Olivia. I want to watch you and my grandson exchange vows as you embark on the next step in your life. I know you were planning to have a ceremony where you exchanged rings in a few more weeks, but I won't be around for that." His hand tightened around mine. "Please, this is all I want."

I glanced up at Trace and we both had the same look in our eyes. How could we not grant Gramps' dying wish?

"Of course," we said simultaneously.

"I'll talk to Lily and see if we can move things up," I croaked. You'd think eventually I'd run out of tears to cry but they kept flowing. "We'll do whatever it takes," I promised.

"I know you will, sweetie." He craned his neck, trying to kiss my cheek. I lowered my head and his papery lips pressed softly against my skin. I was surprised by how cold his lips were.

"Gramps, there's something I need to tell you," Trace started.

I looked over at him and released Gramps' hand. "I'll step out and talk with your mom."

"No!" he cried. "No," he said in a softer tone. "I need you here too. You should hear this."

"What's going on?" I tilted my head to the side as I looked at him.

"Let's sit down and get comfortable." Trace was already pulling a chair up to the side of Gramps' bed.

I eyed him nervously, but sat down. I took Gramps' cool hand into mine once more.

"What is it?" Gramps asked, eyeing Trace questioningly. "You look like you're going to throw up. Whatever it is, I'm sure it's not as bad as you think it is. Spit it out, boy."

Trace took a deep breath. "I don't want to take over the company, Gramps. I *can't* be a CEO. It won't make me happy and I refuse to be miserable for the rest of my life. I'm sorry. I really am. I *tried*. But it's not for me. I hate to disappoint you, but I have to do what's right for me."

Gramps let out a sigh of relief and then began to laugh hysterically. "It's about damn time you grew a pair and told me," he chortled. "I would've never let you take the company, knowing you hated it. *But* I wanted you to come to that decision yourself."

"You mean—" Trace started but Gramps cut him off.

"Yes, I knew you hated it. I've known this life wouldn't be for you since you were a small boy. No matter what you do, I'll always be proud of you. When I'm gone, I'll be smiling down on you from above, proud to call you my grandson, even if your hard headedness drives me crazy."

"I love you," Trace sobbed, standing and kicking the chair back as he hugged Gramps.

I watched them hug each other, two generations of Wentworths, and it killed me that Gramps was leaving us. Why did he have to get cancer? Why did he have to die? It wasn't fair!

I couldn't take it anymore, I had to get out of the hospital room. I opened the door and fled down the hall as far and as fast as my feet would carry me. I hadn't made it far when I collapsed onto the floor, sobbing hysterically. I rested my back against the wall and drew my knees up. Burying my face in my hands, I let myself cry. Not just a few tears, but a torrent of them. I let them cleanse me and try to heal the pain I felt inside. But I knew I could never really be healed. There would always be a hole in my heart where my love for Gramps was held and so brutally cut out.

Someone sat down beside me and arms wrapped around me. Trace's scent enveloped me and I grasped his shirt in my hands.

My tears were waning and anger was replacing sadness.

"It isn't fair." I smacked his solid chest as hard as I could, like this was his fault. "Why? Tell me why he has to die. This isn't right. He doesn't deserve this," I cried, hitting him repeatedly with the sides of my fists. I had never felt anger like this before, not even after Aaron tried to kill me.

Trace didn't say anything as I hit him. When my fists fell to my sides, he pulled me onto his lap and rested his chin on top of my head.

"Life is never fair," he whispered, "and it really fucking sucks."

I clung to his shoulders, getting tears on his shirt, but he didn't seem to mind.

He ran his fingers through my hair in an effort to soothe me.

When I was calmed down, I laid a hand over his heart. "I'm sorry for hitting you," I whispered, ashamed of myself. "I shouldn't have done that." My hair fell around me to conceal my face.

"It's okay. I understand. I feel like punching a wall, so I get it." He pressed his lips lightly against my forehead.

"Did you really mean what you told Gramps? You're not going to take over the business?"

"Yeah," he sighed. "I meant it. You were right, God, you're always right." He leaned his head against the wall and gazed at the ceiling. "I need to do what makes me happy. Being a mechanic does that for me, and there's something else I need to tell you ..." he paused, taking a deep breath.

"What is it?" I cupped his stubbled cheek in the palm of my hand.

"A week before we left, Pete called me into his office to

talk. He's older and not in the best shape, and he wants to sell the shop ... to me."

"To you? Like, to own?"

"Yeah." He nodded. "Pete said he trusts me to take it over. He doesn't have any kids and he wants it to go to someone who really cares about cars. Apparently, I'm his only choice. If I tell him no, he'll close down the shop for good."

Despite the situation we were currently surrounded by, I found myself smiling.

"I'm so proud of you." I kissed his chin.

"Proud? Why?"

"For being the man I love and a person I can respect." I traced a finger over his collarbone.

He kissed me lightly and stood, pulling me up with him.

"Let's go find my mom and get this wedding figured out." We turned down the hallway and a nurse directed us to the waiting room.

Lily was asleep in one of the chairs, her neck tilted at an uncomfortable angle. She'd definitely be feeling that later.

"Mom." Trace shook her knee.

She came sputtering awake. "What? What? Did something bad happen?" She looked around hastily.

"No, nothing like that, Mom." Trace crouched in front of her.

"What is it, then?" She rubbed her eyes. "You ready to go?"

Trace didn't hear her. Instead he was looking around the large waiting room. "Where's Grammy?"

"I had Trent take her home. She was tired and wanted to stay here, but being in this place isn't going to do her any good."

"Right, of course. Anyway, we need to talk to you about

something," Trace explained as I took the seat beside Lily. Before she could question him, he continued, "We need to move the ceremony up. Do you think you can have something ready in three days?"

"Three days?" she gasped, startled. "Trace, are you crazy? Three weeks is pushing it. Three days is impossible."

"Make it happen."

Her mouth gaped open.

"Mom, he doesn't have much time and Gramps wants to be there. Move it up. I know you can put together a beautiful wedding for us." He reached for me and took my hand. "The *whole* family needs to be there."

Rubbing her face, she eyed each of us tiredly. "You two better love me a lot." I knew asking Lily to plan a wedding so quickly was unfair, especially with Gramps in the hospital, but it needed to be done.

"Thanks, Mom." Trace hugged her tightly. "You're the best mom anyone could have." He planted a loud kiss on her cheek. "Now, can you do me another favor and take Olivia home and go home yourself? I'll stay with Gramps."

"Are you sure?" she asked. "You have to be tired from your flight."

"I'm fine," he assured her. "If I go home all I'll do is worry and keep Olivia awake."

"Okay." She stood and hugged him. "Call me if you need anything. I'll be here as quick as I can."

I kissed Trace goodbye and followed Lily outside. We were both quiet as she drove me to the apartment, but when we reached the parking lot and she parked, she said, "Promise me you'll be there for him through this. Since Trey died, Gramps has been like a father to Trace. I'm worried about how he'll react. He needs you."

"I'll be there for him, no matter what," I promised, even though I wasn't sure I could do it.

"Thank you." She patted my cheek.

I dug the key to the apartment out of my purse and grabbed our bags from the trunk, hobbling up the steps.

When I opened the door, a streak of black ran at me, knocking me to the ground.

A long pink tongue flicked out and swiped over my cheek. "Ace!" I cried in delight. "I missed you, buddy!" I hadn't been expecting Ace to be here, but sweet Trent had brought him home since he knew we were back. He was getting a big hug for this. Now, I didn't have to be at home alone and I had my fur baby to comfort me. After Ace had thoroughly licked my face, he looked over my shoulder for Trace. "Sorry, Ace, but Daddy isn't home yet." I scratched his ears. It's just you and me tonight. Are you going to keep me safe?"

At my words the large lab ran over to his basket of dog toys, grabbed his Jabba the Hutt squeaker toy, and ran into the bedroom. A second later I heard the thump as he jumped on the bed.

Shaking my head, I got to my feet, and carried the bags into the room.

After a quick shower I climbed into the bed. Suddenly, I was exhausted. I'd been running on adrenaline since the moment we got the phone call and the day's events had finally caught up with me. Curling my body against Ace's, I promptly fell asleep.

CHAPTER TWENTY-ONE

A banging on the front door had me sitting up and instantly alert.

"What the hell?" I groaned, looking at the clock. It was after nine in the morning, but after everything I'd been through yesterday, I wanted to sleep till noon.

I grabbed a jacket and tugged it on as I headed to the door. I opened it to find Avery standing there, her hair blowing in a slight breeze with sunglasses holding the long strands back, and there was a huge smile on her face.

She hugged me. "I missed you!"

"I missed you too." I hugged her back, a bit surprised by her exuberance since she'd been such a downer before we left. She stepped away from me and I took a moment to study her. Her hair was more vibrant and her skin had a rosy hue.

"You seem ... happy," I commented as I closed the door.

"Luca and I are back together," she beamed. "We had a heart to heart, and I told him that I couldn't live without him. He's it for me, Livie. I was being stubborn and fighting what I felt for him. But I realized that he and I ... We're perfect for each other."

I rolled my eyes. I'd known that since the moment they met

each other. I couldn't believe it had taken her three years to figure that out.

My eyes landed on the shirt she was wearing and I began to laugh.

"What? You don't like it?" She plucked at the red garment.

"It's very you." *I'm the Maid of Honor B*tch*, I read the shirt over again.

"I thought so too." She smiled, doing a little twirl. "You need to get dressed. We have to go dress shopping. Lily knows a place in Tysons that should have something beautiful and in your size so we don't have to worry about alterations."

I hurried into the bedroom and changed out of my pajamas into clothes. Avery stood in the doorway, looking at her bright red fingernails.

"You know," she said, "I should really still be mad at you for getting married without having me there. I mean, I'm your best friend, Livie. But I'm so happy to be back with Luca that I don't care."

"It's not like everyone else was there and you weren't invited." I shimmied into a pair of shorts. "It was only Trace and me."

"Do you think that matters?" She fluffed the ends of her hair. She smiled slowly. "I'm sorry, I'm not mad ... anymore. I just like to give you a hard time."

"I know you do." I opened a drawer and grabbed a shirt. Before I could put it on, Avery yanked the fabric from my hands. "Avery!"

"Seriously, girl, we're going into the city. You can do better than this and shorts."

"You're wearing shorts and a t-shirt!" I accused.

"But I'm the Maid of Honor. I can't outdo the bride," she reasoned, going through the closet.

"Isn't that just on the wedding day?"

She turned to me, rolling her eyes. "If I tried to look my best, I'd outshine you."

My mouth fell open.

"I'm *kidding*, Olivia. Geez, I'm not that much of a bitch. Honestly. Haven't you known me long enough to know when I'm being serious and when I'm not?"

"Yeah, sorry." I tucked a piece of hair behind my ear. "I'm going to go brush my hair and what not while you pick out my clothes. You know, since you seem to think I'm your doll or something."

"Damn straight, and you're a pretty little doll."

Shaking my head, I wandered out of the bedroom and into the bathroom. I put on makeup, still having to hide the slightly yellowed skin around my eye, and let my hair hang down instead of braiding it out of the way.

When I came back into the bedroom Avery had a peach dress laid out on top of the bed with a pair of brown cowboy boots. I'd swear neither were from my wardrobe.

"Where'd you get those?"

"Your closet, duh." She looked at me like I was stupid. "Where else would I have gotten it?"

"I don't know." I shrugged, fingering the soft fabric of the dress. "I just don't remember this."

Avery shook her head, fighting a smile. "That's because you wear the same thing all the time."

"I don't like getting dressed up." I frowned. "It's not comfortable."

"You're ridiculous." She put her hands on her hips. "Now

get dressed and meet me in the car. We'll stop for breakfast on our way." With that, she flounced out of the room and outside. The front door slammed closed behind her. It wasn't the first time I was glad we didn't have neighbors.

I got dressed and grabbed a cereal bar before joining her outside. Knowing Avery, she would forget to stop for breakfast and I'd be left starving. At least the cereal bar would be *something*.

"Hurry up, biotch," she called from inside her red Volkswagen Beetle convertible. She slid her sunglasses on and waved me forward.

I reluctantly made my way down the steps and slid into her car.

"Ready to have some fun?" she asked.

"Yes," I said, even though inside I was screaming *no*.

"Let's find you a wedding dress." She grinned, speeding out of the parking lot.

"How about you drive like a sane person so I don't throw up on all the pretty dresses when we get there?" I retorted.

Her foot eased off the gas pedal. "You're such a party pooper. First, no strippers, and now you won't even let me speed."

"You'll thank me when you don't have a speeding ticket."

"Oh, whatever." She turned the blinker on, making a hasty turn. "You're still a fun sucker." She grabbed a pack of gum from the center console and unwrapped the stick, tossing the wrapper into the back of her car. "You want a piece?" She held the pack out to me, already snapping away.

"No thanks."

"So, besides getting married, what else did you do while you were gone?" she asked, getting on the interstate.

Make memories. "Oh, you know, just had fun."

"Come on, girl. You've got to give me more detail than that."

"We went bungee jumping," I replied, looking out the window.

"Bungee jumping? Like, where you jump off a bridge?"

"Yeah, that."

"You're insane," she gasped in disbelief. "I would never do that. I'd be afraid I'd die."

"I didn't want to, but it was worth it." I shrugged. I knew there was no point in keeping the information from her, after all they'd be at the wedding, so I found myself saying, "Trace found my grandparents."

"*What?*" she exclaimed. "Like, Derek's parents?"

I nodded. "Yeah, they're great. I met my uncle too. He looks so much like Derek that for a moment I thought my mom had lied and he was still alive."

"Wow, that's intense."

"They're coming to the wedding," I explained. "I hope my mom doesn't get mad."

"Why would she?"

I shrugged. "I don't know."

"You worry way too much, Livie." Avery shook her head. "Just chillax." Straightening her shoulders, she said, "I'm excited to meet them."

"They're really amazing." I smiled proudly. "Margaret, my grandma, and Douglas, my grandpa, own a store in their town. It's the cutest place ever. She loves to make things, especially origami. She taught me how to make origami stars and even gave me a jar full of ones made by my dad. It's like I finally have a piece of him." After I'd showered last night, I'd taken the jar out of my bag and sat it on the coffee table in the living room so I could look at it every day.

"Wow, that's really amazing." Avery smiled at me, and I knew she truly meant it. "I can't even begin to tell you how happy I am that you've met them."

"Thanks." I fiddled with a piece of hair to busy my fingers. "So, where exactly is this place in Tysons?" I asked. I'd lived in Winchester for four years and had only been in the city area a few times. Tysons was close to Washington D.C. and had a bunch of fancy shops. It was a nice area, but not exactly my cup of tea. I preferred simplicity.

"I'm not sure. Lily gave me good directions so I doubt we'll get lost, plus I have a navigation system if that happens. I think it's near the mall, though."

"Is it going to be super fancy?"

"Um, we are shopping for a wedding dress so probably." s

I wrinkled my nose. "I'm warning you now, Avery. I *do not* want some fluffy dress that looks like it belongs in a museum, not on an actual bride. I want something simple and flowy, since the wedding will be outside at the Wentworth mansion. Understand?"

She frowned. "At least try one on." She waved a single finger in front of my face. I smacked her hand down.

"Not happening." I crossed my arms over my chest. "I'm not wasting my time trying on a dress I'll never wear."

"You suck." She stuck her tongue out at me.

Wanting to get the topic off of me, I asked, "So what happened with Luca?"

"I decided to stop being an idiot and tell him how I really feel. I told him everything."

"And by everything, you mean ...?" I prompted.

"Olivia" —her hands tightened on the steering wheel— "this is something difficult for me to talk about. It's why I push people away, and it's why I fucked random guys for like … ever."

"Okay." I swallowed thickly, preparing myself for what she had to say.

"God, I don't want to tell you this." She kept her eyes on the road and away from me.

"Avery," I spoke her name softly, "you don't have to tell me anything you don't want to. I'm not going to hate you if you keep secrets." Even this many years later I had never told Avery about my *Live List*. Before I met Trace, I had been embarrassed about it and I knew if I told her she'd try to cross everything off in one night. But once I met Trace and confessed my list to him, it sort of became *our* thing and I didn't want to share it with anyone else.

"No." She shook her head. "I need to tell you. But you have to understand something—no one but Luca knows this. It's taken me a long time to admit that what happened to me was real. But it happened and it sucks. But you move on. Talking about it makes me feel better." She sighed deeply. "My only hope is that you don't look at me differently once I tell you."

"Gosh, Avery. Look at what I went through with finding out about my real dad and then after Aaron tried to kill me. I can handle it," I told my best friend with the utmost sincerity.

"It seems weird telling you this in the car." She forced a laugh. "But I don't have a choice now."

"You always have a choice, Avery. You can wait."

She took a deep breath to steady herself and continued like I hadn't said anything. "You remember how I told you growing up that my parents were gone a lot?"

"Yeah." I nodded, my brow furrowing.

"When my parents left on their extended business trips and whatnot, my dad's sister and her husband would stay at the house with us. They couldn't have kids so they said they didn't mind." She began to tear up and my heart clenched. "One time, when I was eleven, my uncle said he was going to take me up to bed and read me a story. They always read a story to me, but that night Ray didn't read me a story."

"What did he do, Avery?" I asked, not really wanting to know the answer.

She turned her head toward me slightly before her eyes flicked back to the road.

"He pushed me on my bed and he raped me. I screamed and tried to fight him, but he held me down and nothing stopped him." She was crying now and her teeth were clenched.

"Didn't your aunt hear you scream? Your brothers?" I gasped, horrified by what she told me. I had known there had to be *something* to make Avery the way she was. But I'd always assumed it had to do with abandonment issues from being left by her parents all the time. Never, in a million years, had I ever suspected something like this.

She shook her head. "They were all in the basement, watching a movie. No one heard, unfortunately."

I didn't know what to say. Frankly, there wasn't anything I *could* say. I didn't understand how anyone could do something like that another person, let alone a child.

"Avery," I started and words failed me.

"It's okay." She looked over at me. "For a long time, I blocked it from my mind. After that, I put up a fit and my parents didn't ask them to watch us anymore. Actually, shortly before graduation I saw them. It was the first time I had seen Ray since he'd—" she paused, then forced the word out through clenched teeth "—raped me. Up until then, it had been easy for me to pretend it hadn't happened. But seeing him sent all those memories rushing back at me and I felt so *helpless*. I lashed out at you and Luca, because you're the two people I care about the most." She swallowed thickly. "I was really mean to him and so we broke up. He told me he'd be waiting when I decided to tell him what the fuck my problem was. So, I finally told him. If I expect to have a future with him, he needed to know everything." She glanced over at me and it was like a weight had been lifted off her shoulders by telling me.

"Oh, Avery." I desperately wanted to reach over and hug my best friend but since we were driving that wasn't exactly the best idea.

"It's okay, Livie. I knew I needed to tell you, so you would understand why I was being so distant. Seeing Ray made me want to close myself off from everyone and I'm sorry about that. It's the only way I know how to deal with things. That and fucking guys. But I'm a new woman now." She squared her shoulders, turning into a parking lot. I looked up, surprised to see that we were already in Tysons. I guessed we'd been talking longer than I thought. "Luca changed me. No, that's not right. *He* didn't change me. But the love I feel for him did."

She parked the car and I could finally hug her.

"What was that for?" she asked when I pulled away.

Wiping my tears away, I answered, "You needed a hug."

"I did?"

I forced a laugh. "You definitely did."

"I don't want me telling you this to change things between us." She stared at her hands so she didn't have to look at me. "I'm still me, Livie."

"I know you are." I took her hand, trying to offer as much comfort as I possibly could. "I'm glad you told me, but I'm sorry you had to go through that. No one should ever have to suffer through a tragedy like that alone. I know you probably don't want to talk about it, and that's fine, but if it ever gets too hard you know you can come to me. I love you, Avery." I hugged her again. "You may be slightly crazy," I said as I laughed, wiping away a few stray tears, "but you're my best friend."

"I love you too, Livie." Her chest shook as she fought tears. Shaking her head, she said, "Let's find you a wedding dress."

Leave it to Avery to be the one to change the subject.

I put on a brave face, knowing I needed to be strong for her. Besides she'd kick my ass if I ever looked at her with pity.

I followed her into the fancy upscale store. Everything was white with shiny chrome accents. It kind of reminded me of a museum, where you could look but not touch. I frowned, wondering if I was really going to be able to find a dress I liked here. I mean, I knew they had loads of beautiful dresses, which was obvious from the mannequins scattered about. But would any of them be *me*? I stopped in front of a dress that looked so heavy a crane probably had to be used to lift it. And oh, my goodness, it had feathers coming out of the back. *Feathers*!

"Uh, Avery," I called out, "I think we should go somewhere else."

A hastily cleared throat had me turning around to face Avery and a saleswoman. Oh, crap. "Oh, um, I mean, the dresses are lovely, but you know ... a bit much." I blushed, wishing I could ram my fist in my mouth so I'd stop talking.

"Lily told me you'd be coming," the saleswoman said. Her dark hair was pulled back into a severe bun, reminding me of a schoolteacher from many years ago, and I feared she might pull out a ruler to smack me. "She mentioned you wouldn't like some of the more outlandish dresses we sell. I have a room set up for you with some dresses I've already pulled."

"Oh, great. Are they ..." I looked over my shoulder at the feather Cinderella-style ball gown, "Not so big and feathery?"

She laughed and it softened her features. "You're funny." She reached for my hand and began pulling me along behind her.

"I wasn't trying to be," I mumbled.

She dragged me into a large room and once Avery was inside she closed the door.

"I also have some dresses laid aside for your Maid of Honor." She wrinkled her nose at Avery's shirt. "As well as your mother and Lily."

"Are they coming?" I looked between the saleslady and Avery.

"Later," Avery answered.

"Oh, and how rude of me. My name is Louise." The saleswoman held out a hand.

I took it, giving it a light shake. "Olivia."

"I hope we can find the perfect dress for you and make all your wedding dreams come true."

I tried to hide my laugh at her words. Avery shot me a glare, which made it even harder not to snicker.

"Come, come." Louise took me over to a rack of gowns. "Browse through these and see if anything catches your eye."

I flipped through the dresses, surprised that most of them were fairly normal looking. Lily definitely did tell her what I liked. I would have to thank her for that later.

"Let's try this one." I pulled out a dress with a small train with antique lace and short sleeves.

"Seriously, Livie, *that's* the one you choose?" Avery wrinkled her nose, glaring at the dress.

"It's pretty and I like it." I held the dress close to my body.

"It looks like something my great-grandma would have gotten married in," she scoffed. She pushed herself up from the chair and began to look through the rack. She pulled out a tight-fitting mermaid style gown with a low neckline. "You should wear something like this. It's sexy."

I rolled my eyes. It amazed me that Avery could confess something to traumatizing to me one second, and be talking about sexy wedding dresses the next. I wanted to talk to her about it more, but I knew that would probably never happen. Avery had never been one to sit around and talk about her feelings.

"Yes, so while we're saying my vows my boobs can pop out and Trace can get a preview of what's to come," I said sarcastically.

Avery rolled her eyes and put the dress back on the rack. "It's not like he hasn't seen them before."

"And I'm sure the rest of the guests would enjoy the peep show as well?"

"Whatever. Don't try it. But at least pick something not so grandma-ish. You're twenty-two, Livie. Act like it."

"I'm trying it on." I turned my back on her and handed the dress to Louise who was currently pretending that she hadn't been listening to our conversation.

Louise helped me into the dress and onto a raised platform. I stared at my reflection in the mirror, marveling at the fact that I was wearing a freakin' wedding dress. I knew we were already married, but seeing myself in a dress made it even more real. I smoothed my hands down the lacy fabric and turned so I could see the back of the dress. It was beautiful and I loved it, despite Avery frowning in the mirror's reflection, but I knew it wasn't the one. I wanted to take Trace's breath away the first time he saw me in my wedding gown, and I knew this dress wasn't the one to do that.

"This isn't the one." I shook my head at my reflection and stepped off the platform.

Louise unzipped the dress and hung it back up.

I tried on an A-line style next but thought it was a bit too fancy and big for an outdoor wedding. Oh, gosh—I really hoped I didn't get as hot as I did at my mom's wedding. That had sucked.

"Do you have anything really simple but pretty?"

Louise laughed at my vague description. "Let me go check the stockroom and see if we still have the one I'm thinking of. I'll be right back," she excused herself from the room.

"If I was getting married, I'd wear something like that." Avery pointed to a dress in the corner of the room on a mannequin. It was on the risqué side with a low-cut top and high slit on the side.

"That's an interesting dress," I replied. I wanted to tell her it was slutty, but I thought that would be rude so I kept my mouth shut. Besides, she wasn't getting married ... yet. I could talk her out of something like that when the time came.

Louise returned, closing the door behind her. "We still have it and it's in your size. We might need to shorten it a bit if you like this one."

"Let's see it." I smiled kindly.

Louise held the dress up and my jaw dropped. It was exactly what I had seen in my head. Everything about it was *me*.

"Oh, my," I gasped, reaching out to finger the fabric.

"Do you like it?" Louise dared to ask.

"It's beautiful," I gasped.

She smiled wide and helped me into the dress. When I looked in the mirror, tears sprung to my eyes. "This is my dress." I spun around giddily. It fit my curves perfectly and didn't swallow me whole like some dresses. It was flowy with a small train and strapless. It had a sweetheart neckline that showed off a little bit of my chest but I didn't feel like I was going to fall out of it. The top also had really pretty beaded detailing. I felt like a fairy princess in it.

"Excellent!" Louise clapped her hands together. "Let me go grab one of the seamstresses so we can bring this up a bit." She pointed to the hemline I was bound to trip over. "Would you like a veil? Headband?"

"No." I shook my head.

Louise hadn't been gone long when the door cracked open.

"Mom!" I exclaimed, hopping off the platform and running toward her. I hugged her tightly. I hadn't realized how much I missed her until now. "Look at you!" I gasped at the size of her stomach.

She placed a hand over the bulge. "Four more months until little Abigail joins the family."

I paused, repeating her words in my head. "Abigail?" I said hesitantly. "The baby's a girl?!"

"Yeah, another little girl." She smiled as I hugged her again.

"I can't believe this," I gasped. "Abigail is such a pretty name too."

"We're going to call her Abby," she explained, hugging a teary-eyed Avery. Obviously, this was news to her too.

"Hi, Lily." I smiled at my mother-in-law as she entered the room.

"Hey, gorgeous." She chuckled. "Oh, my God! That dress is beautiful!" Lily exclaimed, looking the dress up and down, and then forcing me to turn around so she could see the back. "Please tell me this is the one you're getting. It's exquisite."

"Yeah, this is the one." I spun around in circles so the dress fanned around me.

"It's so gorgeous, Liv," my mom gasped. "You couldn't have picked a better dress." Avery would probably have liked to argue that I *could* have found something better, but she kept her mouth shut, resolving to the fact that I wasn't going to wear anything scandalous.

Louise joined us once again, wheeling in another rack of dresses. A seamstress breezed in behind her and over to me. I stood on the platform and let her measure me and begin to place pins where adjustments needed to be made.

"Olivia?" Lily asked, shuffling through the dresses on the new rack. "What color were you thinking for Avery's dress?"

"I don't really have anything specific in mind. Something light colored, though."

"I think this will be perfect." Lily pulled a dress out and held it up. "Do you like this one?"

It was a short blush-colored dress with flower detailing on the side and a black ribbon around the waist. "That's perfect!"

Louise took the dress from Lily and helped Avery into it.

I thought the dress looked absolutely gorgeous on Avery. It hugged all of her curves and the color looked pretty with her pale skin and red hair.

"What do you think?" I asked her, hoping she didn't turn into a total diva.

"It's perfect, as long as you like it," she replied, looking at her reflection wistfully.

"I do love it. We'll take it," I told Louise.

The seamstress finished marking the alterations and informed me I needed to change. Once I was out of the dress, she took it and hurried from the room. "I'll have the alterations done in an hour or so," she called before the door closed behind her.

Since we'd found a dress for Avery and myself, that left Lily and my mom. I hoped they had something my mom would like and still be comfortable in.

Louise pulled a few dresses for Lily. The first two were horrible and so I decided to intervene.

"Do you have anything that isn't so ... frumpy?" I asked. "Lily isn't old, and even if she was, she doesn't need to dress like it," I explained, hoping I didn't hurt anyone's feelings. But honestly, the current dress she had on looked like a box. I never knew fabric could look so square.

Lily laughed. "Oh, Olivia, I love you so much."

I blushed. "It's the truth."

Louise left the room and returned with a floor-length amethyst gown. I knew as soon as it was zipped that it was the one.

"What do you think, Olivia?" Lily asked as she assessed her appearance in the mirror.

"I think we've found a winner."

Finding a dress for my mom took a longer amount of time, but Louise finally found a maternity gown that fit and looked good on her. The Kelly-green color looked amazing with her glowing complexion and the Grecian style fit her growing belly.

I was so relieved that in a matter of hours we'd managed to find dresses for everyone. I'd been really worried that planning something so last minute would result in less than satisfactory dresses. Thank goodness for Lily and her connections.

By the time we'd left, all the alterations had already been made and we were able to take the dresses with us. We all stopped to eat a late lunch together before heading our separate ways.

When Avery dropped me off at the apartment, I left my dress with her so that Trace wouldn't see it and headed inside.

I called out for him but there was no answer. It didn't look like he'd been home to shower or anything. I hated to think he'd been stuck in the depressing hospital all night and day.

I tended to Ace and grabbed my car keys.

Twenty minutes later, I walked into the hospital and up to Gramps' room.

Gramps wasn't lying in his bed. Instead, he was sitting in a chair and they were using the bed as a table.

"What are you two doing?" I laughed as the door clicked closed behind me.

"Playing chess." Trace chuckled. "I'm going to win."

"Not a chance," Gramps warned.

I pulled up a chair and sat down to watch them finish their game. I wasn't surprised when Gramps won.

"What are you doing here?" Gramps asked me as Trace

helped him back in the bed. "Surely you're not just here to see me. I'm not that handsome to look at anymore."

"I think you're very handsome. I know where Trace gets all his looks from." I poked my husband's cheek.

"Yeah, well, he certainly didn't get his smart mouth from me," he chortled.

"Oh, please, Gramps. Don't act like you aren't a smartass." Trace chuckled, adjusting the blankets around Warren.

"Can you believe my grandson talks to me like this? I don't know why you married this fool," he shook his head. "You could do so much better."

"Thanks, Gramps. Way to make me feel loved," Trace put a hand to his heart.

Ignoring them, I gripped the footboard of the bed in my hands and leaned forward. "There's something I need to talk to you about."

"Oh," Warren cleared his throat. "Of course."

Trace eyed me, wondering what was going on.

"I know you're sick and probably aren't up to it but …" I took a deep breath. "I don't have a dad to walk me down the aisle and I was wondering if you would …?" I bit my lip nervously as I waited for him to reply.

He pushed himself up in the bed. "I don't care if it takes me ten whole minutes, I *will* walk you down that aisle, sweet Olivia." There was a determination in his eyes that had been missing before.

I swallowed thickly. "Thank you."

Having Gramps walk me down the aisle meant the world to me. It was a memory I would be able to hold close to my heart and cherish for the rest of my life. Looking at him now, it was difficult to believe that the doctors didn't think he'd live past the end of the week. I didn't want to say goodbye. In fact, I refused to. Saying goodbye implied that something was ending, and I knew that Gramps' life was really just beginning.

"Don't cry." Gramps frowned at me.

I reached up and felt my cheek. My fingers came away damp. I hadn't realized I was crying. Maybe my body had become so used to the emotion that it didn't even register it anymore.

"Sorry," I mumbled, taking the tissue Trace handed to me. "I don't mean to cry. I want you to know that it means a lot to me that you're going to do this."

"I'm *honored* that you'd ask me, Olivia." His words ended in a cough and when he pulled his hand away from his mouth, blood stained his lips.

"Gramps!" Trace exclaimed, jumping up and cleaning his mouth free of the red stain. "Are you okay?"

"Yeah." Gramps waved his concern away. "That happens sometimes. It's normal."

"That doesn't seem normal," Trace said.

"What's normal about cancer?" Gramps countered.

Neither of us could argue with that, but Trace still told me to find a nurse.

The nurse I found was quick to come and check on Gramps. She assured us that he was fine and we had nothing to worry about. I wanted to argue that the man was dying so we had plenty to worry about, but that would've been rude.

"Trace, you should really go home and get some rest."

He took a deep breath and let his head fall forward into his hands. "I can't."

"How about this, go home and shower, eat, take a nap, and

then come back in a few hours? I'll be here. You know I'll take care of him," I assured him.

Trace looked between Gramps and me. "I don't know."

"Trace, the last twenty-four hours have been extremely stressful. Go home and relax for a little bit. You're no good to anyone if you're dead on your feet." I eyed the dark circles under his eyes. I hated seeing him this tired and stressed.

"Fine," he reluctantly agreed. "I'll be back tonight."

He hugged Gramps goodbye and gave me a soft kiss. I handed him my car keys and he chuckled. "I get to drive the purple chick car?"

"Don't diss my car. It's cute." I laughed.

"Kittens are cute. Cars are meant to be sexy."

"Whatever," I laughed, taking the seat he had vacated so I'd be closer to Gramps.

"See you guys soon," he called as he left.

Once the door was closed, Gramps let out a pent-up breath, and said, "Good, he's gone. I thought he'd *never* leave."

I snorted at that. "Was he driving you nuts?"

"Are you kidding me? He was like a silly little nursemaid." Miming Trace's voice, he continued, "Gramps, are you thirsty? Are you hungry? Can I fluff your pillow? Do you need anything? I was tempted to ask the nurse if she could give him a tranquilizer so he'd shut up."

"Gramps," I laughed, "that's not very nice."

"At least you're pretty to look at!" he exclaimed.

"I'm glad I can be of some service to you." I leaned forward. "Are you thirsty?" I asked to mess with him.

He narrowed his eyes. "Don't start now."

"Sorry, I couldn't help myself." I giggled. Crossing my legs,

I asked, "Are you really okay walking me down the aisle? If it's too much just say so."

"I'm walking you down that aisle, sweetheart. Don't even try to talk me out of it now that you've asked. I don't even know why they still have me in here." He pointed to the bare white walls of the hospital room. "There's nothing more they can do for me." He looked at me sadly.

"We can hope." I reached for his hand. "When you think there's nothing left, there's always hope."

"I wish that was the case, Olivia. But my time has come to an end. I'm not ready, but I've accepted it. I *am* going to see you and Trace get married, though. I *will* make it through that."

I scooted the chair closer to the bed, so that I didn't have to reach so far for him.

"How can you be so sure?" I asked, my eyes roaming over all of the wires hooked up to him.

"Because I'm a Wentworth, and we're a stubborn breed of male. I may be dying, but I'll go when I say I'm ready."

"You're something else." I shook my head.

"My grandson is a lot like me." He chuckled. "Are you prepared to handle that for the rest of your life?"

"Yes," I answered without hesitation.

"Good. I do have one request of you ... Okay, actually two," he coughed.

"What is it?" I asked.

"First off, I'd really appreciate it if you *wouldn't* name your firstborn son after me. Warren is a really bad name and I'd hate for the poor fellow to be stuck with it just because I had to go and die before my time. Don't name him Trey, either. Give the kid his own name," he said gruffly, shaking a finger warningly at me. "Trace will want to be sentimental and that isn't fair to the kid."

I couldn't help but laugh at him. "What name would you suggest for this future firstborn son?"

He pondered that for a moment. "Dean," he finally said. "Dean Wentworth has a nice ring to it."

"I like that." I smiled. "Dean is a good name."

"Glad you like it." He smiled and there was a twinkle in his eye that had been missing earlier. "The second thing I need you to do is take these." He reached over to the opposite nightstand and grabbed two letters in envelopes. He handed them to me and I saw that one had my name on it while the other had Trace's. "I want you to read these when ... when I'm gone." Tears pooled in his eyes. "I'm giving them to you, because I knew Trace would rip them up if I gave them to him."

I stared down at the letters in my hands and my heart felt even heavier than it had before.

"Gramps," I choked, overcome by emotion.

"I don't mean to make you cry." He pressed a shaky hand against my cheek. "But I had to give them to you."

I nodded my head in understanding. I tucked the letters away in my purse and wiped my eyes. "No more talk about dying or babies." I cracked a smile. "Let's do something fun, but not chess. I suck at that."

"There's a room down the hall where the nurses have board games for patients. If you ask one of the ladies at the desk they'll take you to it."

"Okay." I stood. "Anything in particular you want?"

"See if they have Clue." He smiled, pushing the button on the railing of the bed to raise it.

I stopped at the nurses' station outside the room and one of them led me down the hall to a storage closet full of odds and ends. On the top shelf I spotted Clue, but since I was so short I had trouble reaching it. I found a stepstool and even with that I had to stand on my tiptoes to reach the box. I grabbed it off the shelf and headed back to Gramps' room.

"Look what I found," I sing-songed, waving the box in front of me. When I lowered it, I saw that Gramps had fallen asleep. "Well ..." I set the box on the table. "Another time then."

I settled in the chair, hoping Trace had made it home and was actually relaxing like he needed to. But knowing him, I was sure that was the last thing he was doing.

CHAPTER TWENTY-TWO

"Olivia."

I hadn't been in a very deep sleep and I jolted awake at the sound of my name.

I looked around the darkened hospital room, rubbing my eyes and smearing my makeup.

"Trace," I yawned. "What time is it?"

"Three." He shrugged. "I meant to be back by midnight but I slept longer than I wanted."

I glanced at Gramps' sleeping form and then up at my husband. "I'm too sleepy to drive back so I'll sleep on the couch." I pointed to the couch covered in plastic in the corner of the room. I knew it wouldn't be comfortable, but I didn't want to leave. My reasoning had nothing to do with driving, like I'd told him. It was because he looked so sad, and no one that looks like that should ever be left alone.

"I can take you home and come back." He started to pull the car keys from his pocket.

"No." I shook my head hastily. "That's silly. I'll be fine here. Besides, Gramps and I are going to play Clue."

"Oh, are you now?"

"You wanna play?" I asked, grabbing a pillow and blanket. "You can be Colonel Ketchup."

"Isn't in Colonel Mustard?" He chuckled.

"Well, yeah, but I figured you'd like Colonel Ketchup better," I reasoned, lying down on the couch.

"That does sound like a wicked cool name. Think my mom would mind if I changed my name to Ketchup?"

"I think she might be a bit mad."

"Yeah, you're probably right." He stretched his legs out, tapping the heels of his boots against the tile floor.

He looked better than he had earlier, but I knew he was still tired. His shoulders were slumped and his eyes were heavy as he fought sleep.

"Trace," I called.

"Yeah?" He looked over at me, massaging his temples.

"I know this isn't the biggest couch, but come lay down. Gramps is sleeping and you're no good to anyone if you're tired."

He looked over at Gramps and back at me. "Fine, but only because I'm really sleepy."

He climbed behind me on the small couch and spooned my body against his.

"I missed you last night," he whispered, pressing a light kiss to the back of my neck.

"You didn't have fun worrying the crap out of Gramps?" I giggled.

"What did he tell you?" Trace groaned. "Whatever it was, he exaggerated it. I swear."

"Just that you were fussing over him."

"Of course I was. Silly old man. He acts like no one should be worried about him."

"You know how you Wentworth men are." I wiggled against him, trying to get comfortable. "Stubborn and unwilling to take help from anyone."

"You have us all figured out, don't you?" He chuckled softly.

"In all this time, I better know a few things."

Trace cleared his throat and I knew it was a classic stall tactic of his.

"What is it?" I prompted.

"I've been thinking—" he brushed my hair away from my face with a sweep of his fingers "—about our vows for the wedding."

"And?"

"I think we should write our own."

It took every ounce of energy I had left in me not to yell. "Trace," I groaned, "you know I'm not good at that kind of thing."

"We already did the traditional vows at the courthouse. I think this would be more special. Think about what it would mean to Gramps," he pleaded.

"We're getting married in two—tomorrow," I corrected myself, realizing that it was now morning time. "How do you expect me to come up with my own vows by then?"

"You're an English major, Olivia. This should be easy for you. Or, you could do what I plan to do, which is speak from the heart."

Ugh, when he said sweet things like that it was really hard for me to argue with him.

"Fine," I found myself agreeing.

"You could sound more excited about it." He chuckled, brushing his lips over the curve of my ear and sending a shiver down my spine.

"Woohoo," I feigned enthusiasm. "I'll be fine as long as I remember to speak when it's my turn, not yours."

He laughed openly at that. "That was the most adorable thing ever."

"I'm glad you think my mistakes are adorable," I grumbled, still embarrassed about my outburst in the courthouse.

"I think everything about you is adorable."

"That's what every twenty-two-year-old woman wants to be told, Trace," I said sarcastically.

"My bad. How about beautiful?" His voice grew husky.

"That's better." A small laugh escaped me.

"Sexy?" he questioned, leaning up to look down at me. He swiped a thumb over my bottom lip, his eyes warm and full of love.

"Even better." I smiled, my eyes falling closed.

"Goodnight," he finally whispered, his lips brushing against my ear as he settled back down.

"Night," the word left my lips as my body succumbed to sleep.

"IT WAS PROFESSOR PLUM, in the kitchen, with the knife," I announced proudly, knowing I'd solved the murder.

Gramps and Trace looked at their cards, shaking their heads. "Here." Trace slid the yellow envelope my way.

I grabbed it, pulling out the three cards I had correctly guessed. "I win!" I cheered.

"And you've also won the last five games," Trace grumbled, shuffling the cards.

"Aw, someone sounds like a sore loser. Does this make it better?" I kissed his stubbled cheek.

He grinned crookedly. "A little."

There was a knock on the hospital door and then Lily stepped inside. She smiled widely when she saw the three of us.

"Having fun?" she asked, setting her purse down.

"Yeah, except Olivia keeps winning."

"That's because women are smarter than men," Lily quipped.

"Thanks, Mom," Trace chuckled, pretending to be wounded by her words. "You wanna play?" he asked.

She shook her head. "I actually need to steal Olivia for a bit."

"Steal her?" Trace put an arm around my shoulders and tugged me toward him. "I kind of like her, Mom."

"You're so full of it." She rolled her eyes at her son.

"What do you need me for?" I asked, not wanting to leave Gramps.

"You have to pick the cake today and get your nails done."

I wrinkled my nose in distaste. Picking out a cake would be fine, but I hated getting my nails done. "Do I have to?"

Lily laughed. "Yes, I'm sorry."

I frowned, looking for any excuse not to go, but came up

empty. "Looks like I have to leave," I apologized to Gramps. "I'll be back later if I can."

"Don't worry about me," he assured me, opening his arms for a hug.

I wrapped my arms around his body, wishing I never had to let go.

"I love you, Gramps." I kissed his soft wrinkled cheek.

"I love you too, sweet girl."

I said goodbye to Trace and followed Lily out of the room. Trent was coming down the hall as we left and I waved to him.

Lily drove us to a small bakery in Kernstown. I wasn't picky when it came to cake, so I was more concerned with getting something Trace would like, but I knew he was like me and didn't really care which made my job more difficult. How was I supposed to pick one flavor when we'd like any of them?

"I don't know." I frowned at the half-eaten samples in front of me. I had to make up my mind fast so they could get the cake ready for tomorrow evening's reception. On the way over, Lily had told me that we would exchange vows at sunset with the reception taking place right after. "What do you think, Lily?" I asked my mother-in-law.

"They're all really good," she agreed, "but I'm thinking the chocolate."

"Chocolate sounds good to me," I quickly replied. Next, we had to pick out the type of frosting and decorations for the cake. We settled on a white buttercream frosting with flowers going down one side.

"You got it." The baker jotted some notes down on a piece of paper. "I have everything I need. If I've forgotten anything I'll be sure to call you."

We shook hands with her and headed to the nail salon

next. I was tempted to climb out of the back of the car and run away, but Lily probably wouldn't appreciate that, so I was stuck having to tough it out.

Avery and my mom were already in chairs starting their pedicures. Lily and I headed over to join them.

"You look tired," Avery commented as I took the chair beside her.

"I am tired. Sleeping on an uncomfortable hospital couch will do that to you." I rubbed the back of my neck.

"You need to get some sleep tonight, you know, with tomorrow being the big day and all." She wiggled her toes under the water, watching the bubbles foam around her feet.

"Um, the big day has already passed."

"Yeah, but this is like the real wedding," she reasoned.

"Oh, shit!" I exclaimed suddenly, causing Avery, my mom, and Lily to turn my way. Their eyes were wide as they stared at me in shock. I wasn't one to cuss and had taken them all by surprise. "I don't have a ring for Trace," I exclaimed, fighting tears. How had I forgotten to get him a ring? I was the suckiest wife ever.

"It's okay," Avery assured me. "I'll take you to Marcy's when we leave here."

"Thank you," I breathed a sigh of relief. "Wait, where is everyone?" I looked around the eerily empty nail salon. "Aren't there normally more people getting their nails done?" I gulped, imagining that people had contracted some strange nail fungus, never to return to this place again.

Lily laughed at the expression on my face. "I rented it out for a few hours so it would only be us. You have nothing to be worried about."

"Oh." I wiggled in the plush seat, feeling silly. "That was nice of you."

"Avery said you hate getting your nails done so I thought this might make it a little more tolerable."

It warmed my heart that Lily had taken that into consideration. I was lucky to have married into her family and I was glad that we didn't have a relationship like some daughters and mother-in-laws.

It took a few hours to get our nails and toes done. I ended up choosing a sheer pink color.

As we left the nail salon I followed Avery to her red car.

On the way to Marcy's store, I told her about Trace wanting us to make up our own vows.

"I think that's a great idea," she beamed. "It's really sweet and romantic."

I narrowed my eyes at her. "Where's my best friend that would normally gag at something like this? I think I want her back."

"I'm in love too." She laughed. "I understand it now, and I think you should."

"I don't even know what I would say." My head dropped forward into my hands.

"Speak from the heart," she replied.

"You make that sound so easy." I glanced at her between my fingers. "But you know how I am, and I don't like the idea of expressing my feelings in front of a bunch of people."

"You're not. You're telling them to Trace. *He's* the only one that matters in this situation. You need to get up there and forget that everyone else exists. Look at him and tell him how you feel. That's it, Livie."

"When did you get so smart?" I laughed.

"I've always been this smart," she replied with a wicked smile, "you just prefer not to take my advice. Which is ridiculous, because it's really good advice."

"Like not wearing a sweatshirt?"

"I can't help it that Trace is immune to the sweatshirt rule. You must be really good in bed or something. I don't understand it."

We ended up giggling at her words. I was so happy to have my best friend back. Before we left on our road trip I'd feared that the Avery I knew and loved was gone forever. She had never been so depressed before. I was glad that she'd told me why and we were able to move past it. I hated what happened to her, but it really did explain so much about her personality.

"I've missed you." I reached over to hug her once she parked at Marcy's shop.

She hugged me back. "Missed me? I've always been right here, Livie."

I shook my head. "No, for a while there you weren't, and I really missed you."

"Don't make me cry, Livie, this took a while." She pointed to all the makeup on her face.

I rolled my eyes and opened the car door.

Alba was working in the front of the store and when she saw me she called for her mom.

"You're back!" Marcy exclaimed, coming around the counter to hug me.

"I'm so sorry that this is so last minute but I need a ring for Trace ... by tomorrow." I bit my lip nervously, worried that she might be mad.

"Tomorrow?" She raised a brow.

"Yeah." I nodded, tucking a piece of hair behind my ear.

"You see, Trace's grandpa is dying and we kind of got married while we were gone, but we're having a ceremony tomorrow so the whole family can be there. I want you and Alba to come, of course. There wasn't time to send out invitations. I'm sorry. Please, don't be mad at me," I rambled uncontrollably.

"Silly girl." She patted my cheek like an affectionate mother. "You have nothing to be sorry for."

"I feel bad."

"Nope, no feeling bad."

"Do you think you'll be able to make a ring that soon?" I asked, wringing my fingers together.

"I hope you don't mind, but when Trace got your rings I, uh, felt inspired and I kind of already made one for him. If you hate it, I'll make a new one today. Don't be worried about hurting my feelings." She took my hand, dragging me to the back of the store. Avery followed behind me, gawking at all the unique pieces of jewelry.

Marcy opened one of her desk drawers and pulled out a black box. She took the lid off and dumped the ring into the palm of her hand.

"Here."

I gasped when I looked at the ring in my hand. It was perfect for Trace. It was so unique, I had never seen anything else like it, but that was Marcy's specialty so I shouldn't have been surprised.

"It's made of pure titanium, that's what gives it that brownish gray color, and those stripes there are rose gold," she explained.

"It's beautiful, Marcy." I wrapped my arms around her in a tight hug. "Thank you, it's perfect." I stared down at the ring in awe once more.

"Are you sure?" she questioned, eyeing me. "If you don't like it, say so. You're not hurting my feelings."

"Honestly, it's exactly what I would have wanted him to have."

"Good, I'm glad." She clapped her hands together. "Now" —she leaned a hip against her desk— "what do you expect me to wear to this last-minute wedding?"

I frowned, feeling bad that everything had to be so rushed. "I don't care," I said with sincerity. "Wear that if you want." I pointed to her rainbow-colored hippie skirt and white top.

"I'm just messing with you." She squeezed my arm. "I have a dress somewhere that will be suitable, and I'll drag Alba with me kicking and screaming if I have to."

"You won't have to drag me," Alba spoke up from behind me.

"Good, then maybe you'll see their wedding and decide it's time for you to have one of your own." Marcy eyed her daughter.

"Mom," Alba groaned, "I'm not even dating anyone."

"My point exactly. You're not getting any younger and neither are your ovaries."

"Mom!" Alba exclaimed, her cheeks flushing in embarrassment. "My love life is none of your business."

"Well, I wouldn't have to fret over it so much if you had one. Then I'd leave you alone."

"Oh, please." Alba rolled her eyes. "I doubt that."

"Get a man, then we'll see who's right." Marcy smiled triumphantly when Alba rolled her eyes and left the room. "So, Trace's grandpa isn't going to make it?" She turned back to me with sadness in her eyes.

"No." My lower lip trembled as I fought tears.

"Aw, sweetie, I'm so sorry." Marcy hugged me. "Y'all will get through this just fine. I know it."

"I know we will."

But how long will it be before we're okay again?

I SPENT the rest of the afternoon and evening at the hospital with Gramps, Trent, and Trace. The doctor didn't want to let Gramps leave tomorrow, but he was adamant.

"I'm going home, walking this beauty down the aisle, eating cake, and then getting in *my* bed to die. Don't mess with my plan," he warned the doctor with a steely gaze in his eyes.

"Mr. Wentworth, I'm not so sure that's a good idea. You need—"

"You have no right to tell me what I need. I'm dying and I refuse to do that in this bed that sounds like it's breathing. Forget tomorrow, I want out tonight." He started trying to pull the IVs from his arm.

"Gramps." Trent tried to restrain him. "You can't do that."

"I can do whatever the hell I want and I want out of here," Gramps demanded. "I don't want to be in this place a second longer. We all know I'm dying, so why must I be stuck here? I'm going home, and going to bed."

The doctor pinched the bridge of his nose. "I'll see what I can do."

"And while you're at it, can you get someone to take this needle out of my arm?"

The doctor shook his head and left the room. I was sure they'd never had a patient quite like Warren.

"Gramps, stop that." Trent pried one of Gramps' arms away from the other. "You can't do that."

"I want this out and I want to go home." He tried to push himself into a sitting position.

The door opened to the room, yet again, but instead of the doctor, it was Ellie. I knew from Trace that she'd been here this afternoon. I kept missing her when she was here and I wondered how she was holding up. The look on her face told me she wasn't taking this well. She looked like she'd aged ten years in a matter of days.

She strode over to her husband and kissed him, despite the audience.

"How are you feeling?" she asked, looking him over.

"Like I want to go home." He coughed. "And I really want this stupid thing out of my arm." He tugged on the IV wire.

"I'll get you out of here." She smiled at her husband, her eyes roaming over every feature like she was trying to memorize him.

An hour later, all the paperwork had been signed and we wheeled Gramps out of the hospital.

Trent said goodbye and headed over to his own car.

Trace and I helped Ellie get Gramps into the car and then watched them drive away.

Trace draped an arm over my shoulder and pressed a kiss to the top of my head. "Let's go home and get Ace then stay the night at the mansion."

I nodded. "Sounds like a good idea to me."

Once we were home, we showered and packed a change of clothes. Ace watched us curiously as Trace gathered up his food bowl and toys. "We're going on a short trip," Trace explained to the dog, and I watched him while trying to hide my laugh. "What?" he asked, when he noticed me snickering by the door.

"Nothing, I just think it's cute when you talk to the dog like that."

He shook his head, fighting a smile. "The dog deserves to know what's happening."

Ace looked between the two of us, tilting his head, like he knew exactly what we were saying.

"You got everything you need?" Trace asked, carrying his bag over to the door, along with the stuff for Ace.

"Yeah, that's why I'm standing by the door ready to go."

"Oooh, someone's being sassy, maybe I should spank you for that." He curled his body around mine, grabbing my butt.

"Down boy." I pushed a hand against his chest.

"Aw, you ruin all my fun." He nuzzled my neck

"Just trying to keep my virtue intact until tomorrow night," I joked, wrapping my arms around his neck.

He chuckled, nibbling on my chin. "Baby, I'm pretty sure I ruined you a long time ago."

"It was worth it," I whispered, my eyes falling closed as he pressed his lips lightly against mine. "Everything with you has been worth it."

"Everything?" His lips skimmed down my neck and his stubble scratched my skin.

I nodded.

He grabbed my legs and forced them around his waist. "I really wish you were wearing a skirt right now, so I could take you against this door."

I shivered at his words, instantly turned on. "When has that ever stopped you?"

"Good point," he claimed my mouth with his.

It really hadn't been that long since he'd held me and kissed me like this, but it felt like forever. My body craved his like flowers needed the sun to survive.

We were both frantic, clawing at each other's clothes like wild animals. We'd *never* been like this before. I kind of liked it.

We were so desperate that most of our clothes stayed on. He yanked my shorts and panties roughly out of the way and before I could get my bearings he was thrusting inside of me.

"Oh, fuck," he groaned against my neck, steadying his hold on me so that we didn't go tumbling to the floor. "You feel so good." He kissed me and whispered against the skin of my neck, "I've missed you so much."

"Why?" My breath came out raggedly. "I've been right here."

"I know, but with everything going on …"

"I understand," I interrupted, wishing he'd shut up.

He seemed to get the message.

Minutes later, or maybe it was hours, we found ourselves slumped on the floor, exhausted. I was cradled on his chest, with my head tucked beneath his chin. I was so tired that I didn't plan on moving until I absolutely had to.

"That was …," he started.

"Amazing," I finished.

He chuckled. "I was going to say 'different' but that works too."

He brushed his fingers through my hair and my eyes closed sleepily.

"We should probably go," he announced.

"I'm not moving." I locked my arms around his neck. "You can't make me."

"Oh, I can." His fingers inched under my shirt and he began to tickle me.

"Trace! Stop!" I giggled, squirming and falling off of him.

"Get your pants on, we have to go." He chuckled, standing and pulling his pants up with him and fastening the belt.

"I did have my pants on, until you took them off." I pouted, still on the floor.

He grabbed my shorts and panties from where they'd been tossed and dropped them on top of me.

"Thanks, you're so nice," I said sarcastically as I put my clothes back on.

He smiled boyishly and held out a hand to haul me up. "I am nice. I counted three orgasms."

"What does that have to do with you being nice?" I raised a brow, prying myself from his arms before we got carried away again.

"You know, it proves that I'm a very generous lover."

"God." I rolled my eyes. "You are so full of yourself."

"That's what you like to tell me." He opened the door and picked up our bags.

"Does your mom know we're coming?" I asked.

"No." He shrugged, stopping outside the door to look at me. "But it's technically my house, so it's not like I need to call and ask for permission. I'll text her if it makes you feel better."

"It would. I don't want them to think someone is breaking into the house, and we didn't mention to your grandparents that we were coming so it's not like they told her."

"Take a breath. I'll let her know. You have nothing to worry about."

"Sorry." I forced a laugh. "I'm being silly, aren't I?"

"Kind of." He started down the steps. "Get Ace and meet me at the car."

I turned to find Ace watching me with curious eyes. The poor dog had watched everything that had gone down between Trace and me minutes before.

"Sorry, bud, but he's hot and I can't seem to help myself around him." I squatted down and scratched behind his ears. "Let's go."

CHAPTER TWENTY-THREE

I cracked my eyes open, taking in the unfamiliar surroundings. We'd stayed at the mansion a few times in Trace's childhood room, but it still seemed strange to be here, surrounded by high school memorabilia and trinkets of his past.

I sat up, shoving the sheets off of me, and drawing my knees up to my chest.

I'm getting married today.

Okay, that wasn't right. We were already married, but I had no idea what the proper term for this would be.

But I was giddy, knowing that this time our families would be present. I really hoped Gramps would be okay to walk me down the aisle. I hated to think that he might be pushing himself. I knew he was stubborn, though, and nothing, not even his cancer, would stop him from walking me down that aisle.

"What are you doing up?" Trace asked groggily, lying on his stomach.

"I'm excited." I shrugged.

He cracked a smile and eased his eyes open. "It would probably be a bad sign if you weren't."

"Yeah, especially since I already married you." I trailed a finger down his bare back and he shivered.

"Good point." He rolled over onto his back, staring at the ceiling with a serious look on his face.

"What's wrong?" I asked.

"Nothing." He shook his head. But then explained, "I was thinking about how before I met you, I never thought about getting married or anything like that. But once I met you—" he rolled to his side and pulled me down beside him "—all of that changed."

"Why do you think that is?" I asked, staring at his chest so I could avoid his intense gaze.

"Maybe," he began as he rolled on top of me, staring down at me as I squirmed beneath him, "there are certain people that are meant to be together. If that exists, I know we are." He cupped my cheek. "We were waiting for each other."

"Like, soul mates?"

He shrugged. "I don't know, that sounds a bit too far-fetched, but ... maybe."

"I believe we were meant to be, too," I told him. "And I'm happy that we didn't rush into a relationship. We got to know each other as friends first, and that's made us a stronger couple. Don't tell Avery, but you're my best friend. I know I can tell you anything and you won't judge me. You'll listen to what I have to say and give me your honest opinion. A lot of couples don't have that, but we do. We're lucky, Trace."

"I know. Believe me, I know."

After we'd all eaten breakfast together, Lily insisted on separating Trace and me. It wasn't long until Avery, Luca, my mom, and Nick arrived.

"Hi," I greeted Luca, hugging him.

"Hey."

"I'm glad to see you two got things worked out," I whispered in his ear, so Avery wouldn't overhear, and let him go.

"Me too."

"Trace is in his room." I pointed at the stairs. "Lily told him he had to stay in there until she told him he could come out."

Luca chuckled, running his fingers through his wavy light brown hair. "Is he in trouble or something?"

"I think she's afraid he might try to see me in my dress. But the wedding isn't until tonight, so I don't know why she'd be so worried about that."

"I'll go hang out with him." Luca started for the stairs, but turned around and kissed Avery.

My heart melted at the look he gave her. Luca was weird, but he was a nice guy, and I knew he loved Avery. If she messed up their relationship again I wouldn't be able to stop myself from kicking her.

"Why are you guys already here?" I addressed Avery, my mom, and Nick.

Nick held his hands up in surrender. "Don't look at me."

"We're here to help you get ready." Avery rolled her eyes. "Why else would we be here?"

"It's ten in the morning, the ceremony isn't until eight-thirty tonight." I looked at my watch, calculating the hours. "It's not going to take me that long to get ready."

"Oh, yes, it is." Avery took my hand, dragging me upstairs.

"How do you know where you're going?" I asked. As far as I knew, Avery had never been here before, at least not with me. But maybe she'd come with Luca.

"Who do you think has been helping Lily with *everything*? Honestly, Livie, you can be so dumb."

She opened a set of double doors that led into a guestroom. The bag my wedding dress was in already laid on the bed, along with Avery's garment bag. There was even a hair and makeup station set up.

"Go shower." Avery pushed me toward the bathroom, handing me a robe to put on. "The hairdresser will be here within the hour."

She closed the doors behind me and I was left alone in the massive bathroom. I looked around at the expensive touches, wondering why on Earth anyone would spend so much money on a *guest* bathroom. I guess when you had billions of dollars you didn't think about those things.

When I'd found out about Trace's family, I'd wondered why he didn't live so elegantly. An apartment above a garage was hardy the typical billionaire bachelor pad, but that was Trace for you. There was nothing typical about him. The whole family didn't act any different because they had money and you had to respect them for that. So many people let money go to their heads, but not the Wentworths. In fact, they were some of the nicest most caring people I had ever met. I think they understood that money isn't everything. For them, family was the most important thing.

Once I was clean and my whole body smelled like vanilla, I stepped out of the shower, dried myself off and wrapped myself in the fluffy robe.

When I opened the door, Avery stood there with her fist raised and ready to knock.

"'Bout time." She flounced away.

I shook my head and smiled at the woman I assumed was there to do my hair. My mom and Lily lounged on the bed, looking at jewelry.

"I'm Nikki." The woman held her hand out to me. "I'll be doing your hair and makeup, as well as theirs." She motioned to the others in the room. "Do you have anything in particular in mind?"

I sat down in the chair, facing my reflection. I hadn't given it much thought. "Um ...," I stalled. "Could you do something with a braid, but leave some of it down?"

She nodded. "Sure."

She went to work drying and curling my hair. I kept my eyes closed so I wouldn't overthink what she was doing and freak out.

She began to twist my hair to the side, braiding it, and left a few pieces to frame my face.

"Open your eyes," she said a few minutes later.

"Oh, wow," I gasped, turning my head from side to side. She had done an amazing job and I knew my minimal details had been less than helpful. "It's beautiful, thank you."

"I'm glad you like it. Now what about for your makeup?"

"Something soft and romantic," I answered before Avery

could spit something out. She sent a glare my way for ruining her plan. "Nothing dramatic," I begged.

I closed my eyes once more and let Nikki go to work.

The more time that passed, the giddier I felt. It didn't seem like we were getting married *again*, it felt like the first time, which made me both excited and nervous.

Nikki finished with me and then started on Avery's hair and makeup.

I sat on a chair in the corner, nervously tapping my fingers on the arms.

The door to the room cracked open and I gasped. "Grandma!"

After the news of Gramps being in the hospital, and having to plan a wedding in a few days, I'd completely forgotten that Trace said he'd fly them out. I couldn't believe with everything he'd been dealing with that he'd been the one to remember.

I hugged her tightly. I was so happy to see her and I hoped she knew that. "Everyone, this is Margaret, my grandma. Grandma, this is my best friend, Avery." I pointed at my best friend who was currently getting false lashes glued on. I was glad I hadn't had to do that. "Lily, Trace's mom. And lastly, that's my mom, Nora."

Margaret surprised me by striding right up to my mom and hugging her. I don't know what I'd been expecting, but it wasn't that.

My mom's eyes widened but she was quick to return the hug. "It's nice to meet you, Margaret."

"Call me, Maggie, please."

I smiled, pleased to see my mom and grandma getting along. I had feared there might be some animosity there, since my mom had kept me a secret from them.

"Your grandpa and Dex are with Trace." Maggie turned to me. "And Ella is here too. Cecilia, I believe her name was, took her to the kitchen to get something to eat."

"I can't wait to meet, Ella." I thought of the cute little girl in the picture Dex had shown me.

"She's very excited to meet you." Maggie smiled. "I need to go find, Trace. I'll be right back."

"Why do you—" The door closed behind her and it was too late for me to finish my question. "I wonder what that's about."

Deciding not to dwell on it, I sat back down, glancing at the clock. It was close to lunchtime, and there were still hours until the wedding, but suddenly I wished I could make time go faster, even though I was going to have to say my own vows. I still didn't have any plan for what I would say, but I wasn't nervous about it anymore. Once I got up there and saw him it would come to me then.

The door opened again and Cecilia entered with a tray of food for everyone and a small girl clinging to her legs.

Wide dark brown eyes met mine and I crouched in front of the girl.

"Hi," I said softly, "are you Ella?"

She nodded her head slowly, looking up at Cecilia for reassurance. I held out a hand and she placed her smaller one in my palm. "I'm Olivia. Do you know who I am?"

She nodded again and let go of Cecilia. "Daddy says you're my cousin," her voice was quiet. She was the cutest kid I had ever seen. She couldn't have been much older than five.

"That's true." I smiled warmly.

"What does that mean?" she asked.

"It means that my daddy and your daddy were brothers."

"But Daddy's brother isn't here." She tilted her head questioningly.

"No, he's not." I didn't elaborate, since I was unsure of how much Ella knew about Derek.

"You're pretty." She touched the side of my face with her small hand, then touched a piece of my hair. "I want to look like you when I grow up."

"Well, thank you." I laughed. "That's a very nice compliment."

"Do you know where my grandma is?" She looked around the room.

"She left for a bit but she'll be right back," I explained. "Would you like to wait with me?"

She nodded, clutching my hand tighter.

She looked over at Avery as Nikki pulled her hair into a bun with braids on each side.

"Can she make my hair pretty?" Ella asked me.

I looked to Nikki for confirmation before I said anything. "Sure, sweetie."

"I want my hair to be pretty like yours." She gently grabbed one of the springy curls.

"I can make that happen." Nikki smiled at the little girl.

"Thank you," Ella squeaked, hiding shyly behind my legs.

"You want to meet my mom?" I asked her.

She nodded and let me lead her over to the bed. "That's my mom, Nora, and Trace's mom, Lily."

"Hi, Ella." My mom smiled kindly at the little girl.

"Ella is such a pretty name," Lily said.

"Thank you." Ella poked her head out from behind my legs. "Who's Trace?"

"Trace is going to be my husband," I explained.

"Oh." Her small lips formed an O. "Can I see your dress?"

"Sure." I helped her onto the chair. I unzipped the garment bag and held up the dress for her inspection. "What do you think?"

"You're gonna look like a princess." She clapped her hands together. "I want to be a princess when I grow up and live in a biiiig house just like this. Are you really a princess? Is this a castle?" She looked around in awe.

"Nope, not a princess." I shook my head. "And this house is really big, but it's not a castle."

She frowned. "It would be cool if you were a princess."

"That would be cool," I agreed. "I like your shoes." I tapped the end of her toes, covered by shiny pink sandals.

"My mommy got them for me."

Maggie came back into the room and smiled when she saw Ella and me together. "Look at my two girls," she beamed.

"Grandma, that lady is going to make my hair pretty like —" She looked at me questioningly, unsure how to say my name.

"Olivia," I supplied.

"Like Olivia's." Ella nodded proudly, pleased that she said my name correctly.

"Isn't that nice." Maggie clapped her hands together.

"What did you need to see Trace for?" I asked, still curious.

"Oh, nothing."

I sighed. I should have been used to the fact that no one ever wanted to tell me anything.

I had forgotten about the sandwiches Cecilia had brought into the room, but when my eyes landed on them I was suddenly ravenous.

"Do you want a sandwich, Ella?"

She nodded her head, pushing her thick bangs out of her eyes. I grabbed a plate for each of us and sat down on the floor beside her.

Nikki did my mom and Lily's hair and makeup then they left to help set up for the wedding. I wanted to see how everything was coming together, since I really hadn't had much part in anything, but Lily insisted on it being a surprise. Even Trace didn't know what it would look like, which made me feel a bit better about being left out of the loop.

Nikki braided Ella's hair to the side and added some pale pink gloss to her lips so she didn't feel left out. She even took the time to work her magic on my grandma.

I tried to keep my eyes away from the clock, but it was hard not to. Especially when the sounds of guests arriving echoed through the large home.

My mom and Lily returned to get in their dresses and before I knew it, it was time to put mine on.

They buttoned the back of the dress and I eyed my reflection. I looked like a bride—that was kind of the point, but seeing the whole look come together left me breathless.

Lily handed me a bouquet of orchids and said, "Showtime."

I swallowed thickly, trying to gather my breath.

"Gramps will meet you downstairs." Lily took my arm, guiding me out of the room. Maybe I looked faint or something and that's why she felt the need to hold onto me. I didn't feel like I was going to pass out, but my stomach was definitely upset.

Lily handed me off to Gramps, and Avery was the only one left behind.

"Ready, baby girl?" Gramps asked me, smiling proudly at me.

I nodded.

"Trace is going to piss his pants."

That got me to laugh, which was what he was aiming for.

I threaded my arm through his and said, "I'm glad you're the one doing this. I wouldn't want anyone else."

He smiled, his eyes crinkling at the corners. His skin was still unusually pale, but he actually looked healthier than he had in the hospital. "I'm honored." He kissed my cheek.

"You look nice." I took in his light gray suit. An orchid that matched my bouquet was stuck in the lapel.

"Not as nice as you. All eyes will be on you."

That's what I was afraid of. I gulped at his words as we followed Avery to the open French doors.

We stepped outside onto a walkway made of white rose petals, it snaked around the property, and when we reached a certain point Avery stopped, waiting for our cue to continue forward.

Luca sauntered up and offered her his arm.

"Breathe," Gramps whispered.

The air gusted out of my lungs at his words. I had nothing to be nervous about. I took a deep breath, raising my chin.

The music started up and butterflies fluttered in my stomach.

I was glad I had Gramps at my side. He was the one dying, but he was also the one keeping me strong.

We followed the flowered pathway and I gasped when we rounded the trees.

Jars, covered in different colored tissue paper, had little candles lit inside them. They were everywhere, casting the yard with a pretty glow.

The chairs had flowers wrapped around them and at the end of the aisle, Trace stood on the steps of a wooden gazebo. The gazebo was wrapped in twinkling lights and flowers. But my eyes were glued to Trace. He was looking at me with his mouth slightly open. He wore a pair of black dress pants and a white button-down shirt. Even though I'd joked about him wearing a tux, I was glad he was more casual. His hair was slightly damp and brushed away from his face. Stubble still dotted his cheeks, but not as much as had been there this morning.

"Told you." Gramps chuckled at my side.

We walked slowly down the aisle as Gramps struggled to put one foot in front of the other, but I didn't mind. I wanted Gramps to be the one to do this and if it took us ten minutes to reach Trace, so be it.

Luca stood beside Trace and leaned over to whisper something in his ear. Trace punched him roughly in the arm for whatever he'd said. Luca's lips quirked up into a smile as he shook his head

Finally, we reached the gazebo, and since there was no need to have anyone officiate the wedding Gramps kissed my hand before placing it in Trace's. "I love you both." Gramps coughed, a single tear falling down his cheek.

"I love you too," I whispered, kissing the tear away.

"Love you, Gramps." Trace kissed his other cheek. Cameras snapped somewhere, capturing the moment.

I stepped up beside Trace and Gramps sat down.

"You look beautiful," Trace murmured, his eyes gazing over my whole body.

"You're not too bad yourself," I whispered.

He chuckled, shaking his head. He glanced out at the

crowd and back to me. "I guess we better get on with it. You know, since they're waiting and all."

"Oh, right." I blushed, glancing out at the guests. Geez, did we really know all those people?

"Olivia," Trace spoke loudly so that everyone gathered heard his words, "when I met you, I didn't know I was going to fall in love with you and make you my wife, but I did know that you were going to change my life." He squeezed my hands. "You were so shy when I first met you, and I loved making you blush—" He released one of my hands and rubbed his thumb over my cheek. "I *still* love making you blush. I love making you smile and laugh. It makes my life worthwhile. *You* make my life better, Olivia. I didn't know what I was missing until you came into my life. I know you think that I've taught you how to live, but it's the other way around." He swallowed thickly. "You own my heart, keep it safe."

He took my left hand and slipped a ring on. It was beautiful and elegant, with diamonds going all the way around it. His words were still sinking in and my emotions were getting the best of me.

"You made me cry." I released his hands to dab at my face. The guests laughed at my words, but I didn't care.

"Sorry." He smiled, and I was surprised to see tears in his eyes too.

I took a deep breath and let the words spill out of me. "There's not much I can say after that—" I took his hands once more "—but I'm going to try." I closed my eyes and wet my lips. "I believe that fate brought us together, because we both needed each other. You intimidated me at first with your cocky flirtatious remarks, but I saw past that to the guy underneath and I fell in love with him ... with *you*. I was scared of the things I felt for you, since I'd never experienced anything like it before. But I let myself fall, and it's been the most exhilarating ride of my life. I love that you push me to try new things. I love that you listen to me, trust me, and respect me. We're equals in every way. And today, I vow to love you with my whole heart, for the rest of my life." I took his ring from Avery and slipped it onto his finger. It filled me with satisfaction and love to see that symbol of our union on his finger.

"God, I love you." He grasped my face between his large hands and kissed me passionately.

Claps, catcalls, and laughter echoed around us, but, in that moment, it was just the two of us.

He pulled away and placed a soft kiss on the end of my nose. Taking my hand, we started back down the aisle.

"She's Mrs. Wentworth now!" he yelled, raising our arms in the air. Everyone cheered at his words and I, of course, blushed at the unwanted attention.

"Wasn't I already Mrs. Wentworth?" I looked up at him.

"Yeah, but now you have my ring on your finger, so it's official," he reasoned.

We didn't make it very far before we were confronted by a photographer, eager to begin taking pictures of us and the rest of the family.

I smiled and posed as directed. Lots of pictures were taken with Gramps, and it made me sad knowing the reason why. But at least when he was gone, we'd be able to look back at these pictures and smile at the fact that we got to share this moment with him.

After nearly an hour of photo taking it was time for the real party to begin.

Tables were set up on the expansive property and more jar

lanterns covered the tables and grass. I gasped at the all the silver origami stars adorning the tables. "Did you get my grandma to do this?" I asked Trace, clinging to his hand as he led us to the largest table.

"Of course." He grinned. "I thought it was appropriate."

"There's so many." I eyed all the tables. "It must have taken forever."

"A few hours," Maggie said from behind me.

"Thank you." I hugged her. "They're beautiful and special."

"I had fun making them." She shrugged nonchalantly. "Plus, it makes me feel like a piece of your dad is here with us."

I smiled at that and sat down in the chair Trace pulled out for me. He took the seat beside me with Gramps and the rest of his family beside him. My grandpa was on my other side, then my grandma, mom, Nick, Dex, and Ella.

I knew I did the right thing having Gramps walk me down the aisle, but I felt bad for my grandpa. I mean, he was my own family and I hated to think I might have hurt his feelings by not asking him.

"Grandpa?" I leaned over and whispered in his ear.

"What, sweetie?" He smiled kindly, leaning back as servers set plates on the table.

I clasped my hands together, my fingernails digging into my skin. "I hope you aren't mad that I didn't ask you to walk me down the aisle."

I looked down, avoiding his eyes.

"Of course I'm not mad." He forced my chin up with a finger. "I understand. Now, if you don't dance with me tonight, I might get mad then." He chuckled so I knew he was messing with me.

"I think I can manage a dance," I assured him.

"I'm looking forward to it." He patted my cheek affectionately.

I spotted a family at a nearby table and elbowed Trace in the side. He choked on a bite of food and glared at me. "Woman, couldn't you have waited for me to finish?"

"Sorry." I laughed as he took a sip of water. "But is that Marcus and his family?" I pointed to the man that looked suspiciously like the one that had helped talk me into jumping off a bridge.

"Yep." Trace smiled proudly. "I flew them in." Shrugging, he explained, "I know they're not family or anything, but meeting them on the road and connecting with them was nice. I wanted them to come."

"You're a good man, Trace Wentworth." I grasped his knee and leaned over to kiss him softly.

"Because of you I'll *always* try to be a better man," he whispered, gazing at me thoughtfully.

I leaned my head on his shoulder, unconcerned about eating my meal. All that mattered to me was this moment that we were surrounded by everyone we loved.

The cutting of the cake went about as well as I expected. Trace shoved cake in my face and I got mad and tried to climb on his back. We both ended up falling on the floor, much to the amusement of the guests. But hey, that was Trace and me for you, and we definitely weren't normal.

After we cleaned our faces of cake, and Trace changed his shirt since cake got smeared on that, it was time for our first dance as a couple.

When they announced us as Mr. and Mrs. Wentworth, my heart skipped a beat. I still wasn't used to the fact that I was married and he was my husband. It seemed so surreal. How had I gotten so lucky?

I guessed the fact of the matter was I *wasn't* that lucky. I hadn't had the best childhood, the man I'd believed was my father tried to kill me, and there had been plenty of other bumps in the road. Despite everything I had been through, I still felt blessed, and it was because of the man that stood at my side.

"Shall we?" He held out his hand for me and guided me onto the dance floor that was made of more white rose petals. Lily had done an amazing job of making the wedding simple but elegant. Wedding planning might be her superpower.

He swayed us to the music, looking into my eyes. His gaze sent a shiver down my spine.

"You know," he whispered, his lips brushing over the curve of my ear, "now that we're married, there's something I should probably tell you."

"Tell me what?" I eyed him worriedly.

He smiled crookedly. "I lied."

"You lied," I repeated. "About what?" My heart raced in my chest. What could he have possibly lied about?

"When I said I can't dance, that was a lie," he whispered.

I snorted, relief flooding my veins. "I've seen you dance and it looks like you're having a seizure."

"Yeah, well, I like to dance like that because I can. But growing up here" —he gestured behind me to the mansion—

"we were always having fancy parties so Trent and I had to know how to dance."

I laughed, shaking my head. "So, all this time you wanted me to believe you couldn't dance?" I asked him.

"No. I enjoy dancing like I've lost all control of my body." He chuckled. "It's freeing. Formal dancing is boring, but I *can* do it."

"Any other secrets you should let me in on?" I tilted my head as he swirled me around.

He shook his head. "You know all my secrets now."

His fingers found my wedding ring and he twisted it around my finger unconsciously, a ghost of a smile on his lips. "You like that, don't you?" I suppressed a laugh.

He nodded, looking down at me. "Even more than this." He took my hand off his shoulder and kissed my wrist where the tattoo of his name was emblazoned. He'd said the same thing when we'd gotten engaged. It pleased me to know that he was happy to be married to me.

"I have to agree with you." I smiled, laying my head against his chest as more couples began to join us on the dance floor.

"Good." His chest rumbled against my ear with the word.

We danced to two more songs and then my grandpa was tapping on Trace's shoulder. "May I have a turn?" he asked.

"Certainly." Trace handed me off and left the dance floor.

"Hey, Grandpa." I smiled. "I'm really glad you guys could make it."

"That husband of yours is pretty amazing." He shook his head. "He made sure we got here okay."

I looked over my shoulder at Trace, smiling as I watched him introduce himself to Ella. "I love him."

"And he loves you," my grandpa said. "It's obvious in the way he looks at you."

"So, when are you guys heading back?"

"Our flight leaves tomorrow." He frowned. "Maggie can't be away from the store too long."

"Of course. I understand. I hope we can see each other soon." My grip on his shoulders tightened. I hated to say goodbye to them again. It seemed so unfair to finally have them in my life, only to live so far apart.

"I hope so too." His eyes crinkled at the corners as he smiled.

I was then passed off to Marcus, who I was really happy to see.

"How did Trace talk you guys into coming?" I asked him.

He chuckled. "Free plane tickets and a place to stay are pretty convincing." He winked. "Plus, I really like you guys. And Sarah wanted to see Trace, so there was that."

I laughed, looking to my right where Trace was dancing with the little girl. Ella had moved on and was dancing with her dad.

"Should I be worried that she's trying to steal my man?" I joked as the little girl batted her eyelashes at Trace.

Marcus laughed. "I think she's a bit too young, so you're safe."

Next, I danced with Dex. His graying dark hair hung in his eyes and he hadn't bothered to shave.

"I feel like I need to give you *the talk*," were the first words out of his mouth when we started dancing.

I blushed, looking at the ground. "I think you're a bit late for that."

"I was afraid you'd say that." He shook his head. "You know, you might be Derek's daughter, but I feel protective of you and I don't even know you that well," he admitted sheepishly.

"I guess it's the bond of family."

"Maybe so." He smiled and his eyes crinkled at the corners. "At least you picked a good guy." He tilted his head in the direction where Trace was dancing with both Ella and Sarah. Sarah didn't look very pleased at having to share, which made me giggle. "That way, I don't have to punch him and threaten him to treat you right."

"You have nothing to worry about," I assured my uncle.

"I've still gotta scare him a bit." Dex glared over my shoulder, I assumed at Trace.

"There's no need for that." I shook my head.

"Sorry," Dex chuckled, shaking his head as he fought a smile. "I feel like I have to stand in for your dad."

"You don't think he would've approved of Trace?" I frowned.

Dex laughed. "He would've liked him all right, but you'd be his little girl. Daddies with daughters are very overprotective. Ella isn't dating until she's dead," he added.

"Poor Ella," I laughed.

"If any guy tries to come near her, I'll beat them away with a baseball bat, don't doubt me."

About that time, we were interrupted by Gramps sauntering up to us. He grumbled, "It's about time I got to dance with the bride. I am dying, you know."

"Of course." Dex bowed out of the way.

Gramps took my hands, easily picking up on the beat of the song. "I hadn't forgotten about you," I told him.

"I know you'd never forget about me, sweetie. Regardless, I didn't want to miss my chance to dance with you."

My lip began to tremble with the threat of tears and I bit down on it, drawing blood. I didn't want to cry anymore. I wanted to be happy and smiling, but it was hard when I looked at Gramps and knew his days were limited.

Forgetting that we were supposed to be dancing, I hugged him, letting him sway us to the music.

"You have the letters, right?" he whispered in my ear.

I nodded my head against his chest. "I hid them so Trace won't find them." I had stuffed the sealed envelopes in the bottom of the drawer of the table beside our bed. I knew he'd never look there.

"Good girl," he hummed. "I want you to know," his voice grew thick, "that no matter where I am, I'll always be thinking of you and Trace. You can be sure of that. My body might be leaving this world, but never my spirit. I'll always be close to you, Olivia."

"Gramps," I sniffled.

"No tears." He rubbed my dampened cheeks. "Only smiles."

"I don't feel like smiling," I mumbled.

"Silly girl, a smile and laughter can cure anything. It doesn't benefit anyone to dwell on the sad or bad things," he reasoned.

"But it's hard not to." I sighed, my grip on his shoulders tightening. Maybe if I held on tight enough he couldn't be taken away from us.

"I know." He nodded sadly. "Stay strong, my brave girl." He kissed my forehead.

With that, he bled into the crowd. I wasn't left alone for very long as Trace appeared in front of me.

Trace took my hand and pulled me off to the side.

"Are you okay?" he asked, noting my bloody lip.

"Yeah." I nodded. "I'm sad, but I'm fine."

He took my face between his hands. "I don't want you to be sad today."

"I'm trying not to be," I said as I took a deep breath. "But it's hard."

He pressed his forehead against mine and his eyes fluttered closed. "I understand."

He held me for a moment and his presence alone calmed me.

Around us, everyone chatted and danced, having a good time. Some of the kids ran around with sparklers, adding light to the night around us.

It was late and I was tired, but I never wanted to leave. Right now, my whole family was together for the last time.

"Olivia," he said my name warningly.

"Sorry." I looked up into his green eyes.

His tongue flicked out to moisten his lips and his eyes darkened like clouds when a storm was rolling in. "Tonight is about you, me, and our family. We can't worry about what tomorrow might be bring, okay?"

"Okay," I agreed.

We were heading to a table when his mom stopped us. "It's time to release the paper lanterns." She clapped her hands together, smiling giddily.

"What?" My brows furrowed in confusion.

"It's the final event of the night," she explained. "Everyone will release a lantern and then the party's over."

"Oh," I gasped, not realizing how late it was.

Everyone grabbed a lantern and we began lighting the candles inside them.

One by one they lifted into the sky.

"Make a wish," Trace whispered, watching me closely.

I closed my eyes, wishing for the impossible—that I would be strong enough for the both of us.

Once my wish was made, I let it go, watching as it lifted into the air and was carried away.

We hugged everyone goodbye, spending extra time with Gramps. I think I told him I loved him at least twenty times. He probably wanted to strangle me, but I felt it was important that he know how much he meant to me.

Trace and I didn't bother changing out of our formal clothes. In fact, he'd mentioned something about *him* being the one to get me out of my dress.

He rolled the sleeves of his shirt up and opened the passenger door for me. His mom had wanted to get us a limo, but I said that was silly and refused.

Trace slid into the driver's seat and started the car.

"So, " he said slowly.

"Yes?"

He cleared his throat. "Do you, uh, want to go to a hotel?"

"Trace Wentworth, are you blushing?" I giggled, poking his stubbled cheek where I swore I saw the skin stained pink.

He bashfully turned away. "No."

"Why are you blushing?" I asked curiously. "You do realize you did me against the wall the other day, right?"

"I don't know." He squirmed in his seat. "It feels ... different."

I decided to put the poor guy out of his misery. "I don't want to go to a hotel. I want to go home."

He smiled at that. "Home sounds perfect to me."

By the time we made it to the apartment, my stomach was turning in knots. It was silly, Trace was my husband and we'd been intimate many times, but something told me that tonight would take our relationship to a whole new level.

He opened the apartment door and before I could step inside he was lifting me up and carrying me. "The real threshold." He winked.

He kicked the door closed behind us and carried me straight to the bed.

He lowered me down and pressed his lips softly to mine. "I've been turned on since I saw you in this dress." He tugged on the side. "Who knew a fucking dress could get me so excited?"

"You don't look too bad yourself." My fingers made quick work of the buttons on his shirt and my hands splayed across his heated skin.

I sat up and he took his time undoing the buttons on the back of the dress, pressing kisses against my skin. I pulled my hair out of the way, shivering at his touch. I let the dress drop to my waist and my heart beat rapidly in my chest in anticipation.

He pulled the sheets back and made sure my head was cradled on the pillow.

He tore his shirt all the way off and tossed it behind him, along with his pants. He slipped the dress off of me and it joined the rest of the garments on the floor.

I closed my eyes, my breath faltering as his lips skimmed over my chest, down my stomach, and lower.

My fingers grasped his hair as the muscles in my body tightened.

He kissed his way back up my body. His lips connected with mine, kissing me thoroughly. It was like he was devouring me, body and soul.

"I love you," he breathed against the skin of my neck as he sank inside me.

I couldn't reply. The only sound that escaped me was a soft moan.

I clung to his shoulders, scared that I might float away and needed him to keep me anchored here. I couldn't seem to figure out where I ended and he began. For now, at least, we were one person, connected by our love for each other.

"Look at me," he breathed when my eyes closed and I was reminded of our first time together. We'd come a long way in a few years.

My eyes opened and the look in his eyes, of such pure love, was my undoing. *Everyone* should be looked at that way. Like they're special. Like they're loved. Like the other person is incomplete without them at their side.

I raised my head and brought my lips against his. His stubble scratched the palms of my hands and my mouth opened beneath his as I gasped. He lightly nipped my bottom lip with his teeth, grabbing onto the top of the headboard. Sweat dampened his skin and I placed my hands against his muscular stomach, my eyes never leaving his.

I wanted him.

I needed him.

I craved him.

I loved him.

And I was lucky enough to call him my husband.

"Trace," I gasped his name, clawing at his back with my fingernails. Both of our breaths accelerated.

He peppered my face with kisses before laying claim to my mouth.

I thought I might explode from the feelings building inside me.

I found myself gasping his name again in-between kisses.

He grasped my hips, lifting mine to meet his. "Oh, God," I moaned, fighting the urge to shut my eyes.

His teeth clenched together as he sped up his movements.

"Olivia," my name was barely a whisper uttered from his lips. "Olivia," he said my name a bit louder. "Oh, fuck," he groaned, no longer able to hold back.

He slipped from my body, but held me tightly in his arms, our dampened skin sticking together.

He pulled my hair away from my neck and kissed it where my pulse raced.

"Finding you was the best thing that ever happened to me," he breathed.

"You didn't find me. We found each other."

I woke up groggily, something having awoken me. It took me a moment to realize it was a phone ringing.

Trace was sitting up too, rubbing his eyes. His hair stuck up around his head and he looked at me with sleepy eyes. "What the fuck is that?" he growled, the sheet falling to his waist.

"Phone," I answered, looking around to see if it was his or mine. It was five in the morning and I was too exhausted to figure out why anyone would be calling us at this time.

He slipped his boxers on and searched the room for the annoying thing. He found it on the floor, under the dresser.

"Hello?" he answered, scratching the back of his head.

I watched the color drain from his face. He didn't say anything to the person. Instead, he took his phone and threw it against the wall. I watched as it shattered into pieces. He lowered his head into his hands and his sobs filled the room. I had never seen anyone look so completely and utterly broken before and I hated that it was Trace of all people. He didn't deserve to go through this. No one did.

I slowly rose from the bed and approached him like one would a frightened animal.

"Trace," I whispered his name so I didn't startle him.

His chest heaved with desperate breaths and he refused to look at me. "Trace," I repeated.

When he didn't lower his hands, I responded by wrapping my arms around him. That got him to move. His hands left his face and he hugged me against him. My tears dampened his skin. I tried to dam the back, to be strong, but it was pointless.

"He's dead," Trace murmured unnecessarily. "Gramps is dead." His voice was flat with no emotion. I knew he was processing the news and wishing it wasn't true. His sobs increased and I didn't know what to do to fix this. I was pretty sure there was *nothing* I could do, but that didn't keep me from wanting to try. Trace was always so strong and never the one to get so emotional. I had never seen him quite like this—so broken and helpless. It tore me apart. I loved him and wanted to heal everything that hurt. But I didn't know what to say or what to do. I was clueless.

So, I held him.

And he held me.

Maybe, somehow, we could keep each other together.

"FUCK THIS!" Trace yelled from the bedroom.

I came running into the room to see what the problem was. He stood in front of the mirror and the tie he'd been trying to put on had been thrown on the ground. It lay there in a heap looking sad and pathetic, sort of how I'd looked ever since we'd gotten the call about Gramps.

I picked the tie up off the floor and smoothed it out.

"Here, let me help you." I forced a smile, draping the tie around his neck.

He closed his eyes and pinched the bridge of his nose. "I hate this."

"What? Your tie?" I joked, feeling the need to alleviate the tension in the room.

"He shouldn't be dead. It's not right." He opened his eyes to look at me.

"I agree." I tightened the tie and fixed it into place. "There." I stepped away.

He was dressed in a black suit with an emerald tie that brought out his eyes.

"I don't want to go to this." He stared at his reflection, fiddling with his collar like it was restricting his oxygen even though it was loose.

"Trace ..." I grabbed his hands and held them in my own. "We have to. You'd hate yourself if you missed your grandpa's funeral. It's okay to be sad and angry. It's even okay to cry. It doesn't make you weak. It makes you human."

"You know how my mom wants us all to speak about Gramps?" He waited for me to nod before continuing. "I don't want to," he admitted, looking at me with sad eyes partially concealed by his thick-framed black glasses. I hated seeing him like this, but it was understandable.

"Then don't. She's not going to be mad if you don't. Do what *you* need to do." I caressed his face with the back of my fingers, trying to offer him as much comfort and support as I could. The past two days had been hard on the both of us, but

Trace was handling things better than I'd imagined. He'd had a few outbursts of anger, like with the tie, and he'd broken down crying last night, but I knew he'd be okay with time.

He glanced at his guitar case leaning against the bedroom wall. "What if I sang a song?"

A genuine smile met my lips for the first time in days. "That would be wonderful and I know it would mean more to Gramps than a speech."

He swallowed thickly, glancing down at the watch adorning his wrist. "We better go."

He grabbed his guitar case and left the apartment, not bothering to see if I was following.

All I wanted to do was make him feel better but I didn't know how to do it. There wasn't an instruction book for something like this. All I could do was love him, no matter what.

With a sigh, I opened the drawer in the nightstand beside the bed and pulled out the letters Gramps had written to Trace and me. I tucked them into my purse, planning to give Trace his after the funeral. I was sure I'd end up reading mine then too, but a part of me wanted to leave it unread. I didn't want to know Gramps' final words to me. If I didn't read them, then it was like he wasn't really gone.

"Bye, Ace." I pet the dog affectionately on the head and closed the apartment door, making sure it was locked.

Trace was already in the car and he didn't say anything as we drove to the cemetery.

Even though Gramps had known lots of people, we'd chosen to keep the funeral private. My mom, Nick, Avery, and Luca would be there, but that was it outside of the immediate family.

I followed Trace through the grass, around the headstones,

to a spot under a large oak tree. Gramps' casket was closed, on a platform above the freshly dug ground where it would soon be lowered. I was glad they'd chosen to keep the casket closed. I didn't want to see Gramps like that. I wanted to remember him like I knew him when he was alive—smiling, laughing, and strong.

Trace set his guitar case down and his mom eyed it with a question in her eyes, but didn't ask.

Everyone else soon arrived and a man I'd never met before began to speak about Gramps. It was clear the man hadn't really *known* Gramps, so I found myself tuning him out.

After he was finished speaking, we each took turns saying a few things about Gramps.

When it was my turn, Trace stood up with me. He entwined our hands together and I knew then, that we were united, and we'd really be okay. Greif had a way of making you forget that in time you'd heal.

You live.

You love.

You lose.

You heal.

You move on.

I held my head high as I spoke. "Gramps, is one of the most remarkable people I've ever met. He welcomed me into the Wentworth family with open arms. He made me feel comfortable, but most importantly, he made me feel loved. And I loved him back, like he was my own grandpa. I spent a lot of time with him over the years and he became not only my family, but a friend as well. When I say I'm going to miss him, it doesn't encompass the magnitude in which I'll feel empty. There will always be a part of me missing because of his loss. But I won't dwell on his death. Gramps wouldn't want me to do that. I'll remember him often and I'll always love him." I squeezed Trace's hand, letting him know I was finished speaking.

I expected us to sit down, but he tightened his hold on my hand so that I couldn't move. He swallowed thickly and a heavy breath gusted between his lips. "Gramps was more than a grandpa to me. After my dad died, he helped fill that role. I was in a bad place for a long time after my dad died, but Gramps *never* gave up on me. I put my family through hell, but they stood by my side, and with Gramps' help I found my way back home, and I eventually found the love of my life. Without Gramps, there are so many things I wouldn't have today. I'm not going to lie, I'm angry that he's gone. Really fucking angry. But that's life, sometimes bad things happen and we have to decide how to deal with them. I'm not the same person I was when my dad died." He stopped, taking a moment to compose himself. "I was a boy then, but now I'm a man. I've grown a lot since then, and I won't let this break me. Like Olivia said, I'll always remember and love him."

We sat down together and everyone was silent, soaking in our words.

Grammy began to cry beside Trace and he released my hand to hug her. "It's okay, Grammy." He rubbed her back. "We're all here for you."

When he turned back to me, I said, "I thought you weren't going to say anything?"

"I wasn't. But after you spoke, it would've been wrong not to say anything."

After Trent gave a short speech, Trace opened his guitar case.

"I'd like to sing a song to honor Gramps' memory." He cleared his throat.

His mom smiled.

He pulled his chair out and turned it around so he was facing everyone.

He strummed the guitar lightly, closing his eyes as his teeth bit into his bottom lip.

"Somewhere Over the Rainbow" began to float from his lips. I closed my eyes, listening to the song and soaking in the words.

When he finished singing, I heard Grammy sniffling and even his mom was crying. There was a lone tear on my cheek and I swiped it away.

"That was beautiful," I told him as he packed his guitar back up. "That was different than the original," I stated. "Did you change it yourself?"

"No." He shook his head. "That's Jason Castro's version."

"It was perfect." I placed a hand on his arm. "Very fitting." We stood, standing by the casket.

"Yes, it is." He skimmed his fingers over the mahogany top. "Gramps is with the rainbows now."

Everyone was hugging and saying goodbye. I managed to keep Trace from leaving, saying I wanted a moment longer. When everyone was gone, I pulled his letter from my purse. Trace watched my movements carefully, eyeing the letter with apprehension.

"Here." I handed Trace his. "Gramps gave me this when he was in the hospital." His hands gripped the envelope tightly and I feared he might rip it. "I don't know what it says, but I think you should read it. There's one for me too." I pulled the second letter from my purse.

He took a deep breath, staring at his name scrawled on the envelope.

"I don't know if I can do this," he confessed.

"I don't know I can, either," I admitted. "Maybe we should do it together?" I suggested.

He nodded and we sat beneath the tree. The leaves cast shadows over us and we both stared at the sealed envelopes, reluctant to open them. He looked at me and I looked at him. At the same time, we ripped the envelopes open.

I pulled the piece of paper out carefully, like it was a precious artifact I was worried I might damage.

Tears leaked out of my eyes as I began to read.

Olivia,

If you're reading this then that means I'm dead. Sorry about that. Some things cannot be helped. I held out for as long as I could. I fought hard, I promise you that. I'm sorry I wasn't strong enough to stay longer, but my time has come to an end and I must say goodbye. I love you very much. I know you know that, but I felt the need to say it again. I couldn't have picked a better woman to steal my grandson's heart. You bring out a side to him that's been missing since his dad died. You make him smile and laugh. You've shined a light into all his darkest places and driven away his demons. I can't thank you enough for that. You don't know what he was like after his dad died … I feared he lost his way. I worked hard to bring him back, but you didn't have to work at it. You're his soul mate, Olivia. Soul mates are hard to find, but I managed to find mine in Ellie. Hold him close, and never ever let go. Live your life, Olivia. Don't dwell on the bad things. Move past them, together.

That was one of the most important things I learned while married to Ellie ... together, we could solve any problem and conquer any hurdle. I want the best for you and Trace. I know you're both bound for great things. I'm proud of Trace for following his dream and choosing not to take over the company. He should be admired for making the less easy choice. If he ever doubts his decision, remind him of this. As for you, my sweet Olivia, write that book. Don't let life get in the way of your dreams. Our dreams can take us anywhere as long as we let them. So, spread those wings and fly baby girl.

All my love, forever,
Gramps.

A Few Weeks Later ...

"WHAT DO YOU THINK?" Trace took a step back with his hands on his hips, assessing the new sign on the garage.

WENTWORTH WHEELS

"It's ... interesting." I eyed the name now emblazoned on what was once Pete's Garage.

"You don't like it." He frowned, his brows furrowing together.

"No, I do." Actually, I thought it was ridiculous, but I didn't want to hurt his feelings so I kept my mouth shut. Two weeks ago, Pete had handed the business over to Trace. It had been shut down since then as Trace prepped to open the garage under its new management. Pete had left him all of the equipment since he didn't need it, but the place had been in need of a serious makeover. Now, it sparkled with renewed life.

The last few weeks had been hard, since we were still mourning the loss of Gramps, but Trace was better since he'd been putting so much time and energy into opening the garage as his own. It was a welcome distraction for him.

"Don't lie."

"I'm not lying." I laughed. "I wasn't expecting that, though." I shrugged, pointing at the sign.

"I thought it was catchy." He crossed his arms over his chest. "Better than Trace's Garage, at least."

"Yeah, this is better than that," I admitted. "I'm really proud of you." My voice brightened as I smiled at him. I knew it had been hard for Trace to admit that taking over the family business wasn't for him. He wanted to please his family, but he would've been miserable leading his family's company. Instead, his mom had stepped up to the plate and filled Gramps' shoes. She had worked for the company after she married Trace's dad and after he'd died she'd continued to put in hours.

"Thanks." He slung his arm around my shoulders and pulled me in for a kiss.

After looking at the sign for another minute, we made our way into the apartment.

Trace stopped in the kitchen, leaning a hip against the counter. "I noticed you canceled your job interviews."

"Yeah." I bit my lip, remembering the words Gramps had written in his letter. *As for you, my sweet Olivia, write that book.*

Don't let life get in the way of your dreams. Our dreams can take us anywhere as long as we let them. So, spread those wings and fly baby girl.

After reading Gramps letter, I knew taking a job teaching wasn't what I really wanted to do. Writing a book would be hard, and I might not ever do it, but I wouldn't know until I tried. So, for the time being I'd continue to work at Marcy's store and write in my spare time. Who knew where it would go, but at least I'd be happy, and happiness was the key to everything.

"So ... does this mean you're going to write that book?" he paused, waiting for me to respond. When I didn't say anything, he grabbed an apple and bit into it. He arched a brow as he eyed me from across the counter.

There was no point in not telling him my plan. I knew he would support my decision. Besides, this is what he'd wanted me to do all along. I strode forward and grabbed my laptop. I plopped on the couch and opened the lid of the computer. "Yeah, I am and I'm going to start right now." My voice shook nervously with fear. Admitting this was a big step for me.

"And what story are you going to write?" His eyes sparkled and his lips threatened to turn up in his signature cocky grin.

"Ours."

EPILOGUE

ONE YEAR LATER ...

I stared out the window of our new home, smiling at the white picket fence and the idyllic setting. The new house was close to the garage, but we wanted to get an actual house so Ace would have room to run around a yard. Plus, with the baby due any day now, he kind of needed his own bedroom. The apartment would not have been a great place to bring a baby home to.

I turned, picking up the picture on the side table. It was of Trace and me, kissing Gramps' cheeks at the wedding. I couldn't believe he'd already been gone more than a year. His loss still felt fresh but we were moving on and we were happy. We had everything we could ever ask for and more.

"Done!" Trace called from the nursery.

I waddled inside, my hand on my rounded stomach.

I closed my eyes, stifling a laugh. "Really, Trace? *This* is what you've been doing in here all afternoon? Now I know why you told me to stay out." I shook my head, fighting a smile.

"What?" He frowned. "You don't like it."

"'*I am a Jedi like my father before me*'," I read the decal he'd affixed to the wall. Shaking my head, I couldn't help but laugh. "Starting him young, aren't you?"

"You're never too young to have a love of *Star Wars*," he defended.

I wrapped my hands around the bar of the crib, smiling at the mobile my grandma had made the baby. It was made of pale blue and white origami stars. I was happy the baby would have something made by family to look at and not something from a store.

Trace lowered to his knees in front of me and I gazed at him quizzically, wondering what he was up to.

He lifted my shirt up and placed his hands on my stomach.

"Buddy, it's Daddy," his breath tickled my bare skin as he spoke. "I really want to meet you, so I wish you'd come out already. Plus, Mommy's getting really tired and cranky." He grinned up at me.

"Hey," I laughed. "You'd be tired and cranky too if you had to carry this around all day." I pointed at my large stomach.

"Come on, buddy, it's time for you to come out," he coaxed and the baby kicked against Trace's hand.

"Nice try," I sighed. "But I gave this kid an eviction notice a week ago and he has yet to vacate the premises. He's stubborn, like his daddy." I smiled down at Trace, running my fingers through his hair.

"I'm ready to meet him. I want to know if he looks like you or me. I bet he looks like you." He smiled wistfully, rubbing my stomach.

I laughed, placing my hand against his to still his movements. "Trace, he's not a genie in a bottle. You can't rub him out."

"I can try." He grinned boyishly.

About that time, I felt a gush and my eyes widened.

Trace looked up at me and his eyes were full of panic. "Is that what I think it is?"

I nodded.

He rushed out of the room, grabbing the bag with baby clothes and ran down the hall to our bedroom. He came back with the baby bag slung over one shoulder and my overnight bag on the other.

"Baby time." He smiled, but there was fear in his eyes too. I'd have been lying if I said I wasn't scared. "Do I need to carry you?" He looked at me skeptically.

I rolled my eyes. "I can walk."

"I can carry you if—"

"Just get me to the hospital," I said calmly, because I knew one of us had to stay calm in this situation and it definitely wouldn't be Trace.

He helped me to the garage and into the large SUV he'd insisted on buying the day after I told him we were going to have a baby.

"Did you have to get a SUV that was so high?" I grumbled, as I tried to scramble my way into the car. I was having trouble between my short legs and the boulder that was currently my stomach.

"This was the safest car for the baby," he defended.

After some help from Trace, I managed to get seated and stretched the seatbelt across my stomach.

I think he broke at least ten traffic laws in his haste to make it to the hospital.

By the time I was admitted into a room and my doctor came to check on me, I had dilated six centimeters. "More than halfway there. Things are moving really fast. You'll have a baby to hold soon."

Trace was pacing nervously back and forth across the room as he called our family. When he hung up, he continued pacing. I was tempted to shuck something at him to get him to stop. He was making me more nervous than I already was.

"Please, for the sake of my sanity, *sit down*," I begged.

"Sorry." He took the chair beside me. I reached my hand out to him and he took it. With his long fingers, he spun the hospital band around my wrist. He stopped, focusing on something. "Is that little man's heartbeat?"

"Yeah, it is." I smiled at the sweet sound. Nothing was as precious to me as our baby's heartbeat.

"It's beautiful." Tears welled in his eyes and I reached out to cup his cheek.

"You've heard it before," I stated.

"I know, but it gets to me every time. It's our baby."

I knew what he meant. When I'd found out I was pregnant, I couldn't even begin to describe how elated I was. When I saw the baby on a sonogram for the first time, I cried for ten minutes. Hearing the heartbeat ... There was nothing else like it.

"I never could have imagined that a year ago that we'd be here." He looked around the room. "It seems so surreal that we're here ... That you're having my baby."

"Believe it." I rubbed my stomach, grimacing as a contraction rolled through my body. "I hate you for this," I hissed, so overcome by the pain that I forgot how happy I'd been a few moments ago.

"I'm sorry." He sat up to kiss my forehead. "If I could switch places with you, I would."

I evened out my breathing as the pain faded away.

From that moment on the contractions quickly escalated. Apparently, little man had decided it was time for him to make his grand entrance. I begged for drugs but there was no time. Trace brushed my hair away from my face, murmuring sweet words.

Gripping Trace's hand, I pushed our baby into the world. Tears leaked out of both our eyes as we saw our son for the first time. Even covered in goo he was the cutest thing I had ever seen.

"I love you so much," Trace murmured and kissed me deeply.

"I love you too," I sobbed, watching as they cleaned my son. I held my arms out weakly, desperate to hold the small bundle they were wrapping. He was a part of me, of *us*, and I needed him.

The nurse placed him in my arms. "Congratulations, you two."

My breath left me as I gazed down into the eyes of my son. Dark hair poked out beneath the knit blue cap they'd stuck on his head, and his eyes, although the blue babies were born with, held a hint of green. His nose was rounded on the end, exactly like Trace's, and he even had his dad's pouty lips. I think I'd given birth to Trace's clone. Little man would be breaking hearts all over the place.

"He's real," Trace gasped, reaching out to rub the baby's head.

"Of course he's real." I laughed. "What did you think had been growing inside me the last nine months?"

He chuckled. "It doesn't seem like this should be possible. That he's ours."

"He is one-hundred percent ours. Crying, screaming, and dirty diapers included." I smiled up at him.

"Thank you," he whispered.

"Thank you? For what?" My brows furrowed together in puzzlement.

"For giving me this gift." He ran a finger over the curve of the baby's cheek. "He's perfect."

"I have to agree with you there." I smiled as the baby yawned. I was sure there had never been a cuter baby. His eyes closed and he opened his mouth in a small yawn. I didn't want to let go of the baby, but I knew Trace deserved to hold his son. "Here, take him." I held my arms out so he could take the baby. Family would be arriving soon to meet the baby and I wanted Trace to have time with him first.

The baby looked so small in Trace's large hands. He stood, rocking the baby in his arms. Slowly, he lifted the baby up and leaned his forehead against our newborn son's.

"Hey, buddy, I'm your daddy," he whispered to the sleeping baby. "I'm new at all this so you'll have to bear with me," he continued. "But I want you to know I love you and I'll always protect you. No one will ever hurt you." He kissed the baby's nose and murmured, "I love you, Dean."

Tears welled in my eyes once more as I watched Trace with Dean. My son had the best dad in the world, I was sure of that.

Cradling Dean in his arms like a small football, Trace grinned. "Well, what are we going to do now?" His eyes strayed back to Dean, then to me again as he waited for me to answer.

I thought for a moment before answering, smiling at my husband and newborn son. I had everything I wanted right in front of me, so in my eyes there was only one answer.

"Anything we want."

ACKNOWLEDGMENTS

First off, I want to say that I loved writing this book so much. Trace and Olivia hold a special place in my heart and I was so happy to be continuing with their story. But it's bittersweet, because now I have to say goodbye. At least I know, that they'll always live on the pages of these books.

I can't thank the fans of Trace + Olivia enough. When I wrote *Finding Olivia* I was so worried that people wouldn't understand Olivia's Live List or hate her for her shyness. But you guys embraced both characters and hearing from you and how much you love them warms my heart. I hope you've loved this book just as much and are happy with where they ended up. I know I am.

I have to thank my beta readers, Haley, Kendall, Stefanie, and Alexis. This was the first time I've ever had beta readers and you guys really made me feel better and helped talk me down from quite a few ledges. Maybe eventually I'll stop freaking out with each book, but that isn't likely. Seriously though, you guys are awesome and I can't thank you enough for helping me.

Of course I have to thank the fabulous Regina Wamba for creating the gorgeous cover as well as taking the cover photo. Your talent is mind-blowing and I'm honored to get to work with you.

This wouldn't be complete without thanking Kim and Luke for bringing Trace and Olivia to life. You guys are my perfect Trace and Olivia and I'm so happy to have you on my covers.

Emily, (you know who you are), you've become a very special person to me and I love that you've become one of my best friends. You're always there to talk to me about whatever, whether it's talking to me about my latest book crisis, or just gushing over Reign. I know you have my back, and I've got yours.

Last, I have to thank my family. I know a lot of people out there don't have a family as supportive of their dreams as you guys are. It means the world to me to know that I have you all by my side.

www.ingramcontent.com/pod-product-compliance
Lightning Source LLC
LaVergne TN
LVHW031608060526
838201LV00065B/4775